Prophets have risen up many times through the ages, claiming to have the gift of seeing the future. Whether certain ones could or not is a debate for another day. What's not debatable is the most common response by society: to condemn them as insane, with often horrific results.

The screen went blank for a second, and Anne wiped her eyes, hoping the horrible movie was over. She didn't ever want to come back to this library again.

Then she saw dots slowly lighting up and glowing, coming to life scattered around the screen. There weren't very many, not even twenty of them. Lines formed on the screen, and after a second Anne realized those were the lines of the continents. The dots were on the land.

She could see a few on each continent, and only five in all of North America.

Her fear drew back a little as her curiosity started to recover. What was she looking at? They weren't near any of the cities she knew.

"What is it?" she whispered.

The lines of the continents faded in the middle, right around the Atlantic Ocean, and words floated to the surface. Pale blue words.

Remaining Human Population.

Dreaming the Storm: Book One of the Storms of Future Past Series

Copyright © 2018 by Kari A. Kilgore

All rights reserved

Published 2018 by Spiral Publishing, Ltd.
www.spiralpublishing.net

Book and cover design copyright © 2018 by Spiral Publishing, Ltd.
Cover art copyright © 2018 by SÃ¸ren Sielemann | Isoga1 |Dreamstime.com

ISBN-13: 978-1-948890-07-6
Library of Congress Control Number: 2018910624

To Carolyn and Linda

For countless hours of friendship, learning, and laughter.

DREAMING THE STORM

BOOK ONE OF THE STORMS OF FUTURE PAST
SERIES

KARI KILGORE

SPIRAL PUBLISHING, LTD.

DREAMING THE STORM

PART I

BEFORE THE STORM

When a country, a society, or an entire planet is hit with catastrophe, an event that changes everything from that point forward, humans are driven to try to find out why.

What have we done to deserve this?

How can we get back to normal?

And did anyone know this was coming?

That last one is more than idle speculation by the unaffected, especially if there *are* no unaffected.

The mistake people make, the wishful thinking that leads them to pursue The One Who Knew, is assuming such a person could have made any difference. That she could have done one thing that would have kept all the bad things from happening.

Or, more darkly, that this mythical person knew and decided to do nothing.

Prophets have risen up many times through the ages, claiming to have this gift of seeing the future. Whether certain ones could or not is a debate for another day. What's not debatable is the most common response by society: to condemn them as insane, with often horrific results.

Is it any wonder, then, that people who do know - who can *see* - so often choose to hide their knowledge and themselves?

Is it any wonder that knowledge frequently torments them in solitude until they truly are as insane as others assume?

The only salvation for one so cursed - through chance, divine intervention, or a quirk of genetics - may be one person to witness their visions. To share in the fear and hopelessness, the struggle and possibility. To simply understand and believe.

The seer lucky enough to find such a witness may not only be able to make a difference in the terrible things to come, but may indeed have the strength to do so.

Anne Fincastle was eleven years old when the dreams started.

Evan Griffith was too young at thirteen to understand how, as witness to her dreams, he would save her life.

Chapter 1

Evan squeezed his hands hard against his ears. He didn't want to hear any more today, not of anything. His clothes crowded close around him, scratchy and soft and smooth, making an even smaller room inside his closet. A room he finally felt safe in.

The black behind his closed eyes turned to shifting red. Someone had opened his closet door.

He pushed against the cold wall, shoes he'd tossed back here and forgotten digging into his backside. Rich scents of grass, dirt, and his own stale feet rose up at the movement. Maybe whoever it was wouldn't see him huddled behind the row of pants and jackets. Evan was afraid his legs showed, though. He should have put the rolled up sleeping bag and heavy winter blankets in front.

The light moved again, and Evan only squeezed his eyes shut until his eyeballs ached. He heard rising and falling sounds through his hands, closer and slower than the shouting. Someone was trying to talk to him. He should be polite and see who it was, but he just didn't want to.

A cold, damp hand closed over one of his and he flinched away. That hand was too small to be one of his parents. The voice was too soft to be either of them.

He risked barely opening one eye.

Gwen, that was his big sister Gwen. Still wearing her school clothes. Stripy pants so wide at the bottom that Evan didn't know how she could walk, and a shirt with ruffles all over. She leaned in close, her long pigtail braids swinging forward. He shifted his right hand the tiniest bit off of his ear. He could still hear the shouting, but not too bad.

"Come on, Evvie. It's time to go."

Evan shook his head and hid his face against his knees. He was almost four years old now. Too big to be a scaredy-cat anymore. But he was scared to death of walking through the house right now.

Gwen leaned so close he felt her warm breath on his cheek, so Evan lifted his hand away from his ear again. A ringing pop brought all the noise back into his head.

"It's okay. Mom will know where we are," Gwen whispered. "She told me to take you with me when this happens." He squeezed his eyes closed again and started to cover his ear. Gwen grabbed his hand. "I'm supposed to take you with me, so come on."

Evan opened both eyes then, wanting to tell her to go away and leave him here in his closet. He felt safe here. If he ran to his bed and got enough pillows to go with his clothes, he could bury his head enough to drown out the whole wide world.

Gwen's brown eyes were right in front of his, and she was crying. He'd hardly ever seen her cry. She was nine, and so much bigger than him that he thought she never cried anymore. She held out her hand.

"We're just going down the street to Mr. and Mrs. Fincastle's house. They'll know what to do. It's okay."

He lowered his hands so he could get up, but a loud shout from his Daddy made him jump and cover up his ears again. Gwen squinted up her face, then put both hands under Evan's arms and lifted him up. She grabbed his fuzzy tan coat with big wooden buttons he could fasten by himself off the floor and wrapped it around his shoulders.

He could tell by her mouth that she was asking if he was ready, but he didn't dare uncover his ears again. Evan nodded, trying his best to be brave and strong. He followed his big sister.

Gwen had on her own coat with long brown fringe hanging from the sleeves and her big denim bag full of school books slung over one shoulder. That bag scared Evan and made him wonder just how long they were going to have to stay at the Fincastle's house.

He stayed as close behind her as he could on the shaggy blue carpet in the hall and on the stairs, so close that he bumped into her when she stopped to open the front door. He thought he heard a crash coming from the kitchen, and Gwen whirled around and looked that way.

Evan was too afraid to look. Now that he was out of his safe closet and almost through the house, he just wanted to get away. Gwen was crying harder now, but she managed to get the door open and pushed Evan through in front of her.

"I'm sorry, Evan," she said, putting her arm around him when the door was closed. He finally lowered his hands all the way, curling his fingers against the freezing cold. But he could still hear his parents shouting inside.

That awful sound was the end of the world to him.

"We'll just go over there for a little while, and Mom will come and get us when things calm down."

"What if they hurt each other?"

This time Gwen didn't look sad or cry at all. She looked really, really angry. Her mouth turned down and her eyebrows made sharp lines pointing toward her nose.

"They never have before." Her mouth was a tiny, thin line now, like his Daddy's was sometimes. When she was mad, Gwen looked so much like his Daddy that it made Evan a little scared. "What Mom told me is to get away and take you with me, so that's what I'm going to do."

They walked just down the block and across the street, Evan holding tight to Gwen's hand. He stopped every few feet to look back over his shoulder. He couldn't hear his parents anymore, but he kept imagining he could.

"What are you looking for?" Gwen said.

Evan stared at Gwen, not wanting to upset her more than she

already was. Mist puffed out of her nose and mouth and her cheeks were bright red from the icy wind.

"What if they do hurt each other, Gwennie?" He didn't say what he was really thinking, what his belly was feeling.

What if daddy hurts mommy?

"There's nothing you can do about that, Ev. They're both grownups. Mom told me once that all I can do is stay out of the way. Now I'm big enough to get you out of the way, too."

Evan closed his eyes, trying to squeeze the tears back inside. Some part of him, a part too old for his mind and body, was crying out that he *could* do something. Not only that he could, but he *had* to.

If he let his parents fight and never did anything about it, whatever happened would be his fault. Evan's fault. He wanted to run away and never look back, and he knew in his bones that leaving them alone screaming like that could only make things worse.

Gwen started up the steps to the Fincastle's house, but Evan hung back again.

"What's wrong?" Gwen said. "We should go inside. It's not good to just hang around out here."

"Will Mr. and Mrs. Fincastle be mad at us too? For wanting to stay here?"

Gwen shook her head and pulled on Evan's hand.

"They never have been before. They're really nice. Don't worry. They know what to do."

Gwen reached up to ring the doorbell, and Evan kept himself from pulling her away. He didn't want to bother anyone. He'd be perfectly fine sitting here on the porch, hidden where no one could see him.

Not being seen made a lot of sense to Evan.

Before he could say a word, Mr. Fincastle opened the door. His big, warm smile went away when he got a good look at the two of them. Evan stared down at his bare, grownup feet poking out of faded jeans that were all strings at the bottom.

"Are you two okay?"

"Yes, sir," Gwen said. "We just need to… Can we stay here for a little while?"

Evan glanced up at the shaky sound of his big sister's voice. She hardly ever sounded scared, even less often than she cried. Mr. Fincastle opened the door wide and stepped back.

"Of course you can. Anne just went down for a nap, so walk quiet as a mouse."

Evan was confused for a few seconds, worried about just how quiet a mouse walked. He remembered a birthday party at Mr. and Mrs. Fincastle's house back during the summer. Anne turned one that day, but she hadn't walked very well at all. What Evan remembered best was how she'd laughed when she dug her small fists into the pink icing on her cake.

He did his best to tiptoe as he and Gwen followed Mr. Fincastle inside.

"Come on back to the kitchen, and I'll get you something to drink. Mom, we have company."

A television with wood all around was on in the living room, but no one was in there watching. Evan saw a man with a big nose and a blue suit talking, a man he'd seen a lot lately. The man waved his arms and said "Well, I am not a crook…" as Evan walked by.

Evan expected to see Mrs. Fincastle when he walked around the corner into the bright gold kitchen. The refrigerator and oven were the same pretty gold as the ones in his house, and the shiny floor under his feet was covered with stripes of brown, blue, and that same gold.

Instead of someone his mother's age, Evan saw an old, old woman sitting at the kitchen table. He blinked and nearly tripped over his own feet.

"Well hello there!" The woman was beaming, her whole face lighting up in a smile Evan couldn't help returning. Now that he could get a closer look, he saw she had gray hair like his own grandmother did, but her face looked smooth and young. Her eyes were bright, and as green and pretty as Mr. Fincastle's. "And who are these beautiful children?"

Mr. Fincastle turned away from the refrigerator with a bottle of what looked like orange juice. Evan hoped it was the same thing the astronauts drank instead. Mr. Fincastle was smiling, but he still looked sad.

"These are our neighbors, Gwen and Evan Griffith. They live just down the street. They're going to visit with us for a little while."

"Oh, I remember Evan now!" The woman held out her hands, and Gwen and Evan each took one. Her fingers were warm and smooth. "And it's lovely to meet you, Gwen. I'm Mary Fincastle, and this is my son, Mike."

Mr. Fincastle sat down with four glasses.

"I don't think you've met Evan, Mom. Dad was still alive the last time… Anyway, I'm sure you remember Gwen. She's been here before."

Mary Fincastle tilted her head, looking so much like a curious dog that Evan had to fight back a giggle. No matter how he felt, he didn't think laughing while his parents were yelling at each could possibly be a good thing.

"You do look familiar, Gwen," she said, smiling again. "But Evan is here a lot. He's just like part of the family."

"He sure is," Mr. Fincastle said. "They both are. Are you two hungry? I can make you a sandwich or something."

"No, sir, not right now," Gwen said, and Evan shook his head. "We just… Our Mom said we should come here."

Her voice had that trembly sound, and Mr. Fincastle seemed as upset by it as Evan was.

"Don't you worry, Gwen, not about one single thing. Want to come into the living room and watch television for a while? Time to change the channel anyway. I think we've all had about enough of Mr. Nixon lately. There has to be something better on."

The shows were very good, and before long Evan's eyes were trying to close all by themselves. He didn't want to act like a big baby in front of grownups, but he was really sleepy. He was still young enough to need a nap, no matter what else was going on.

The next thing he knew, Mr. Fincastle was picking him up.

"I'm sorry…"

"Shhh, don't be sorry for needing a nap. I could use one myself most days."

Evan put his arms around Mr. Fincastle's neck and laid his head against his shoulder. A nap really did sound good. He heard a woman's voice, a younger woman than Mary Fincastle, but he couldn't quite manage to open his eyes.

Mr. Fincastle put him down, and Evan felt something warm beside him. He turned toward that warmth and snuggled up close. The last thing he heard before he fell into real sleep was two adults laughing softly, and one baby girl breathing.

Her breath against Evan's cheek smelled as sweet as flowers after the rain.

Chapter 2

FIVE YEARS later

Rainy summer days were the worst as far as Anne was concerned. Much as she may daydream about it, she never was going to find a magic hallway inside her closet or a hidden trapdoor under the shaggy brown carpet in her bedroom. She'd only see the same pale blue walls, the same dolls and cars and picture books on the same bright yellow shelves, the same songs to sing to herself until she was bored to tears.

The pebbled white ceiling of her room sounded like a constant roar of water, or maybe like her mother was running the vacuum cleaner in the attic. The view of the sky through her windows looked more like almost bedtime instead of not even lunch time. The streetlight she could see through the branches of a maple tree was even on.

Anne didn't understand why Evan loved the rain so much. The only thing she loved about it was when he came over to play on stormy gray days like this.

Then the dolls and cars and bricks came to life like magic, with Evan helping figure out what the next story was until it really was nighttime and he had to go home. Anne didn't usually like the board games her parents played with their friends, but Evan even managed to make those giggly fun.

Anne pulled another skirt out of her chest of drawers, at least the fifth or sixth she'd tried on in the last hour. The others were neatly stacked one on top of the other on her bed. She wasn't sure why she kept changing into different ones. A vague idea of wanting to outgrow her Christmas gifts floated in the back of her mind. Wanting to grow up to six so she could start school just a little bit faster.

The pretty pink skirt with blue flowers and green leaves all over it joined the others in the disappointing fits-me-just-fine pile.

She pulled on a pair of last year's pink pajama bottoms that were indeed a little too small, missed in her mother's regular thinning out of her clothes for sad kids who didn't have any. Anne scrubbed her sock feet on the thick shaggy blue carpet, then touched the metal of her doorknob. Nothing. The trick her father taught her about making sparks with her fingertips only seemed to work when it was cold outside.

Anne pushed the door all the way open and poked her head out into the hall. The blue carpet covered the whole floor and all the way down the stairs, but the walls were a boring grownup white. She couldn't hear a sound in the whole house besides that rumbly rain.

Her mother had said she wanted quiet time for a couple of hours, and that Anne was old enough to entertain herself without help now. The idea that she was old enough for anything usually made Anne happy, but not this time. She wondered if she needed to be a day younger, a month? Or all the way back to her last birthday when she turned five?

Anyway, it didn't seem fair to her.

Even more unfair was Evan visiting family in a far away place called Virginia for ages and ages now that he didn't have to go off to school all day long. The thought of joining him in real school, where the big kids were, delighted and scared Anne at the same time. A few hours of kindergarten hadn't been all that bad. She kind of wished she could go to her school today, but she knew she really was too old for that school now.

At the real school, there would be kids of all ages and sizes, not just little kids like Anne. Evan said it was okay, but he was already seven. She was afraid he knew secrets she didn't know, something his big sister told him when she first went to real school. Gwen was a lot older than Evan, and Anne didn't have a big brother or sister of her own. Maybe that was something no one else could warn her about, and she'd just have to walk in and face it.

Anne jumped at a slow, rolling boom of thunder over her head. Her daddy had said rain all day long and maybe storms. If it thundered, he said she couldn't go outside no matter what because of lightning. No chance to get out or have something fun to do until lunch time.

She put her hands flat on her belly, scowling down at her fingers laced together. Nope, not even hungry. Anne thought she'd been up here for at least four or five hours, but she should have been ready for lunch by now. She shook her head and sighed.

Her mother hadn't exactly said Anne had to stay in her room, only that she had to stay upstairs and be quiet. There wasn't much she liked up here outside of her own room, but she stepped out into the middle of the hall anyway. From her door at the end, she could see a guest room door, a bathroom door, and her parents' door, all shut tight. Only her grandmother's stood open, and in the gloom Anne could make out a glowing light in there.

Anne grinned and headed that way, doing her best not to stomp and make noise. She'd been sure her grandmother would be having quiet time too, not sitting right up here alone herself. If Gemaw took a nap, she almost always kept the door closed.

Anne slowed just before the doorway, listening as hard as she could. Even noisy rain wouldn't drown out her Gemaw's snoring, so she must be awake and bored just like Anne.

"Gemaw?" she whispered, tapping her fingertips on the wooden door frame.

"I'm awake, sweetheart. Come right on inside."

Anne walked through her grandmother's open door, her eyes on the pile of cases in the middle of the room. She'd never seen such pretty bags, shapes and sizes she'd never seen before, and so many different flowers and colors. The ones her parents used, and her own, were plain, hard plastic blue rectangles with tiny wheels on the bottom.

"What is all this stuff, Gemaw?"

"Hello sweet pea! These are just my suitcases."

"They're so pretty. Where did you get them?" Anne touched the biggest case, a dark purple rectangle bigger than she'd ever seen, made of soft fabric.

"I got these when I first got married to your grandfather, a long time ago." She stood beside Anne, one hand on her shoulder. "My mother helped me pick them out special."

"What's this one for?" Anne reached for a round case sitting on top, made of that same purple fabric but with pink designs all over. Initials were sewn into the middle, small m, big F, small e.

"That one was supposed to hold hats, but it doesn't anymore. I put my socks in there, wrapped around all the pretty things you've given me that I don't want to break."

Anne looked around the room then, noticing the walls and shelves were bare.

"Are you going somewhere?" Her grandmother sat on the bed, smiling. It was neatly made, but her special pretty pillows were all missing.

"I'm going on a trip, but everything is going to work out just fine." Anne was drawing breath to ask where she was going when she heard someone out in the hall. Instead of her mother grumpy about her interrupted quiet time, her father walked in.

"What's going on, Mom?" He was smiling, like her grandmother, but his voice sounded strange.

"I just wanted to get everything packed up so it would be easier."

Anne's dad raised his eyebrows, then squatted down and hugged Anne.

"Hi sweetheart. Listen, can you go play for a little while? I need to talk to Gemaw, private adult stuff."

Anne started to argue that she was bored, that she'd come in here to have someone to talk to, but her father had a serious, don't argue look now. Her grandmother was still smiling and seemed happy, and Anne couldn't figure out why her dad wasn't.

"Just for a little while, Anne. Okay?"

"Okay, Dad. See you later, Gemaw."

He pushed the door around when Anne walked out, but he didn't quite close it. She scooted her feet all the way to her own doorway, tapping her non-sparking bedroom doorknob with her fingers. She was still bored and still wanted something to do.

Her dad said it was private, but he hadn't closed the door. She rocked back and forth from her toes to her heels, trying to decide. Playing out in the hall was still playing. She grabbed her favorite doll and her favorite car and walked quietly toward her grandmother's room.

"I don't understand what you mean, Mom."

"Karen has been so kind to me, for a long time now. This will be easier on everyone, Mikey."

Anne sat down and rolled the car back and forth on the carpet, trying to be quiet as a mouse like her dad always said.

"None of us want you to leave. Why would you think that? Karen hasn't said anything to me, not a word."

"Well no, I know she hasn't. But I don't want her to have to." Anne scooted a little closer, her hip dragging the doll along the wall.

"We all love having you here, Mom. Come on, let me help you put everything back. A little mouse out in the hall can help. Right, Anne?"

Anne froze, her face and her whole body feeling hot. How had he known she was out there? Her plans to crawl backward until she got to her own room dissolved when he pushed the door open. He had one eyebrow raised, but he didn't look really angry.

"Gemaw needs help unpacking her bags, Scoot. Want to join us?"

A couple of weeks later, when Anne got up, she saw her grandmother's door standing open. It was another weekend, so everyone could sleep as long as they wanted, but Gemaw was dressed and sitting on her bed.

The pretty cases were all in the middle of the floor again.

"Good morning, sweet pea!" Her grandmother was smiling, looking as happy as a little girl.

"Good morning, Gemaw. Where are you going this time?"

"I'm just going on a trip, nothing to worry about."

"Can I go with you? I really want to go."

Gemaw shook her head and patted the bed beside her. Anne climbed up and scooted close for a hug.

"You can't go on this trip, Anne, only me. You need to stay here until you grow up a little more."

Anne crossed her arms and sighed.

"That's not fair. I want to go on a trip, too."

"Don't worry, pea. You'll get to go on a lot of trips when you get bigger, but it will all work out just fine."

Anne jumped when her father spoke from the open door.

"Morning, girls. Heading out again, Mom?"

"Good morning, Mikey. Yes, it's almost time to go."

"Well, come downstairs and have breakfast first. We'll check the schedule and make sure."

Everything got put away again after breakfast, but Anne's grandmother didn't seem upset at all. She thought her parents were only pretending to be happy, though. They all went to the park that afternoon, and Anne almost forgot all about it. When she came downstairs to kiss her parents goodnight, they were sitting in the living room talking. The TV was on, but it was turned down low.

She took the stairs one at a time, quiet as a mouse.

"I haven't said a word to her, Mike, not a word."

"You know how she picks up on things. If you wanted her to move, you should have said something to me. I had no idea."

"Then she doesn't either, so let's just forget about it."

They were quiet for a few seconds, and Anne had decided to go back upstairs after all when her daddy spoke again. She had to listen really hard to hear his words.

"She kept saying it would be best, now she's saying it would be best for Anne. Where else would she be getting that, Karen?"

"I told you I didn't say anything, and I didn't. If you're determined to get into this with me right now, I'll tell you right now she might have a point. These things get harder over time, not better. It might not be best for Anne to see that."

Anne stood up, forgetting that she wasn't supposed to be listening at all.

"Mommy? You want Gemaw to leave?"

Her mother stood too, but she didn't move toward the stairs. Her face was bright red.

"Anne, I've told you about sneaking around and listening to grownups!" Anne drew back at her mother's shout. "You need to get back upstairs and go to bed, now!"

Before her father could say a word, Anne ran back up the stairs as fast as she could. After she cried enough to feel a little better, she heard voices coming from downstairs, loud voices. The TV must be on louder now.

Just as Anne was about to fall asleep, someone knocked on her door.

"Anne, sweetheart?" her mother whispered. "Are you still awake?"

"I'm awake, Mommy."

Both of her parents came in and sat on the bed, one on either side of her. When her daddy turned on the light, she saw both of them had red eyes like they'd been crying.

"I'm sorry I yelled at you, Anne," her mother said as she stroked Anne's cheek. "I was surprised you were there, but I shouldn't have yelled."

"Your Mom and I were talking," her daddy said. "Private grownup talk. You know what that means, don't you?"

Anne wished she could hide her face under the blankets.

"I know. I'm not supposed to listen. I'm sorry. I'll try to do better." Her mother scowled, but Anne caught her father's smile. "Can I ask you something?"

Her mother and father looked at each other, then back at her. "Sure, hon," her daddy said. "But it is bedtime, so not too long."

"Is Gemaw going away?"

Her father brushed back her hair and sighed.

"I don't know, Anne. She will someday, you know that. Like Grampaw did."

"Yeah, I know she'll be gone someday, but I mean is she going to live somewhere else."

"How would you feel about that?" her mother said.

"I don't want her to go," Anne said. "She makes me feel better when I have bad dreams."

Her father moved closer and Anne put her head in his lap.

"What do you mean?" he said. "When do you have bad dreams?"

"I have bad dreams a lot, not every night, but a lot. Gemaw comes in and tells me everything will be okay. Sometimes I go into her room, but most of the time she finds me before I even get up."

Her mother's face scrunched up for a second, but her daddy only had a little smile. His eyes looked sad instead of happy.

"Well, no one's going anywhere right now," he said. "Gemaw did that for me when I was your age too, sweetheart, but you can come to us if you have bad dreams. You know that, right?"

"I know, but I don't want her to go. Please? I really want her to stay here."

"Enough talk for one night." Anne's mother kissed her forehead, then stood and turned out the light. "We all need to get some good sleep, and we all need some sweet dreams."

After a couple of quiet days, Anne's grandmother packed up her pretty bags again. She did that more and more often. For a while, she and her daddy made a game out of it, seeing how fast they could help her put everything back, and her grandmother played along.

Anne knew the second when everything changed. Her daddy never had to tell her a word. His whole face and his body and his heart changed. Her grandmother never did seem to be upset or sad when they were helping her put everything away, but after getting more and more upset every time, her daddy gave up.

He didn't make her unpack anymore, and he didn't try to talk her into staying. Her grandmother just slept on the boring bed in the empty room, her cases all piled up in the middle. Anne was too scared about what her daddy giving up might mean to ask questions, but something deep down in her chest knew what would happen.

Her Gemaw moved out into a huge, scary building before Anne had time to turn seven.

She never quite believed the promise that everything was going to work out just fine.

Chapter 3

By the time Gwen went away to college when he was eleven, Evan didn't need to hide in the closet from all the shouting anymore. He knew how to take himself away when a really bad fight got going, either to Anne's house or just out into the yard most of the time. Gwen had told him to keep himself out of the craziness however he could, and she'd helped by leaving her bulky old portable radio and tape player.

Unless things got really bad, Evan could stuff a towel against the bottom of his bedroom door, turn up the music, and pretend he lived in a normal house without all the yelling.

Or at least a house where the yelling didn't happen quite so often.

Everything between his parents had been quiet lately, at least while he was at home and awake. A stretch of calm over an entire weekend was unusual enough that Evan was able to dig into his homework instead of having to go to the library or to Anne's house. Once he got comfortable at his rarely-used desk, he enjoyed the change of pace.

His usual pop music station from the city was on, but not nearly as loud as usual, and he even had the door and the window open. A warm early summer breeze floated the Major League Baseball curtains he'd gotten for Christmas into the room every few minutes. He was tempted to go out there and enjoy the day, but he was almost finished with his report for school. He wouldn't admit it to much of anyone, but Evan enjoyed writing history papers more than just about any other homework. This one about the mysterious Cahokia Mounds, a few hours south just outside of St. Louis, was one of his favorites so far.

A stack of library books and a couple of his encyclopedias sat on the broad, scratched surface of his mother's old desk, but Evan rarely needed to look back once he'd read about something. If it caught his attention, the facts seemed to stay in his mind forever without much effort. He swung his feet just above the ground, lost in the words and the thoughts that drove them.

Evan didn't notice the soft footsteps out in the hall or the knock on his door. He blinked at the sound of his mother's voice. He hoped he wouldn't have to go to the library after all.

"Hey Ev, can I talk to you a minute?"

Megan Griffith stood just outside the door, gripping the handle even though it hadn't been closed. She wore her usual jeans and a bummy t-shirt for a working around the house day, so she wasn't planning to go anywhere. Her dark hair was caught back in a loose braid, and her cheeks weren't red or blotchy like when she was fighting with Evan's father.

She smiled, but her eyes looked tight and sad.

"Sure, hang on," Evan said. "I'll be right there."

The strange knot in Evan's belly faded when he focused on the paragraph he was in the middle of writing, then came back full force after he closed his notebook. His parents hardly ever interrupted during the rare times he did homework at home, not with something besides the shouting. He tried to convince himself that whatever his mother wanted wouldn't be that big of a deal without much luck.

She waited in the bright, sunny kitchen, but she wasn't reading or cooking or working on anything else she usually did. She was pacing back and forth, and Evan would have sworn she was talking to herself. She didn't notice him at first, then jumped when he spoke.

"What's going on?"

"Oh, hon, you startled me."

Evan sat beside her at the round kitchen table, pale wood spotless and gleaming. The knot in his belly was bigger now. And it was twisting.

"Listen," his mother said. "I wanted to tell you. I'm going to Chicago to visit with Gwen for a few days."

"You're… When are you going?"

"I'm leaving tomorrow morning."

"But this is Saturday. I can't miss the whole week of school."

She looked away from him, rubbing the side of her face.

"I'm going alone, Evan. You'll stay here with your dad."

He reacted before he had a chance to think.

"No! I'm not staying here with him, you'll just have to wait."

"Don't shout, son, please listen to me. I need to get away for a little while, that's all. It might be good for the two of you to have some time together."

"Good? There's nothing good about me spending time with Hurricane Ed!"

Evan wished he could get the words back, and he could feel his cheeks burning. Gwen would kill him if she knew he'd spilled their secret name for their father. He risked a glance up at his mother, expecting her to be upset with him.

She had one hand over her mouth and her eyes were watering, but that wasn't an angry look. His mother was trying her best not to laugh and doing a rotten job of it.

"Evan, you shouldn't… You shouldn't say things like that. At least not where I can hear you." She took a breath deep enough to regain her stern mom voice. "It's just for a few days, son. You two will be fine."

Evan shook his head and stared out the window into the back yard, trying to keep from getting even more upset. He didn't like to spend a few minutes alone with his father, much less a few days. He was more comfortable with complete strangers. At least the strangers weren't always looking at him like he'd let them down somehow.

And the strangers didn't spend so much time either fighting with his mother or not saying a word for hours on end.

"We're not exactly the best of friends, Mom. I think he'd be a lot happier if you took me with you and he stayed here."

"You never talk to each other," she said, her voice barely loud enough for him to hear. "How could you possibly be friends? This might be a good chance to try."

Evan shook his own head but kept staring out the window. He didn't want his mom to see the tears in his eyes.

"Dad doesn't like me, never has. No matter what I do, I'm some kind of disappointment. There's nothing we can talk about."

"That's not true, hon, of course he likes you." The sound of her voice made Evan turn around. She didn't sound like she was lying, not quite, but she didn't sound sure of herself either. "You just need to get to know each other."

"Why are you so determined to go right now? Does Dad know? Are you even going to tell him?"

Evan ignored the whispery voice saying he was mad at the wrong person. He didn't particularly care about being fair at the moment. What he cared about was being dumped and left behind. His mother leaned her elbows on the table and held her face in her hands.

"No, I'll tell him. Don't say anything about it. I'll tell him tomorrow. I just need to get away for a little while."

"Yeah, away from me." When she turned to him, her blue eyes flashing, he knew he'd said one thing too many. For the first time, he didn't care.

"No, Evan, *not* away from you, but that attitude isn't helping. I'm not leaving you, and I'm not leaving your father. I'm taking a break, I'm leaving tomorrow, and that's all there is to it."

Evan's heart ran cold at the idea of her leaving his father. What if this little break or whatever is was turned out to be something she liked? That would explain why she didn't want him to say anything.

He had several friends with divorced parents. There were times when he didn't understand why she stayed with Ed, but he hadn't really considered the reality of anything else.

"Leaving Dad? Is that why you don't want me to say anything? Is that what's going on?"

She blinked and tried to hide it, but Evan saw tears in her pale blue eyes. He'd seen his own eyes in the mirror too many times to mistake that.

"I'm sorry. I shouldn't have said that. Telling him anything like this is my job, not yours. I just can't deal with the hassle tonight." She squeezed her lips into a line and took a deep breath. "You're not a kid anymore, Ev. You know things have been a little rough around here lately. We've both been busy at work, and everyone's trying to get used to Gwen being gone. This feels like a time to take a break."

"I might need a break too, did you think about that?" Evan wiped at his cheeks, but he knew he wasn't hiding a thing. "What if he decides to take it all out on me with you and Gwen gone? That doesn't exactly sound like a break to me."

She leaned forward and hugged him, and after a few seconds Evan stopped trying to get away. The stray tears had turned into real crying now, but he didn't try to stop. She stroked his hair, just like when he was little.

"Come on, it's going to be okay. There's no reason he'd want to fight with you. Gwen pushed him as much as he did her, and you never have. You can always go over to Anne's house, any time you need to. You've always done that."

Evan sat back, grabbing for a napkin before his nose started running.

"I don't think he'd like that very much, Mom. I wouldn't be getting away from the shouting, not with only two of us here. I'd be getting away from him. I'm sure he'd notice if I just walk out the door."

"Well, truth is that's his problem, not yours." She brushed the hair back from his forehead, something else she hadn't done in ages. "You'll be at school most of the time, anyway."

"When will you be back?"

"Sometime over the weekend, probably Sunday. I can talk to

Anne's parents before I go. I'd bet they'd be happy for you to spend some time with them on Saturday. Okay?"

Evan shook his head again, but inside he knew there was no point in talking about it anymore. She was going to go, and he was going to have to deal with it. Getting more upset and yelling wasn't going to change a thing. It never did between her and his father.

"I guess so. I'm going to go finish my homework." When he stood, she caught him in a quick hug.

"Thanks, Evan. We'll plan to go up together soon, just you and me. We'll leave Hurricane Ed here by himself and see how much he likes it."

PART II
DREAMS BEGIN

Chapter 4

Anne opened her eyes inside a massive library, the biggest one she's ever seen, even bigger than the one at the university in the city. The wood and metal shelves stretched away in all directions as far as she could see. Even when she leaned her head back far enough to feel dizzy, she couldn't see the tops of them or the ceiling.

Only hundreds, thousands, millions of books in every shape, size, and color.

Well, stacked impossibly high and forever out of reach in what she was starting to suspect was a dream, they were still books. More than she could read in her life, in a hundred lives. Anne smiled and hugged herself, turning in a circle to look at as much as she could. She breathed in the warm, welcoming scent of all that paper without even a hint of the dust or sharp cleaners that made her eyes and throat hurt in a real library.

There was no door or checkout desk, not that she could see. A few scuffed and scarred tables were shoved together in a clear spot beside her, with green cushioned chairs poking up here and there. She walked on thin gray carpet that made her footsteps silent, running her fingers along the row of books closest to her.

Warm scratchy fabric. Cool slick plastic. Rough bumpy paper. None of the spines she touched had any words on them, only flashes of color and pictures she couldn't make out. They all had a feel to them, a hit of sensation. She didn't have to read the titles to know which books would be scary, sad, boring, or exciting.

Anne wanted to find something happy to read. She'd been feeling very unhappy lately, even in her dreams, filled with something she could only call dread. She couldn't say why, but asleep or awake, she was sure something bad is going to happen. She wanted to escape, just for a while.

A huge book caught her attention, almost too heavy for her to pull off of the shelf she has to reach up to. The book was almost as long as from her waist to the top of her head, but it didn't weigh nearly as much as she thought it would. She managed to get it down and stagger toward one of the beat up tables. Even with her arms wrapped around the warm, pebbly surface, Anne couldn't tell how this book would make her feel besides curious.

The book landed with a huge, echoing bang, but no one shushed her. No one else seemed to be in this giant building but Anne.

She stared at the book, wondering why this was the one she had to read. Bound in well-worn leather, dark brown and fragrant. She smelled the old, slightly uneven paper when she ran her fingertips across the closed pages, one of her favorite smells in the world.

There was no picture on the cover, but she finally saw writing. Two words embossed in heavy gold took up most of the space.

The Future.

Anne grinned, hoping she'd found a new science fiction book. That was her favorite thing to read by a long shot, that and fantasy. Anything with spaceships and robots and dragons and magic sent her right into another world, so deep that she wanted to stay there forever.

She lifted the cover, wanting to get a look at the table of contents so she could try to guess what the stories were about. Instead of single pages she could turn, half of the book fell to each side. In the middle was a screen as long as Anne's arm. She could still see the edges of the pages on either side, but a strange, tiny, flat TV seemed to be jammed inside somehow.

She wasn't sure how to read it, but she was even more curious than before. The outside still looked like a normal book. She ran her fingers all around the sides, but she couldn't see any way to make the book work. She hoped the battery wasn't dead, if it even had a battery like a flashlight or a toy. She finally touched the middle of the screen.

Anne drew back as the screen came to life. She couldn't see any images, but the black was illuminated, a brighter version of nothing. She put her ear close to the book and heard the faintest hum. She remembered how her Gemaw's old television had to warm up sometimes, but Anne was sure a tiny flat television like this didn't exist.

The screen finally lit up.

A swarm of bees, crawling all over honeycomb, in and out of the picture.

Anne jerked her hands away even though she was sure it was only a movie. Even in her dream, she knew the things on the screen couldn't hurt her.

She'd never liked bees since she got stung a few years ago, one of the earliest things she still remembered. That bee had been on the rim of the glass Anne was drinking out of, and it crawled up into her nose and stung her before she could react. The pain had been horrible!

Her mother and father both tried to tell her that was a yellow jacket, not a bee, but the damage was done. Anne didn't kill bees. She just did *not* want to be around them.

The image shifted down in a fast movement that made Anne dizzy to show the ground at the bottom of the hive. There were piles of bees, drifts of them, and all of them were dead. Anne didn't see a single one stirring now.

The movie pulled back, and now she saw two hives with dead bees.

The image doubled to four, then again and again and again until the whole screen was filled with piles of dead bees. Despite her fear, Anne was terribly sad. Even though she didn't much like them, she knew bees did a lot of good.

What had killed so many of them?

The next picture showed a small green plant with tiny purple flowers, rows and rows of them. The flowers were moving, changing. They came out, dried up, and fell off, over and over again. Nothing ever sprouted from them. They just died. Eventually the plant turned brown, then it crumpled into the soil.

The same thing happened with different kinds of plants, this time with white and yellow blooms. They looked healthy, but the flowers just shriveled up.

People stood in huge crowds, and these people weren't real like the bees had been. They looked like drawings that moved, like old cartoons Anne and Even watched sometimes in the afternoon.

The cartoon people watched the plants trying and trying to make fruit and vegetables, but nothing ever grew. The people were silent for a long time.

Now all Anne could see was that crowd of people, but they were shriveling just like the flowers. Each person got smaller and smaller, thinner and thinner, then they crumpled up and blew away.

When blank spots opened up in the crowd, they started shouting at each other, screaming, clenching their fists, drawings of blue veins standing out on their necks. Anne wanted to close the book and make the movie stop before someone got really angry.

She was too late.

One drawing woman pushed a man and he fell down. Then the whole crowd was fighting, punching and kicking and clawing and biting. Some of the people had guns then, and when they shot, whole groups of people puffed away into dust.

Anne needed to close the book. She needed to put it back on the shelf and run out of the library and never come back again. But she couldn't move.

The scene shifted again, and she saw a lake. Not a regular lake, not like the one she went swimming in sometimes.

This lake was inside a big metal circle, a giant one, and bunches of other little round lakes were all around it. Some kind of machinery worked away in the middle of the groups of round lakes, and she could see the water moving. It flowed from one circle to another, getting less cloudy and dirty and more clear and sparkling with every move.

A low, droning noise grew, drowning out the noise of the machines, getting closer every second. The camera tilted up, making her stomach roll. Anne wanted to shield her eyes from the harsh light.

An airplane flew out of the sun, a huge plane, bigger than she'd ever seen. It seemed to hang in the clear blue sky without moving. When it was overhead, the belly of the plane opened up and dust fell into the water.

In just a few seconds, the water in every one of those lakes turned from clear, cool blue into a sickly, diseased green. The machinery strained, then chugged, then it finally fell silent with smoke floating around it.

A little girl much younger than Anne, maybe only two or three years old, walked along the edge of the lake on a metal sidewalk. The lake held real water, but the little girl was a drawing just like all the dead people.

She stopped and lay down on her belly, reaching her hands into the foul water.

"No! Don't drink that!" Anne shouted, her voice echoing in the vast library. "Can't you see it? It will make you sick!"

The girl drank anyway, but before she could sit up she clutched her throat. She coughed and clawed at her neck, then that little girl curled up on the metal sidewalk. She turned to dust and floated down into the water.

Anne moaned as the camera drew back to show hundreds of children around each of those lakes, all curling up and dying.

And she saw hundreds of lakes, round metal lakes and real, outside lakes.

And she saw thousands of them, blending into rivers and seas and oceans.

Around every single one of them, piles of dust as high as the dead bees were shifting and moving. Fish floated up to the top of the real lakes, drawings of fish with Xs for eyes. The fish turned into dust too, cartoon dust that covered the real water.

Anne knew that wasn't dust. That was dead things, dead things the poisoned water had killed. The dead things made the poison worse.

The screen went blank for a second, and Anne wiped her eyes, hoping the horrible movie was over. She didn't ever want to come back to this library again.

Then she saw dots slowly lighting up and glowing, coming to life scattered around the screen. There weren't very many, not even twenty of them. Lines formed on the screen, and after a second Anne realized those were the lines of the continents. The dots were on the land.

She could see a few on each continent, and only five in all of North America.

Her fear drew back a little as her curiosity started to recover. What was she looking at? They weren't near any of the cities she knew.

"What is it?" she whispered.

The lines of the continents faded in the middle, right around the Atlantic Ocean, and words floated to the surface. Pale blue words.

Remaining Human Population.

Anne gasped. She knew enough from school to recognize the vast, empty stretches where great cities were supposed to be. Millions and millions of people weren't there anymore. Chicago was gone, and so was St. Louis. The single, pale dot of her town was the only thing left in the whole Midwest.

Anne closed her eyes and shook her head, then covered her eyes with her hands to make sure. That was enough. Whatever this book was, she didn't want to see anything else it had to show.

Not now. Not ever.

She stood, keeping one hand over her eyes, the other held out to make sure she didn't run into anything. She backed away until she felt the shelf behind her. She walked slowly, hoping she could finally find the door in this awful place.

Sometimes in her dreams, she could run and run without ever getting anywhere. Anne was afraid she'd go crazy if that happened now, if she got trapped in this horrible place. The kind of crazy that waking up wouldn't even solve.

When she'd taken about ten steps, she peeked through her fingers.

She *did* see the door, a long way off through the stacks and tables and chairs. She lowered her hand and walked as fast as she could. The walkway out of this row of books and tables was getting more crowded by the minute. More chairs, desks, and even tables were everywhere, and she kept having to push them out of the way.

When Anne got to the end of the row, she stopped. She didn't want to look. She didn't want to see any more.

She had to look. If she didn't, she felt like she'd get trapped in this dream forever.

She held on to the shelf with one hand and a table with the other, and she turned her head slowly enough that she heard her neck creaking.

The huge book was still on the table, but it was closed now. Anne let out a breath she'd forgotten holding. A worried voice inside her head muttered that she should have put the book back in its place on the high shelf, but she didn't care. As long as it was closed, she wouldn't have to see anything else inside of it.

When she turned back toward the door, the path was even more full of chairs. She squared her shoulders and started walking, moving things out of her way, climbing when she had to.

If she didn't have to look at that book anymore, she wasn't going to let a little thing like getting out the door scare her. Sweat ran down her face and arms and legs, and all her muscles ached, but Anne kept moving faster.

When she finally jumped over one last chair and grabbed the cold metal handle with both hands, tears joined the sweat on her face.

The door to the outside closed behind her with a bang.

Anne sat up, wild-eyed, desperate to make sure she was still out of the library. She could barely see, even when she blinked and rubbed her eyes. A blue glow, way too close to the horrifying dots on that

TV screen, washed across her hands and arms. About the time her heart stopped pounding in her ears, she finally recognized the ceiling and shelves of her own bedroom.

Her face and her whole body were covered in sweat, so bad she could smell it. The sky was still dark outside. The clock beside her bed, the source of the glow, showed she had two more hours to sleep.

Sleep that might very well include more nightmares.

"Forget it," she whispered, swinging her legs over the edge. "Not worth it."

She dumped her pajamas in the hamper in the bathroom, thinking she'd probably need to do the same with her sheets. At eleven, she was pretty sure she was old enough to start doing her laundry herself, if nothing else to stop her mother from deciding to donate or throw away Anne's clothes without warning.

Right now she had to get in the shower and get the stink of the dream off of her skin.

Anne turned the water up as hot as she could stand it, until steam was pouring over the top of the sliding shower doors. She stepped in, hissing when the spray hit her, but she didn't turn the temperature down. She wished she could stand to turn it up a little higher, beyond the immediate reddening of her chest, arms, and belly.

Maybe enough scrubbing and soap with that scalding heat would get the reek of that library out of her pores.

After washing every inch she could reach and rinsing her pink washcloth until her fingers got wrinkly, Anne decided to go ahead and wash her hair. Might as well get ready to go to school, even if she had to try to sneak a nap during her afternoon classes.

She'd never had a nightmare quite like that one, and she'd had bad dreams as long as she could remember. It hadn't felt like a dream at all, not really. Anne was sure if she pulled the clothes she'd been wearing in the dream out of her closet, they'd be covered in the same musty smell as that library. She decided to hold her breath and dump them into the hamper under her sheets just so she wouldn't find out the truth.

Scrubbing her hair hard with a towel, hard enough that she knew she'd be combing out knots and tangles, didn't quite drown out the low hum lingering in Anne's ears. The same hum that awful book had made. She attacked her teeth just as roughly and with too much toothpaste, listening as hard as she could to the scratching of the bristles.

Anne started humming to herself when she walked back into her bedroom, and that finally replaced the sinister noise in her head. Or maybe her tuneless song only covered it up, but she didn't care.

Her eyes went to the row of spiral-bound notebooks on the shelves above her desk. She often wrote down her strange or scary or disturbing dreams when she woke up, and the good ones she remembered sometimes too.

Evan had given her the idea not long ago, when they were talking about her Gemaw moving out. He'd said she could write them down and that might make her feel better. And if that didn't work, she could take the notebook and tell her grandmother the next time they visited.

Anne was surprised at how often just writing it down helped, and she'd taken a bunch to read to Gemaw over the years as well.

She shook her head, humming a little louder without realizing it. She didn't want to write this dream down. The captured words and images, black ink following the pale blue lines on the paper, would give an already too real dream even more weight and substance.

That felt a big step too close to making it come true.

Chapter 5

A HUGE, echoing boom kicked off the dream next time.

Anne stood with her back against the door to the library, and she knew without trying that the door wouldn't open for her, not yet. She didn't want to be here, not here. The same library with the awful moving book was the last thing she wanted to see.

Anne took a few steps forward, determined to control something before bad things started to happen. Everything was so much larger than before, so big that her mind cried at trying to understand. The rows still went on as far as she could see in every direction, and the shelves again stretched so tall she couldn't make out the top of them against an invisible ceiling. The building still *felt* bigger, somehow.

Maybe this library was as big as the whole wide world.

If that was true, what if she got lost and couldn't find the door again?

The same stinky sweat covered her body, and Anne felt drops running down her scalp under her hair. She knew she'd wake up from the dream. She always had, even from the worst nightmare.

Still, this had the disturbing hint of reality, like she could open her eyes a thousand times and never be able to leave this place.

Well, she'd just have to stay within sight of the door and find something else to read. Eventually the door would have to open.

Anne turned the opposite way from where she'd gone the first time, when she'd had to climb over a thousand chairs and tables to get away from the huge reference books that now looked much taller than she was.

She spotted a shelf full of picture books only a few steps away from the door. These were all small enough to hold in her hands, books for children. Several tiny, brand new tables and chairs sat on a rug covered with blocks of vivid colors, and a fake hot air balloon in the same colors hung overhead.

Anne was her full size and age of eleven even in the dream, a little too old for such things. But she felt safe looking at them.

Most of all, and no matter how old she was, she needed something happy to look at. A clammy, dark feeling that something awful was going to happen kept rising up from under her bare feet, creeping slimy and cold up her ankles.

Anne needed something good to make her smile, to make her feel warm and silly. Not more terrible movies from the book about the future.

She took one more step away from the door, deciding losing sight of it just for a second would be worth the risk. Stepping under the balloon and onto the warm carpet dulled the echoes of the vast space around her, like she'd walked into a safe little tent. She pulled a bright book out from the low shelf that didn't even come up to her waist, one she remembered checking out herself just a few years ago. It was one about the moon.

She'd driven her parents crazy asking them to read it and renew it until they'd bought her a copy. She moved around the knee-high tables until she could see the door, then sat in the much too small chair. Her knees felt like they were as high as her shoulders. Anne laughed, the sound echoing too much for inside her sheltered tent.

The noise escaped into the unseen roof and bounced around, getting louder for several seconds before fading away. She was afraid a thousand little girls were laughing, just out of sight where she couldn't see them.

Anne squeezed her eyes closed tight, knowing the doorway out of the dream still wouldn't work yet. She vowed to keep quiet, opened her eyes, and started to read.

The words didn't quite make sense, but the soft, pastel drawings of flowers and castles and sweet animals were just what she needed to see. She gradually forgot the door, the awful book on the other side of the library, and the gigantic space all around her.

Her feet again felt like they were sinking into cold, sticky mud, right through the cheerful carpet, but she managed to ignore that for a while.

A loud click from behind her made Anne jump. She turned and blinked at a gigantic old wooden television on a metal cart she hadn't noticed before. Her teachers sometimes rolled a TV into the classroom for them to watch, like when the space shuttle launched, but this one was way too big.

Anne recognized her Gemaw's old set, the one in a cabinet that was big enough to sit on the floor and still be waist-high on a grownup. That couldn't possibly balance on top of the thin metal cart, but in a room bigger than the whole world, anything could happen.

Anne could hear the wood creaking and shifting as the huge TV warmed up.

Remembering the way the book had turned itself on, the bad book, she tried to get up and leave. Once again, she was held tight, unable to move.

"No," Anne whispered, trying to force her gaze away from the screen. "I don't want to see any more."

The black screen exploded into shapes and colors, and Anne couldn't stop herself from letting out a small scream at the swarms of bees. Her voice echoed again, getting louder and louder until she clapped her hands over her ears to block it out. All she could hear then was her own racing heartbeat, and sweat ran down her back despite the cool room.

Everything on the screen was the same, at least until the people with the guns showed up.

The people suddenly didn't look like drawings anymore. They looked like real people.

This time when the bad people shot, the groups of the dead didn't just turn into dust.

This time they were covered in blood that sprayed everywhere, and they were all screaming.

Anne squeezed her hands tighter over her ears, but she could still hear them. The same thing happened to mobs of people by the big round lakes, the only thing Anne knew more about now. She'd looked in her encyclopedias, too afraid to go to a real library. The first things the giant airplane had poisoned were for cities to clean their water, to make it safe for everyone to drink.

This time when the little girl drank the green water, the real little girl, she didn't just turn into dust. She turned green herself, then her body started to swell and look rotten.

Like in the first nightmare, the camera drew back until Anne saw hundreds of children beside the metal lakes, all drinking and falling and dying.

Even in a dream, Anne knew she couldn't possibly be smelling those tiny rotting bodies, but the thick stench coating her nose, mouth, and throat told her otherwise.

Finally the carnage on the screen stopped, with the cool, blue words floating in the middle of the Atlantic Ocean. The dots on all of the continents looked the same, and the words floated to the surface.

Remaining Human Population.

"How many are left?" she whispered.

The blue words in the middle of the ocean shifted and rearranged themselves.

Less than one million.

Anne covered her mouth, trying to keep breathing now that the stink of death was clearing. She knew a world with over four and a half billion people, and now there were less than one million?

She needed to get out of here before she saw more, and before the chairs completely blocked her path. She managed to raise one shaking hand and did the simplest thing she could think of. She pulled the plug.

When the TV went dark, Anne started to cry.

~

ANNE SAT STRAIGHT UP in bed, gasping for air. That awful dream, the same one as before? Barely a week had gone by since the first one. She'd finally started falling asleep without being afraid of it coming back. As soon as she'd let her guard down, she was right back there.

"You sound as crazy as Gemaw," she whispered, rubbing her eyes. "Talking to yourself isn't much better."

She dumped her pajamas in the hamper again on her way to the shower. Getting up two hours early had gotten her through the day the first time, but she didn't want this to become a habit.

She'd heard about recurring dreams somewhere, but she'd never had one. Why did it have to be a nightmare coming back? Why not a *good* dream?

Anne thought about her grandmother as she scrubbed and tried to steam the awful scenes and smells away. Calling her Gemaw crazy made Anne feel guilty, but it didn't feel far from the truth.

Her dad's mother was very sweet and very kind, just as when she'd lived here and comforted Anne after her ordinary bad dreams. Gemaw also didn't seem to understand what was real and what wasn't. Gemaw's mind ranged through time, like everything was happening at once. She was eight years old, she was in her thirties, she was her current age in her late sixties, she was twenty.

All of that in just one short visit.

Anne's dad said Gemaw had always been different, kind of unusual, but this had gotten worse as she got older. Anne had heard her mother talking about it to her Uncle Walt once though, and she'd told a very different story. More than any of the other times Anne had listened in to her parents and their grownup conversations, she regretted hearing what her mother said about Gemaw the most.

Her mother said Gemaw had always been nuts, that she'd never been right in the head. That the worst decision she'd ever made was to let someone like that move in where she could affect Anne. And the best had been when she agreed with the old woman that it was time for her to go.

Anne couldn't remember Gemaw living anywhere besides with them before she'd moved into her group home, though Anne's dad said she'd lived in her own house about an hour away until Grandpa died. Anne didn't really remember her grandfather either.

She didn't mind visiting Gemaw at all. It was like watching an actress play out different roles all in one movie scene. The thought of a movie made her shudder as she turned the water off.

That dream had been bad enough the first time, when the people looked like drawings. It had been creepier that way, really. More eerie than gory.

Seeing real-looking flesh and blood people was so much worse.

Anne got dressed for school, deciding to start writing down what she did before she went to sleep. She was still too afraid writing the dreams down would make things worse somehow, and she'd never tell her Gemaw about such awful things, anyway.

If something she was doing made those dreams happen, she might be able to change her habits. Her father had warned her about eating weird things or watching scary movies before bedtime. Her mother didn't want her reading too much before bed, either.

Anne hoped her parents were right. She was afraid of never getting free of the end of the world library, and of what that might mean for her mind and her sanity.

Chapter 6

Anne fell to her knees, hugging herself, tears streaming down her face. Not again.

Please, *please*. Not again.

She was in the same library, the same one she'd been dreaming of for weeks now. Sometimes the building was normal sized, like the one she never went to in town anymore. Sometimes it was gigantic, big enough to hold the whole planet.

Lately it had been tiny, making Anne feel like the room had been built with her flat on her back, close enough to keep her from drawing a deep breath. Books no bigger than her pinkie fingernail lined shelves pressed all along her whole body, and the ceiling pushed against her nose and stomach.

None of that mattered, not once the movie started. Realizing she was dreaming didn't make any difference at all. The moving scenes showed up no matter where she went, and they were getting worse.

The black and green computer screen the librarians used had revealed hand to hand fighting with knives and bullet impacts from the guns, all in close-up nauseating color and detail.

The encyclopedias had changed the shriveling people into starving people, and they weren't just getting thinner. Their flesh wasted away and sores grew on every part of their bodies. Their hair and then their teeth fell out before they finally fell. Horses, cows, chickens, even dogs and cats, joined the horrifying scenes, drinking the poisoned water with the same heartbreaking result.

In the claustrophobic space compressing her entire body, the white ceiling tiles with tiny black dots transformed into a screen. Anne was forced to watch people eating poisoned food, sometimes the poisoned animals, then throwing up until blood came out, then parts of their bodies followed. That smell, forced into her compressed nose, was by far the worst.

Anne had written down and tried changing all of her bedtime routines, but nothing had helped. At least a few times each week, and sometimes every single night, she was in the dreadful library.

"I have to change something in here," she whispered, wiping her eyes. "I've tried everything else."

She got to her feet and looked around, but today every section in the regular sized building looked exactly the same. The children's section was gone, the computers were gone, even the TVs that seemed to appear from nowhere were nowhere to be seen. Shelves and stacks of books stretched away from her, all of them dull and grey without any writing on the spine at all.

Anne looked to the right, where she'd found the TV screen book. She hadn't seen it again after that first dream.

"Maybe that's the problem," she said with courage she did not feel.

She walked toward that long, scuffed up table, trying to ignore her shaking legs. She had to do something to get the dreams to stop. Her schoolwork was suffering from the lack of sleep. She knew that even here. Her parents kept asking her what was wrong, though Evan had given up after a couple of weeks.

She knew she wasn't fooling anybody just as well as she knew she couldn't explain this. And she was afraid this dream was going to drive her crazier than she was already feeling.

She saw the original book, *The Future*, on exactly the same high shelf where she'd first found it.

Anne pulled it out, managing to get it onto the table without too much noise. Her stomach was twisting inside of her before she even got it open. The same screen was there, and the same touch of her fingers activated it.

Maybe it would be different this time.

Maybe it wouldn't be the ever worsening nightmare that wouldn't leave her mind all day long.

When the swarming bees appeared on the screen, Anne cried out and sat back in her chair. She knew she wouldn't be able to move or look away. She never could do that here.

The scenes played out again, each just a tiny bit more gory and graphic. The starved people and animals and war dead were piled up and burned in giant pits, and the smell and sound and even heat rose all around her.

By the time the blue letters appeared, declaring the world population at less than five hundred thousand this time, Anne was swallowing convulsively to keep from throwing up all over herself.

This had to stop, please.

"When is this going to happen?" she said, her voice trembling. "Will I be alive then?"

The letters faded before scrambling all over the screen, moving too fast for Anne to read. She waited, afraid to see the answer but afraid to turn away.

If she blinked, if she looked away for just a second, she could miss it. She could miss her chance to know what was going to happen and when, and maybe her only chance to stop the dream loop. The letters finally stopped moving.

You will be long gone, Anne Fincastle.

Anne tried to breathe deeply to stop the tears that kept welling up into her eyes. So many people dead. So many animals. So many children. No water to drink, no food to eat.

Deep down in her belly, Anne was relieved she would never see it. At the same time, she was terrified, and anger knotted up her face and her muscles.

This thing knew her *name.* This thing knew the way into her *sleep.*

This thing *never* left her alone anymore, even when she was awake.

If the dreams started happening during the day, too, Anne knew what little life she had now would shatter into useless pieces.

"Can I do anything about it? Can I save them?" She paused, then shouted loud enough to hurt her own ears. "Why do you keep showing this to me?"

You are the only one who can stop it. You are the only one who must. If you fail to act, all of humanity will perish.

The letters faded, and the outlines of the continents were again bright and clear. A few scattered dots on each land mass showed the pitifully few humans left on the Earth. Anne closed her eyes for a second, but when she looked back, she was sure some of the dots were missing.

Yes, one just went out, somewhere in Australia. They were going out on the other continents too, one after the other.

When all of the dots in Australia were gone, the outline turned red.

Anne gasped. The people were dying, all of them were dying. She tried to close the book, not wanting to see any more, but the screen now weighed a ton. She couldn't move it an inch.

The dots continued to go out, all over Europe and Africa, in China and India, then throughout South America. Anne kept trying to close the book, sweating and straining with the effort. It still wouldn't budge.

She watched, helpless, as each continent went red, one after the other, even the islands all around the oceans turned crimson. North America was last, with the lights fading from the coasts inward.

"No! I don't want to see this!"

When only two dots were left on the whole planet, one in Illinois, where Chicago should be, and one to the southeast where Evan went to visit his family in Virginia, Anne could finally move the book. She dug her fingers under both sides and pushed as hard as she could.

The book closed with a tremendous boom, far louder than before.

The floor shook underneath her, and she heard the other books rattling on their shelves.

The awful movie was finally gone.

THIS TIME ANNE woke with tears running down her cheeks and her pillow soaking wet. On one or two other nights, she was sure she'd screamed in her sleep, so this could be called an improvement.

The clock showed three hours before the sun would even come up. Waking up so early on a Saturday made her want to cry even harder.

She was so, so tired. Every part of her ached with exhaustion. Good nights were getting so rare that they seemed like a distant memory, like some kind of good dream she'd had years ago. She staggered into the bathroom and turned on the light.

She thought she looked nearly as old as her Gemaw now, like she'd skipped over turning twelve and gone straight on to sixty. Her green eyes were puffy and red, and she couldn't pretend the dark circles under them didn't show anymore.

Too many people had asked her about that.

Evan had noticed before anyone else did, even before her own mother.

Anne wondered sometimes if Evan liked her, not like a friend but like a girlfriend. She wasn't sure if she wanted him or anyone else to like her that way. It seemed like an awful lot of trouble to the adults she knew.

And if she was losing her mind just like her grandmother, no one would want to put up with that, anyway,

She washed her face and went back into her bedroom. She didn't think she'd be able to get back to sleep, but maybe she could figure it all out if she tried yet again. Anne sat down at her desk and got out her notebook, her special private notebook. It looked like a regular spiral notebook, and that was exactly what made it safe.

She was old enough to know writing *Private!* and *Keep Out!* and *Do Not Touch!* would only draw her parents to it like a beacon. This way, no one had any idea what was inside.

She turned to the last page with writing on it, nearly halfway through. She hadn't done anything special before falling asleep, and that never seemed to make any difference anyway. The dream seemed to be random, even though she was getting less and less of a break from it.

Nothing seemed to cause it, and nothing seemed to keep it away. That didn't make her feel better.

Anne drew a line under the last entry and started writing. She didn't note what had happened on the screen. She was still too afraid to do that, though she was running out of other ideas. She couldn't stand to try to remember it more clearly. Flashes of the dying and dead in her mind all day long were bad enough already.

She wrote down what she'd done in the dream, like she had the last several times. The one thing she hadn't done to try to change the pattern, the one thing she could think of to try, was just what she'd done tonight. Getting that original book down off the shelf hadn't improved anything.

All she'd learned was she was supposed to do something about it, and that even the survivors weren't going to last long. She put then pen down and rubbed her burning eyes, laughing under her breath.

"What am I supposed to do about a bad dream?"

As it turned out, she already had made the difference, at least for a little while.

The dreams stopped, but before a week had passed Anne would have welcomed them back. Now she was having visions, and not just at night.

She was having visions of the end of the world all day long. And the visions weren't just scenes like a movie, as awful that was.

Now Anne *lived* in the visions, she was part of scene. She heard the screams, smelled the blood and the fear. She felt the heat of the burning pits of human bodies.

More than Evan or her parents or her teachers were noticing something was wrong with her now. She knew she seemed to zone out and stare into space when she saw the visions. Evan had told her that, but she couldn't figure out how to stop them. At least with the dreams, she knew she'd be alone when they happened.

Now she never knew when a vision would hit her.

People on the street seemed to stare at her even when she wasn't having one, but before long Anne couldn't be sure about that.

Not once she stopped seeing the faces of people around her.

The first time it happened, Anne ducked into the girls' bathroom before anyone could notice. Her gym teacher, one of the few who took the time to make sure Anne participated in classes anymore, played the victim. Ms. Denton no longer had short curly blonde hair and a ready smile, or at least Anne hadn't seen that.

Most of Ms. Denton's head was missing, and part of her legs were, too.

Anne somehow knew a plane crash tore the woman out of life just as it tore her body.

She didn't have to fake throwing up that day, and for once she didn't hide the reaction. Her mother picked her up from school. Anne wasn't sure if staying in her room the rest of the afternoon kept her from seeing more.

Not until she left the house the next day and saw the faces of the dead everywhere.

Instead of a man walking into a store, she saw a soldier dying with blood gushing out of his belly. Instead of a little boy running across the playground, she saw a starving shadow of a human being, his head huge and his belly distended.

And worst of all, instead of a little girl walking into the kindergarten room she and Evan walked by on the way to their classes, she saw a skeletal, ill version of the girl, clutching and clawing at her throat as the water poisoned her.

Almost every person Anne saw turned into a death mask, some version of how they would eventually perish. She didn't know when it would happen, or even *if* it would happen, and she didn't care. She couldn't stand to see any more.

She kept her eyes down and hurried from class to class, then she rushed home and went upstairs to her room. Even her parents, even their faces were dead and cold and lifeless to Anne. She could hear them talking, but they looked like cold, badly made wax figures instead of people. She was grateful she couldn't see how they were going to die, but seeing them dead was bad enough.

The only person she could stand to be around was Evan. She could actually see his face, hear his voice, look into his beautiful pale blue eyes. He could talk to her, or at least talk at her, even though Anne could hardly ever manage to say anything back to him.

She was so glad he kept talking.

She felt bad for ignoring him, but she couldn't stand to be away from him or around anyone else. She wondered why she couldn't see his death or even her own in the mirror, but she was afraid to wonder too hard.

The last thing she could stand would be seeing his face disappear behind his particular version of the end.

After a month of the visions, she knew she had to talk to Evan about them. No one seemed to notice she never spent time with anyone else when she could possibly avoid it. But even with him walking beside her every morning and every afternoon, cheerfully talking nonstop the whole time, Anne was starting to get terribly lonely.

She hadn't really talked to anyone in so long, not since the nightmares first started months ago. And she'd realized that was the one thing she hadn't done to try to stop the dreams or the visions.

She hadn't told a living soul about them.

Maybe if she did that, maybe if she talked to her best friend in the whole world, the only friend who'd stayed by her side, the visions and the dreams would go away. Maybe if she brought it all out into the light, it wouldn't be able to torment her any longer.

She was so afraid he would start to look at her the same way other people had, at least back when she could see other peoples' faces.

She didn't know what she'd do if Evan stopped spending time with her, or if she started seeing his face disappear.

But she was too scared and lonely to keep it all to herself any more.

Chapter 7

Evan's nearly empty backpack banged against his shins every few steps, but he didn't bother slinging it onto his back. The early spring weather was just warm enough that it made him feel way too hot. As he walked toward home with Anne silent beside him, he enjoyed the hot sun on his face after a terribly long and cold winter.

He'd grown used to the sound of his own voice on these walks over the last few months, and the lack of any response from his friend. Evan talked about his day, all the trivial little details he was sure no one else in the world would want to hear. From the second he'd parted company with Anne that same morning, he filled in all the minutes and hours in between.

Each class, every conversation, even the thoughts that wandered through his mind when he was bored.

Once he ran out of daily chatter, Evan switched to the walk itself. He pointed out how the daffodils were lining the sunnier yards and driveways, joining the redbuds in an early show of color and new life. He mentioned how many trees held the first pink flush of budding, with only the stoic oak trees refusing to respond to false warm weather. A car that he didn't recognize passing them on the residential street made it into his comments from time to time.

Evan wasn't naturally given to so much inane conversation. He was far more likely to want to listen most of the time. But since Anne had started to withdraw over the winter, turning into a pale, barely there whisper of the friend he'd grown up with, Evan couldn't stand the silence between them.

It never occurred to him to spend time with someone else, someone who would talk instead of leaving him running his mouth constantly.

Because somewhere inside, he was afraid if he turned his back on Anne, she'd fade away into nothing. Evan was somehow even more afraid of sinking into withdrawal with her and disappearing.

He slipped his worn flannel shirt off as they walked onto a sunnier street, getting close to the park where they'd spent hours playing in happier times. Evan knew he was probably going to feel too old for such things in the fall when he started high school. He couldn't remember ever seeing kids that old in the sprawling public park, at least not near the playground equipment.

He sometimes saw them in twos or in groups huddled in the picnic shelters, surrounded by low conversation, loud music from giant silver boomboxes, or floating clouds of smoke.

The move to a new building wouldn't be all that far or dramatic once the coming summer passed and Evan joined those crowds of older kids. He'd even still be able to walk to school with Anne and have lunch with her, though his big sister Gwen told him that wasn't the best idea, hanging out with a middle school kid.

Evan nodded and let Gwen talk, but he couldn't imagine purposely avoiding Anne, either on this walk or in the cafeteria the middle school and high school shared.

Being in a different building than Anne all day long was going to be more than enough change for him.

They were just about to turn the corner toward their street when a low whisper startled him.

"I need to talk to you."

"What? Did you say something, Anne?"

Evan turned to look at her, certain he'd imagined hearing her voice. She hadn't spoken to him for what seemed like weeks now. She was looking right at him instead of at the ground, her green eyes wide and frightened. She slowed, then stopped. Anne fidgeted for a second, then grabbed Evan's arm.

"I need to talk to you."

She pulled him back the way they'd come, continuing on into the playground. Evan was too confused to do anything but follow. He watched her straight brown hair shifting over her shoulders, flat and lifeless as it had been for a while now. She kept pulling him past the redbud trees in full violet bloom and stopped beside the swings.

Anne kicked at the ground and stared at it too, not meeting Evan's eyes, for several seconds.

"Okay then, talk," Evan said, dropping his backpack. "You haven't said a word to me in ages."

Anne dropped her own backpack and sat on one of the swings. Her feet finally reached the dusty groove underneath instead of dangling above it, but she just sat there. Evan sat beside her, wondering what in the world he was supposed to do.

He'd been worried about her for a long time, everybody had, but she'd resisted everything he'd tried to figure it out. His constant chatter wasn't working, so he decided to be quiet until she decided to say something.

He didn't have to wait long.

"I've been seeing things, Evan."

He was relieved she was still staring at the ground instead of watching him. Her seeing him scowl when she finally started talking wouldn't help either one of them.

"Seeing things? I don't know what you mean."

"Dreams, like I always had, but worse," Anne said, her voice a little louder. "Visions. Nightmares. I don't know what to call them, but they're happening all the time now."

Evan stared at her, afraid to move. He didn't remember anything like that happening to his sister several years ago when she was eleven. He did remember some of the awful dreams Anne had told him about over the past few years.

Until she stopped telling him much of anything.

"What are you seeing?"

"The end of the world," she whispered, finally looking into his eyes. "I keep seeing the end of the world."

"You mean like in the Bible?"

"No, this isn't like that." Her eyes and mouth wrinkled, but not like she was going to cry. She stared over his shoulder for a few seconds before looking at him again. "This is people, people do it. At least part of it. The air is poison and the water is poison and nothing ever will grow anymore."

Evan blinked, casting around desperately for anything to say. All his words had left him, and most of his thoughts had too. All he had inside was fear.

"Is it something you've been reading? A book or something?"

"No, not a book, not a Bible, not a movie or a TV show," she said, her voice rising as she scowled at him. "It's not fake at all. It *happens*, Evan. It's going to *happen*."

Now Evan was starting to get a little mad to go with his fear. Was she just trying to prank him, to make him ask her stupid questions and then laugh and tell everyone? That had happened to him before. He wondered for a second if it was April Fool's Day, but that was a few weeks away.

Something in his gut told him Anne would never do that to him.

"Why do you... I don't want to hurt your feelings, Anne, but what makes you think this is all going to happen?"

"I can see they way it happens, and it already has. Remember I told you about the woman in the room across from my grandmother, where she lives? I started seeing her face hurting and blue, like she choked to death, for days before it she really did die that way. I never saw the body, but I heard my parents talking about it. That woman, she had food hidden in her room when she wasn't supposed to have anything crunchy. She choked to death, Evan."

"You didn't tell me all of that," Evan said. As unbelievable as this whole conversation was, he had to force his brain, and his heart, not to focus on her keeping secrets from him on top of not speaking for weeks. "Why didn't you tell me that when it happened?"

Anne stared at him, her eyes bright with tears nearly falling. He was afraid he'd already said too much.

"Would you tell anyone about this, Evan? About crazy dreams, about predicting when an old lady was going to die? If I'd said something about seeing her choke, maybe they would have found the food and stopped it, but I never did!"

Evan shook his head, the pain in her voice almost making him cry. He rubbed her shoulder, wishing he had the courage to hold her hand.

"You don't know," he said. "Maybe she had it hidden really well. Or maybe she would have just hidden more later. I'm sorry. This is visions, not just dreams? Or did you dream about her too?"

"No, I didn't dream about her. The dream is always the same, about the end of the world." She took a deep breath, her chin and lips quivering. "But now I can see the way everyone is going to die. Every person. People don't look like people to me anymore. They look like they're dead. And the same people look the same way, all the time."

Evan's stomach fell past his feet. He couldn't imagine anything more awful. No wonder she didn't look at anyone anymore. She was looking at him now, though, right into his eyes.

"What about me?" he said, his voice trembling. "How am I going to die?"

"You look normal to me." She nodded once. "You're the only one left. That's why I want to walk to school and home with you. To get a break from everyone and their dead faces."

Evan looked at Anne again, really looked at her, and he saw something about her for the first time. He knew she would never tell him something like this to trick him, or fool him, or scare him on purpose. Without having to ask, he knew she'd never told anyone else about this. Not her parents or a teacher or any other soul.

Anne trusted him.

She was scared to death, and she was still trusting him. Even if nothing she was saying made any sense to him, he couldn't turn away from her.

Not now, not ever. Evan's fear went deeper, driving cold through his whole body.

And his heart left the secure place in his own chest, something he hadn't even suspected it could ever do.

Evan's heart belonged to Anne from that moment forward.

"Okay, Anne. You see the end of the world. Tell me how it's going to happen. Maybe we can do something about it."

Chapter 8

A NNE COVERED her mouth with her hand, trying to stop what had to be her hundredth yawn this afternoon. Her watering eyes blurred the drawing of one of the blue-ridged mountains Evan constantly talked about after his visits to Virginia. The sharp colorful pencil lines morphed into a shimmering watercolor, then back.

The thick crust pizza the teachers had brought in for lunch sat heavily in her belly. Anne was afraid she'd start burping up pepperoni even worse than her smelly garlic breath any second now.

Evan sat next to her, his elbow occasionally brushing against hers. He hated drawing, and at thirteen he was two years older than everyone else in the class. Every time she glanced at him, he was scowling and chewing his lip.

Knowing he was only there because of her stirred up warmth in Anne's chest.

No one else at school knew how often Evan and Gwen came to Anne's house when their parents were fighting. Less than when they were all younger, sure, but more than he'd want anyone else to know.

Evan was the only person on earth who knew about her dreams, and the only one she could imagine ever telling. Talking to him helped somehow, forced most peoples' faces to go back to normal.

Anne yawned again, shaking her head to try to wake herself up as the teacher started talking about distance and perspective. The freezing cold classroom raised chills on her bare arms and legs but didn't help her fight off an intense need for a nap.

Evan grinned at her, his pale blue eyes merry, then went back to his labored drawing.

He was too nice to point out how this mid-summer art class had been Anne's idea in the first place, but here she was falling asleep. He'd never do that, not when he knew how little she slept at night.

Anne's eyes drifted closed, her fingers dragging a purple pencil through the middle of her pale green mountain lake. The teacher's voice faded. She tried one last time to shake herself, to stop the dream paralysis from taking over. For a second, she was more upset about falling asleep in front of everyone than whatever the dream might turn out to be.

That feeling didn't last out her next breath.

A woman sat in a bright yellow kitchen, her face buried in both hands. This didn't look like the things Anne been seeing during the night: strangers starving and fighting and dying in lands she didn't recognize. The woman and the house looked familiar, and she realized they felt familiar too.

Evan's house, and Evan's mother. Evan said she'd been home all week with awful headaches she got sometimes.

Mrs. Griffith looked up, and her face was all wrong. Her skin was pale and tight, like her whole body was clenched up. Like her whole body was tearing itself apart.

Anne tried to scream, no longer caring if everyone in the classroom heard her, but the sound never reached her throat.

She couldn't watch this. She'd seen too many people die in too many different ways in her visions and nightmares. She knew the look.

Evan's mom picked up her coffee cup and got to her feet. She grimaced and staggered, trying to catch herself against the counter. She fell hard, the cup shattering around her. She didn't move anymore.

Anne was caught, frozen, unable to even try to scream again. The other deaths she'd seen play out in her mind had been gory and sharp and horrible, but none were even close to this.

She knew this woman.

Evan's mom had always been kind to Anne, and Evan adored her. They were so much more alike than he was like his moody sister or his scary father. Now something awful had happened to Mrs. Griffith, and Anne couldn't remember what was going to happen next.

Couldn't *remember*? That didn't make any sense, but it did feel right.

This didn't seem like a nightmare anymore, far in the future, surreal and too vivid. This felt more like a memory, but Mrs. Griffith had seemed fine when they'd left Evan's house that morning.

Was this happening right now?

The horrible image inside Anne's mind got a thousand times worse when it split into three. In each one, Evan's mom was on the floor, her black hair covering her face. Motion in all three at once made Anne's head hurt.

She knew, somehow she *knew* she had to pay attention to everything.

Evan's father Ed walked into the kitchen, dropped his black briefcase, and knelt beside his wife. He touched her throat right below her jaw, then sat cross-legged beside her. He started to cry, the first time Anne had ever seen him do that. Ed was much more likely to shout.

He sobbed, rocking and holding his sides. After what seemed like hours and hours, he slowly got up and walked out of the kitchen.

When he came back, Anne couldn't quite make out what he had in his hand. Something black and metallic. He sat down again, with the thing in one hand and the other on his wife's shoulder. He looked at her for a long time, then brushed her hair back from her face.

Her eyes, pale blue like Evan's, wide and staring at nothing.

Mr. Griffith leaned down and kissed her. He put the thing in his mouth, and just as Anne realized what it was, a crashing boom jerked his whole body. She remembered that sound too well from too many nightmares. He slumped forward over his wife's body, a dark red lake growing all around them.

The last thing Anne saw was Evan, walking into the room alone.

At the same time…

Evan found his mother. He shouted and fell sobbing to his knees beside her. Anne saw herself in this memory, walking into the kitchen, panting from running through the painful heat outside. When Evan turned toward her, his broken, terrified eyes made her want to disappear.

In that instant, seeing how her friend was falling to pieces, she understood why Mr. Griffith put the gun in his mouth.

At the same time…

The third memory was the worst, so bad that Anne tried to keep herself from seeing it at all. Evan got home after his father, but not so long after. He walked in to catch his dad getting the gun out of the hall closet beside the front door.

After staring at Evan for a long time, ignoring the questions, Ed Griffith's face turned hard and empty. He hugged Evan, something else Anne had never seen him do, then put an arm around him as they walked toward the kitchen.

Anne tried to reach out somehow, to stop them, to get Evan's attention, to make even one small thing change. In the end, at least she didn't have to watch. She only saw the kitchen door swing closed. Evan screamed a second before the crashing boom. She heard a second shot.

It was all over.

In the same instant, Evan's father got home alone. Evan got home alone. Evan walked in the front door and saw his father with the gun.

In the same instant, Evan's dad slumped over his wife. Evan fell to his knees beside his mother. Two gunshots rang out.

They were all memories.

They were all true.

None of them had happened yet.

"Hey, wake up!"

Anne jumped, focusing on the room around her, on the voice of her friend.

Evan.

He still didn't know, he didn't know anything. His mother was dead, but that was the least of it.

He was going to go home and his father was going to be dead, too. He was going to go home and find his mom, lying cold and still. He was going to go home, and his father was going to kill him, then kill himself.

Anne couldn't let any of those things happen. She couldn't imagine how she could stop them.

Anything she did might make the worst memory come true.

"Where've you been?" Evan said, waving his hand in front of Anne's face.

She blinked, then turned toward him. Her eyes were dazed, like she wasn't seeing him at all. Evan didn't think she'd met anyone else's eyes for months, not since she'd started having nightmares almost every night. She hardly ever looked at anyone besides him anymore.

He touched her arm.

"You okay, Anne?"

She gasped and finally focused on him. He started to move his hand, but she grabbed it. He was a little scared by the tears in her eyes.

"Evan," she whispered. "Don't go home."

"What? Why would I go home? We're here for another three hours. This crazy class in the middle of vacation was your idea, remember?"

She shook her head, still staring into his eyes.

"Listen to me. Evan, you have to listen to me!"

She let go of his hand, but before Evan could be disappointed, she was hugging him tight. His heart pounded, and other parts of him responded, too. Kids glanced at their table, looking confused or smirking, all of them younger than he was.

Before he could decide what to do, Anne whispered, her warm breath against his ear giving him goosebumps.

"Don't go home. Don't go home, please. Don't go home."

Evan forgot about all the other kids and the teachers too.

"Anne, you're scaring me. Come on, don't do that."

What Evan wanted to do was hold her as long as she'd let him. She felt so warm in his arms, so perfect, and her hair smelled like the sun. But he hadn't been lying about being scared. Anne knew how much he hated that. He held her shoulders.

"What's going on? We're supposed to wait here for your dad to pick us up. Why can't I go home?"

She wiped at her eyes, but the tears kept falling. One of the teachers was going to notice everyone looking in their direction. Evan was sure he needed to know what was upsetting her, even if he got both of them into trouble.

"Just stay here, and you can go to my house later." Anne was nodding, her words running together. "My parents never mind when you come over. That will be better."

"No, tell me what's wrong," Evan whispered when he wanted to shout. "Tell me now."

"Ms. Fincastle? Mr. Griffith? Is this class boring you so much that you must interrupt everyone else?"

Evan shook his head without looking at the teacher. He should just apologize, get back to work on his terrible drawing, and worry about all of this later.

Something in Anne's eyes warned every nerve in his body.

"Stay here, Evan," Anne said, her breath hitching in her chest. "Don't go home."

Evan stared at her, trembling starting in his belly and moving up to his heart and brain.

If he left now, he could make the walk in about ten minutes. Less if he ran.

That was exactly what he needed to do. He needed to run.

Another teacher spoke from right behind him.

"Both of you get back to work. Your parents paid good money

for you to learn something, not for you to cut up and disrupt everyone else."

His parents.

Evan's jaw dropped. Anne's eyes squeezed closed, and she was crying harder, her mouth turning down. He barely heard her, but she was still whispering.

"No, don't go home. Don't go home."

He grabbed his backpack from under the table and shoved the chair out of his way.

"Evan!"

He ignored her and kept walking. He made it out of the classroom and halfway down the hall before he started to run. Evan pushed the doors open with both arms straight out in front of him. The midsummer Illinois heat hit him like a suffocating blanket, but he kept going.

By the time he got to his block, he had to slow to a walk, grabbing at the cramp in his side. No one else was out, everything still and quiet in the terrible heat. He wiped sweat from his eyes and face and kept moving.

Evan imagined everything that could be happening, from a robbery to a fire to his sister coming home from college to throw some kind of fit. He saw no smoke, but he was still relieved when he didn't see fire trucks. His sister's car wasn't there either.

Evan's flesh felt like it was going to boil off his bones. No thief would possibly be out on an afternoon with the air over one hundred degrees and soaking wet.

Walking up his driveway, still pressing his hand against the sharp pain in his ribs, Evan didn't need Anne to tell him something was horribly wrong.

～

BY THE TIME Anne made it to the big double doors, Evan was gone. He'd been out the classroom before she could even grab her own bag. She groaned at the blast of summer air and fierce sunlight, making her head pound after the freezing cold classroom.

Keeping both of them inside was one of the reasons their parents had agreed to the expensive class, but Anne wasn't worried about that. She was worried about not being able to see her friend at all.

She started walking, but before she left the school grounds she was running. Evan was two years older, several inches taller, and much faster. She'd never be able to catch him.

The awful memories of Evan's father getting home first hadn't faded at all inside her.

What if Mr. Fincastle decided to go home early today? What if she hadn't seen hours later, but what was going to happen in just a few minutes? Anne felt like she was drowning in the humid air, but she kept running. She had to make sure.

Please, don't let it be one of the other memories. Please.

Anne was gasping by the time she saw Evan's house. There was no car in the driveway. She stopped with her hands on her knees. No car.

Mrs. Griffith parked around back.

Evan's father wasn't home yet, not unless he had walked for some crazy reason. He worked in the city, so that probably meant he wasn't here. He might not know yet, but he could still show up if Evan called him or called the police or an ambulance.

The memory of Evan's face in all three memories, his broken and haunted eyes, got her moving again.

Evan turned the key in the lock, still listening for the imagined burglar. Cool air hit as hard as the hot air had, raising chills all over his sweaty body and making his head pound.

Too cold, it was way too cold with no one home. His parents always adjusted the thermostat when they were all out.

"Anyone here? Hello?"

He closed his eyes for a second, holding on to the door. He heard his mother's voice in his mind, warning him about coming into a cold house after running around outside. Warning him he could throw up or pass out and hit his head. His head was indeed swimming, his stomach turning slow, sickening loops.

He remembered how pale his mom's face had been that morning, even though she'd planned to go back to work today. He dropped his backpack and walked toward the kitchen, keeping one hand on the wall in case he got dizzy again.

"Mom?"

The house was silent except for the rumble of the air conditioner, straining to keep up with the heavy air outside. Something didn't feel right. Evan was covered in chills again, this time unrelated to the cold.

He wished he'd listened to Anne, that he was still beside her, failing miserably to draw anything even he could recognize.

He should have waited. He should have thought this through like his father constantly said, called home or either of his parents instead of charging in here by himself. He'd never even thought of stopping at the pay phone he ran by in the hallway at school. Now it was too late to leave.

His guts knotted up and he was afraid he was going to be sick after all. He pushed the kitchen door open.

"Mom!"

She was on the floor, broken pieces of her coffee cup all around her. Evan fell to his knees, not noticing the shards that cut into his jeans and his palms.

He didn't need to check her pulse or her breathing.

He knew.

"Mom, please!"

Evan rolled her onto her back anyway, and her head rolled with her. Pale blue eyes just like his were open and staring at nothing. Evan's breath caught exactly the same way Anne's had, and he reached out with a shaking hand, touching right under her jaw.

Her flesh was cold, so cold.

Nothing inside her was moving anymore.

Chapter 9

ANNE CLOSED the door to Evan's house quietly, not sure why at first. Then she knew.

Anne still saw all three of those memories; she *felt* all of them.

Evan alone. Evan's dad alone. Evan walking in on his father with the gun.

Mr. Griffith wasn't here yet, but disaster was still coming. She looked at the closet beside the front door. Evan had never mentioned his father having a gun, but that didn't matter.

Anne opened the door, blinking when the bright light came on. She stepped up onto a grimy tackle box. She closed her eyes, trying her best to focus on just one memory.

All three of them were still playing in her mind, still rushing toward her with devastating force.

She leaned up as far as she could, calf muscles cramped from running in the heat, grasping the doorjamb. Right there, she'd seen Evan's father reaching right there. Her fingers felt something heavy, like bumpy leather instead of the steel she'd seen. She stood on her tiptoes and got the whole thing into her grasp.

Anne held the handgun from her memory. The light brown leather holster, embossed with some kind of western design with a dark EG in the middle, covered it almost completely, but this was the same gun. She touched the cold, oily barrel.

In her mind, she heard the crash as it fired: once, twice.

She stepped down and closed the door. Anne let her backpack slide down onto her elbow and unzipped the biggest compartment. The gun made her bag way too heavy, but it fit. She zipped her pack up, then carefully put it down beside Evan's.

Anne concentrated on the images still screaming through her head. Evan turning his face up to her was clear and substantial, and her own tears started. The other two, the memories with the gun, felt a tiny bit lighter.

Maybe she was making some kind of difference after all. She took a deep breath and walked toward the kitchen.

When she reached up to push the door open, Anne felt an odd tingling. She stared at her hand, surprised she couldn't see tiny blue lightning racing over her flesh. Nothing like this had ever happened to her before, but it wasn't exactly scary.

She had a sense of anticipation, of completion. No matter what happened when she opened the door, it was going to be terrible.

But Anne knew it was going to be right.

～

"Evan."

He turned at Anne's voice, sinking back to sit on his own heels. She was as red and sweaty and overheated as he'd been a few minutes ago, and she was crying again.

"You knew about this?" he whispered, looking back into his mother's eyes.

"I saw…I saw this. Right now. I remembered seeing you beside her. I didn't know what to do."

"When?" Evan wondered at the blood on his palms, still not feeling the cuts. "When did you see it?"

"When I told you." Anne knelt beside him, avoiding the broken cup. "Not until then."

Evan looked up at her, into her lovely green eyes. She was shaking her head and crying harder.

"I couldn't stop it, it was too late, your mom, I mean, but I thought if I could stop you from coming home, it wouldn't hurt you so bad. I couldn't let this be even worse."

"Hurt me." Evan couldn't understand her words or his. He stared at his hands again.

"I'm sorry, Evan, I'm so sorry. I couldn't make it stop."

He turned back to Anne, his movements and his thinking painful and sluggish.

Something. He had to do something.

His mother was…

His mom, she was…

"Be careful." Anne held out her hands. "You're going to cut yourself."

"My mom," Evan whispered, unable to find any other words. "My mom."

"I know, Evan. I'm so sorry."

Evan finally moved, crawling toward Anne, desperate to get to her before something inside of him broke.

He could feel it, a dam overflowing and cracking down the middle, failing to hold back a torrent that would drown everything and everybody in its path.

He grabbed her around the waist and held on for dear life, wondering if he would still exist after the flood.

ANNE SAT beside Evan on the couch in his living room, trying not to stare at Mr. Griffith. He'd charged right through the house without saying a word, staying in the kitchen for a long time. He'd only staggered back out when the paramedics arrived with grim faces, soft voices, and a stretcher piled up with all kinds of equipment she didn't recognize.

Evan's father had paced for a few minutes, still without speaking. Anne was terrified he would walk right to that closet and look for his gun, even with her sitting there. He'd glanced at the door every time he passed by, but he made no move to open it.

Once he finally sat in his favorite recliner across from them, her fear only worsened. Mr. Griffith stared at the coffee table between them, as if he was deeply offended by the piles of books and magazines that were always scattered across the surface.

He was still wearing his gray jacket, but he'd loosened his tie and unbuttoned his white shirt. Anne had never seen him looking so bad outside of her own strange memories, his thick brown hair standing up and his face blotchy. He started asking the same questions over and over again as soon as he sat down, but that wasn't what bothered Anne.

Evan's father vibrated like a cartoon character who'd been hit on the head with a giant hammer. She was sure it was one of her visions, something only she could see. His clothes didn't move, and neither did his hair or the chair he sat in. But to Anne's eyes, his face, eyes, and hands shuddered and flashed, shifting before she could figure out what was real.

She saw the red face, the messy hair. She saw his face pale and white, his son's blood splattered across his cheeks and forehead. She saw his eyes rolled up and empty, much more blood and gore welling out the top of his head.

The gun was still too close. Anne hadn't done enough to change what was coming. But she knew Evan's father would stop her if she tried to get away now.

"Your class was supposed to last all day, wasn't it?" he said. "Why were you here so early?"

Ed Griffith had asked that question already. He didn't seem to be hearing or seeing anything around him. Anne didn't know if she'd ever be able to explain what she'd seen back in the classroom to Evan, much what she saw now. She knew she'd never be able to explain any of it to Mr. Griffith.

She was too afraid her jittery vision meant the gun was the only thing he *could* focus on.

"We were bored with the class, Dad," Evan said, trying again with the same lie. "We decided to come home. We were going to get something to drink because it was so hot. Anne's parents weren't there yet. Then I…I called you when I saw."

Evan's dad covered his face with his hands, shaking his head.

She couldn't understand why she still saw the memories that hadn't happened, any more than the unnerving appearance of him. The memories with the gun. She hoped those would fade away. At least his voice sounded singular, steady.

"You should have stayed at school, son. You were supposed to stay there all day. That was the plan." Mr. Griffith got louder with every word. "That was what you told me. I would have never wanted you to see this. If you wanted to come home, you should have called me."

Evan turned to Anne, tears running down his cheeks again. She wanted to hug him, but not with his father there.

"I didn't think about calling. We just left. I'm sorry."

"That's just it, Evan, you didn't think!" Ed Griffith shouted, clenching his fists and glaring at his son. "You never think anything through!"

Evan's face went white. Anne finally understood why he and Gwen called their father Hurricane Ed.

"I think it's time for you to go, Anne. Your mother…" Evan said, his voice breaking. He held his breath for a second. "Your parents are going to be worried."

"Maybe that's best," his father said, looking at the floor. "I shouldn't have shouted like that. We've got a lot to take care of before your sister gets home."

Anne didn't need the memories to know that was going to be awful. Gwen was as likely as Mr. Griffith to get angry when no one expected it, much more so than Evan or his mother were.

His mother *had been*. Mrs. Griffith would never *be* anything again.

Anne hated to leave her friend, but she wanted to see her own parents very badly.

She took Evan's hand and stood beside him. He squeezed hard enough to hurt her fingers, but she didn't let go. Evan picked up her backpack, but he didn't seem to notice the extra weight. Anne was afraid to say anything to stop him.

"Thank you for staying, Anne," Mr. Griffith said, still looking down. "I still don't understand why either of you were here so early, but I'm glad Evan wasn't alone."

"I'm sorry," Anne said to Evan instead of his father. "I wish I could do something."

All three of them jumped when the kitchen door opened.

"I'll walk you home," Evan said, and they left without looking back.

He didn't let go of her hand or say a word on the walk, two doors down and across the street. They sat on the swing on her porch, facing away from his house.

Anne didn't want to watch the paramedics wheeling his mother out. She didn't want Evan to see either. Neither of them spoke until the silent ambulance drove by.

"Are you going to be okay tonight?"

"I don't know, Anne. I've never had one of my parents die before." He looked at her for a second, then he hugged her hard. "Thank you for trying to stop me."

He was down the steps before she could say a word. Anne stayed where she was, staring at the oak tree beside her house, not wanting to watch him go back home.

She remembered now that Evan and his father were going to have a terrible night. It would only get worse when Gwen got there.

She kept waiting for the other memories to calm down, but they were still strong within her. The crashing boom echoed through her mind, and Anne knew she had to get rid of the gun. If she took it into her house, her parents would find it. They'd guess where it came from too, with Mr. Griffith's initials on the holster.

The early evening was still uncomfortably warm, but she grabbed her backpack and walked around to the garage to get her bike.

~

THE SAFEST PLACE she could think of, a huge row of dumpsters behind a strip mall, was only a couple of miles away. Anne was dripping with sweat by the time she got there. She'd only passed a few cars along the way, and no one else was out walking or riding in the damp heat.

The sky was still light, but no one was behind the stores either. There weren't any windows on this side, only a solid row of cinderblock and stacks of empty wooden pallets. Sometimes Anne saw teenagers back here smoking. Cigarette butts, empty liquor bottles and beer cans, and food containers drifted against the dumpsters. If any of the stores had cameras, she was sure no one bothered checking them.

She got off her bike and walked down to one of the huge bins for the grocery store. That would be a great place with so many bags jammed into it each day. She lifted the lid, wrinkling her nose at the rotten stench even when it was mostly empty. She got the gun and holster out, then she froze.

She'd seen more than kids smoking back here. She'd seen grownups, sad and dirty grownups, rummaging through the grocery dumpsters. No, she couldn't put the gun here.

She walked her bike past three more dumpsters until she got to one behind a department store that always had discounts and sales going on. When she raised the lid, Anne saw a bunch of hangers, packaging, and empty boxes. Not much worth digging around in.

This one didn't really smell bad, but Anne still held her breath as she reached in for a huge wad of plastic. She took the gun out of the holster and wrapped it up. By the time she was finished, the gun was only a stain in the middle. She tied some long, white plastic strips around the whole thing and dropped it into the dumpster.

Anne turned the holster over in her hands. Nothing would link it to Evan's father besides the initials, but she still didn't want to leave it here. If someone found this, that could lead right to the gun, and the whole thing might end up back in Evan's house.

She smiled, surprised she could with her heart breaking for her friend. She knew exactly the right place. She put the holster in her backpack and rode away.

Less than ten minutes later, Anne stood on a bridge outside of town.

The road didn't even have lines on it because no one lived out here. The pavement went on for another mile or so, then it was just a gravel farm road passing through endless rows of corn and soybeans. Anne knew it wasn't possible, but she and Evan had ridden far enough out there that she was halfway convinced the road never ended. It only branched off into dirt roads and kept going on forever.

The river beneath her flowed fast with recent storms. The holster wouldn't sink to the bottom to be found someday during a drought. It would float away, with any luck ending up in the next county before it ever washed ashore. Anne had a feeling the muddy water would take care of the initials long before then.

She braced her hip against the concrete rail and threw the holster into the middle of the river. It sank for a second, then resurfaced several yards away. She closed her eyes and counted to ten. This time it was only a pale brown blob, so far away she wouldn't have known what it was.

Anne sighed, holding on to the hot, pebbled concrete as her whole body sagged. Seeing the holster floating away was only part of it. The memories, the two awful memories, had shifted somehow. They didn't seem real anymore, like they were waiting right around the corner.

The images were still vivid and terrible, but they felt like dreams now, normal dreams instead of nightmares. No longer deep and heavy and threatening, the scenes of Evan's father and the gun were now light as campfire smoke.

Evan's mother was still gone, and his family was going to suffer terribly over that. Evan most of all. But everything had changed.

As soon as Anne saw Evan's house on her way home, she remembered all the things he would do and every word he would say to her over the next few months. She couldn't do a damned thing to stop it, or change it, or make it easier for him. All she could do was wait and listen when Evan needed to talk.

He would need to whisper and shout and groan and cry, and he would need to be still and silent for longer than he ever had. As bad as the long days ahead would be, she knew everything could have been so much worse.

Anne hoped remembering what didn't happen would give her the courage to go through everything that did.

Chapter 10

For the first time in her life, Anne was relieved when school started. Not because the classes were a little better than the year before, though they were. Having an art class and a music class made a huge difference, choices she finally had getting into middle school.

She didn't even mind getting up so early, not as long as she got to sleep in plenty of time. The whole summer seemed like an effort to stay up as late as she could for some reason, with her body in an ongoing rebellion.

That disruption did have benefits, with Anne noticing a few changes she'd started to despair of ever happening. A few stray hairs in her armpits and lower down. A hint that she may actually need a bra at some point in her life. Increasingly oily skin and a few pimples around her nose seemed like a small price to pay if she was finally going to grow up a little bit.

She glanced at Evan, walking beside her in silence, no longer filling in the space with chatter about how his school day had gone. They'd gotten into the habit of walking the path around the park near their houses a few times before going home this year. Anne didn't have to ask why Evan wanted to take the extra time.

Living with only Hurricane Ed wasn't getting easier with passing time.

Her friend seemed to have talked himself out over the past few months, trying to adjust to his new reality without his mother. Anne missed the constant updates, the peek into what she could expect in whatever grade Evan was passing through.

She missed his light and happy company. Knowing he'd probably felt the same when she sank into silence the spring before only made her feel worse.

Anne saw other changes in Evan, even though she saw him so often over the summer that it was hard to notice. His voice settled into a deeper range, and she'd noticed how much hairier his arms, legs, and armpits were when they went swimming. He was growing even taller now, getting stronger in his back and shoulders. Once in a while Anne wondered if he was growing hair she couldn't see, like she was.

She would never admit it to another soul, but spending so much time with her friend was the main reason Anne was relieved about school. The separation she'd dreaded, with Evan going to the high school building instead of the one she was in, gave her the distance she hadn't realized she needed.

They still walked to and from school together, like always, and they ate lunch together most days. But the hours and hours of listening to him, mourning with him, had taken a toll on Anne. She was tired in a way even the constant dreams last spring couldn't manage. She hoped she hadn't exhausted Evan by telling him about the dreams in the first place.

The dreams and visions left her in peace, at least for the moment. That weary part of her felt like it was slipping somehow, like the nightmares had only retreated after the living nightmare of Evan's mother dying. Anne was sure they lingered still, waiting to see if she would recover enough to hold them back.

"I had to talk to the counselor today," Evan said, startling Anne. "They pulled me out of gym class for it."

Evan looked at her, rolling his eyes. He kicked a rock out of the way.

"Ms. Fleming? What was she like?"

"A waste of time. I hated it."

Anne had seen Ms. Fleming watching her at the end of the last school year, when she started to have the awful dreams. That was one reason she'd tried so hard to keep her school work at some kind of reasonable level. She was sure Ms. Fleming was nice enough, but her constant smile made Anne nervous.

"What happened?"

"She gave me this big lecture all about how it was okay to be sad, that no one was going to think I was weak for that. Does she really think I don't fucking know I'm sad? My Mom died!"

Anne was surprised at Evan talking that way, but she didn't want to upset him even more. She'd heard plenty of older kids using that word, but she'd never heard it from him. She sometimes forgot that he *was* two years older.

Evan sighed, a harsh, painful gust.

"She spent the rest of the hour digging and digging at me, trying to get me to tell her about the day it happened."

"What did you say?"

"I didn't want to say anything, that's private. No one knows about that day but you."

Anne felt her own cheeks turning red at that. He was right. No one else knew what had really happened, and even he didn't know all of it. She didn't know if she'd ever be brave enough to tell him, especially about his Dad and the gun.

"I told her Mom had an aneurysm," Evan said, "and that was it. She kept asking who found her, who found her, and of course she already knew. Why else would she ask that to begin with?"

They walked on for a few minutes, and Anne had no idea what to say or do. Evan had talked about that day for hours on end, to her. He'd had plenty to say.

"I think she was trying to get me to cry, to see if I would or something," he finally said, watching a bunch of kids playing soccer. "Like that would prove I was doing better, if I could cry on command for her."

"Did you?"

"Of course not!" Evan glanced at her, his eyes and mouth drawn in. "I'm sorry, I'm not mad at you. But I wasn't going to tear up because she wanted me to. I just looked her in the eye and answered her questions. She finally let me go, but she wants to see me a few times a week."

"Why?"

"I'm guessing my father wants her to," Evan said, pushing his hair off his face. "He has to be the one who told her about me finding Mom. And that keeps him from having to deal with me now that Gwen's back at college. I guess it keeps me from having to deal with him, too."

"I'm sorry, Evan. I wish I could help."

"You do help. I would have gone crazy stuck in that house with the two of them all summer. And I do need someone to talk to, just not them or Ms. Fleming. You don't make me feel like I have to pass some kind of sadness test so I'll be normal. I just feel how I feel with you."

He smiled at her for a second, then he looked back at the path. Anne knew Evan was able to cry, and that she could too. She'd been afraid he'd never stop a few times over the summer.

"Dad could stand to find someone to talk to," Evan said. "He needs it way more than I do. I wonder if Dad's making Gwen see someone."

"Think she'll cry on command?" Anne said, trying to imagine either Gwen or Ed showing that much emotion that wasn't anger.

"She'd probably scare anyone to death who tried. I'd like to see that, though."

Chapter 11

Evan saw the trouble before Anne did. Gwen's tiny blue Chevette was in the driveway, earlier than she normally would be on a Friday. He hadn't expected her at home at all this weekend, so it couldn't possibly be good news.

Anne caught on before he had a chance to say a word.

"Looks like you can ask Gwen about the counselor."

"Yeah. No need to wonder. No need to wonder how my weekend's going to go, either."

Anne smiled up at him, but her eyes were more tired than anything. Guilt he'd been feeling more and more curdled in his stomach, guilt at taking up too much of his friend's time and energy.

"Will you be okay, Evan?"

"I'll be fine, don't worry. Crazy as they both are, they're my family, I guess. We have to get this worked out sometime. Maybe I'll see you tomorrow?"

She stopped, her body facing her own house, face turned toward him. Evan tried to keep his eyes on hers, but he kept watching her chew her lip. Just a little tic of hers, nothing she even noticed doing. But he never failed to notice when she did.

"Call me later if you need to," she said with the first real smile he'd seen all day.

Evan watched her run across the street, stop to wave from her porch, then disappear into her house. Into her typical, normal family. Mother *and* father, no dramatic older sibling, no shouting he could hear from down the street.

He hadn't forgotten Anne's dreams or her strange visions, and he certainly hadn't forgotten her somehow knowing what had happened to his mother. But Evan envied Anne's family more with every passing second.

Standing out here on the sidewalk wouldn't be the best way to meet his father coming home, especially not with his sister already inside. Gwen knowing what was going on before everyone else did might make things calmer for her, but Hurricane Ed never seemed to like surprises.

Evan didn't like *any* of this, but he walked the few steps home anyway.

Gwen met him at the door before he could even drop his backpack or take his shoes off. She'd changed her look again, with some kind of pale makeup and dark eyeliner to match her dyed black hair. Her ripped jeans and faded black t-shirt seemed fairly normal, but Evan would have bet his allowance that she wore stranger things when she was at school.

"Did he make you talk to a shrink?" she said, blocking Evan's path away from the door.

Evan ducked around his sister, noticing he was almost as tall as she was.

"Good to see you too, sis."

"Yeah yeah, happy family reunion and all. We'll talk later." Gwen followed him into the kitchen nearly on his heels. "Come on, before he gets home. Did you have to see someone?"

Evan grabbed a bottle of soda out of the refrigerator, hesitated, then got two glasses out. He only poured for himself, though.

"I had to talk to the counselor at school today," he said. "I don't know if she's a real shrink or not, but she sure thinks she is."

Gwen filled her glass to the rim with the rest of the soda. She crinkled the bottle slowly enough to make Evan want to scream before she dropped it in the trash.

"He made me see one, too. Or at least he made the arrangements with my advisor. This one's real, I guess. A real graduate student. Poor guy deserves better than me for his first time out."

Evan tried to stop it, but the idea of some poor almost doctor, barely more than a kid himself, trying to make Gwen cry on command got to him. He laughed with a mouthful of the bubbly dark liquid and somehow managed not to inhale or spit it all over the floor.

"I doubt Ms. Fleming was ready to deal with the mood I've been in lately, either."

They both turned at the slam of a car door outside.

"Hurricane warning," Gwen said, draining her glass and closing her eyes. "I'm sorry, Evan. I know you hate this kind of shit."

"For once, I'm glad to have the excuse to get into it with him. Don't worry. I'll let you take the lead."

The two of them walked into the living room, arranging themselves on the couch without having to say a word. Gwen sat across from their father's recliner, leaving Evan a few feet farther away. Angry as he was, Evan didn't mind the distance.

Telling Ms. Fleming he needed help, telling her anything about Evan's personal, private life, was a step too far for his father to take. If Evan was ever going to speak up about anything, now was the perfect time.

He felt that way for all of about fifteen seconds, until Hurricane Ed opened the door.

Ed Griffith stopped as soon as he spotted his children, one hand on the doorknob, face stony and emotionless. He closed the door and leaned against it, locking gazes with Evan.

"What a nice surprise," their father said, voice flat, face still not showing any emotion. "Two for the price of one. Good to see you, Gwen."

When Ed finally focused on his sister, Evan's whole body started shaking and sweat broke out all over him. Without raising his voice or even saying anything directly to him, his father managed to terrify him to the core.

Ed had never hit him, and as far as Evan knew, he'd never hit

Gwen or his mother, either. But even the promise of confrontation, a promise he was certain his sister was going to keep, turned Evan into a trembling mess.

"Great to see you too, Dad," Gwen said, as if she could read Evan's mind. "Can't say I liked the surprise you sent for me today all that much."

Mr. Griffith stowed his briefcase and jacket in the closet by the door, then took his time loosening his tie before he turned around or answered.

"Is that all it takes to get you to come home for a visit these days?" he said, glancing at Gwen and Evan in turn. "I'll keep that in mind."

He walked into the kitchen, as if everything was normal and no one was upset at all. Evan couldn't imagine his father missed the thick, painful air in the room, like someone had dumped dust full of broken glass into the vents. His own lungs resisted drawing as much as a breath.

"Relax, Ev," Gwen said in a low voice when he turned to her. "All part of the game. He's trying to piss us off enough so we'll give up. Don't let him."

She looked calm enough, no more upset than their father was. When Ed walked back in, carrying a glass of water instead of his usual evening beer, Evan forced his body to stay still.

"Looks like you both have something to say," their father said as he settled into his recliner. "Let's hear it."

"Are you seeing someone?" Gwen said. "A shrink, I mean?"

"Not right now. I talked to a psychiatrist over the summer. That's what they're called, Gwen. They're doctors. He's the one who suggested I get help for you two."

"Someone who never even met either one of us," Gwen said, her voice still as cold as their father's. Evan felt like his whole body was on fire. "This guy can just decide what's best without a word to either one of us. He must be good."

Ed's eyes flashed, but he still sounded calm.

"That would be *me* knowing what's best for you. In case you forgot, that's my job. Making sure you kids are okay. And that's what I'm going to do whether you like it or not."

"I haven't even lived here for two years! That's the part you're missing, Dad. I'm twenty years old, not a kid you have to walk across the street. Evan's not a baby anymore, either."

Evan drew back from his sister's shout. Far from being ready to face any of this, all Evan wanted right now was to run and hide.

"That so, Gwen? All grown up now, no need for me to bother myself with you as long as the university cashes my checks? How about you, son? Ready to set off for the big city yourself if I'm going to interfere in your life? The way, oh, I don't know, a father might do?"

Evan tried three times before any words came out. Gwen let him down by keeping her own mouth shut while he struggled.

"I don't need to talk to Ms. Fleming," Evan said. "I don't think she can do any good. All she wanted to do was try to make me cry."

Ed frowned and raised his eyebrows at the same time.

"Well, if she's no good, I'll find you someone who is. You can talk to my guy. But you're going to talk to someone. Both of you."

"Or what?" Gwen said, leaning forward. "Sounds to me like you're threatening to stop paying my tuition if I don't waste hours spilling my guts to some grad student. Gonna decide my major now, too?"

Evan's ears, mind, and body braced for the outburst of horrible noise he knew was coming. His father sipped his water, then lowered his chin before he answered in a normal voice.

"That's a choice you have, Gwen, to give up on the education your mother and I worked so hard for. Just quit and get a job as a waitress or a cashier. Throw all your potential away. I've never said a word about what you want to study, and as long as you work hard at it, I never will. But you're going to let someone help you through this."

"Why do you think neither of us ever talks to anyone?" Gwen said. "Do you really believe we don't have any friends? How do you think we got through all the bullshit around here *before* Mom died?"

"That's enough!" Ed slammed his fist on his own leg, but Evan flinched away. "Whatever happened before doesn't matter, not any more. All the ways your mother or I messed up are in the past. You want to drag that up someday in the future, be my guest. We're all going to have to adjust to right now, whether we like it or not."

"Or else, huh?" Gwen's voice broke, surprising Evan more than his father's shout had. "No matter what we might want."

"In this case, that's exactly right," Ed said. His tight voice and face reflected his anger. "Like I told Evan, if you don't like the person you're talking to, we'll find you someone else."

Evan's voice and mouth acted without consulting his brain.

"For how long?"

"I guess that depends on you, Evan. I think until the end of the year is a good start. Then we'll see. Just promise me you'll tell me if you need to talk to someone besides your counselor."

"I do talk to someone," Evan said, his voice not much above a whisper. The energy that pushed him to speak without warning had deserted him. "Every day."

Their father shook his head and sighed. "Yeah, that's part of the problem. She's kind of a weird kid, Evan."

"Well so am I!" Evan shouted, fists clenched, halfway standing. "You had your psychiatrist! I only got through the summer because of her!"

Heat boiled up from Evan's stomach, out through his whole body. This time he knew the effect his words would have, and he didn't regret a damn thing. He would have said more if Gwen's fingers weren't gripping his shoulder.

"You finished, son?" Their father's voice was calm again, but bright red spots against his tight, pale cheeks said otherwise. "Got more to say to me?"

"Listen, maybe we do need help," Gwen said in a sharp tone that didn't match her words. She didn't let go of Evan. "Maybe all three of us should go until the end of the year."

Gwen squeezed harder, pushing Evan back against the couch. Ed could have been a statue staring into his son's eyes.

Evan waited for the air to crack and shatter inside his lungs and against his skin.

"Will you talk to someone too, Dad?" Gwen said. "You're right, we all have to adjust. All of us."

Ed stared at Evan for several more seconds before he spoke.

"Sure, Gwen. If that's what it takes." He stood, holding his glass of water. Evan had never seen his father hit anyone, but he'd seem him throw plenty. "You kids need to think this through, think about what this has been like for me instead of just yourselves."

Ed Griffith turned away, stopping before he left the room. He spoke without looking back.

"I'll get the grill going for dinner. Think you can handle the rest?"

Gwen let go of Evan, but she held him just as firmly with her gaze.

"Sure, Dad," Evan said. "We can handle it."

Their father nodded and walked toward the kitchen.

Evan fell back against the cushions, his heart pounding in his ears and even his vision. The only thing he could feel in his whole body was the sharp depressions of his sister's fingers. The rest of him may as well have been floating a thousand miles away.

"What the hell, sis? Trying to break my shoulder?"

"Trying to keep the two of you from breaking each other's heads." Her eyes flashed exactly the way their father's did. "What were you trying to pull? You know what he's like."

"I wasn't trying to pull anything. He just… That was too much. You said I'm not a kid anymore. I have to stand up to him sometime, Gwen."

She shook her head, then stood and pulled Evan to his feet. He doubted he could have managed on his own.

"Maybe someday, sure. I don't like the way he looked at you, Ev. I've seen him angry more than I should have, but nothing like that. Do me a favor?"

Evan followed her into the kitchen. Ed stood in the back yard beside their waist high brick grill, staring into flames still far too high for cooking anything.

"Tell me what it is first," Evan said.

"Don't get into it with Ed, not unless you have to. Not without me here. Okay?"

"What am I supposed to do when he gets like that?" Evan turned the oven on. "Let him walk all over me? Or maybe ask if he can wait 'til you get here?"

"You know the answer." Something in his sister's smile irritated and embarrassed Evan at the same time. "Go the same place I always took you when things got bad around here. Sounds to me like Anne wouldn't mind any more than you would."

"Run off across the street for the next five years, huh, Gwen? Don't you think he'll notice if I just disappear?"

Gwen walked around the small table in the kitchen, lining up plates and silverware.

"If he knows where you are, he'll be fine. Give him a chance to cool down, and you do the same. That five years will pass faster than you think, kid."

Chapter 12

Anne caught herself staring at the huge maple tree outside her bedroom window, trying to count how many leaves were orange instead of yellow. Weeks of the school year passing and frost in the mornings surely sent the number into the thousands.

Her mind wandered to how she could create a formula to figure it out, if only she got an accurate count of one branch then counted all the other branches. Algebra was taking over her brain, not that her grades reflected that.

And daydreaming all evening about ways she could do better, how she could impress her teacher with her revolutionary new maple tree theory, would never get her homework finished.

She turned her desk chair away from the window, scooting the legs from one set of impressions in the shaggy blue carpet to another. Her mother and father talked about wanting to replace the carpet in the whole house sometimes, maybe with thinner carpet or even smooth linoleum.

Anne hated that idea, but she'd never figured out how to explain why to her parents without sounding silly. The thought of losing all the impressions of her, from her chair to her bed to the flat tracks in her room and in the hall where she always walked, felt like she could disappear from everywhere.

The room did change around her, usually in ways she wanted. The shelves were now a crackled red and black instead of yellow, and filled with more books, sketchbooks, and notebooks than toys. Posters of her favorite singers and movie stars had replaced the faded and tattered drawings from her grade school years.

Anne's mother still patrolled her closet and drawers, making sure clothing that either didn't fit or wasn't worn often enough went to girls who really needed it. Anne didn't care enough about her clothes to argue about that anymore, not that arguing had helped much when she was younger.

She forced her gaze back to the history book on her desk, searching for answers to an endless list of questions she had to turn in the next day. Just like the past few weeks, Anne's eyes started to drift closed within minutes.

Ever since the horrible dreams came back, she'd struggled to stay awake once she escaped from the discomfort of acting normal at school. Sometimes she stood with her books propped on a shelf to get as much done as she could. Sometimes even that didn't work.

She spent more time trapped in the awful empty library, forced to watch movies about the end of the world, than she could ever manage to spend on her homework. If only the dream would let her work on classwork in there, she'd have straight As like Evan always seemed to.

Anne had tried that trick, focusing on her studies, several times before she accepted that the dream was going to have its way with her no matter what. The routine and predictability of the nightmare helped a little with getting through it night after night.

One thing she was thankful for was she hardly ever saw the death masks over people's faces when she was awake anymore. Only when she was more tired than usual or upset about something else. She was scared the masks would come back like the dreams had, but not so far.

Anne jumped at a knock at her door, realizing her eyes had closed all the way that time, long enough that they were dry and scratchy.

"Come in."

Her dad opened the door, and she could tell from his face this wasn't going to be good. He was smiling a little, but his eyes were wrinkled in the wrong way.

"I know you're busy, got a minute to talk?" he said, standing in the doorway.

"Yeah, for a little while. I have a lot to do."

He sat in the chair beside the window, the chair Anne used for reading when she could stay awake for it. He kept glancing at her, then looking away. At the floor, at the ceiling, anywhere to avoid her eyes. She didn't think she'd ever seen him so jumpy.

"We were talking, your Mom and I…" He shook his head and looked right at her. "Anne, I'm worried about you. Your school work, and other things, too. You were having trouble before what happened to Evan's mom, but now it seems to be getting worse."

Anne's chest churned out what felt like enough jittery heat to keep her awake for days on end.

"I'm okay, Dad. I talk to Evan a lot, and that helps."

"I know that part, hon. His dad says that's really important to Evan. I'm glad he seems to be holding his own after such a rotten thing. I'm more worried about you."

Anne scowled, trying to imagine Hurricane Ed saying anything that nice about her. Whether Evan's father liked her or not, talking about what Evan had been through usually worked to keep her own father from worrying too much about her.

"Evan's dad doesn't like me."

"Well, I don't know about that." Anne's father rubbed his eyes for a second before he looked back at her. "What I'm saying, what I mean to ask is do *you* need someone to talk to? Someone older than Evan?"

Everything inside of Anne stopped, frozen solid and scared to death. This was exactly the kind of attention she did not want on the shaky state of her own mind.

"Someone at school, like the counselor?"

"No, Ed told me how Evan feels about that. He sees a doctor now, too. You know that. A doctor who knows how to really help with things like this. You can talk to me and your Mom about anything, like always, but someone with training might be better."

Evan did hate going to the counselor at school, but he liked Dr. Lewis a lot more. Anne thought talking to two different people only made things worse for him, not better. She wasn't sure a doctor would be any different for her.

"I don't know what I would talk to a doctor about."

"Anything. How you're feeling, what happened to Mrs. Griffith, things at school, whatever you're worried about. You can talk to her about the dreams you've been having too, if you want."

Anne stared at her father as painful chills ran up and down her body.

He knew? He knew about the dreams?

"What dreams do you mean, Dad?" she whispered.

He reached forward and patted her knee. "I've heard you getting up in the middle of the night for months now, and your Mom has heard you crying. You look tired all the time, Anne, and you've been getting more quiet. Your schoolwork isn't nearly what it was last year. Something's causing you trouble. Maybe talking to a doctor will help."

"I didn't know you knew about the dreams," Anne said, and now she was the one looking everywhere but at her father. "Do I have to go?"

"I'm not going to make you go, no," her Dad said as he stood up. "Talk to Evan about Dr. Lewis if you want. But I am worried about you, hon. I'd like you to. I really do think it will help. Will you try it, just a few times?"

Anne looked down at her hands in her lap. If her parents knew about the dreams, they might know about the visions and the memories too. She glanced at her special notebook sitting closed on her desk. Maybe her father had figured out which one to read after all, or her mother on one of her prowls through Anne's clothes and shoes.

Finally telling Evan about the awful things she saw, at least some of it, had made her feel so much calmer and less upset last spring. Maybe talking to a doctor would do the same.

If she could just get more sleep it would be worth it.

"I'll try, Dad. At least a few times."

Chapter 13

THE WAITING room for the psychiatrist looked more like a family living room than a doctor's office. They were inside a house with a yard instead of a brick office building like most doctor's offices. Two toddlers were even sitting on a thick brown rug over a shiny hardwood floor playing with a set of plastic blocks. Their clinking and loud giggling made Anne's shoulders more tense with every passing second.

The furnace was on too high, and the huge brass vent on the wall gave off a hot, dusty smell every time the floor rumbled and warm air rushed out. Anne's father had quickly shed his coat, jacket, and tie before he settled down to fill out a stack of paperwork.

Anne wondered how he could write so much about her, check off so many little boxes, without asking her any questions. She was grateful he didn't want to talk, though.

Across from the row of hard, curved plastic chairs where Anne and her father sat, a wooden staircase took up all the space above the vent. She hadn't seen anyone go up or down the stairs, but she heard movement above her head. Despite Evan's reassurance about Dr. Lewis, Anne wasn't looking forward to climbing up into the unknown with someone she'd never met before.

Her father flipped all the papers with his thumb, then tapped the stack against the brown clipboard to even them up. He gave all of it to the receptionist sitting in a little office hidden behind the staircase. Anne heard them both speak, too low for her to hear, before her father sat beside her again.

"Should only be a few more minutes," he said. "Do you want me to go with you? I don't have to, but I'd be glad to."

"Not this time, Dad." Anne closed her eyes, wishing she could take back the sharp sound of her voice. "I don't mind, really, but I guess I should go by myself today."

Her father nodded, and the worried lines around his eyes and mouth relaxed a little.

"I'll be right here if you change your mind."

The ceiling creaked again, then Anne heard two sets of footsteps. They were moving toward the top of that mysterious staircase. Unless Dr. Lewis was going to talk to those little kids, it was almost her turn.

Both of them stopped playing, moving quickly to put the bricks and all the other toys away. By the time Anne saw blue jeans and white tennis shoes coming down the stairs, the children waited, coats in hand. Dark green pants and brown loafers followed the tennis shoes.

"Anne?" the receptionist said, smiling with her eyes and her voice. "Dr. Lewis is ready for you."

Anne stood so fast her head swam for a second. Her father grabbed her hand and squeezed, but he let go right away. She smiled toward him, but she was busy watching for Dr. Lewis's face.

The jeans and tennis shoes belonged to a young woman, and the children chattered as they joined her in front of the receptionist. Dr. Lewis stood on the second step, leaning down far enough to peek at Anne. He had brown hair with gray at the sides, an almost all gray beard, and little round glasses. His smile and his eyes behind the glasses were warm, and most importantly to Anne, he had no trace of a death mask.

Dr. Lewis's office at the top of the stairs looked even more like a room in a regular house. A small desk was tucked behind the door, but there was a couch, a recliner, and three other chairs scattered around a big round rug with bunches of colors. A few more toys were in a box in the corner, and even more books than Anne had filled a whole wall of shelves.

The doctor waited for Anne to sit cross-legged in one of the chairs before he sat across from her.

"I'm Dr. Lewis," he said, shaking her hand. "So, Anne, tell me what's going on with you. Why are you here?"

Anne stared, not sure what she was supposed to say. Dr. Lewis was nice, much more friendly and honest-looking than Ms. Fleming at school.

But she kept thinking about how Evan hated talking to the counselor. He'd never been able to figure out what she was looking for or how to make the regular meetings stop. If Anne didn't handle this first one right, she might be stuck talking to Dr. Lewis for years.

"Um, my Dad wanted me to talk to you."

"Of course, that's how I usually meet new people," Dr. Lewis said, smiling. "But parents have usually noticed something changing, something that bothers them. They don't understand, so they come to me. I want to hear from *you*."

Anne opened her mouth, then she couldn't figure out what to say. She had too many secrets, too many things she kept to herself. She hadn't even told all of it to Evan. Well, her dad had mentioned the dreams. If he knew about those, Dr. Lewis probably did too.

"I've been having dreams," Anne said, staring at her the tips of shoes poking out under her knees. "Really bad dreams, for a while now."

"When did they start?"

"Last year, last school year, I mean. Before the summer."

"Are you still having them?"

"Yeah, but not as often. Did my Dad tell you about that?"

"He talked to me about that, yes," the doctor said, looking down at a folder in his lap. "But I want to hear from you."

Anne looked into the doctor's eyes, wondering what all she should say.

"I dream about… I dream about the end of the world. About people dying."

"What causes the world to end in your dreams?"

Anne blinked, once again unsure of what to say. Dr. Lewis had reacted the same way Evan had, not the way Anne had expected. Neither of them had laughed or said she was crazy. They both just asked how it happened.

Maybe she could trust this doctor, too.

"The bees die and people starve," she said, feeling shaky and hot. "Then there's a war, and the water gets poisoned."

"A lot of people are afraid of those things happening. Is the dream always the same, Anne?"

"Yes," she whispered. "That one's always the same."

"Have you read a book or seen a movie like that? Sometime before the dreams started?"

"No, nothing like that. I just saw the same thing in my dreams. It was like a drawing at first, but now the people look real."

"How often do you have these dreams?"

"Just once in a while at first, then I started having them every night," Anne said, catching a tear before it could get away. "They stopped for a while when I started writing them down. That and talking to Evan so much over the summer, I think."

The doctor nodded, turning a page in his folder.

"Yes, I know Evan. He's your friend?"

Anne smiled, a warm feeling in her belly pushing a little bit of her nervousness away.

"Yes, my best friend. He lives on the same street we do."

"Your Dad mentioned Evan's Mom too, that she died over the summer. That couldn't have been easy for him, or for you."

"No. We talked about it a lot. We talk about a lot of things."

"Does Evan know about your nightmares too?"

"He was the first person I told about it, before the summer."

"Have you talked to Evan about anything else? Anything that bothers you or upsets you, Anne, that you might want to talk to me about?"

This was the first time Anne felt like she shouldn't say anymore. Maybe she'd already said too much. The doctor looked the same, that part hadn't changed at all. He didn't have a death mask. Still, Anne was starting to get an odd feeling in her head.

Something in her mind was going to split, double or maybe even more. She was about to see another memory, just like the day Evan's mom had died and a few times since then.

"Nothing in particular," Anne muttered.

"It's okay, Anne. I'm not going to get mad or anything. Listen, I don't want to hide things from you. I know something happened the day Evan's mom died, something that worried Evan's dad and your dad too. Can you tell me about that?"

Now Anne's heart was pounding so hard she could hear it. She couldn't believe Evan would have said a word about her knowing something was wrong during their art class. He would never do that.

"Did Evan tell you that?" Anne said. "Did he tell you what happened that day?"

"I can't tell you what Evan and I talk about. Whatever he says to me is confidential, Anne, just like whatever you say to me will be. I won't even talk to your parents about the specific things, not unless I'm afraid you're going to hurt yourself. Okay?"

Anne nodded, a reflex, like shaking the doctor's hand when he held it out. If Evan didn't tell Dr. Lewis, someone else had to. But who? No one else knew.

Then she remembered the teacher standing right behind them then, telling them they needed to stop causing trouble. Mr. Adkins, that was his name. He wasn't one of Anne's teachers, not now, but he was the art teacher at the high school.

He'd still been standing right there when Evan and then she had run out of the room. He might have told Evan's dad. Or one of the other kids, they'd seen everything too.

"I just, I had a bad feeling that something was wrong. I tried to stop Evan from going home."

"How did you know that, Anne?" the doctor asked, looking into Anne's eyes. "What happened?"

"I don't know," Anne whispered. "I just had a terrible feeling. When Evan left, I followed him. We found his mom there, then he called an ambulance and Mr. Griffith."

She knew she was answering the wrong question, but she had to get the doctor off the track somehow. That was too much, too close to the truth. She had never even told Evan about the three different memories of his mother's death. She'd never told anyone, not one person.

Anne stared at Dr. Lewis, cold washing over her.

She had written it down.

She'd written the whole thing in her notebook. All of it. If her parents had read that notebook, if they'd told Dr. Lewis about what was in her notebook, it might already be too late.

"Are dreams and strange feelings all you have that's different, Anne?"

Anne gripped the chair arms, fighting her screaming need to get up and run out of the room. If her father hadn't been outside waiting, if she hadn't promised him she'd at least try, she would have done just that.

"That's all, and that doesn't happen much anymore."

Dr. Lewis looked at her for a long time, not saying a word. Anne felt sweat on her face, and she smelled her own armpits. The doctor's warm brown eyes and sensible glasses felt more like huge spotlights and microscopes, with Anne pinned like the frogs her class had dissected last week. She couldn't move, and she couldn't think.

"Anne, I'm not trying to trap you, and I'm not trying to hurt you. Your parents aren't either. We just want to see if there's anything going on we can help with. That's all. But to help, we need to know what's going on."

"Did you read my notebook?" Anne said in a shaky voice, staring at the thick rug on the floor. "Do you already know?"

"I didn't read your notebook. I wouldn't do that unless you asked me to." Dr. Lewis closed the folder and looked at Anne.

"But my parents did."

When the doctor was silent again, Anne leaned forward in her chair.

"You told me you didn't want to hide anything, Dr. Lewis. Did my parents read my notebook?"

The doctor sighed.

"Your father knows enough to be worried about you. Do you want me to ask him to come in and talk to you about it?"

The odd feeling in Anne's mind got deeper, like the twitching muscles she sometimes got around her eye. She closed her eyes for a second, and she was in front of the massive screen in the library. She didn't see three different things this time. She saw only one.

On that screen, Anne was in a building, white and cold and lonely. She was sitting in a room on a bed, rocking and staring at the wall. She only saw that single image, but it was jumpy. Her movements seemed to skip and catch like a broken videocassette, and a jagged noise roared all around her.

"Don't I have any choices?" she whispered.

"I'm sorry, Anne, I couldn't hear you."

The doctor's voice was soft, but Anne jumped. She was back in the office, but the empty white room still hung in her mind. Every other time she'd seen a memory coming, more than one thing was there. More than one way it could go.

Now all she saw, all she felt, was herself in that terribly empty room.

"Are you going to put me in a hospital?"

Dr. Lewis drew back and blinked, and Anne felt a tiny bit better.

"That's not what your parents or I want. We just want to see if we can help you through a rough time. That's all."

"What do you think is wrong with me?"

"I don't think anything is wrong," Dr. Lewis said. "This isn't like you have a bad cold or ear infection. We'll just talk and see if I can help. I think there are medicines that may help you sleep, and maybe help with the rest of it, too. If you want, I can bring your father in and we'll talk more about that."

Anne nodded, fighting not to cover her ears. The roaring, broken noise in the empty white room was all she could hear.

PART III
A MIND BREAKS

Chapter 14

Much as he hated the noise and chaos in the shared cafeteria, Evan still looked forward to his time there every day. The grade school kids with their shorter school day were already out of the way by the time he and everyone else in high school got to the vast, echoing room.

Harsh overhead lights with bumpy plastic covers, an entire wall of windows, and white tiled floors magnified every noise and movement. Rich, sometimes overcooked food smells suppressed his appetite more often than stimulating it. Evan brought his own lunch when he remembered to pack it.

He'd forgotten today, so he waited in line, hoping something edible would be waiting for him. He couldn't see Anne at any of the big round tables in the middle of the room or the rows of long tables along the walls. She usually sat far in the back, though, away from the chatter and bustle.

Evan found her at a lonely table against the back wall, sitting with her back to the crowded room. He never could stand to sit that way, with his back exposed, if he could avoid it. By the time he joined her, the rectangular, greasy cheese pizza was nearly as cool as his soda. At least he wouldn't burn his mouth.

"Hey Anne. How's your day?"

She glanced up from her half-finished hamburger, shrugged, and stared at the floor.

Evan was dying to ask her how her appointment with Dr. Lewis the day before had gone. He liked seeing the psychiatrist on Tuesdays a lot better than Ms. Fleming on Thursdays. Anything was worth cutting down the times he was pulled out of class to talk to the school counselor.

He didn't want to push Anne, any more than he wanted his father or sister to push him about his own appointments. After a few minutes of eating in silence, Anne covered the remains of her meal with a napkin.

"Does Dr. Lewis make you take drugs?"

Evan grabbed his napkin, trying to contain the bite of congealed pizza he'd almost spit out.

"*Make* me take drugs? My dad's more concerned with *stopping* me from taking drugs. What happened yesterday?"

"I guess he's not making me. Not yet." Anne poked at the white napkin with her fork, pushing it into the puddle of ketchup on her plate until the red bled through. "He wants me to, though. Because of the things I see."

Evan tried his best to keep his face still and calm. He'd known that day he was making a mistake, deep down in his gut and his heart. He never should have told Dr. Lewis about Anne seeing death masks. But he'd also believed the doctor's promise that he wouldn't tell anyone else.

"My parents read my diary," Anne said. "My notebooks. I was so stupid. I never should have written all of that down."

Evan breathed out as quietly as he could manage, trying to hold on while his body floated and sank at the same time. What he'd done still wasn't right. But the consequences he'd face for that would all be his own.

"They want you to take drugs for that? What kinds of drugs?"

"Dad called them anti-psychotic, but they both kept saying I wasn't psychotic. Dad doesn't want me to take them. I think my mother does."

The word drifted and crashed around Evan's mind, repeated over and over again in his father's voice with that one extra word. *She's a psychotic kid, Evan…*

"If they think you're going to hurt people like John Wayne Gacy or some other murderer, they're the ones who are crazy."

Anne smiled, only a brief shadow, but enough to make Evan feel a little better.

"That's what I thought, too. They had to tell me what it meant so they could tell me I don't have it." Her eyes meeting his were too bright, and her chin trembled. "But it means people who have breaks with reality. People who don't know what's real and what's not. How can they say that's *not* what I have?"

"*I* say that's not what you have!" Evan tried to keep his voice down, but several kids glanced their way. "What you saw about my mom was true. Didn't you tell me your grandmother knew she was going to have to move out? That was true, too."

Anne held her face in both hands. Evan was relieved she sat with her back to everyone else. She couldn't possibly see the people behind her, whispering to each other and giggling, then laughing out loud. Evan stared at every single one of them until they at least looked away.

"That's what I don't understand," Anne said. She reached across the table and dragged Evan's key ring around in a circle. "My dad said he didn't want me to take those drugs because of how they affected my grandmother. He said they only made her lots worse. But Dr. Lewis still thinks we should try it."

"He only mentioned antidepressants to me, the first couple of weeks. I know my father's been taking them, and Gwen might be. I probably should." Evan held his breath for a second, hoping he wasn't about to make everything worse for his friend. "Do you think the medicine might help, Anne? How do you feel?"

"It's not what I feel, Evan. It's what I see. When my parents started talking about it when we got home, I saw the library. The one from my dreams. The one with screens inside?"

She took a shaky breath.

Evan wasn't able to breathe at all.

"I saw my parents fighting over me taking the drugs," she said.

"Dad said he was afraid it would get worse. Mom said how much worse could it get? I saw you and me sitting right here, like now, but I couldn't move. You tried and tried, but nothing helped. I saw my Dad in the kitchen, with a bottle of pills with my name on it."

"I can help, Anne," Evan said, fighting the urge to take her hand. "You spaced out a few times last year, remember? I can get you out of that, every single time."

"That's not how it works this time. I haven't had any as bad as this will be. All three of those movies in my head ended in one place. I'm in some kind of hospital, worse than the place my grandmother's in. That doesn't change, no matter what.

"Then maybe I can go with you," he said, scared of the idea but more scared of losing her. "I've been having trouble too, and I'm sure Ms. Fleming would tell them I need to go. She can't figure out what else to do with me. Dr. Lewis already wants me to have drugs, too."

"You don't want to go there," she said, shaking her head. "It's for crazy people. Not for people like you."

"You're not crazy! Don't say that. Don't let them make you *believe* that."

He wanted to say that enough people were already saying it without her pitching in, but he didn't want to hurt her feelings. Of course she knew, she knew what people were saying about her.

Evan couldn't pretend it wasn't true about both of them, not with even more kids staring at them now.

"It's not exactly normal to have the same dream over and over again." Anne scooted her chair back, making a harsh scraping noise. "Or to see how everyone around me is going to die. Maybe if something like this happens, all of that will stop. Maybe I could be normal after that."

"How long?" Evan said, not bothering to hide how his voice shook. "How long do they think you'll be there?"

"They keep saying we don't want that, we don't want that. I don't think what they want matters. I can't tell from the visions. When I see myself there, I look the same way I do now. It might not be long at all."

Evan wished he was the one with his back to the room as tears spilled down his cheeks. The only time he'd been away from Anne for more than a day was on trips to visit family back in Virginia. He didn't want to imagine weeks or months on end.

Or years.

"Let me help, will you?" he said, scrubbing at his face with the greasy, tattered napkin. He was afraid his aching heart would stop inside his chest. "Even if it's all going to go bad, just let me help."

He clenched his fists to keep from grabbing her hand when she stood.

Anne stared at him for several seconds before she turned and walked away.

Chapter 15

THE DREAM CAME BACK before Anne's father even had a chance to fill the prescriptions, and the dream was so much worse. Something had changed.

Anne walked into the gigantic, echoing library, the same as before, but giant screens were everywhere now. The shelves held screens, dozens of oversized computers sat on every surface, and the walkways were choked with rolling TVs. Even the table tops and the ceiling were massive screens.

She froze, afraid to take another step. Seeing more people than she could count dying on one was bad enough. She didn't know if she would be able to stand watching on dozens of screens at once.

She closed her eyes, breathing deeply, then screamed as loud as she could. Instead of bouncing around the space and getting louder with every repetition, Anne's voice didn't make it past her own ears. She dug at her arm with her fingernails, hard enough to draw shiny black dream-blood, but she may as well have been tormenting a rag doll. She never even felt it.

Anne jumped at a sudden electronic pop and hum as all the screens powered on. As afraid as she was, not watching might be even worse.

All the screens were still dark, but they were activated. All of them, even the giant one overhead, came to life at the same time. Anne walked into the jumble of tables and chairs in the middle of the floor, the trembling in her body forcing her to sit down.

The whole room filled with images of swarming bees, and the sound was deafening. The sudden silence when the bees all died made her ears ring even worse.

Anne forced herself to keep watching, hoping desperately for some kind of change, any kind of difference in the dream. Agreeing to let the doctor try to help her had to change something.

She covered her ears against the screams of dying people, the roar of gunfire that shook the floor, and the droning airplane that made her bones vibrate. Anne cried out when the screens went blinding white.

All of the screens, every single one of them, showed her sitting on the bed in the hospital room. The roaring static noise was back too, loud enough to make her teeth hurt.

One Anne on the screen started rocking, and all the others followed, one after the other. They were all a little off, just a second or two, and the various movements made her sick. Anne focused on the screen closest to her, one of the rolling televisions.

All she could think to do was count, each time she saw herself rock forward on the screen.

One. Two. Three.

The static got louder, but she could still hear a new sound, one she hadn't heard in the doctor's office when this memory first came to her. Anne on the screen was humming, low and quiet, then higher and louder when she rocked forward.

Both noises got louder, the static and the humming, until Anne squeezed her eyes closed and covered both ears again.

"Stop!"

This time her voice came back to her, hundreds and thousands of times, louder and higher pitched every time. Just before all the glass in the library surely would shatter, including the hateful screens, every noise stopped.

After a few seconds, Anne thought the sound wasn't going to come back. She slowly moved her hands, and the room was silent.

All she could hear was the soft buzz of so many screens. She opened her eyes, not sure if she would still see the lost girl or the dying people.

Instead she only saw scattered dots on all of the continents of the earth. Cool blue words hovered in the middle of the Atlantic Ocean.

Remaining Human Population

Anne drew in a shaky breath. At least this part she'd seen before. She even nodded to herself when the dots started to disappear, first in Australia, then all across the planet.

When only the two in North America were left, one north and a little to the east of where Chicago should be, one around Virginia far to the southeast, the tense muscles in her shoulders started to relax. This was where the dream always ended.

She still had no idea what she was supposed to do, but at least it would be over for now. The same thing had happened here dozens of times over the past few months, then she had woken up. It was almost over.

The northern light went out.

Anne gasped, looking at every screen she could see to make sure she hadn't imagined it. By the time she looked back at the screen right in front of her, the southern light had gone dark too. North America glowed just as red as all of the other land on Earth.

She didn't want to know. She couldn't ask the question. But she knew she would never wake up until she did.

"How many are left?" she whispered.

Remaining Human Population: Zero

A larger word filled the entire screen, all the screens, blocking out all the land, all the people, everything that had ever happened in the whole world.

Extinction

Anne curled forward and wrapped her chilled arms around her stomach, trying to keep cold facts from finding a place to stay in her mind.

Everyone. Every person on the planet. All of them dead. Her Dad and her Mom and Dr. Lewis had all tried to tell her it was just a dream. Only a dream.

If that was true, why was her heart falling to pieces in her body? Why did she feel the failure and devastation in every part of her? Not just a general failure that she couldn't understand, but *her* failure.

Only she could have stopped it.

Only she had failed.

The sobs were strong and deep, starting in her belly and ripping their way out through her throat and mouth.

Anne didn't quite realize she was rocking.

Chapter 16

For the next couple of weeks, Evan tried to pretend everything was going to be okay. He went to classes, did his homework, did his best to stay quiet at home and out of his father's way. He walked to and from school with Anne, and neither of them spoke of her dreams or the medication he was sure she'd started taking.

Even when he saw the dark circles under her eyes, same as when the dreams were so bad before, Evan pretended.

He revived his habit of talking about nothing to fill in the spaces when Anne withdrew into silence. That was returning to a kind of normal, right? The way things had been before.

Back when his mother was still alive.

His grip on the delusion, fragile to begin with, nearly slipped a couple of times when Anne seemed to disappear right in front of him. She stared straight ahead, her face and her eyes blank and lifeless.

Evan managed to get her attention without anyone else noticing, touching her arm, talking directly into her ear. The relief each time was strong enough to let him pick up his imaginary armor and keep pretending.

Somewhere inside, an echo of Anne's glimpses of the future, Evan never really believed his own pathetic pretense.

This was nothing more than a waiting game. A game he knew he and his friend were going to lose no matter how badly he fought to deny it.

The game ended in the worst possible place and time, leaving both of them with nowhere to hide.

Evan barely heard his own voice at times like this. His running commentary about his morning classes blended into the general drone of conversation in the noisy cafeteria. He paused long enough to pop his last potato chip into his mouth and glanced at Anne.

He didn't need to ask to know she hadn't heard a word for the last several minutes. His friend had disappeared right in front of him.

"Anne? Come on, don't do this. Don't leave me here."

Evan touched Anne's shoulder, squeezing and then shaking her gently. She seemed to be looking down at her half-eaten lunch, but he knew she was really staring into space he couldn't see. She wasn't seeing or hearing him or anything else.

"Listen to me. You're at school. Wherever you think you are isn't real. I know you can hear me."

Just as they had during that art class the day his mother died, kids were turning to look at them. Evan saw them out of the corners of his vision. He heard the whispers, rising around the room like ocean waves, drowning out all the other conversations.

"You've got to help me, Anne," he whispered, squeezing her arm a little harder. "Everyone can see. They're going to take you away from me."

Someone walked toward them, and he didn't even have to look. He recognized the clacking noise of Ms. Fleming's shoes. Someone had certainly warned her about the new medication Anne was on, and the woman still watched Evan like a hawk.

The two of them would never be able to hide.

"She's going to catch us," he said under his breath, reaching up to touch her cheek. "Stay with me, please!"

"Mr. Griffith?" Ms. Fleming said from across the table. "Evan? Anne? What's going on here?"

"Nothing, we're just fine," Evan said, forcing himself to look at her. "Just give us a minute."

The counselor clacked around the table and touched Anne's cheek herself. She leaned down to look into Anne's face, then jerked back up.

"How long has she been like this?"

"She's fine," Evan muttered, closing his eyes. "She's going to be just fine."

"How long?" Ms. Fleming said, the sharp tone in her voice forcing Evan to answer.

"A couple of minutes. She's always come out of it before."

"This happened *before?*" she said, getting a tiny notebook out of her bag. "No one told me that. How long is she out of it like this?"

"Usually only for a few seconds," Evan said, touching Anne's shoulder again. "Never like this. Can you help me?"

Ms. Fleming waved toward someone in the hall. Evan didn't see who walked in, but the flat tap of the shoes sounded adult. He heard the word *catatonic.* The sound of those four syllables chilled every part of him.

The counselor finished her whispered conversation, tore a sheet from her notebook, and pushed the other person away. Evan finally focused on her.

For the first time, he saw what looked like real compassion in Ms. Fleming's face. This wasn't on any of the scripts she seemed to follow in her meetings with him. She also looked only a few years older than he was.

"I'm hoping someone will be able to help her, Evan. Can you stay with her for a minute? If she comes out of this, she might be disoriented."

Evan nodded. Anne usually was confused at first, then she got embarrassed. She still hadn't moved, even with all the motion and noise around her.

She'd told him this would happen. She'd tried to warn him.

Evan wasn't ready.

He didn't want to be ready for this.

"She sees Dr. Lewis," he said, still staring at Anne's unmoving face. She hadn't even blinked since Ms. Fleming got there. "Same as me. I should call her Dad."

"Would you do that, please?" Ms. Fleming said, glancing around the room before she raised her voice. "Everyone finish up and get ready to go. Your next classes start in a few minutes. Everything is under control here."

She was lying.

Evan knew it, everyone around them knew it. He couldn't imagine she was fooling anyone, not even herself. But he couldn't think of anything to do to stop it or change it.

After weeks of trying to make it all okay, trying to fix whatever was going wrong with Anne, Evan finally admitted to himself that he needed help.

She needed help he couldn't give.

He still couldn't imagine what he was going to do, how he was going to face the walk home without her by his side. How he was going to walk to school alone tomorrow morning, and for who knew how many mornings after that.

But some part of Evan was exhausted from trying to do all of it himself. That part had always suspected he was too young for this, too weak and inexperienced. Even Ms. Fleming looked scared to death.

No matter how hard he'd tried or how impossible the task, Evan knew he would always feel like he'd failed his friend.

Chapter 17

Anne felt her life grind to a halt.

The world continued without her.

The tingling in her body that warned her of a memory rose to a scream that wanted to drag her into nothing. Everything was a blinding glare of white. She heard Evan's voice, still chattering away, not aware she was frozen into her memory.

"Anne?"

Evan's voice could have been coming down a long, twisting tunnel instead of right beside her. That one word drew out, echoing, doubling back on itself until it sounded like dozens of boys were speaking at once.

Still she couldn't move.

Anne sat on a hospital bed in a cold, white room. She couldn't hear or smell anything around her. This was a trap, a horrible trap she might never get out of. The memory kept her body frozen, but her mind was thrashing, trying to break free.

"…wherever you think you are isn't real…"

She couldn't tell if he'd spoken those words five seconds ago or five hours ago. Every syllable, every sound drew out, stuttering from his lips to her ears.

Anne had given up a long time ago on trying to figure out if things were real or not.

All she could focus on any more was whether or not they were true.

"The drugs…" Anne-within said, the words echoing around the hospital room like Evan's voice had.

That part was true, deeply horrifyingly true. Something about those pills her father was so afraid of kept Anne from breaking out of the memory.

Evan touched her, squeezing her shoulder, but it felt like she was wearing a dozen thick winter coats instead of a regular shirt. His hand gave her an odd sense of pressure, but no warmth at all.

The tone of his voice changed. He was talking to someone else. Ms. Fleming.

Anne screamed inside her own head, trying to force some part of her body to respond.

"…catatonic…"

That was Ms. Fleming, and Anne knew exactly what that word meant. Her breaks from reality were so deep now that she couldn't hide them.

Evan couldn't help her, and he knew it. Everyone knew.

She didn't have to see Evan's face or even hear his voice. She could feel the change from wherever she was.

"No!" she screamed, her ears ringing. "I'm still in here!"

"Can you help her…"

Her friend, her dear friend who had never turned away from her. He was being pushed away, and he was going. She felt him disconnecting, pulling things she needed back into himself.

If she was going into that lonely hospital, and she couldn't see anything that could stop that now, she would be going without Evan's support. She herself had told him he couldn't go with her, and of course he couldn't.

Saying that to him and feeling the reality as he pulled back from her weren't even in the same kind of human experience.

Anne's heart pulled out one tiny sinew at a time.

"Evan! No! Please don't go! Don't give up on me!"

Anne's throat grew raw with screaming. Anne's throat was perfectly calm as her body stared at the table. Everyone around her got up and shuffled out of the cafeteria, trying to see as much as they could on the way.

Evan sat still, touching her shoulder. Anne willed every part of her, every ounce of her body to try to move, to twitch under his hand. To cry, to scream, anything to let him know she was there.

"Evan. You should go on to your next class," Ms. Fleming said, her voice rising and falling like a terrifying fun house clown. "You don't want to see this."

"Yes I do!"

His voice was clear and loud, coming from her ears instead of down that narrow, dark tunnel. The last word continued on, getting lower the longer it lingered in her mind.

"Where are they taking her?"

Anne knew, she'd seen it, she was there now. She'd tried to tell Evan, but he hadn't believed her.

He never believed the bad things she told him until they came true.

"They have to get her out of this first. Then they'll probably take her to a hospital in the city."

She heard Evan's breath catch, the same way she had so many times over the summer. He was trying so hard not to cry.

He didn't always make it, no matter how hard he tried.

"I'm going with her."

"No, that's out of the question. Her father is going to meet her at the hospital, and you need to stay here. In fact, you need to be getting to your next class."

"She can't go alone! She won't understand what's going on if she wakes up alone. I know what to do when she comes out of this."

Anne started rocking in her hospital room, leaning forward, over and over. The springs on the hard bed squeaked, grating on her nerves. She hummed, trying her best to drown out the noise.

She didn't have any choice about rocking. Her body did it without asking.

Her body stayed frozen, staring at her half-eaten lunch.

"Listen to me, Evan. The doctors know what to do for her. They've been doing this for years. They understand what's wrong and how to help."

"No, they don't know," Anne moaned, rocking harder. "They don't understand. All they can do is make it worse!"

The screen was back in Anne's head, three scenes active and moving and changing.

Evan sat beside her motionless body, head in his hands, shoulders shaking. Ms. Fleming stood behind him with her hand on his back. The paramedics, the same two who had helped Evan's Mom, walked into the cafeteria.

Anne sat on the bed, rocking and humming, light glaring off of the white walls all around her. And the world slowly ground to a halt as billions of people died of starvation, poisoning, or war. Anne kept rocking, but she was crying now.

The dots scattered all over the continents started to go out.

Evan tried to hold on to Anne's shoulders, but Ms. Fleming and one of the paramedics pulled him away. He stood watching them for a second, then turned and slowly walked away.

The last light, the last surviving human population, went dark.

"Evan! Please don't leave me! Everyone is going to die!"

Anne's voice echoed off of the brutal white walls, forcing her to rock faster. Her voice got rougher, her throat more painful.

Anne wondered about losing her voice inside of her own mind. She knew a sore throat in the real world would eventually go away.

Would she ever get her voice inside back again?

The paramedics carefully lifted Anne, making sure to hold her head steady. They put her on the gurney and covered her with a blue sheet. One of them reached under the gurney and grabbed huge straps with metal clasps. She wrapped them around Anne's body, catching the ends and pulling them tight.

Anne wasn't sure why the woman bothered with that. She couldn't feel her body, much less move it. She didn't care to move it anymore.

Evan had walked away from her. Everyone was dead. Moving her body was the least important thing she could imagine.

Rocking was all that kept Anne aware and in the world. If she stopped, even for a second, she could slip back into that awful nightmare. Watching so many people die, over and over again, knowing there was nothing she or anyone else could do, pushed Anne down into a dark pit she could not find the bottom of.

She considered letting go to see just how deep it went. Maybe once she finally found the bottom, she wouldn't have to see anything anymore.

Ms. Fleming walked with the paramedics to the cafeteria door, and Anne was surprised to see she was crying. She never would have imagined that, not over her. All the counselor ever did was smile at Anne, not cry.

"If she wakes up… When she wakes up, tell her Evan is thinking about her," Ms. Fleming said, then she turned and walked away.

The paramedics rolled Anne out into the bright sunlight. She wished one of them would remember to close her eyes. That light hurt, and her pupils didn't seem to be getting smaller. Going blind in her body wouldn't give her mind any relief. Losing her eyesight wouldn't break the screen inside her head.

She only saw two scenes now. The third had gone black when Evan walked away from her.

Anne rocked in the hospital bed, her humming getting louder with every motion forward.

The map of the world showed nothing but red, all of the land on the planet dead and empty.

The gurney bumped the back of the ambulance, shifting Anne's body against the thick straps. The paramedics didn't notice that any more than they'd noticed her eyes. With a shove, they rolled her up into the small space.

Ms. Fleming had told Evan they'd be taking her downtown, to a hospital downtown. Anne didn't know where they would want to put someone like her. Her grandmother lived out near where Anne and her family did, not in the city.

Was she too young to stay with her grandmother? If she couldn't be with Evan, her grandmother might be all right. At least she'd have someone to talk to, someone who never looked at Anne like she was crazy.

"Have her parents been notified?" the man driving said.

"The counselor said he would meet us there." The woman sitting beside Anne finally pushed her eyes closed. "Poor kid. What do you think happened to her?"

"Probably drugs. Seems to get all of 'em now, no matter where they live."

Anne felt like laughing instead of sobbing or screaming, though she still couldn't move her body.

Yes. Finally someone could see what was going on, even if he was saying bad things about her, the wrong things.

The drugs. Her father had been right to be afraid of the drugs, but now the damage was done. It hardly mattered if Anne never moved her body again.

Everyone was going to die.

Evan had walked away from her, and they were all going to die.

Getting better felt like too much work.

Anne let go and slipped into the void inside.

Chapter 18

EVAN BLINKED when the afternoon sunlight hit his eyes. He realized he'd stepped outside of the high school, onto the stairs heading to the front lawn. Same as he did every day. But when he got to the sidewalk today, he turned left to walk home alone instead of right to meet Anne in front of the middle school next door.

He shook his head, trying to remember the last few hours. He couldn't say it passed in a blur. A blur would be something, anything he could recall.

Evan's afternoon had passed in a blank.

One foot in front of the other was all he could concentrate on now. He had to trust his feet and the rest of his body to get him home.

"Evan."

Evan wasn't totally sure he'd actually heard that voice out in the world, the one he heard most inside his own head. Well, second most, behind Anne's.

"Back here, son."

He finally noticed he'd walked right past his father's sensible blue sedan. His dad was standing by the driver's side, elbows on the roof. Evan hadn't even noticed. He'd walked right past the entire afternoon without noticing after they'd taken Anne away from him.

"What are you doing here?" he said without thinking of how it sounded. "I mean, I'm glad to see you."

He headed back toward the car as his father got back inside. This was long before he should be home from work. Evan couldn't remember his father ever picking him up from school. His mom used to, but she'd worked in town, not so far away in the city.

Hurricane Ed dropped Evan and sometimes Anne off in the mornings, before they were old enough to walk or in bad weather. Never in the afternoon though.

"I heard what happened today," his father said when Evan shut the door. "I wanted to make sure you're okay."

"Oh." Evan looked down at his hands. "I've been better."

"Do you understand what happened? I know you're not a baby anymore. You're a damn smart kid. Problems like this aren't easy for anyone. Might be a good thing, though."

"No, I don't understand," Evan said. "I don't think it's good, not at all."

His father sighed as he started the car. He seemed to do that when he didn't want to say what he was thinking, as if that could fool anyone.

Evan had caught on a long time ago.

"She was sick, son. Same thing as last year, but worse. She wasn't getting better here, she was getting sicker. Maybe where she is she can finally get some help."

Evan squeezed his eyes closed, willing himself not to cry. He was in high school now, way too old to cry, even when his heart was tearing into a million pieces. He wanted to shout, to scream the words circling through his mind, without worrying about who could hear him or what they would think.

She doesn't need a hospital. She needs me! She kept me from going crazy after Mom died. I can't let her down. I'm the only thing that keeps her calm anymore, and I'm not with her!

"She's not sick, Dad. She's confused. She's not crazy."

"No, no one is saying crazy, Evan." His father's fast words and red cheeks told another story. "But she was unhappy. I know you could see that. I know you want her to be happy."

Evan looked out the window, and the tears got away from him. Of course he wanted Anne to be happy. That was one of the things he thought about most, how he could possibly make her happy.

He hadn't been able to for a while now, and that was keeping *him* from being happy anymore.

"Can I at least go see her?" Evan whispered.

"Maybe in a while. Not right away, no. She needs to think about getting better right now. You need to focus on your schoolwork."

"How long will she be there?"

"No one can say with these kinds of things. I hope she'll be there as long as she needs to be. She's young, so there's plenty of time."

Evan didn't have to ask who his father was thinking about. Anne's grandmother. He barely remembered her living with the Fincastles, and he'd visited her with Anne a couple of times.

He loved spending time with Anne's Gemaw. He knew she had to stay in the group home where she was, though. She'd been there a long, long time.

"Who told you about what happened?"

"Mrs. Fincastle called. She's worried to death about Anne, but she wanted to make sure you weren't too upset."

That was something else Evan didn't have to ask about. He'd overheard the conversations his father and Anne's mother had sometimes. Both of them were scared Anne would end up like her grandmother, even though Anne's father wasn't at all like that.

Evan hadn't been scared of that until today.

"Did her father go see her?"

"They're both probably there by now."

"Did Anne's mom say how she's doing?"

Ed parked in their driveway and turned to look at Evan. His eyes and mouth seemed pinched in his face. He took a deep breath.

"She didn't know when she called me. They probably won't know anything for a while. Now, I have to ask you a hard question, one I know you're not going to like."

Evan turned toward Anne's house for a minute, not wanting to hear whatever it was. The day had already been hard enough.

Both cars were gone, and the house looked empty and abandoned. He finally turned back toward his father.

Evan was sure he wasn't going to like the question either. His churning stomach matched his shaking hands. At least he wasn't numb anymore.

"Was Anne on some kind of drugs, son? Was she drinking or doing anything like that?"

Evan was horrified to have to bite his cheeks to keep from laughing. Drinking? Drugs? Who did his father have Anne mixed up with?

And if Ed thought she was doing those things, what did he think of his own son?

"No, Dad, she wasn't on anything. As far as I know, she's never had a drop of alcohol. The only drugs she's taking are the ones Dr. Lewis gave her. She's afraid of those."

His father blinked and leaned back a little, raising his eyebrows. "Afraid of them?"

"She's been afraid they would make everything worse. She's been afraid of going to the hospital for a while. She was right about both."

Evan barely got the words out before he was crying again, turning away but not before his dad saw.

"I know this is a lot for you to handle, especially after... after the summer. There's nothing anyone could have done. If the drugs were making it worse for her, the doctors will figure that out, too."

Evan wiped his eyes before he turned back to his father. Ed Griffith looked years older than a few months ago, the day he'd come home to find his wife dead and his son and the odd neighbor girl there waiting for him.

The lines around his eyes and mouth hadn't been there before, and dark circles under his eyes never seemed to leave now. Several grays glinted in his thick brown hair.

Evan didn't want to cause him any more trouble. He was also terribly worried about his friend.

"Will you tell me when you hear anything?"

"Of course I will. Come on, we better get ready for Hurricane Gwen. She'll be here in a couple of hours."

Evan finally did smile, and his belly twitched with concealed laughter. He wasn't sure whether the nickname suited his sister or his father more. Or who would be more annoyed by it. Hurricane Ed put one arm around Evan for a second, the closest he got to a hug these days.

"You can talk to your sister about this, too, you know. She might not always show it, but she likes you most of the time. She likes you a hell of a lot better than she likes me."

Chapter 19

Anne was confused by the noise at first. That didn't sound like the echo of the library where she'd been trapped for what seemed like years. That sounded like it came through her ears, her real ears.

She'd given up on her real ears working a long time ago.

"Anne, hon, I'm here."

The scent washed over her then, not just in her nose but all over. The dry aroma of thousands of books in that library and the warm, acrid scent of all the screens had numbed her sense of smell. Now smells overwhelmed everything else.

Her own skin, sharp citrus cleaner, something made with chicken, maybe, and… and something so familiar, so welcome, that it made her eyes and jaws ache. A musky smell and a flowery one, and just underneath, a faint, almost vinegar trace.

"Dad?" she whispered, her voice strange and rough. "Gemaw?"

"Yes, sweetheart, we're both here," her father said, tears in his voice. "We're both here. Everything's going to be all right."

Anne tried to open her eyes, but everything was too harsh and bright. The library was always dim unless all of those screens were on. That light wasn't like this though. That light was cold and blue. What she saw behind her eyelids was more warm and yellow.

Warm. Yes, warm, she could feel that light against her face.

Warmth like the sun, but it was too much for her eyes. She turned her head a little, rolling against softness, like a pillow. That was better.

"We're right here, and we're not going anywhere." A woman's voice. Her grandmother's voice. "You just take your time."

Anne opened one eye a tiny bit, and though it was still so bright, she could manage. She opened the other one a little and saw white walls. She wasn't surprised by that. She'd been seeing those same walls for weeks now, since long before she'd gotten trapped in that library.

This didn't seem like one of her dreams or one of her visions. She felt her body in the bed now, felt both of her hands. She didn't have to see to know who was holding each one. Her right was almost engulfed in both of her father's big hands, and her left in the dry, papery grasp of her grandmother.

"How long?"

"Three days," her dad whispered.

Anne forced both eyes open so she could see him.

Three days sounded like a miracle to her. She would have believed three years. Or thirty.

She'd wandered every corner of that damned library, looking at every single book on the shelves. She never found a door that opened. Only more books than she could count.

Some of the books were blank, only more screens. But she'd found and read dozens of books trying to keep herself sane, waiting for the awful movies to start up again all around her. Anne couldn't remember all of the stories in the books right now, but she hoped she'd be able to someday.

Her father didn't sound nearly as relieved as she felt. He sounded like three short days had been an eternity.

"Three days isn't that long, Dad," she said, her voice still raspy but stronger.

He laughed, and tears filled his eyes. Anne was amazed at how green his eyes were, at how much her grandmother's were just like his. She felt like she hadn't seen such a vivid color for a lifetime.

Her father looked awful, almost as bad as Evan's father had the day Mrs. Griffith died. His face was puffy and his hair stood on end. She wondered if he'd slept at all in those three days.

"Well, it might not have been that long to you, sweetheart," he said, wiping his cheeks. "But it's been a while for us."

"Are you hungry?" her grandmother said, not sounding nearly as upset. "They brought you lunch a little while ago."

Anne blinked and focused on the table beside the bed. A silvery dome sat on top of a tray. That was where the smell of chicken was coming from. A glass of water and a glass of milk made her throat ache. Her stomach was already aching.

"I'm starving. I haven't eaten in three days?"

That got her father laughing, and a second later Anne and her grandmother joined in. When she started to sit up, her Dad shook his head, still smiling.

"Hang on, let me raise your bed up."

He grabbed some kind of remote control, and the flat bed moved under her. In a few seconds, the bed was more like a giant recliner, and her grandmother rolled table closer.

"They've been feeding you," her father said, touching a shiny plastic tube that went into her arm. "I'd imagine you're ready for something solid."

"What happened to me?"

Anne had the fork in her hand before her Dad could uncover the food. Once the full aroma hit her, her stomach rumbled.

Three days? When you thought about three days without solid food, it did seem like a while. She ate tiny bites, trying not to go too fast.

"They think it was a bad reaction to the medication." He sat back and rubbing the back of his neck. "They've got you off all of it now. They said it would take a few days to clear out of your system."

"That happened to me, too," Anne's grandmother said, nodding.

"It did, Mom. That's one reason we knew to be careful with Anne."

Her father tried to hide it, but Anne saw his eyes. Not worried like before. He looked scared to death.

"What now?" Anne said, pausing to take a long drink of milk. "Am I going home with you?"

"Not just yet, no," her dad said, shaking his head. "With you having such a bad reaction, they want to make sure you're better before you come back home."

Anne stopped eating for a minute, staring at him, then her grandmother. They both looked perfectly fine, with no trace of the scary masks she'd seen on other people's faces. She didn't have any sense of a memory right now either.

Nothing hovered around her, and nothing seemed to be moving toward her.

The nightmares were another question that she wouldn't be able to answer until she went to sleep, but she felt better than she had for a long time. Her mind felt tired and foggy, as if she really had been asleep for days, but she wasn't afraid at that moment.

"I'm feeling better right now," she said, watching his face.

"I know, and I'm more relieved than you can imagine. What happened to you was pretty serious, hon. Everyone just wants to make sure you're okay."

He looked right into her eyes. He didn't seem nervous at all, just sad. Anne turned to her grandmother. Her face still had that small smile and her eyes were warm and merry.

"How long do I have to stay here?"

"I don't know," he said. "I'll talk to your doctors a little bit later on and try to figure it out, but we can't be sure yet. Don't worry about it right now. Just worry about getting better."

"Where's Mom?"

"She had to get a few things taken care of at work today, but she'll be here tonight. That's why I brought your Gemaw."

Anne didn't want to say it out loud, but she was much happier with her Gemaw there than her mother.

Anne hadn't forgotten her mother shouting that Anne needed the medication because she couldn't get any worse. She'd remembered that before it ever happened, but even knowing what was coming didn't let her avoid overhearing it in the first place.

She hadn't wanted to hear that, and not just because she knew it wasn't true. She knew she would get a whole lot worse. Her mother's words hurt so much she'd never mentioned it to anyone. Not even Evan.

Evan. He had to be scared to death too. His face the day she got trapped haunted her now that she was awake. And he was the only person in the world who made her feel more calm than her grandmother did.

"Can Evan come visit me?"

"Just immediate family for now," her dad said. "You need to get a little better first."

Anne ate for a few more minutes, thinking it was one of the best meals she'd ever eaten. It was just chicken and rice and vegetables, and not all that spicy, but the warmth in her middle was fantastic. She was wondering if they'd give her more when her father spoke again.

"What do you remember, Anne? About the day this happened?"

The fogginess had cleared with the food, but Anne knew she needed to be careful here. Telling the truth about her dreams and visions, or at least having the truth read from her notebook, got her on the medication to begin with. Only Evan knew she remembered things before they happened.

She didn't need a clear head to know telling her dad she'd remembered the day she got trapped for weeks before it happened wouldn't be a good thing.

"I remember going to lunch. Then I couldn't move." Anne pushed the table with the empty plate away. "I could still hear everything, but I couldn't say or do anything."

"Do you remember coming here?" he said, his voice soft.

"I remember them putting me into the ambulance, but then I think I must have fallen asleep. Everything got jumbled up once they put me in there."

So far she hadn't lied, and she hoped she wouldn't have to. Anne got so confused sometimes between the visions and the dreams and the memories that hadn't happened yet. The last thing she needed was to have to keep a bunch of lies straight in her mind.

"Do you remember anything after you got here?"

Anne thought for a second, trying to be honest again. She remembered being here, sitting up in this bed and rocking, humming to try to drown out the sound of the springs. But she didn't know if that had really happened or not.

That might have been one of the false memories, like the ones she'd had about Evan's father. She couldn't think of a way to ask without having to answer a bunch more hard questions.

"I don't really remember anything, Dad," she said, draining the last of her water. "I might have had some dreams, but I'm not sure. Have I been asleep the whole time?"

He closed his eyes for a second, and his eyebrows wrinkled toward his nose.

"I think today is the first time you've been all the way awake," he said slowly. "You weren't really asleep, but I don't think you knew where you were. That's one thing the doctors will talk more about when you're ready."

She knew then that the memories had been the truth, even if she hadn't experienced them directly. She *had* sat in the bed, rocking and moaning, going over the different memories over and over and over again in her head. She didn't remember anyone being in the room with her, but she was sure at least her dad would have been.

"I'm sorry I upset everyone so much," Anne said, drawing her knees up against her chest. "I didn't mean to."

"Don't you dare apologize for a damn thing," her grandmother said in the loudest voice Anne had ever heard from her. "Every last one of us does the best we can, sweetheart. If we're not hurting someone else on purpose and we keep trying, we're on the right path. Don't let anyone *ever* tell you different."

Her father blinked and smiled at his mother, then he leaned forward and hugged Anne hard.

"She's right, hon. You don't have anything to apologize for. You just think about getting better."

Chapter 20

EVAN'S BEDROOM felt like a bomb shelter to him sometimes, especially on the weekends. Even more so when his sister was home. He kept the door closed more often than not, usually with the radio on.

Same as when his mother was still alive, the volume changed depending on what was going on in the rest of the house.

The curtains and bedspread decorated with her beloved St. Louis Cardinals rather than the home state Cubs or White Sox was probably a little young for Evan. But so far he wasn't willing to let that much of her fade into the past.

He'd carried one of the framed photos of the two of them upstairs not long after she died. Evan-at-ten grinned into the camera, his mom kissing his cheek, her own cheeks rosy and happy. If his father noticed the picture's new home on Evan's nightstand instead of the living room wall, he hadn't said a word about it.

More books than anything crowded the shelves, spilling onto the floor recently. In contrast to the little boy sheets, the walls held maps ranging from ancient explorer's fantasy versions with dragons hiding in the oceans to modern, colorful images from airplanes and satellites.

Evan never could decide if he loved history or science more. He wanted to learn everything about both.

Regular bomb fallout from Gwen and Ed or not, Evan was starting to wonder if he stayed in his room way too much since Anne left. That feeling of withdrawal, of retreat, bothered him more than he admitted to Dr. Lewis or Ms. Fleming.

Nothing else made sense to him right now, though. Evan decided as the weeks passed that as long as he kept his grades at top marks, whatever he did to get through was fine with him.

Not even an hour after Evan settled down in Ed-free weekend peace to read, Gwen's voice pulled him out of the story.

"Let's go."

Evan looked up, surprised to see his sister standing in his doorway.

"Go where?"

"I'll tell you on the way," she said. She plucked his book out of his hands and closed it.

"I was working on something," Evan said, not sure if he should be annoyed or excited.

"It's Saturday, you dweeb. Much as I think they should, I doubt they assigned you *Dune* for ninth grade English. Come on, we haven't got all day."

Evan got up and grabbed his jacket, deciding on excited.

"What's your big rush on a Saturday, Hurricane Gwen?"

Gwen rolled her eyes, but she walked out the door, Evan close on her heels. She looked as much like their father as he did their mother, with her light brown hair and eyes. She acted a lot more like Ed, too.

Evan had often felt like he and his mother were calm ports in the storms that constantly tore through their family until Gwen left for college. Now he had to try to keep himself safe and out of their paths. And he'd lost the only person in the house who could see just how much alike Gwen and his father were without getting offended by it.

"Well, even though you know I hate it when you call me that, I'll still take you with me."

She ran down the stairs and out the door faster than Evan could keep up. By the time he locked the front door, she was already in her cramped, beat up blue Chevette. She had it started and in gear before he could close the door.

"Seriously, what's the hurry?"

"Hurricane Ed's only out for a few hours." She rested her hand on his cracked vinyl seat as she backed out. "We have to be home before then, or at least back in town."

Evan's head bounced off of the seat when she shifted into drive while the car was still going backwards, the same way his father did. With only a quiet protest from the transmission, they headed out.

"Here, you're good at navigation," Gwen said. "I think I know where this is, but help me keep an eye out."

She handed him a wrinkled piece of notebook paper, the edge ragged from the spiral binding. Evan absently pulled the twisted scraps of paper off as he stared at the scrawled lines, squinting in an effort to read his sister's writing.

When he deciphered directions leading into Chicago, with the ninth floor as the final step, his belly twisted. He could only think of one reason they'd be taking a forbidden trip that required extra secrecy.

Gwen was downright fidgety, looking in her rear view mirror, checking her watch, looking all around them until they were on the interstate heading toward the city. She took a deep breath then, and Evan wondered if she knew how much she even sounded like Hurricane Ed.

"Okay, enough with all the mystery, Gwen. Where the hell are we going?"

She accelerated around three cars and got back into the right lane before she glanced at him.

"I talked to Anne's father this morning."

Evan's heart leapt. Anne had been gone for three weeks now, and he hadn't even spoken to her over the phone. All his dad would tell him was she was doing better, and Evan hadn't seen her parents around.

"What did he say? How is she?"

"She's doing a lot better, Ev. They've cut way down on her

medication, and she seems to be pretty stable now. He said she's been hoping you would visit her."

"What? Dad told me just last night she can't have visitors yet! I've been asking him every day!"

Evan knew how loud his voice was in the cramped car, but he didn't care.

"That's exactly why we're going to see her right now. You know I normally try to stay out of these things, but this is just too much of an asshole move by Ed. She's been having visitors for a couple of weeks now."

"Goddamn it," Evan whispered, looking out the window to hide his tears once again. "Did Dad know that?"

"Mr. Fincastle told him as soon as he knew. He's been spending a lot of time taking his mother to see her, that's why he hasn't been around."

"Why didn't Dad tell me? Why?"

Gwen shook her head and glanced at Evan again.

"He's had a bug up his ass about Anne since Mom died, you know that. I don't understand why. I always thought she was a sweet kid. Her parents couldn't have been better to you, or to me. They kept us safe when Mom couldn't. Probably kept us as sane as we are."

"Did Ed tell you Anne was there? That she was with me when I found Mom?"

Gwen hummed low in her throat.

"Let me guess. He decided you both did something wrong. He never told me you were both there. He said you called him, but he didn't mention Anne at all. I'm glad she was with you."

"Dad thinks she's crazy, just like her grandmother. And I think Anne's Mom does too, or at least she's afraid of that."

Gwen snorted.

"Yeah, Ed and Anne's Mom are a lot alike that way."

"Did Mr. Fincastle tell you what's wrong with Anne? What happened to her?"

Gwen was quiet for a while, pretending to study the signs over the highway. They had sixteen miles before they had to exit. She was just stalling. Evan's heart pounded, and sweat sprang up all over his body.

"They're not sure, Ev. They think she did have a bad reaction to the medication, and getting her off of that has helped a lot. But they're not sure what's causing the nightmares or the rest. Has she ever told you much about what's going on with her?"

Evan glanced at his sister out of the corner of his eye, wondering how much he should tell her. She'd been home more often on the weekends since their mother died. Even though that too often led to sparks between Gwen and Ed, Evan knew she was worried about him.

She'd never tried to be his mother, not once. He was grateful she seemed to be turning into his friend. Gwen wasn't likely to side with their father, either. She never really had, not as long as he could remember.

"She told me about the dreams last summer," he said, now looking at the road ahead of them. "She has nightmares about the end of the world. She has for a long time now."

Evan hoped she wouldn't ask him any more. He felt strange about telling her that much.

"And they put her on medication just a few weeks ago," Gwen said, almost to herself. "Well, I'm no psych major, but if stopping the meds helped, maybe it's not anything permanent. And you're not going to catch it even if it is. A visit will do both of you good."

"Thank you, Gwen," Evan said, tears building up again. "Thank you for taking me."

"You're welcome, Ev. I'm sure I don't have to tell you not to mention this to Hurricane Ed. He gets on my last damned nerve, but he's paying for college. If he stops, I'll have to move back home."

"And no one wants that."

Traffic grew heavier and slower as they descended into the city, gray and silver towers rising to block out the pale sun. Evan tried to keep up the conversation, but the closer they got to the address on the paper he was now smoothing against his leg over and over again, the more nervous he got.

He'd tried to convince himself years ago that he didn't really like

Anne that way, not like a girlfriend. Even after she'd trusted him with her secret, he'd tried to deny it.

On the worst day of his life, the day his mother died, Evan had given up fighting how he felt about Anne. That was his one bright memory from that awful day, that whole awful summer. He didn't know if she felt the same way, and he wasn't sure what he'd do if he did know.

The thought of seeing her after almost a month turned his whole body into a manic swarm of butterflies.

"Ready, Ev?"

Gwen's voice jerked him back to the present. They were in the depths of a run down parking garage, an endless sea of cars stretching into the gloom. They'd gotten into the city faster than his father ever did, or his mother. No surprise with his sister driving.

Evan was surprised to catch himself wishing he had those extra few minutes to calm himself down. His heart raced and his palms were sweaty, and he knew his pale face wasn't hiding one tiny bit of the flush climbing up from this throat.

"Yeah, let's go."

Evan's feet never touched the ground as he followed Gwen across cracked, filthy concrete and iridescent puddles. The stink of exhaust and rubber coated the back of his throat.

By the time the dingy fake wood elevator door opened, he was afraid to look at his sister. If she saw how he was feeling, he was afraid she'd tease him for being such a baby and take him right back home.

He stepped forward and jabbed the cracked and stained button marked nine before she could.

Gwen set a quick pace along speckled yellow tiles in an endless white hallway, then stopped in front of window set into the wall. Silver wires crisscrossed the glass, and a grouchy looking woman wearing pink hospital scrubs stared at something on her desk.

As soon as Gwen pushed a glowing button between the window and a gray steel door, the nurse looked up. Her warm smile transformed her face and everything around her.

"We're here to see Anne Fincastle?" Gwen said, sliding her

driver's license through a gap at the bottom of the glass. "Gwen and Evan Griffith."

Evan held his breath, hoping neither of them would ask him any questions. He was afraid his voice would come out in a squeak if it came out at all. The nurse checked Gwen's driver's license against a printed list, then pushed it back through.

"Anne will be happy to see you," she said, winking at Evan. "Come on back."

She touched a buzzer under her desk, and the door to their left clicked. The silence in the hall dissolved into a chorus of beeping, ringing, and low conversation. A shorter hall, this one pale green with bright, cheerful paintings all along the walls, stretched back to a room that looked like the teacher's lounge at Evan's school.

Several doors with windows at the top were closed, with only a few standing open. Evan wondered which one Anne was behind, even as he seriously doubted his legs would carry him that far.

"What do we need to know before we go back?" Gwen said.

Evan watched the nurse, trying not to miss a word she said. The last thing he wanted to do in his whole life was make anything worse for Anne.

"Just talk to her, act normally," the nurse said. She handed each of them a yellowed plastic holder with Visitor on a blue piece of paper inside. "She's doing a lot better. Not quite ready to leave us yet, but don't feel like she's going to fall to pieces. Both she and her father have mentioned you, young man."

Evan managed to smile back at her, but he couldn't hide how badly his hand shook when he took the badge.

"Anything we shouldn't talk about?" Gwen said.

"Well, we're not quite sure when she's going home, so don't bring that up. She's worried about her school work, too. We've been telling her she'll have all the help she needs with it when the time comes."

"I'll help her," Evan said, his voice far too loud.

"I figured you might," the nurse said, smiling, and now his ears burned. "She's in room seven, and her door's open. Just go on back. Visiting hours go until eight pm, so you have plenty of time."

"Thanks," Evan finally said in a fairly normal voice before they were too far away.

Now his feet felt like lead and concrete. Everything was too loud, especially his pounding footfalls. The shaking had moved out from his hands through his entire body.

Before Evan was ready, Gwen stopped in front of the fourth door on the right. The room beyond was narrow, nothing visible but another of those silver-laced windows. His sister's smile made his face hotter when he didn't think that was possible.

Gwen looked like she knew a secret Evan couldn't even guess at.

"Here," she said, taking the badge out of his hands. "You're going to be just fine. I promise I won't spy on you or bother you. And everything is between us."

Before he could say a word, Gwen knocked on the door. Someone called out, a voice Evan hadn't heard in a thousand years. His sister walked him forward, her hand a gentle pressure between his shoulders.

Evan's pounding heart stopped.

Anne was there, she was right there, sitting at a wooden desk by the window. Hair clean and shining in the sunlight, falling in loose waves past her shoulders. Her face curious and unafraid. She looked more vibrant and alive than she had for a long time.

Anne was more beautiful than anything he'd ever seen or imagined.

"Evan!"

She jumped up and ran over to him, hugging him so hard he was sure he felt his spine crack. He squeezed back just as hard, breathing in her sweet scent, trying to make it part of his own body. His heart lurched into life again, and he knew she would feel it beating against her own.

"Anne," he whispered, unable to say anything else.

Evan would have been happy to pass the rest of his life in her arms, no need for anything or anybody else on the entire planet but the two of them. He didn't remember anyone else was in the room until Anne spoke, her breath against his ear sending hard chills all over his body.

"Gwen, thank you for coming."

It took every ounce of strength and courage he had, but Evan managed to let go. He didn't want to be rude to his sister, but more than that he didn't want Anne to let go first. She smiled at him, wiping her eyes with her sleeve, then stepped forward and hugged his sister.

She didn't hold on to Gwen for nearly as long.

"You look great, kid," Gwen said. "I'm happy to see you."

Before Evan could gather enough of his wits to move, Gwen picked up a light, spindly plastic chair and carried it toward the door. She glanced back at him with that same secret smile before she stepped out into the hall, but he didn't care one bit about that now.

"Come sit down, come talk to me," Anne said, grabbing his hand. "I haven't seen you in forever!"

"Forever and a day."

PART IV
EYE OF THE STORM

Chapter 21

Ordinary routines. The daily grind. Boring repetition.

The things most people complained about turned into the anchors for Anne's sanity. The doctors in the hospital in the city told her that, over and over again while she was there.

Look for the normal. Look for habits you can depend on.

Hour after hour at first, then day after day.

Worry about longer than that later. Much later.

The hospital kept a routine for patients for a reason, they said, and too many people forgot that after they went home.

At first, Anne thought that advice was crazier than she felt during those weeks away. She kept a long list of what she would do to break the monotony as soon as she walked out the door.

Stay up all night instead of getting up early. Eat hamburgers for breakfast and pancakes for dinner. Wear her clothes backward and inside out.

That was before the anxiety and fear she never expected hit her, right after the doctors said she could go home in a week. Anne's imagination twisted her silly ideas then, turning them into a trap instead of salvation.

Years ago her mother had scolded Anne for a sour expression, warning her that her face would freeze that way. Anne didn't quite believe that any more, but she was terrified her habits would do the same thing if she messed everything up on purpose. What if she threw up if she tried to eat her meals in the right order, or broke out in a terrible rash if she put her clothes on the right way? Or what if she forgot how to put her clothes on at all?

Anne surprised herself by spending that last week making new lists in her mind and on paper.

Anne's List of Boring Routines.

The other change in those last few days in the hospital would have made her mother proud if Anne ever figured out how to tell her about it. She studied her face in the metal mirror in her room any time she was alone, making every expression she could think of. Months of experience seeing all those death masks gave her more to choose from than most people.

She was determined to find Normal Face. The expression she could manage to hold onto no matter what she saw around her. What she felt inside her. The perfect arrangement of her features that didn't shout *blank*, or *anxious*, or worst of all, *crazy*.

Anne wanted less attention, not more. The best way she could think of to make that happen was to appear relentlessly *normal*. Hour after hour, day after day.

She knew she had it when the nurses, doctors, and even other patients started saying how great she looked, how healthy and happy. Her parents agreed, and her teachers did too once she got back to school.

Anne held Normal Face so carefully in place that her muscles felt funny when she tried to relax her features.

She practiced doing that at least once a day, though, making whatever expressions she could think of when she was alone. As much as Normal Face helped her get through the days and even *feel* normal, she was still a little worried about her face freezing that way.

The only person who didn't seem totally fooled by Normal Face was Evan. Anne caught him staring at her, brow wrinkled and a tiny frown on his own face.

Instead of scaring Anne, like anyone else catching her would have, knowing her friend saw through her made her feel better. In the middle of all her new routines and habits, she was glad this one thing hadn't changed.

Another thing that hadn't changed was the effect her smile, her honest and real smile, had on Evan when she caught him staring. His answering grin, and blush, made them both feel better.

No matter what everyone else seemed to think, Anne knew Normal Face wouldn't last forever.

THE STRANGEST REFUGE Anne found in her ordinary routines over the next four years was visiting Dr. Lewis. She couldn't quite drop Normal Face, no more than she could anywhere else but with her grandmother or Evan. But her psychiatrist seemed immune to constant worry about Anne, at least during their appointments. Relief from the stress of someone else's expectations turned their appointments into a weekly oasis.

The only apparent change by the time Anne was almost sixteen was Dr. Lewis didn't tower quite so much over her. The bigger change was the request Anne had planned, one she'd never made before.

Unwilling to break the routine too quickly, the safe routine, Anne waited for Dr. Lewis to ask all the typical questions first. Her time was running out, but no need to rush things. The last question was the opening she'd been waiting for, and dreading.

"Anything new going on this week, Anne?"

"I need an increase in my prescription."

As usual, Anne tried to figure out what he was thinking. She'd never managed so far. Not being able to when she knew how so many things were about to go wrong in her life made her feel a little bit more normal.

"What's going on?"

"I'm starting to feel anxious again," Anne said, staring at the floor. "A lot like I did before."

"You mean when you had such a bad break? When you were eleven?"

Anne nodded, still looking down. She'd been pretty honest with Dr. Lewis, certainly since the hospital. But she'd kept this particular vision to herself. She'd kept it from Evan, too, but not for much longer.

Her grandmother's death was going to upset everyone and everything around her, and Anne didn't want to make it worse. It was already going to be terrible.

"Are your dreams getting worse?"

"They're the same as always, just happening more often now. Right now I see a few people surviving most of the time, at the end."

"And are you having trouble seeing people's faces again?"

"Not everyone. Some people still look normal." Anne looked up, making sure. "You do."

"This hasn't happened for a long time, Anne," the doctor said, closing his notebook. "Do you have any idea what's different?"

Anne had rehearsed this over and over again in her mind and on paper, trying to get ready for this moment. She wasn't sure that had done her any good at all. She was more afraid of stumbling over her words and sounding like an idiot than ever.

And she was scared to death she was going to sound as crazy as some people already thought she was.

"A bunch of things are going to change over the next few months is all I can figure out. I've been thinking about that a lot lately."

"Are you worried about taking your driving test? That's in a couple of months, right?"

Anne smiled, relieved she could be honest again. She wasn't worried about the driving test at all. It wasn't gong to happen in a couple of months.

As far as she had ever remembered, that was never going to happen.

"I'm not worried about that. I'm more worried about getting a job this summer. And about graduation."

"That's right, you have a few friends getting ready to leave, don't you?" Dr. Lewis said, flipping the notebook open again. "Evan's graduating, isn't he?"

"Yeah. He'll be leaving for college in the fall. I'll hardly ever see him after that."

"That's not going to be easy for either of you. I'm sure you'll see him when he comes home for breaks and such."

Anne didn't say a word, afraid of giving too much away. Evan wouldn't come back to their neighborhood at all for breaks. Not even one time.

His father was going to sell their house before Thanksgiving and move into the city. She didn't think Ed had decided to do that yet, not consciously. He was gong to though, and no amount of protest from Gwen or Evan was going to make a damn bit of difference.

"Maybe," she finally said, knowing Dr. Lewis would sit there for ages waiting. "I'm getting a little worried about making it through the next few weeks of school myself. Finals especially. If I'm already having bad dreams, I won't be getting enough sleep. That always makes everything worse for me."

Dr. Lewis looked into her eyes again, and Anne was careful not to flinch or look away. She knew very well that the medication wasn't going to solve anything. It might even make things worse in the long run. But she had to do whatever she could to make the blow easier for herself and everyone else.

If she fell apart herself before her Gemaw died, she would escape the pain and upheaval. But everyone she cared about would have an even worse time.

Especially her father. She had to stop that if she possibly could.

"You remember as well as I do how you reacted to stronger medication before," Dr. Lewis said. "We won't try the same drugs, but I'm going to ask you to keep a journal just for this. Make a note of how you're feeling every morning and night. Every day, without exception. Don't try to make anyone feel better or keep them from worrying. Be honest. Can you promise me you'll do that?"

Anne looked down at her hands for a second, then back up into the doctor's eyes. She knew she would do that. She would dutifully write it down, at least what she promised to write. Every morning and every night.

Anyone reading what she wrote wouldn't have any reason to

suspect what was coming. Even people reading it afterward, including Dr. Lewis, wouldn't be able to find the clues they were looking for. The medication would help Anne get through the next few weeks a little more easily.

No medication on the planet would help her avoid another trip to the hospital for a much longer stay this time. But right now, she could look her doctor and anyone else in the eye and tell the truth.

"Yes. I promise I'll write it all down, Dr. Lewis."

Chapter 22

Spending time with her grandmother had been one of Anne's favorite things as long as she could remember. Now the visits left her perfectly balanced between sorrow and pleasure. Joy and dread.

Her Gemaw's time on earth was growing dreadfully short, and Anne felt that change in her own body. But she wanted to spend as much time as she possibly could with the only person who understood her odd experience of life so far.

Gemaw hadn't been back to the Fincastle's house for years, not even for a short visit. The last visit was not long after Anne returned from her stay in the hospital. Anne thought her mother was relieved by the end of the visits, when the nurses said the time away left Gemaw too agitated and confused.

Anne didn't have to ask her father how sad that change made him.

The two of them visited once a week, more often when they could. Even if they only stopped by for a few minutes, Anne and her father enjoyed the time as much as Gemaw did. The longer visits on the weekends and during summer were even better.

That window of peace, of not having to pretend at all any more, always helped Anne stay calm no matter what else was going on around her, or inside of her. If either of her parents dropped her off and went to run errands, she didn't even have to bother with Normal Face at all.

The spring before she turned sixteen, when she knew her grandmother was about to die, the visits only intensified Anne's problems. Before she got to the long, low brick building full of rooms and tiny apartments, noise and static started up.

Inside her head sounded like all the screams and crashes of all of Anne's nightmares at the same time.

When she walked into her grandmother's little apartment, the noise stopped, every time. Anne could sit on the blue loveseat with her Gemaw, chatting and laughing. She could pretend to be normal for however long the visit lasted.

As soon as she stepped back out into the world, the bedlam inside her head started up again. It wasn't loud all the time, thank goodness. But that low, disruptive background never went away outside of her grandmother's nursing home.

As on so many other visits, Anne sat with her grandmother on the overstuffed loveseat while her father sat in a matching chair close by. The beige walls had almost no empty space, and the shelves, coffee table, and chest of drawers were just as crowded.

Every painting, photo, and memento Anne had watched her grandmother pack over and over again had come with her to this smaller space. From that bedroom down the hall from Anne's room so many years ago to the four walls she shared with so many others, Mary Fincastle kept as much of her life and her memories around as she possibly could.

Anne understood that up to a point. She spent hours wishing she didn't remember all the horrible things that hadn't happened yet. If some kind of witch or scientist or even a priest offered her the chance to trade some of her real life memories to stop others crowding around her, Anne knew she'd likely jump at the chance.

Her Gemaw seemed perfectly healthy to Anne's eyes and ears, not much different than she always had. Her short wavy hair was almost completely white now, with barely a trace of brown left. She wore her thick pink-rimmed glasses all the time now instead of just when she read.

But her laughter was every bit as warm and strong as her grip on Anne's hand, the same as when she'd lived in the same house with them. Her face was firm and unlined enough that guessing her age would have been tough if she'd worn a wig or a hat.

Anne hoped she aged half that well, at least when the visions didn't have her convinced she'd never live half that long.

Anne's father leaned forward and smacked his thighs with both hands, a sure and predictable sign that he was getting ready to go somewhere. The memory slotted into place in her mind, strangely reassuring. Knowing the conversation a beat before it happened often let Anne relax.

"Mom, Anne wants to sit with you a while so I can get some errands done. Is that okay with you?"

"Of course she can sit with me!" the older woman exclaimed, her eyes sparkling. "There will never be a time when I don't want my beautiful granddaughter with me."

"Good. Walk me to the door, Anne?"

Anne waited by the door, watching her father hug his mother. Seeing her father as someone's little boy was disorienting and sweet at the same time. Even without the memory lining up in her awareness like a targeting scope, she would have known what he was going to say when he joined her.

"Are you sure you'll be okay here?"

"I'll be fine, Dad. I want to spend some time with Gemaw. You know how much it helped for her to sit with me in the hospital. I can't ever really pay her back for that, but I'm happy to try."

"I didn't mean to bring that up," he said, then he closed his eyes for a second. "Is an hour too long?"

"Two hours wouldn't be too long."

Mike Fincastle smiled, the worry leaving his eyes for a brief moment. He kissed Anne's cheek.

"All right. You already know this, but just use the nurse call button if you have any trouble."

"I will. And we won't."

Anne watched him walk down the hall, returning his wave

before he turned out of sight, before she went back to sit beside her grandmother.

She wondered if her Gemaw's different way of seeing the world kept her looking so young. Gemaw's skin was smooth, her eyes bright and clear. Her loose grasp on time and reality kept her living in a facility like this for years, but maybe there were benefits too.

Anne hoped the benefits were worth it in case she ended up in the same place.

"Where are we, Gemaw?"

Her grandmother laughed and took Anne's hands again. This was her favorite game, one Anne's mother hardly ever let her play. The answers ranged widely, with no way to predict the place, the company, or even the decade.

"We're holding a tiny little boy, one so laughing and happy I can't believe they've let me take him home."

"Who is he?" Anne said, though she thought she knew.

"Well, he's your son, my dear."

Cold washed over Anne, taking the fun out of the game and making her head pound. Familiar memory or not, she hadn't expected that answer.

One of the dreams that had tormented her during the last few weeks after the memories started getting worse was of a little boy dying, abandoned and lonely, starving to death in a small, dark room.

That little boy had had the exact same eyes Anne was looking into now, and the same ones she saw in the mirror.

"Do you think maybe that's my father instead of my son? Maybe that's your son."

Her grandmother looked at the floor and tilted her head, her mouth working just a little. She was talking it over, but Anne had never figured out who with.

Her brows drew down in concentration, and Anne wished she hadn't said anything. That had just been too close to her terrible visions. Her grandmother looked back at Anne then, and her eyes were happy.

"You're right, that is my son! The best little boy anyone could have ever wanted to meet."

"I like him too," Anne said, nodding and smiling. "I'm glad he's my Dad."

"I was a little confused, that's all. Your babies have the most beautiful blue eyes I've ever seen, blue like a robin's eggs."

Anne's jaw dropped, and everything inside of her ground to a halt. She'd had that exact thought when she first saw a shell from a robin egg on the ground, how Evan's eyes were the exact same color.

She hadn't thought of Evan or anyone else that way, like a boyfriend, for a long, long time. Knowing she was going to have to go away again, even though she was going to warn her friend before it happened, made thinking that way feel like an even worse idea.

"I don't have any babies, Gemaw," Anne whispered.

She dreaded seeing the confused look again, but it never happened. Instead her grandmother smiled and laughed, then she actually winked.

"Don't you worry, you will. They'll be safe and happy no matter how strange it seems to you. Trust me. I might not know much, but I know all about this."

Her enthusiasm was irresistible, and despite her fear, Anne smiled back. She knew it wasn't a good idea or even what she particularly wanted. But what could the harm be in letting her grandmother believe it? Her memories of the two of them talking were almost all in the past now.

"I'm glad they'll be happy then," she said. "How do they turn out?"

"They're both so smart and strong, and just beautiful," her grandmother said, her eyes unfocused but still happy. "And they're going to have so many babies, generations of them. You're going to live on forever, sweetheart."

Anne stared at her grandmother, at a complete loss for what to say. She knew better. The dreams and visions had been telling her differently for more than five years now. Too many other things had come true for her to be able to doubt it any longer.

The storm was coming, the terrible crash of almost one hundred percent of the human population. And that was the optimistic version of her nightmares.

Sometimes the storm took out everyone. Not a single human was left alive at the end of that one. Of course Anne wasn't going to live forever, but she could never say that. She couldn't say that any more than she could tell her grandmother she herself wasn't going to live out the rest of this spring.

"That sounds wonderful, Gemaw. I'm glad to have something to look forward to."

"You have more to look forward to than you know," she said, leaning forward to pat Anne's hand. "You have some rough times ahead, but you'll have sweetness in the end."

Anne's eyes filled with tears. That was exactly what she was trying to do. Give her Gemaw some sweetness in the end.

She hadn't been lying to her father about that. Her grandmother sitting with her through so many endless hours in that hospital had let Anne walk out of there with some part of her own mind still intact.

"Gemaw, can you tell me what happens to you? When you move through time? What is that like?"

"Why would you ask me such a thing? Is that what happens to you?"

She didn't sound angry or upset. Only confused and curious. For the first time in her life, Anne didn't mind the question.

"No, not really. I have a lot of dreams about the future, but I know I'm not really there. What I see is a long way off, nothing I'll be alive for."

"I'm really there," her grandmother said, nodding. "I know I'm sitting here with you, and I know I'm in every other time. All at the same time."

"Are you afraid?"

"Not at all. I've had so many wonderful lives and adventures, but I always get to go to sleep right here in my own bed. How could I be afraid of that?"

Anne smiled, unable to argue. She didn't seem to have any sense that her life was about to come to an end. Anne was relieved for her, but she wished she didn't know either.

"Are you afraid, Anne? Of what you see?"

She thought, wondering how much she should tell her grandmother. Any of her secrets were safe here, and they always had been. She'd never doubted that. But Anne didn't want to scare her grandmother or make her sad.

"I am sometimes, Gemaw. I don't want to see so many people get hurt. But I have wonderful memories too, things to really look forward too."

"I used to be afraid sometimes too, when I was younger. When it first started and I didn't know what was going on. Your father never seemed to have that part of it, or any of it really. Your aunts didn't either."

"I wonder why I do?"

Anne had asked that question more than she cared to count, and she knew everyone around her had done the same since the nightmares started.

Why had this horrible curse or sickness or mutation, whatever it was, skipped an entire generation and landed full force on her?

"Maybe you're the first one to come along who could handle it as well as I do." Her grandmother nodded, then burst out laughing.

Anne stared at her for a second before she was laughing too. She leaned over to hug her grandmother, and the two of them laughed until they were both wiping tears from their cheeks.

"See, that's all you have to do," Anne's grandmother said, sitting back. "Just figure out how to laugh at it and you'll be just fine."

"I'll remember that, Gemaw."

"How is Evan?"

Anne smiled, trying not to lose the lightness of such a lovely moment. Evan was just fine right now. He wasn't going to be in a few short weeks. Anne would have a lot to do with that. No matter how badly she wanted to, she wouldn't be able to stop it.

"He's doing great. He's leaving for college in a couple of months. I'm really going to miss him."

The older woman leaned over and patted Anne's hand.

"It's going to be fine, Anne, don't worry. He'll come back to you. He always will."

Anne's breath caught, and she was suddenly fighting back entirely different tears. She'd never seen a happy ending for herself or for Evan. She still didn't know how either of them were going to die, thank whatever gods had given her this terrible sight to begin with, but there was no happy ending.

She was afraid to hope her grandmother saw something she herself could not.

"I hope that's true, Gemaw," she whispered. "I really do."

Chapter 23

Anne sat in her bedroom, hands over her ears, eyes squeezed closed. Her head was buzzing, shrieking, echoing with every kind of noise she'd ever heard.

This was the static of her dreams turned up louder than she could possibly tolerate. And she couldn't do anything to make it stop.

The noise had been growing louder over the past several days whether she was awake or asleep. Her head had turned into some kind of organic alarm clock that got louder with every passing second. She was terrified of what would happen when that alarm finally went off.

Her journal and pens were on the desk beside her. She'd gotten everything ready a few days ago just in case. When it happened, she was going to be out of time, and she had to say something. She had to let her father know how sorry she was to be causing such a problem again.

Anne had tried everything she could think of to stop another break in her mind from happening. All she could do now was apologize while she had the chance.

Despite her covered ears and roaring head, Anne jumped when the phone rang downstairs.

That was it.

That was the alarm she'd been dreading for weeks now. She winced, wondering if her flesh and bone ears would bleed when the noise got even louder.

Every trace of sound stopped instead.

Anne held her breath, wondering if this was only some kind of calm before the storm, the eye of the hurricane raging inside her brain.

Silence. She slowly lowered her hands and opened her eyes. Her father stood in the doorway to her room, crying harder than she'd ever seen him cry before.

"Anne," he said, gasping for breath. "Your grandmother… your Gemaw…"

She walked over to him, not wanting him to force himself to say another word. For once, her wretched memories would help another person, even for a second.

"You don't have to say it, Dad. I'm sorry. I'm so sorry."

He cried harder, sobbing against her shoulder, and Anne stood calm and strong. This was the one chance she would have to comfort her dad, no matter how much she might want to again. She was barely going to make it through the next few days. Then she was going to make everything even harder for him.

"I'm so sorry," she whispered.

Anne listened to her father as he stepped back and started talking. Every word matched up with her memory, every pause and hitch in his chest.

Gemaw had died in her sleep, no signs of any suffering. He and Anne's mother were making the arrangements today, but he thought the funeral would be in a couple of days. People had to travel to get here.

So many people loved her.

Then he looked at her, his eyes still red and streaming, his heart broken from losing his own mother. But he had to be worried about his daughter.

"Are you okay, sweetheart? Are you going to be okay?"

Anne had to tell the best lie of her life.

"I think I'll be fine, Dad. Don't worry about me."

He nodded, hugged her again for a second, and left. Anne walked back to her desk and picked up her favorite pen. Gemaw had given her this pen a few years ago when she'd come home from the hospital in the city. It was the only one Anne owned that she could refill and keep using for a long time.

She hoped she never lost this one. She needed to keep her grandmother with her for the rest of her own life.

She wrote slowly, squinting through her tears, making the words as clearly as she could.

Dad.

I'm sorry to cause more trouble for you, especially right now. Please forgive me. I tried everything I could to keep it from happening again. There was nothing I could do.

I love you.

I'm sorry.

Anne tore the sheet out, then carefully folded it so the writing didn't show. She wrote Dad on the outside even though Evan would know who to give it to.

He was going to read it himself. She didn't mind that at all.

She did mind causing her friend more upset and stress when he was already anxious about leaving for college. She at least needed to warn him what was going to happen, especially since she was depending on him to give the note to her father.

She slipped the paper into her purse, then got up to get ready. They were going to the funeral home in a little while. Anne's mother would indeed be sad, but her relief would come through loud and clear too. Anne and her father would help each other get through the next few days and through the funeral.

He would be on his own after that, same as Evan would.

And so would Anne.

ANNE'S dry eyes and skin told her some kind of huge fan ran over her head, hidden by tasteful beige tiles, working hard to keep the funeral home air circulating. But even right by the glass front doors, the smells turned her stomach.

Mounds of dying flowers competed with too much perfume and cologne. The chemical stink of brand new carpeting fought with suits and shoes that normally stayed confined in a closet.

Anne was relieved she hadn't bothered with breakfast.

"Oh, honey, I haven't seen you since you were a tiny little thing!"

She turned toward the elderly man who had spoken, yet another person she had no memory of. Her whole morning had consisted of greeting people who knew far more about her than she did about them.

"Thank you for coming," she said, grasping his frail hands. "I'm sorry for your loss."

"Your grandmother was such a dear woman," he said, shaking her hands before he walked away.

Anne nodded, then looked back out to the full parking lot. Her father hadn't been exaggerating about the number of people coming into town for her grandmother's funeral. Every space she saw in the vast parking lot was full. She wondered how far away Evan's father would have to park.

She remembered Ed and Gwen would bicker all the way over here, and Evan would be more desperate than usual to get away. She spotted them at last, Evan and his sister walking fast to keep a few steps ahead of their father.

She made sure no strangers were swarming toward her, then darted outside to meet them. The cool spring air, fresh and lively after overnight rain, drove the musty funeral home smells away.

"Anne, I'm sorry about your grandmother," Gwen said, putting an arm around her before she walked inside.

Evan smiled at her, but he stood to the side. Anne smiled back, just for a second, then turned to his father.

"Thank you for coming, Mr. Griffith."

He surprised Anne by hugging her, a real hug. The first she ever remembered from him.

"Of course. You holding up?"

"We're all right, as much as we can be."

"Let me know if you need anything," Ed Griffith said, patting her on the shoulder before he followed Gwen.

Anne met Evan's wide blue eyes, and the two of them tried to keep a most inappropriate giggling fit under control. They walked off through the sea of cars before any of the adults smoking around the entry could notice.

"What was that all about?" she whispered.

"You got me," Evan said. "I've never seen him act like that either."

"Something about me and the Griffith men."

He smiled, pulling her into the one hug she'd been waiting for in a day filled with random physical contact.

Evan was still taller than her, that much hadn't changed. But at seventeen his shoulders and arms were warm and so much stronger around her, his voice deeper than her father's. He spoke softly, almost into her ear.

"How *are* you doing?"

"I'm okay right now, Evan, but I need to talk to you. I'm afraid I'm not going to be for long."

His answer unspooled backward in her head, far too long and slow to be his natural voice. Anne dreaded the fear in that voice when Evan's words caught up with her memory.

"What's going on?"

"I can't talk about it right now," she said, trying to fight the echoing mess in her head. "Take me for a walk tonight and I'll tell you."

Evan held her shoulders, and Anne couldn't look away from his pale blue eyes. No matter what else was going on around her, or inside her, she could always see her friend's eyes. He touched her hair.

"I'll hold you to that, Anne."

His words, and his smile, got her through the rest of the horrible afternoon.

Anne hoped she'd remember everything about him when her mind fell apart.

Chapter 24

Evan paced back and forth on the front porch at Anne's house, waiting for her to make her escape. He'd stayed inside as long as he could stand the noise and crowd, long enough to speak to both of her parents. He never had enjoyed huge crowds, certainly not for anything like a funeral.

He couldn't stand to see Mr. Fincastle looking so sad, either. His eyes were too much like Anne's.

Almost an hour later, Evan wasn't about to leave knowing she needed to talk to him. It seemed like everyone inside had decided to linger all night long. The wait was getting to him.

He could see Anne when he passed by the front windows, standing in a group of people he didn't recognize. Probably relatives from out of town. She didn't seem particularly happy, but she didn't have the desperate look he'd seen at the funeral that morning either.

He was at the far end, thinking about sitting on the porch swing, when he heard the door open.

"Thank you for waiting," she said, walking right past him and down the steps. "Let's go before someone else grabs me."

He followed her and they turned down the street, heading away from his house. No need to tempt his father or give him something else to ask about. Hurricane Ed had been more and more full of questions and advice as each day passed this semester.

Mostly about Evan *Leaving For College* in the fall.

College felt too far off and strange, like a daydream, to worry too much about for now. All Evan wanted to do was get through the next few months. If he could do that without too much struggle with his father, he'd be a happy young man.

The only thing interfering with his eagerness to get away was walking beside him right now.

Anne groaned, more annoyed than upset.

"If one more person tells me a story from when I was three years old, I'm going to scream."

"I remember that from when Mom died. I guess it makes them feel better, but I never knew what to say to them."

They continued on to the playground. After so many years, they'd never found a better place to escape. To talk. Evan was definitely too tall for the swings anymore, but the habit just felt safe.

A few kids were trying to stretch out the last few seconds of sunshine on the soccer field, but no one else was around. The two of them sat on their usual picnic table, feet on the splintery bench.

Evan noticed Anne had brought her purse out of her own house for some reason, but he didn't say anything.

"I need you do to something for me," Anne said, watching the kids playing. "Something you're not going to like."

Evan's heart beat too fast to be comfortable. She'd said just that morning that she wasn't going to be fine. He wanted to help her if he could, but he wasn't sure he wanted to know what that would mean.

"What's going on?"

She opened her purse and pulled out a folded piece of paper. It was blank on the outside except the word Dad in her neat handwriting. Evan took it, then looked back into her eyes.

"I need you to give that to Dad in a few days. Not until… You'll know when."

"Why can't you give this to him? What's wrong?"

She looked up at him, and even in the fading sunlight he could see how upset she was. She was scared to death.

"I'm going to have to go away again, Evan. Losing Gemaw, it's too much."

"Have you talked to Dr. Lewis about it?" Evan said, panic working through his heart and out into his body. "There has to be something we can do."

No, please. He couldn't stand this, not now. Not ever.

Not when he was already unhappy about leaving her to go to college. He had to at least know Anne was okay.

"All anyone can do is try to get through this," she said. "I did everything I could to make it easier, but nothing is going to stop it. The last thing I want is for my parents to be more upset. I was able to keep it together for an extra week, until today. After this though, I won't be able to stop it."

"Does your Dad know?"

Anne shook her head, finally looking away.

"I didn't want to make it worse for him right after she died. As long as I could manage, anyway."

"How long have you known about this? When did it start?"

Her dreams and visions scared him, but not as badly as the memories. Nightmares were bad enough, and he'd certainly had his share.

Remembering things before they happened sounded like the ultimate nightmare to him, especially if he couldn't do anything to change the outcome.

"I knew something was going to happen after New Year's," she said. "But not what. I started to see her dying in March. Right after that, I saw myself going away. Once I see something like this, it doesn't change. You know that, Evan. We just have to get ready."

"Well, I'm *not* ready, and I'm not going to be." He stepped back, took a deep breath, and squared his shoulders. "I'm not leaving."

"You can't think that way," she said, scowling at him. "Not because of me."

Anne jumped off the table and started walking. Evan grabbed her bag and followed. It was everything he could to keep a broad grin from taking over his face. Saying those words out loud - I'm not leaving - lifted a ten ton weight from his shoulders, one he hadn't realized he was carrying.

"Does it matter why, Anne? The world won't end if I hold off for a semester, or even a year."

She whirled to face him.

"Do you really expect me to explain why you have to go to college? Now? When I'm about to go back to the goddamn nuthouse?"

Evan drew breath, but her expression stopped him cold. Anne's eyes didn't match her voice. Neither did anything else about her. Angry as she sounded, she looked, somehow she felt, calmer than she had for a long time.

His friend was going through the motions for some other reason, reacting because she was supposed to. He recognized her carefully angry face as easily as her carefully normal one.

"You want me to go in the fall," he said. "No matter what I might want. Just like everybody else in my life."

Anne jammed her fists onto her hips and looked away from him. Chill loneliness Evan hadn't felt since she left him the first time settled into his heart.

"You're going, Evan. That's all. No point yelling or fighting about it. Maybe we're all saying the same thing because nothing else makes sense."

"It doesn't make sense when you're-"

She stepped forward and covered his mouth with one hand.

"This is exactly what I *don't* want. Shouting at each other when no matter what happens, we don't have much time left." She dropped her hand, but Evan still felt the heat of it. "Can you please give the letter to my father?"

"Yes."

"Thank you. Can we not talk about this any more?"

Evan listened to his own teeth grinding together. He hated being upset with her. If she was telling the truth, he wouldn't want to remember an argument as their goodbye.

"Okay."

They walked toward the edge of the soccer field, where only one boy and one girl kicked a black and white ball around. Evan wished he could take both of them back ten years. When getting home in time for supper was all they worried about.

Except he'd never known a time like that, not really. Neither had Anne, not since she turned eleven years old.

"How long?" he said. "Do you know when it's going to happen?"

She shook her head. When she looked up at him, Anne seemed older than her grandmother had been.

"I don't know. Not long."

Not long turned out to be the day after Evan's high school graduation.

Chapter 25

Evan paced around his bedroom, trying to work up the courage to talk to his father. His footsteps echoes around the nearly empty room. He was supposed to be excited. He was supposed to be leaving for college in two days, his first step into his own life. His first steps away from the constant rumble and clash of living with his father.

He'd been daydreaming about this as long as he could remember. Now all he could think about was how empty his life was going to be without Anne.

He sat on his bed, picking up a picture of the two of them at his graduation a few months ago. She'd told him just before she left that she'd already known things were going to fall apart then, but he couldn't tell from the photo. They were both grinning, he in his blue cap and gown, she in a dark green dress that had made him weak in the knees. He was going to pack this last so he wouldn't be without it. Now it was all he had left.

"Come on, Evan, grow the fuck up."

That's exactly what Gwen would say. That's what she *had* said when their father first started telling him where to go to college a year ago.

Don't waste your time, son, go on to the school that's best for you. Go now, start out in the right place.

His father hadn't listened to a word when Evan suggested staying closer by instead of going hours south to St. Louis. Hurricane Ed wouldn't hear a word about community college, either.

No, out of the question. I've worked and saved so you two wouldn't have to worry about this, and I'm not going to let your mother down by skimping now.

Evan stood, taking a deep breath and squaring his shoulders. His father hadn't listened to him about much of anything in eighteen years, not that Evan pushed all that hard. He'd done his best to keep his promise to Gwen, made right after their mother died, to not push Ed any harder than he had to without her around. Evan would have sworn she visited less and less often every year.

This was going to have to start changing sometime. He had to at least try. He walked slowly down the stairs. Dreading this all night and all day tomorrow wouldn't make it any easier. He would either manage to stand up to his father or he wouldn't.

"I need to talk to you, Dad."

Ed Griffith looked up from the television, eyebrows raised. Evan couldn't tell if it was curiosity or if he was already saying no. That didn't matter. He couldn't stop now. He might not ever get started again.

"What's going on?"

He did turn the baseball game off, though Evan half wished he'd be more distracted. He sat down and looked at his hands, then at his father.

"I need to delay going to college for a year."

"And why is that, son?"

"I'm just not ready, Dad. I know I'm too late to enroll anywhere else, but I want to get a job and go to community college in the spring. I'm just not ready to go so far away."

"You'll do fine, Evan. It will be tough at first, but you're going to meet people you'll know for the rest of your life. That's a hell of a lot more important than wasting time around here."

Evan shook his head, scowling at himself. He wasn't getting the words right, at least not in a way his father could hear.

"I know, and I can still do that. I will do that. I'm just not ready yet."

Ed leaned back and crossed his arms. Evan knew in that second how the rest of the conversation was going to go, or at least it always had. When his father crossed his arms that aggressively, he'd made up his mind.

Everything had to change for the first time though, and Evan couldn't give up.

"Evan, you talked about this all year and all summer like you were ready. You've made an awful lot of plans and arrangements for someone who's not ready. You've got your whole first year planned out. You have a job on campus. You've even met most of your professors."

"I know. I'm letting a bunch of people down, most of all you."

"No, son, most of all *you*. I'm not going to let you sit around and waste a year of your life over a case of cold feet. You're going."

"Dad, listen to me," Evan said, trying to keep his voice quiet. "It's not just cold feet. I'm afraid if I go now I'll be making a huge mistake. If my freshman year is a disaster, I might not ever recover."

"Oh come on!" Ed sat forward with his hands on his knees. "You've gotten what, two Bs the whole time you've been in school? The only way this could be a disaster is if you don't go at all."

"You're not listening to me."

"I'm listening, but you're not making any sense. You're not going to derail your life like this on some kind of crazy whim."

Evan closed his eyes, knowing it was no use. His father wouldn't have used that word, crazy, by accident. He confirmed it just a second later.

"What's this really about, Evan? Is it Anne?"

Evan wanted to say no, but he couldn't even manage to shake his head. He was exposed, frozen to the spot, unable to breathe. All he could do was nod.

"You're not leaving her, son. She's already left. She left reality."

"Her grandmother just died, Dad!"

"You've lost two grandparents, and I don't have to remind you you lost your mother when you were thirteen years old. You didn't have to go to a hospital to get over it, and neither did your sister. That's not what healthy people do."

"I can't just leave," Evan whispered, staring at the floor. He was too close to breaking that long ago promise, to getting angry and shouting. That never got anywhere, at least not when he did it.

He'd never been able to figure out why it worked for Gwen.

"You're not responsible for her, son. You're responsible for starting your own life. You're not going to sit around here waiting for someone who might not ever come back. There's no more discussing this. You're going."

Evan stood, trying his best to sound and act like his sister.

"I'm just not going to go then," he said, his voice rising. "You're not going to throw me in the trunk and drag me off to college!"

"Well, that's fine. You're eighteen now, and you can make your own decisions." The calm, hard tone in his father's voice sent a chill through Evan. "But I'm not going to support that either. If you don't go now, I'm not going to pay for college. Not one damn penny. And you'll have to find another place to live if you want to hang around here and get some kind of dead-end job."

"You'd just kick me out in the street? Way to be supportive, Dad."

"No, I wouldn't kick you out. I'd never do that. But I am going to sell this place, Evan. I should have years ago. I was only waiting for you to get finished with high school. You can come live with me in the city if you really want to. You have a home as long as I'm alive. But if you decide to live with me and you don't go to college, you'll be paying rent and your share of everything else. I'll support you any way I can, but I'm not going to support you in wasting your life."

"God dammit, I'm not a kid anymore!"

"No, you're not, son," Ed Griffith said, getting to his own feet. "But you're talking and acting like one right now. You can hate me if you need to, but I will not let you make a mistake this big. You need to get out of here and start your own life, and that's exactly what you're going to do."

He left the room without another word.

A few minutes later, Evan walked back up to his nearly-empty room.

He stared at the picture of himself and Anne until he fell asleep.

Chapter 26

"Anne, you have a visitor. Feeling up to that?"

Anne didn't even turn away from the window. She didn't have to. The deafening static inside her mind had been getting quieter all day long. She had to take this chance while she had it.

"Yes."

She heard the low murmur of voices, and before the door closed she caught some of the words for a change. The nurse was saying Anne had been having a lot of trouble communicating and to be prepared for that. She said the one or two word answers were good signs over the last few days. Anne knew she'd finally be able to manage more than that, at least for a few minutes. Someone stood still, then slowly walked toward her.

"Evan," she whispered.

"I'm so glad to see you," he said, and his voice trembled. "I couldn't… I couldn't leave without…"

Anne turned around in the chair to look at her friend. He was as neatly dressed and put together as ever, with his clothes and hair perfectly arranged. The thing no one would have been able to miss was his eyes. He looked like he hadn't slept in days, and like he wasn't going to sleep for many more.

She knew that was probably true.

"Come sit with me," she said, putting her hand on the chair beside hers. "I want to see you, too."

He took her hand as he sat, and Anne let him. What she had to say wasn't easy. If this small contact made it even a little less painful for him, she wanted to do that.

"You don't have to talk," he said. "I just wanted to see you."

"It's okay. I need to talk to you. I don't think I'll be able to for long. And I want you to talk to me before you go."

"I didn't want to go at all," he said. "I *don't* want to. My father can't hear me no matter what I say."

Anne clenched her jaw. He had to go on with his life, he had to. She couldn't stand to see him get dragged into the mess inside of her.

"He might be right," she said, squeezing his hand. "What would you do around here anyway?"

"I know, I know," he said, wiping away a tear. "It's time to start my life and all that. He was pretty damned clear that he'd cut me off unless I stick to the plan."

"You're ready, Evan. You've been looking forward to this as long as I've known you."

"I'm not looking forward to leaving you here," he said, not bothering to wipe his tears anymore. "I feel like I'm abandoning you, Anne."

Here it was, the thing she'd been dreading for weeks. The memory was as strong as anything happening around her.

"You're not abandoning me. You're ready to go. I have to stay here, probably for a long while this time."

"You're doing better already," he started, but she shook her head.

"I'm doing worse, not better," she said, closing her eyes so she couldn't see his. "I have the nightmares every night, and I can hardly see anyone's faces now. They're not sure what to do with me anymore. The nurse wasn't lying. This is the first day I've really been able to hear anyone or talk since I got here. The noise is too bad."

Evan touched her cheek, and Anne forced herself to look at him. She wanted to remember the color of his eyes, the shape of his face. She didn't want to forget a single thing about him even after she sent him away.

"Can you see me? Can you see my face? Can you hear my voice?"

"You're the only one I can see and hear now, Evan. Now that my grandmother is gone, you're the only one left."

"I can't leave, I can't leave you," he said, pulling her forward into his arms.

Anne squeezed him hard for a minute, willing that moment to go on forever even though she knew it wouldn't. She sat back, taking both of his hands.

"Listen to me. You have to go. You can't stay here because of me. I'm not getting better, I'm getting worse. This is the second time this has happened to me and I'm not even sixteen years old yet."

"Don't say that-"

"I am saying it. They've found the right drugs for now, or at least they're starting to, but that didn't last before. Next time they might not find anything. I might end up in a place like this forever. They want to try shock treatments if I get worse again. I overheard them talking about it yesterday."

"Don't let them do that! If they don't know what's going on, that could make it worse, and you can't reverse it."

"I know, I think so too. And so does Dad. I don't think they're going to do that. I haven't seen it, anyway."

"You're not going to be her forever," Evan whispered, shaking his head, squeezing her hands. "No, that's not going to happen."

"It might already be happening. Look at me, Evan. I'm going to miss you, but I can't let you do this. You have to go. Don't think about me. You have to go find your own life."

"You sound like my goddamn father."

"Sometimes even he knows what he's talking about," she said, trying to find the courage to follow through with the memory. "I don't... I don't want you stay, Evan. I can't see past being in here, and I don't know when I'll ever get out. Knowing you're sitting around waiting will only make it harder."

"I don't think I can do this if I can't even talk to you."

"Listen to me. You can write to me, okay? I'll write back if I can. I can't promise much of anything right now, but I think hearing from you, how well you're doing, will help me a lot. I haven't even been able to talk this clearly to anyone else since I got here. Maybe if you write to me, that will help too."

Evan took a deep breath, looking steadily into her eyes. She knew when he made his decision. He didn't have to say a word. Another memory opened up to her then, and with it she felt a tiny spark of hope. She saw herself with his letters, so many hand-written letters, and those words were the only thing that made sense to her.

She knew the nurses would come in to help her, and she wouldn't be able to see their faces. The doctors would be no different. All she would see was the way they were going to die or some kind of waxen mask. Sometimes she wouldn't even hear their voices over the deafening noises inside her mind. Even her parents were going to look and sound that way for a long time.

But when she read Evan's letters, Anne would be able to see his face and hear his voice. She'd be able to imagine everything he wrote to her as if she were right by his side. She still couldn't see when she would leave this place, but she knew that line of sanity between her and her friend would give her a chance.

"Okay, Anne," he said, sitting up in his chair. "I'll write to you. I promise. I'll do the best I can if you promise me you'll do the same."

Now Anne was crying herself, tears of relief instead of fear. She hugged him again, nodding against his shoulder. This was the first thing she'd felt sure about in a long, long time.

Feeling sure about anything was the first good surprise she'd had all year.

"I will, I promise. I'll do the best I can."

PART V

DARKEST HOUR

Chapter 27

Evan backed out of the crowded common room, feeling like he'd been saying goodbye for at least an hour. The threadbare brown couches and chairs were covered with people in various states of intoxication and relief after the last finals of the fall semester.

Evan knew a little more than half of them. The other half, friends and a more solid support network than he'd ever had back home, made him surprisingly sad to think about leaving for good in a few more months.

The flat white walls had a few more dings and scrapes than when he'd moved in. The even flatter gray carpet would surely be replaced before another year passed. Some stains never washed out. Still, this dorm and the university and St. Louis itself made up the only real home Evan had now.

Hurricane Ed hadn't bothered waiting for Evan's first holiday break four years ago. He'd put their house on the market and moved into the city before the end of September. Gwen joked he hadn't even waited for Evan's bed to get cold.

Evan shook himself, then stepped from dingy carpet to shining green floor tiles. This end of term party was nice and all, but he really needed to get on the road. The drive was long even without holiday traffic and bad weather, and tonight he was afraid he was going to have both. He'd have more than enough time in the car to dwell on the past, and his future.

"Come on, Griffith, what's your hurry?" his roommate for the last two years shouted. "Got a hot date?"

Evan smiled, knowing his face was turning red. He certainly hoped that would be the case.

"Yeah, as a matter of fact I do. I've wasted more than enough time with you ugly fuckers."

Everyone in the room burst into laughter, including his roommate. Evan grinned, waved, and walked away before anyone else could try to stop him. He was going to miss these guys after graduation in the spring.

But he'd never miss anyone here as much as he'd been missing Anne.

The fierce wind drove the fog of nostalgia and the stink of beer and cigarettes from his head. Evan brushed a couple of inches of fresh snow off his car windows and headed north. Before he managed to get onto I-57, his huge, mostly ignored bag phone rang.

Only a handful of people had the number, and all of them knew how absurdly expensive every minute was. Evan could only think of one person who even knew he'd be in the car with the silly thing turned on.

"Hi Gwen."

"You're not driving tonight, are you?"

"Sure, clear as a bell down here. I'm fine, the interstate is wide open."

"You'll stop if you get tired, or if the snow gets worse?"

It wasn't really a question.

"Yes, Mama Gwen, of course I'll stop. I've made this drive a time or two, remember?"

"Right, I'm going to bed, smart ass," she said. "Let yourself in and be quiet about it. Love you, Ev."

"Love you too."

He ended the call, relieved he hadn't been lying about the roads. Snow was still blowing around, but the highway was clear. As long as it didn't come down harder, he'd be able to make good time. Everyone else must have gone early or delayed.

Nothing to do on the vast interstate but drive, listen to music, and think.

Expensive minutes or not, he wanted very much to call Anne, but he wasn't sure of her work schedule this time of year. Between his finals and her being busy, they hadn't talked or written much for a while. He'd see her tomorrow, certainly, and finally get to see her new apartment.

He closed his eyes for a second, no longer worried about hiding what he was looking forward to. Well, what he *hoped* to look forward to, maybe. Even his own thoughts were a jumbled mess.

Anne being nearly twenty was part of that. Evan could admit that to himself, at least inside his own mind. She'd had time to work out her own life a bit while he'd been away. Her having her own apartment certainly didn't hurt.

He was terrified enough of telling her how he felt about her without worrying about her father walking into the room. Mr. Fincastle had always seemed to like Evan, but that didn't change the fact that he was Anne's father.

Evan had seen his own father's reaction when Gwen brought her boyfriends home, how he'd had an eerie sense of who was dangerous to his little girl and who was not. Hurricane Ed had despised Mark on sight, and that never changed until Gwen's wedding day. All of them would deny it, but Evan thought their father's suspicion lingered until his first nephew was born.

Evan wasn't ready to set off those alarms in Anne's father, not just yet. He hoped graduating from college and doing so well would help with all of that.

It wasn't just nerves over Mr. Fincastle by any means. That would at least be typical. Evan knew his own father would never approve of Anne, no matter how much time passed, and even if she'd been perfectly fine that entire time. In the years since his Mom had died, Ed's opinion of Anne had only gotten worse.

Again, going by what he'd seen Gwen go through, it was going to be tough. The fact that Ed already distrusted the woman Evan wanted, assuming she wanted him, would make everything even harder.

Evan shifted in his seat, popping out one cassette and switching another, not quite so energetic. His normal driving music was keeping him too much on edge tonight.

Assuming Anne wanted him. Was anything else in the entire world worth worrying about? Gwen accused him of being a drama queen sometimes, and he supposed she was right. Evan knew he just needed to brood about things from time to time. He'd brooded about this one for a while.

He'd dated on and off, mainly to shut his father up and keep people out of his business, and plenty of his friends had gone through several relationships over the last four years. Just because he wanted Anne more than he'd ever wanted anything didn't mean she felt the same way.

What he would do if she didn't feel that way about him shut his normally active mind down cold.

"There's no hurry, Evan," he said, his voice rising and falling to match the song. "You have plenty of time."

He already had a summer job lined up closer to home, only an hour away instead of several, and he planned to go to grad school there too. He smiled, thinking how relieved his father would be that he already had an apartment arranged close to the university. No worries about asking Evan to move in with him and hoping the offer would be refused.

He had at least two years, more if he ended up with a job somewhere close by. He didn't want to rush Anne or himself, but he didn't want to wait any longer than he had to, either.

The snow was falling again, but the roads were still empty and fairly clear. In any case, he had two weeks on this break to see how things worked out, how he and Anne both felt now. Everyone had grown up, probably more than they should have, over the past four years.

Evan hoped they'd grown toward each other instead of away.

~

ANNE'S APARTMENT building didn't look all that different from some of the newer dorms Evan had driven past less than twenty-four hours ago. A three-story boring tan box jammed in with five or six just like it, nondescript holly bushes scattered around frost-burned winter grass. The biggest difference was the lack of bike racks instead of several jammed full of college commuter specials.

After a furious internal debate with himself, Evan decided to skip bringing flowers, candy, or anything else he hoped Anne might be happy enough to hug him for. No matter how vividly he'd imagined their reunion and hopeful happily ever after, that only existed inside his own head.

His confidence and excitement didn't quite insulate him from fear of a broken heart.

Evan was sure he'd been knocking for an unreasonably long time on the rusty steel door before it opened. He'd been starting to worry about disturbing the neighbors. The sight of Anne drove all thoughts of other people from his mind, but not in the way he'd expected.

"Evan," she said, closing her eyes and sighing. "Come in."

He stood for a second, watching her walk away, too stunned to move. He couldn't remember a time in well over ten years when she hadn't hugged him after they'd been apart, certainly not when it had been most of a year since they'd seen each other. That was the smallest thing in his mind right now.

The biggest was shock over how awful she looked. Her hair was dirty and uncombed, her faded t-shirt wrinkled and stained. She turned then, scowling at him as she sat down at what looked like a battered fold-up card table in the kitchen, probably older than either of them. He closed the door and walked slowly toward her.

The apartment was small but fairly neat, as similar on the inside to Evan's dorm as on the outside. Nothing was quite organized, but no distressing piles of garbage or rotting pizza boxes. What bothered him about the apartment was the smell.

The air was stale and heavily organic. Unwashed. A scent he recognized too well from all-night study sessions. No one here was in school, so unless there were crowds of teenagers playing too many video games, that didn't make sense.

Someone smoked far too many cigarettes, and the cloying sweetness of incense didn't quite cover up marijuana and alcohol sweat in the air.

He sat down at the scuffed table across from Anne, trying not to stare. She hardly looked like the same woman he'd said goodbye to in August. She covered her eyes with her hands, but he could see how pale and unhealthy her face was. She was thin, far beyond her normal slender build and into bony.

Something had gone terribly wrong in a short time. He had no idea what to say or do, alarm shorting out all of his reason. He couldn't just sit here silently.

"I'm glad to see you, Anne."

She never even uncovered her eyes.

"I didn't expect you so early."

Evan stopped himself from looking at his watch, but he knew it was almost two in the afternoon. Everything he could think of to say sounded terribly judgmental and condescending.

"How've you been?" The painful formality made him wince inside.

She grunted, then lowered her hands to cover her mouth. Her lovely green eyes were swollen and bloodshot, and she seemed to be having trouble focusing on him. As thin as the rest of her was, her face was puffy. This wasn't just a one-night drinking binge.

That much alcohol could not possibly be good with her medications, if she was still taking them. She finally took a deep breath, put her trembling hands on the rickety table, and answered the question he'd forgotten asking.

"Just great, Evan. Fantastic. Better than ever. You look like you're doing well."

"I'm good, long drive last night. Going to your parents' for Christmas?"

"Probably not, I have to work both days. Hazards of retail."

She looked away from him as she spoke, and her pale cheeks flushed. She was lying and not trying all that hard to cover it up. He wondered if she was still working at all.

She'd never looked so unhealthy or acted so strangely before she'd gone to the hospital before. He couldn't guess what, but she was on the edge of something.

Evan didn't want to be the one to push her over.

"They'll be disappointed," he said.

"Someone is always disappointed, no matter what I say or do. This way I don't have to listen to everyone harping on about it."

"Have you seen something, Anne? A memory or a vision?"

"Goddamnit, the biggest problem I have is everyone asking me if I have a problem! Maybe I'm just having a bad day, did that ever occur to you?"

"It occurred to me that you haven't hidden anything like this from me since you were eleven years old. Whatever's happening with you is more than a bad day."

"You need to go, Evan."

Reasonable or not, his temper finally caught up with hers.

"Come on, Anne, this is bullshit. I haven't seen you for months, and you're acting like you've never seen me before. What's going on?"

She glanced at him, then covered her eyes with her hands again. The reunion Evan had imagined all the way home had fallen apart before it ever got started.

"Nothing is going on. I'm just busy, that's all. I've got a lot on my mind right now. I don't have time to play hostess."

Gwen called him on being too nice all the time, and other people had too. This was definitely not the time for being nice.

"Hostess? Since when did you have to be my hostess? I offered to take you out to dinner, remember? That's why I'm here. You don't have to do a thing but get ready."

She lowered her hands and finally looked at him, really looked, and Evan was scared to death by what he saw. She was sick or badly hung over, and he wasn't sure it was only alcohol either. Whatever this was could not be a good thing.

"I'm worried about you," he said, reaching for her hand. "You look like you haven't slept in a week."

She jerked her hand away and drew back from him.

"Stop worrying about me, Evan, just stop it. I'm fine. You left to start your life a long time ago. Time for me to do the same. You need to get on with your own life and stop trying to fix mine."

Anne usually knew when things were going to get bad, actually, and she did everything she could to warn people and get ready. Had even that scant blessing failed her?

"I'm not trying to fix you or anyone else. I just wanted to see you, spend some time with you. I miss you when I'm gone, you know."

"I know," she whispered, holding her head again. "I'm sorry, I miss you too. I shouldn't be talking to you like this."

Evan rubbed his eyes, scrambling for what to say. Her mood swings were making his own head hurt. His ideas about having plenty of time seemed to make a lot of sense right now, but he didn't feeling comfortable walking away from her.

"Have you been sick?" he said.

She laughed, and the bitterness and anger in her voice broke his heart. Her laugh had always been light and free, even when it was rare.

"I've been sick since I was eleven years old. You know that. This is just more of the same."

"You look… I'm sorry to say this, but you look hung over. You look awful."

Anne stared at him. He heard his father's voice, his many lectures about thinking things through. This time he'd tried, choosing all of his words carefully, and that only made things worse.

"Are you going to tell me you never drink with all your college buddies?"

"Sometimes, sure. But I haven't drunk enough to get hungover since I was seventeen years old."

"Say it, just say it," she said, lifting her chin. "Go on. And you don't have the same kinds of *issues* I do, right?"

Evan winced. This was more than casual drinking. The Anne he knew would never have thrown that in his face. She knew he hated that part of his father, and that Evan would never repeat those words no matter what happened.

"I wasn't going to say that, Anne. I would never say that. Seems to be on your mind, though."

"Of course it is!" she shouted, leaning over the table toward him, then standing. "We're so relieved you graduated from high school, but maybe you shouldn't go to college just yet. Get a job, but maybe you should stay home. Don't get too stressful a job though, nothing that would possibly give you a way to advance or afford a place of your own. Maybe moving out isn't such a good idea, especially with your issues!"

Evan wanted to cover his ears, close his eyes, maybe find a closet to hide in. He had no idea what to do. He didn't want to upset her even more by leaving, but staying here didn't seem to be exactly keeping her calm.

"Anne?"

They both turned to see a guy standing in the hallway. He was as disheveled as Anne, with his hair standing up and ripped jeans on, but no shirt. His eyes were as red and his face as puffy as hers.

Evan watched as he stumbled across the kitchen and put his arm around Anne's shoulders. She didn't flinch away like she had from Evan, but her face was now bright red. She stared at the floor.

"What's going on in here?" the guy said, staring at Evan with narrowed eyes.

"Nothing, Joe, I'm fine. Just talking to an old friend."

Evan's chest was tight and hot, and his whole body felt like he was trapped in quicksand. He'd never wanted to get away from a place more in his entire life, but he couldn't move. He couldn't blink or look away from Anne's face, not even when she finally met his gaze.

An *old friend*.

Nameless and in the past, not even worth an introduction.

"Yeah, sorry to disturb you," Evan said, his throat aching. "I was just leaving. Have a good holiday."

He pushed himself up from the chair, wondering if his legs would support his weight or function well enough to get him out the door. After that it didn't matter anymore.

If he didn't escape this stinking room, he was afraid his heart would explode within him. He looked into Anne's eyes for a second longer, then he turned away and walked out the door.

He managed not to slam it before he leaned against the wall, his breath coming in sharp, painful gasps. He felt like he'd run up ten flights of stairs rather than walking fifteen feet. His head pounded hard enough that his body trembled in time with it.

Of everything he could ever have imagined, nothing came close to this. His heart had been so neatly ripped out that he wondered why it still beat at all.

He had no idea how long he stood there before his spinning brain finally settled on one idea, the only course of action he could take.

Get out of here. Get away. Don't let one of them open the door.

Don't let her see you like this.

Don't let him see you at all.

Go.

Evan walked down the hall, his head and his heart throbbing. What had happened to her? He didn't try to fool himself that seeing the guy, Joe, hadn't been horrible, but something far worse than a boyfriend had changed in Anne.

Just a few years before, he'd felt sure he could help her, stop the nightmares and the visions and keep her calm if he just stayed by her side.

Just a few hours before, he'd been sure he could love her enough to keep anything from hurting either one of them ever again.

Now he was wondering if anything could stop her from killing herself with drinking or whatever else she was doing.

He drew back from the brutal wind when he opened the door, lowering his head and walking to his car. By the time he shut the door, his face and hands were numb and his eyes were watering.

He wished his heart would go numb.

His heart was still sharp and aching, the scattered pieces cutting his insides to ribbons. Evan was far past the point of tears or anything else he could think of.

He had to get away from here.

Away from her.

Chapter 28

Before Evan turned toward Gwen's place, an idea finally floated to the surface of his jumbled mind. He'd asked about Anne seeing her family for a very good reason. The only other person she trusted was her father, and no one else seemed to understand her like he did.

Evan wasn't so sure he understood his friend anymore, but surely her father still did. He couldn't face his sister in this state anyway. Hurricane Ed would be even worse.

Not even 2:30 yet, that had all happened so quickly. Having the imagined course of his life altered so fundamentally should have taken longer than half an hour.

Anne's father would still be at work this early, and it wasn't far from here. A absurdly expensive call had never been more worth the cost than this one. When the phone on the other end started to ring, Even wondered if Anne's father answering or not answering would be worse.

He was out of time after three rings.

"Mike Fincastle here."

"Hey, Mr. Fincastle, Evan Griffith."

"Oh, Evan, great to hear from you. Are you home for break?"

"Yeah, just got here last night." Evan gripped the steering wheel hard enough to make his knuckles ache. Worry about his friend or not, he knew he'd be crossing a line with his next words. "Listen, have time for a cup of coffee? I'm about twenty minutes away, and I'm buying."

The silence only lasted a few seconds, not even a block at thirty miles an hour. Evan forced himself not to panic.

"Sure, I can meet you downstairs at three. It's called Jolt, but it's a pretty good place."

Evan laughed, hoping it didn't sound as artificial as it felt.

"Cute. Okay, I'll see you there at three."

By the time Evan finally found a parking spot a few blocks away, the lot split between dented and salt-covered cars like his own and gleaming new models, he was feeling a little bit calmer. He still had no idea what he was going to say to Anne's father.

He couldn't think about her being with some other guy, not right now. He was quite sure that would be on his mind more than he could stand for a long time after he wanted it to be.

Right now he had to think about Anne, not himself. He didn't have to be a doctor to know she was in real trouble. Even without what she'd gone through in the past, his friend needed help Evan couldn't provide.

Mike Fincastle sat at a table by the door, and he stood and hugged Evan hard. Evan had to squeeze his eyes closed for a second before he let go.

He'd been expecting Anne to hug him like that instead of standing with some other guy's arm around her.

Some half-naked guy who'd just crawled out of her bed.

"You look fantastic, Evan. How's school going?"

"It's going great, thank you for asking. I'll be graduating in the spring, then heading back up here for grad school."

"Oh, that's wonderful. We've all missed having you around. Are you staying with Gwen?"

"Yeah, crashing on her couch. I'm not sure the boys remember who I am yet, but they were very excited to wake me this morning."

Mr. Fincastle rolled his eyes and smiled.

"What are they, two and four? That's got to be an active household. Are they all doing well?"

"Everyone's great, thank you. How are all of you?"

Just as he'd feared, Mike Fincastle's warm smile faded. He didn't look as cold as his daughter had, but he looked as frightened as Evan felt.

"Have you talked to Anne?"

Evan took the excuse of asking the waiter for a double-espresso, hoping it would slow the pounding in his head. He hoped something resembling words would come out when he turned back.

"I saw her, just a little while ago. I stopped by her place."

Mr. Fincastle nodded, and his mouth compressed.

"Not exactly Shangri-La, is it?"

"No, not really," Evan said, looking out the window.

"Neither her mother nor I wanted her to move out, but short of…well, having her committed or something, we couldn't do much to stop her. How do *you* think she's doing, Evan?"

Evan looked into green eyes so much like Anne's that it made him want to cry all over again.

"Not very well."

The waiter brought his espresso then, giving both men a chance to regroup. Evan was thankful it wasn't boiling hot, or he would have burned the hell out of his mouth.

"I don't think she's doing well either," her father said. "I think she's been drinking."

"Yeah, me too. That can't be a good thing with her medication."

Evan felt like he was gossiping or breaking some kind of bond of secrecy, but neither he nor Anne were kids anymore. He cared too much about her to let her destroy herself without even trying to stop it, even if she didn't feel the same way about him.

Her father covered his eyes the same way she had.

"I don't think she's taking medication anymore. I think she's been drinking instead, using that to keep the nightmares away. I know I never dreamed the couple of times I drank myself blind back in college."

"Not the healthiest way to deal with it," Evan said. "I'm sorry, that was way out of line. That's none of my business."

"Of course it's your business! You're her oldest friend, her closest one, too. If anyone in the world truly understands her and cares about her, it's you. Did she talk to you?"

"No, not really. I wasn't there very long."

"I don't know what to do for her. She's twenty years old and paying for her own room and board somehow. I can't just drag her back home, and unless she has some kind of breakdown, I can't force her to get help. By then it might be too late."

His voice broke, and Evan closed his eyes, not wanting to see the older man's face. He couldn't save Anne, he couldn't comfort her father, and he couldn't calm his own reeling heart.

Maybe he should have just stayed in St. Louis. His life there at least had some kind of order. He accomplished things there, and he knew what was coming and how to handle it. Here it was all he could do to manage not to cry.

"Is she still seeing Dr. Lewis?" Evan said.

"Not for several months now, since a few weeks after she moved out. I don't think Anne wants to hear what he or anyone else would say." Mr. Fincastle sat back in his chair then, taking a deep breath. "Well, I'm sorry your holiday has gotten off to such a rotten start, but I really appreciate you calling me. It's long past time I did something, even if I have no idea what that might be. I can't just keep letting her get worse."

The silence between the two men went unnoticed in the noisy shop.

Dwight, a guy who lived two rooms down during Evan's freshman year had started drinking too much, or maybe he had been before he got there. No matter how much his roommate or the resident or his adviser or anyone else talked to him, he couldn't hear a word of it. Dwight made it through that year without getting suspended, but he didn't come back the next. His roommate said his parents forced him into rehab.

He returned subdued and quiet the next year. He'd told Evan he'd relapsed several times, but he was okay. Dwight backed it up by acing all of his classes, taking extra and steadily catching up on the lost time, but he'd never lost that quiet, restrained manner.

Evan was afraid if Anne didn't make some kind of change soon, she'd never have a chance to see what the other side would be like.

"Listen, I'm sorry to rush off," Anne's father said, startling Evan. "I need to make a couple of phone calls. Thank you again for calling and meeting me here. Can you stop by the house before you head back? I know Karen would love to see you."

"Sure, I'll do my best. I'd love to see her too. I don't know if I can do anything, but let me know, okay?"

"I will, Evan." Anne's father hugged him again. "I will. Speak to you soon."

Evan watched him walk out and duck into the bitter wind. He had an equally cold feeling in his gut that nothing was going to get better.

Not for a long time. Maybe not ever.

Chapter 29

Anne walked out of her parents' house, slamming the door behind her. She pounded on the heavy wood twice, knocking the gigantic wreath and a strand of glittering red and green garland off, trying to keep herself from screaming out loud.

Before one of them could open it, she ran down the stairs and across the street to Joe's filthy Datsun hatchback. He'd refused to go inside as always. This time she was glad he'd stayed out here. She closed the car door a little more quietly.

"Let's go," she said before he could ask any questions.

Anne tried to stop herself, but as Joe pulled away in a cloud of blue smoke, she looked back. Her father stood on the front porch. Even from this distance and moving through the oily haze, she could see him wiping at his cheeks.

Well, that's what he deserved for talking to her that way. She was nothing but glad.

"How'd it go, babe?" Joe said with his asshole smirk. "About like it does with my parents?"

Anne ignored him, turning toward the smeary window. She didn't want to deal with him any more than she'd wanted to deal with her father and his selfish demands.

She was not a little girl that he could order around. Not anymore.

Joe touched her hair.

"You all right?"

She turned back to him, suddenly quite sure who she did want to deal with.

Evan. His damn interfering had gotten all of this started, deciding he knew what was best for her yet again. Evan and her father thought they had everything worked out, typical fucking men.

It was usually her mother trying to force Anne to live her life to suit everyone else.

"I'm fine, Joe. Just fine. Can we stop one more place? It won't take long at all. I promise."

FASTER THAN HE would have thought possible, Evan adapted to the routines of Gwen's household. He didn't have much choice from his central sleeping location on the living room sofa. At the very least, doing everything he could to keep up with two whirlwind toddlers left him tired enough to sleep.

And busy enough to keep his mind off how badly his holiday, and his plans, had gone wrong.

The wakeup giggles had drifted back to quarter to seven that morning, as if the boys were gearing up for their pre-dawn raid on Christmas presents the next day. Evan sat cross-legged on the dark blue hearth rug so he could feed the fireplace, while his nephews created a noisy toy car war with rules only they could understand.

Gwen had the good grace and humor to bring him a huge mug of coffee before she retreated back to her bedroom. The promise of pancakes and maple syrup whenever she and Mark finally got up kept Evan and both boys relatively quiet.

Evan lurched to his feet when the apartment's intercom buzzed, not wanting the harsh noise to wake his sister. They weren't expecting Hurricane Ed yet, and he wouldn't bother with the intercom when he had a key. Evan crossed the room as quickly as he could with pins and needles climbing up both legs.

"Meet me downstairs."

"Who… Anne?"

"Of course it's Anne, you son of a bitch. Meet me downstairs or you'll wish you had."

Evan's jaw dropped at the vicious tone of her voice, but she cut the connection before he could say another word. He walked to the end of the hall and jerked the curtains back. Anne was out there, pacing beside an ancient tan car more rust than paint, glaring at the building every few seconds.

Her words finally sank in, and he dropped the curtain, squeezing his eyes and his fists closed.

Son of a bitch. If she was able and willing to say that to him, she was much further gone than he'd thought.

One of the boys squealed laughter just then, and Gwen's sleepy voice answered. They apparently hadn't heard those awful words, but Evan knew he had no choice but to go out there.

He didn't want anyone in that state of mind anywhere near his family. Especially not those kids.

"I'll be back in a minute," he said as he passed through the living room and grabbed his coat. "I won't be long."

Gwen stood in the living room in her robe, rubbing her eyes.

"Dad will be here soon."

"I know. This shouldn't take long."

Evan managed to close the door quietly, but he was more furious than he wanted to admit. After the way she had treated him two days ago, Anne thought she'd just show up at his sister's house making demands?

And he had *never* reacted well to that particular phrase. Call him a bastard, a jackass, an asshole, whatever seemed to fit. He knew he'd been all of those things at one time or another.

But he he'd never been able to tolerate *son of a bitch*, not from Anne or anyone else. He wasn't about to start tolerating it now.

He crossed the street and was nearly beside Anne before she

noticed him. Evan glanced at the smudged, yellowish car windows and saw Joe, to no surprise whatsoever.

Obviously he would be here too. Things might have had some chance of staying calm otherwise.

Anne turned and strode toward him. Her hair and clothes seemed to be clean, at least. Evan was too angry to hope that was any kind of good sign. From the look on her face, so was she. She stopped just a few inches away, and he tried not to draw back at the liquor on her breath.

"Did you talk to my father?"

"Good to see you too, Anne."

"I asked if you talked to my fucking father!" she shouted, jabbing her finger into his chest.

"Yeah, I did." Evan moved out of range of her hands and her breath. "You're showing me the reason why right now."

"Goddamn you! What fucking business is my life of yours, Evan?"

Evan saw her father's eyes, heard him saying of course Anne was his business. He tried to remember how badly he'd wanted to see her just a few days ago.

Now he just wanted her to go away before his sister heard her shouting like this. Or his nephews.

"It's my business because I care about you, and you're falling to pieces right in front of me. How are you possibly drunk at nine in the morning?"

She stepped forward again, cheeks flushed and eyes blazing.

"I am not fucking drunk, and it wouldn't be your concern if I was. You need to concern yourself with your perfect little life and stay the hell out of mine!"

He knew more curtains than his sister's were drawn back, but he didn't dare turn away. That was the second thing he never would have imagined her saying to him, not in a million years.

She knew better than anyone how *imperfect* Evan's life had been. She was one of the main reasons he'd gotten through it so far.

"Stop shouting or I'm going back inside. And I won't open the door or answer any calls while you're acting like this."

"If you don't like the way I'm acting, maybe you'll reconsider telling my father I need to go to goddamn rehab next time," she said, her voice quieter but no less furious. "You don't know the first fucking thing about my life."

"Who the hell do you think you're talking to, Anne? I know more about your life than anyone else possibly could. I know whatever you're doing isn't working."

"You knew me a long time ago. You ran off to college and left me to rot in that blasted hospital. If I did rot after all, you can fucking blame yourself. I know I do."

The blow would not have been harder if she'd punched him in the nose or kicked him in the balls. He had blamed himself, over and over again, through all the years since she'd started having so much trouble. And he'd nearly driven himself crazy with guilt for months after he'd left for college. Getting through that first semester had been the hardest thing he'd ever had to do, until just this moment.

"You can't… you don't know what you're saying."

"I know exactly what I'm saying, and I should have said it a long time ago. If our friendship meant so much to you, if I was so important to you, how could you walk away and leave me there? Do you have any idea how bad it got for me after that?"

Evan stepped back again, but she followed. His head was swimming, and not just from the horrible smell.

He did know. He knew she'd been there for months that time, much longer than before.

"I had to go, Anne, I didn't have any choice. I couldn't help you. I couldn't do anything."

"I'm sure that's what you told yourself. Just walk away, let someone else handle it, anyone else. Well, they handled it alright. They handled it by drugging me out of my mind for months, and they wanted to for the rest of my life. I wasn't able to think or feel anything again until I moved out of my parents house and got off… the fucking…drugs."

"You told me to go," Evan whispered, tears cutting a hot trail down his face. "You told me I had to go, that I had to."

"You know what? That's exactly what I'm going to tell you right now. Go. Get the hell out of my life and stay out. I don't need the drugs, I don't need rehab, and I don't need you!"

"Anne, please, listen to me…"

"No Evan, fuck off! Stay away from me and don't you ever, ever talk to my father again! Fuck off!"

She got in the car and slammed the door before he could say another word. Joe stared up at Evan for what felt like an unreasonably long time. Right before he finally drove away in a cloud that stank worse than Anne's breath, he smiled.

Evan couldn't move or think. He couldn't cry anymore, and the anger that had driven him down to the street had turned into ice in his belly.

Gone. She was gone. And she'd made it painfully clear she didn't want to hear from him anymore either. Not today. Not ever. There was nothing left for him to do but go back inside before he froze to death.

He had to get through the rest of this visit, Christmas and New Year's Eve and few days after. He had to do all of that without screaming until he sent the rest of his mind to wherever his heart had disappeared to.

He turned in time to see the curtain drop at his sister's window. Gwen. He couldn't imagine Mark or one of the kids wanting to watch this disaster unfold. His sister had seen the whole thing, and she'd probably heard quite a bit of it.

Well, unless he wanted to get in his car and head hours south to an empty campus, he didn't have anywhere else to go. Anne's parents' house and certainly his dad's were out of the question.

Evan had to speed up his pace to avoid a car, and by the time he got to the sidewalk the car slowed and turned into the driveway.

Of course. This couldn't have gone any other way.

Maybe he was just a little early, or maybe Evan's thoughts had conjured him out of thin, freezing cold air. Evan turned his head to wipe at his face, hoping the tear marks wouldn't show. That was the last thing he wanted to be explaining to Hurricane Ed.

"Hey, Dad."

"Evan! What the hell are you doing out here?"

His father got out and hugged Evan briefly, a typical grasp-and-pound guy hug. Anne's father had hugged him like a person, like someone he really cared about.

Evan couldn't be thinking about that.

"I had to bring something out to the car," Evan said, "and the boys were a little loud. Need help carrying anything?"

"The boys are always a little loud. Yeah, I could use some help. I brought a bunch more stuff for them to make noise with. Gwen loves it when I do that."

"You're right, Dad, she does. She told me so just this morning."

Evan ended up making three trips, wanting to give his father the chance to greet his grandsons. He also needed to clear his own mind before he could face everyone inside.

Gwen had seen, but he knew she'd never say a word until their father left. And even then, she'd give him the chance to talk to her instead of prying. That was one of the many things he loved about her.

He didn't know if he'd ever be able to talk to her or anyone else about this. All he could do was keep moving, putting one foot in front of the other. He had to just keep breathing until he could get out of here and go back to where things made sense.

Just before he walked back inside with the last armful, Evan stopped, wanting to duck right back out into the cold. He'd finally realized he might be able to escape in a few days, but he wouldn't be gone for long at all.

In less than six months, he'd be right back here, getting settled into his own apartment and a new job, getting ready for at least two years of graduate school.

He knew six months wasn't going to even let him get started pulling his own heart back into some kind of human shape again. He doubted six years would be able to do that. But once again, Evan couldn't think of anything else to do.

There was nothing else to do.

He just kept going.

Chapter 30

After the joyful furor and disruption of Christmas morning, Evan finally got time alone with his sister. Wrapping cleared away, huge brunch devoured, Hurricane Ed departed, Evan's brother-in-law and nephews crashed early, leaving the two of them stationed by the fireplace.

Both of them referred to this rare time as their annual bitch session, even though most of the time the catching up was positive. Evan hoped she wouldn't mind that this year he really did need to complain and commiserate.

Hot toddies in hand and sharing a plate full of ginger cookies, Gwen assured Evan that their father hadn't acted any worse than normal that morning. She was certain Evan's time away only made everything *seem* worse.

For his part, Evan knew he was arguing too much. Just as well as he knew he had no interest in stopping.

"I don't understand why Mom stayed with such a colossal prick."

Gwen smiled, but Evan didn't like the look in her eyes. The days since Anne had yelled at him then walked away were crawling slower than a snail. All he wanted was to get away from here, get back to school and try to make sense of his life again. Staying anywhere near his father wasn't going to help anyone.

"Mom wasn't such a saint herself, Ev."

Evan a deep breath. Did he want to know this? Did he want to hear anything his sister was so reluctant to tell him that she'd kept it to herself all these long years?

"I know she wasn't, of course not. But I don't think she could live up to such a jerk of a husband."

Gwen shook her head, looking away from his eyes.

"There's a lot you don't remember, kiddo."

Evan scowled, almost as annoyed with her as he was with their father. He'd lived away for almost four years, he was about to graduate from college, where he was doing extremely well. He wasn't a kid anymore.

"Yeah, well, why don't you enlighten me? Your advanced age should give you some kind of advantage. Maybe this is your lucky day."

She scowled back for a second, and he knew she'd risen to his bait. Assuming he couldn't take whatever she was talking about was exactly the kind of shit he was getting tired of from their father.

"All right, but remember you asked me. She had an affair, Evan. Not too long after you were born."

Evan couldn't stop his jaw from dropping, and he knew he was staring at her like an idiot.

"Horse shit. I don't believe it."

"Hey, you don't have to believe it, bro. I remember it, and I promise you Dad does too."

"You imagined it, Gwen. You were still a kid, too. There's no way they told you about something like that."

"No, they didn't tell me, not when it happened. I knew something was bad though, from the way they fought."

Evan sat back in his chair, clutching his borrowed pillow covered with cartoon characters he didn't recognize. Much as he'd wanted to vent earlier, now he only wanted to get away and not hear one more word.

No. She was making all of this up.

"They always fought. Up until the day Mom died."

She nodded, then pulled her legs up underneath her on the couch.

"Sure, of course they did. But not like this. Young as I was, I was scared to death they'd hurt each other."

Evan closed his eyes, his stomach twisting acid into his throat. That part he knew she wouldn't make up. Worse fights than he could remember had to be criminal.

"But you don't know…" he said, then he cleared his throat against the burning. "You don't know what they were fighting about. They fought all the time."

"I didn't know then, no. She told me herself. Not long after I left for college. She drove up to see me for the weekend."

Evan remembered his mother leaving like that, but it hadn't occurred to him to see if from her point of view until just now. He'd always felt like she was abandoning him, leaving him at the dubious mercies of his father.

Thinking about those weekends now, when he sat here desperate to escape his own shattered heart, he understood it differently.

"I remember her doing that. I hated it. I felt like she was dumping me."

"No, that wasn't it. She just needed to get away for a while. I understand that way better than I care to admit now. I'm sure Mark does too. Anyway, that weekend I was pissed at Dad, just like you are right now. And I was pissed at her for staying with him. Sound familiar?"

"And she just told you?"

"Nope, I asked her. I asked her what he'd been so nasty about back then, and why she didn't get the hell out."

Gwen looked out the window, and Evan wasn't surprised to see tears standing in her eyes. He'd regretted getting angry with his mom more than he cared to remember, especially about those visits to Chicago without him. He didn't want to imagine how much worse the extra years of adolescent temper made Gwen feel.

"I was pretty rude about it," she said, "but I don't think she would have told me if she hadn't had a few gin and tonics that night. She was always a lot more…honest after those."

Evan blinked, surprised yet again. By the time he'd gotten old enough to have cocktails with his mother, it was too late. He'd never realized how sad such a simple fact could be.

"She was quiet for a while," Gwen said, "then she said she stayed because you were so little. And that it hadn't all been Dad's fault. I of course argued with her, saying she couldn't have done anything to justify him being such a jackass."

Evan dreaded hearing the words, but the idea had taken root in his mind like a hideous burrowing insect. If he couldn't find a way to contain and control it, he was afraid all his memories of his mother would sour and rot.

"Then she just said it. Mrs. Megan Connor Griffith sat on that nasty old futon I used to have in her tidy little blue traveling dress and said, 'I had an affair.' I reacted about the same way you did, but I knew she was telling me the truth."

"What happened?"

"She probably had postpartum depression, that's what it sounds like to me now. Ed was working more hours than normal, trying to make partner, and she'd been home for a while. This is not about you, Evan. Don't you *dare* think that."

He realized he had been going down that exact road, his brain trying to make it all his fault. Such nonsense, as if he'd had anything to do with the timing or the fact of his birth. But his mind was trying to go there anyway.

"She started going out, taking you with her, finally finding a place she trusted to keep an eye on you. I remember that part," she said, smiling. "She assured me she was just as paranoid with me, and Dad did too. She acted like everyone in the world was going to steal you if she turned her back for a second.

"Anyway, she went to a book club, reading club, something like that, and she met a guy there. She wouldn't tell me anything about him except he paid more attention to her than Dad had for a while. At least she thought so. And all of it got out of hand."

The sympathy for his father was making Evan more sick than his anger had. He wasn't ready or willing to feel any sort of compassion for Ed.

"How did Dad find out?"

"It was stupid, really. I've wondered if she did it on purpose so it would all have to stop, but I never asked her. She told him she was going to visit Aunt Sandy in Pittsburgh. The hotel in Chicago showed up on the credit card bill. That could not have been an accident. She was way too smart for that."

"How long? How long did it go on?"

Gwen shrugged, shaking her head and sighing again.

"I never did get a straight answer on that, and I stopped asking. I think it was almost a year."

Evan felt like she'd punched him in the gut, or like his mother had. A year? An entire year? That wasn't just a betrayal of their father, not at all. She had to have been focused on this mystery guy when Evan himself had needed her most.

"For fuck's sake… A year?"

"I think so, that's the idea I got."

"Did you ever ask Dad about it?"

"You know, I did think about it. I thought about that a lot. By the time I thought it all over and tried to make some sense out of it, I was wondering why *he* stayed with *her*. A year is a hell of a lot different than some random one-night stand. But I never did ask him, and once she died I just couldn't."

Evan rubbed his eyes, trying to keep his tears from falling. Now he knew, he understood so many things.

Gwen coming home from college so rarely, seething and furious. His mother seeming to feel she deserved any amount of screaming Ed or Gwen cared to dish out.

And his father, the betrayed and horrified air he carried to this day whenever anyone mentioned their mother. Had he just been waiting, all those years, for his wife to finally abandon him forever?

A far worse thought than sympathy for his father burst through the mess in his head then, a thought that had been digging around in that muck most of his life.

"Hang on, Gwen. This is going to sound like some kind of adolescent pissed-off fantasy, and it probably is. If I don't ask, it's going to drive me crazy. Are you… Do you believe the affair started after I was born, not before?"

His sister pursed her lips, looking more like Ed than she ever would have admitted.

"I do believe that, Evan. I understand why you would have wished for a different father. I know I did. But I'm afraid you're stuck with Ed, just like I am."

"I don't look or act anything like him, and I don't think he ever did like me. That might be why."

"No, stop this. Even if there were any chance of that, and I'm sure there's not, he raised you. I don't think he likes much of anybody, but I know he loves you and me both. He's your father. There's no reason to dig into a mess like this. Sheesh, I'm sorry, Ev. I shouldn't have told you all of that. You were fine without it."

He shook his head, looking into his sister's brown eyes. Ed's eyes. He wondered then if his dad had always been so tough on him because he was looking into his lost wife's eyes in his son's face.

"Don't apologize," he said. "She wasn't a saint anymore than the rest of us are, but I'm not going to run down and get DNA tests or anything. If he ever even suspected…that, it explains a whole lot of things that have bothered me for years."

"Yeah, I eventually felt that way about all of it. But finding out what happened knocked me on my ass for a long time. Are you okay?"

"I think I'd rather know than not. I've spent a lot of time being angry about her dying, angry at her. And angry at you. You knew her as an adult. I never did."

"That could have been a blessing in disguise, brother."

"You don't really think that, Gwen. Good or bad, I never really got to know her. That's part of her I never had and I never will. Trust me. I'd rather know. Don't try to protect me, old lady."

She laughed a little, then stretched her arms above her head.

"Well, if you're going to sit at the grownups' table now, want to join me in one of Mom's beloved gin and tonics? I get the good stuff though. None of the cheap swill she had to put up with."

"Absolutely. Show me how to make one and we'll see who passes out first."

Evan hugged his sister tight.

"Thanks for telling me, Gwen. I'm glad to know more about who she really was, even if it sucks."

"That wasn't who she was," Gwen said, walking ahead of him into the kitchen. "It was just something that happened. I'm not saying it was justified, any more than Ed acting like such a prick was. She wasn't perfect. Neither was he. Once I got over being so pissed at both of them, I figured that took the pressure off of you and me."

Chapter 31

ANNE WOKE SLOWLY, painfully, her mind dragged up through the darkness and squeezed back inside her far too small skull. A vise, someone had a vise around her skull.

"Anne, come on, wake up!"

The vise shifted until it was driving into her skull through her ears, the points sharp and white hot. Someone shook her shoulder, someone who had been saying her name for a long time. She opened her eyes.

"What do you want?"

She tried to keep her voice from reaching her throbbing ears. The room was dark, thank goodness, but she could still see someone sitting on the edge of her bed. Someone who reeked of cheap cigarettes.

Joe.

"If you want to keep this shitty roof over your head, get up and let's go." He took a long, glowing drag. "You can get it filled again today."

Anne closed her eyes and turned away. The darkness had been good. It had been empty. It had been quiet. So far, the darkness was worth the hangover that came with it.

She'd hoped the hangover would get better with time. Lately it seemed to be getting worse.

"I'm not going to ask you again."

He'd only gotten really angry with her one time, a few months ago. She didn't want to go through that again. She pushed herself up to the edge of the mattress on the floor.

"I'm up. Get out of here so I can get dressed."

"Sure, whatever. Nothing I haven't seen before." He did leave her in peace.

Anne braced herself against the nausea when she stood up, but that part wasn't too bad. Her stomach twisted and clenched, but nothing threatened to eject itself out of her.

Today the headache was going to take center stage. That was easy enough to deal with. More booze took care of that, every single time.

When she turned on the light in the bathroom, Anne caught her reflection by accident. She tried not to look at herself in mirrors anymore.

Her eyes were the same, even bloodshot and swollen. Her face looked puffy and terrible though, as if it had been inflated somehow. And there was nothing in that mirror she could stand to see anymore. The woman staring back at her looked more like forty-four than twenty-four. Maybe fifty-four.

Anne looked away and turned on the water in the shower.

She couldn't go out looking this bad, not if they were going to score. She had enough trouble fooling people as it was. No need to take any more chances, not with Joe's temper stirring up.

More booze, that's all she needed, more booze. Anne stood under the hot water, trying to remember when she'd first had that thought. How long? Two years ago? Three?

Back then, it had only been a drink in the evenings, a new thing to her in her new apartment. A glass of wine, which she didn't love. A mixed drink, which she did.

Shampoo ran into her eyes, making her gasp, and she did remember the first time. It was before she'd met Joe, but only days before.

Five years ago.

She and her roommates had been celebrating something, lost to the fog of so many intoxicated days. Anne had had more to drink that night than she ever had before, and she'd passed out rather than falling asleep.

When she'd woken up the next morning, she'd had her first hangover. That one had been the puking kind. But as soon as she staggered away from the toilet, she realized she'd had her first dreamless night in almost ten years too. Not a single image lingered on her mind's eye, waiting to terrorize her daylight hours.

Anne turned off the water, stepping carefully onto the stained mat.

Stopping the medication had been easy after she'd repeated the experiment a week later. Drink too much, pass out, wake up with no dreams. She'd never even gotten the bottle out of her medicine cabinet after that.

A few days later, when Joe came back to her place the first time, he'd come out of the bathroom bouncing one of her pill bottles in one hand.

"What are these for, babe?"

"I have a lot of trouble with nightmares. I stopped taking them a few days ago. I'm not going to get the prescription refilled again."

"Hang on, let's talk about that," he said, putting the bottle in his pocket and sitting down beside her. "These are solid gold, babe. Do you pay for them?"

"No, I'm still on my Dad's policy. I will be for a few more years, then my doctor said I could get them through the state as long as they're prescribed."

Joe's eyes had widened, and Anne remembered now that his look made her uneasy. Why was he so excited about her prescription? She'd always been quietly ashamed of all the pills she'd used over the years trying to feel normal, trying to act normal.

"Well, listen, I have an idea. How about if you let me see what I can get for these. Don't cancel anything just yet. Then if it works out and you still don't need them, we'll be in business. Real business."

Anne winced trying to brush out her hair. It was too long again, that happened so quickly. She'd have to get it cut, even though Evan liked it better long.

"Where the hell did that come from?" she whispered.

She hadn't seen Evan for a long time now. Almost five years. She doubted she'd ever see him again after the way she'd talked to him the last time.

Well, he had been getting way too damned much into her business, and dragging her father into it too. She and her parents had been getting along just fine until Evan tried once again to fix everything.

He fixed things into a massive disaster. She was better off without him.

She walked into her bedroom to get dressed, wondering what day of the week it was. She could refill her prescriptions on the first, but she didn't know anything beyond that. The booze had taken the nightmares, but it had taken a lot of her short-term memory with it.

She pulled out a blue sundress, one that used to fit her well, and got out a cheap belt that almost matched. She had to have the belt to hide how loose the dress and all the rest of her clothes were now.

Joe was getting pretty good money for her pills, sure, but that didn't mean they had enough to waste on clothes. That's what he told her, anyway.

Anne walked over to her dresser and started opening drawers, looking for her paper prescriptions. That was when Joe had gotten so angry, the one time a new pharmacist asked to see the original prescription. She'd been afraid her parents had ratted her out and she wouldn't be able to get the pills anymore. All she wanted was the original paper scrip.

That short delay, time enough to go back to the apartment and dig until she found it, had been too long for Joe. He made sure Anne never forgot again.

She knew she'd need booze before they left. That trick had taken a while longer for her to learn, using the booze to stop her visions during the day too. At first she only drank at night, just enough to force herself into a deep sleep.

Enough turned into a moving target that never lasted very long, though.

Once she started drinking during the day, she realized the visions were getting weaker. She wasn't seeing the horrible death masks anymore, at least not clearly. All she saw was a shadow, then a hint as faint as Joe's cigarette smoke. And then they were gone.

She was having trouble focusing on their faces by then, but at least she could try. It had been years since she'd reliably seen anyone's face.

Anyone except Evan's.

"Goddamn it, get the hell out of my head."

She finally found the note behind a jumbled pile of socks with too many holes to wear, wondering as she always did why the doctor kept renewing it.

Anne hadn't been to a doctor since she'd started drinking so much. She wondered if her father put Dr. Lewis up to it, hoping Anne would take the pills someday if she still had them.

She wondered if either of them suspected the pills were paying the rent and the utilities and the food and gas for Joe's car.

And the pills payed for the booze. The booze that kept the bad dreams and visions away.

Anne walked into the cluttered living room, knowing Joe would be waiting for her. He would never let her walk by, not today. Not when she could get more of what he needed more and more, or at least the money to pay for it. And she could always tell where he was by the stink of his cheap cigarettes.

He was sitting on the beat up thrift store couch, clouds floating around his head after such a short time. If he was so desperate for money that he had to sell her pills, why did he waste so damn much money on those cigarettes?

Maybe she didn't care so much about his temper today.

"Where did you sleep last night, Joe?"

"I was right here, on this nasty couch."

She shook her head, heading into the kitchen for coffee. She hadn't caught anything from him for a few months, not that she knew of. But three trips to the health department in the last few years had taught her never to trust him again.

"Yeah, right. I'm sure you were on something. Somebody, more like."

"No, I was right here. I can't sleep with you anymore. Your crazy ass dreams keep me awake all night."

Anne froze, barely keeping a grip on her cup before she put it down.

"Dreams?" she whispered.

"Yeah, you toss and turn, kicking and thrashing, making all kinds of damn noise in the middle of the night."

She poured the coffee, having a terrible time keeping most of it in the cup. That was the whole point of the booze, that had been the *only* point of it.

The booze kept the nightmares away.

"When? When did I start doing that, Joe?"

"I don't know, a month ago? Two?"

She turned to get the sugar, her heart pounding in her ears. How could she not know about nightmares that bad? Drinking enough to knock herself out was the first thing that stopped them, the first thing since she was eleven years old.

Her dreams had always been worst right before something terrible was about to happen.

Always.

"I can't even trust my own mind…"

"What? Come on, get a move on. I got a score for these in a couple of hours, but she won't wait. We need to get that filled now."

Anne swallowed too much of the coffee, too hot, tears filling her eyes at the burning in her mouth and throat. She gripped the edge of the counter and drank the rest.

The damage was done now, why try to deny that? She had no idea if she meant her scorched mouth or the dreams.

She opened the freezer and got a bottle of vodka, only a few swallows left from the day before. They were down to only two bottles in there. They'd have to use the money from her pills for more today. She drained it, then dropped it on top of the others in the garbage.

The cold alcohol numbed her mouth and throat. She hoped it would do the same for her mind.

"You got the scrip?"

"Yeah, I got it. I got it."

That was one lesson she didn't have to learn twice. Getting between Joe and his scores for something as simple as needing her original prescription had turned into another kind of nightmare. She followed him out without another word.

While he drove, Anne studied the people on the sides of the road. She looked at their faces, trying to see their features. That was the other thing the booze had stopped, once she'd started drinking during the day. The visions of how everyone was going to die.

She'd had long stretches when she was a kid, months at a time, when she could hardly see anyone at all. She only saw a charred mess, a bloody mess, a blue and drowned mess.

There had been a few times when the only person she'd been able to see was Evan. Those had been right before her trips to the hospital, always. She jumped when Joe spoke.

"Wake up! Get in there in case there's a line. I don't want to miss this one. I think she'll be a repeat buyer."

Anne looked around, finally noticing they were parked outside of the drug store. Joe was still in the car, but he was watching her.

"All right, Joe. I'll be right back."

He never went in with her, not anymore. He'd gotten paranoid about being on the security camera or some such shit. He either didn't think Anne being on the camera was such a big deal, or he just didn't care. He told her it was her scrip and the doctor kept filling it, so why worry about that now?

Anne found she cared less and less about things like that. If she did get picked up, it would be what she deserved anyway, letting him sell her pills. She walked to the back of the store as fast as she could, to the pharmacy tucked away behind windows.

"Yeah, I need to get this filled?"

The pharmacist stared at her, and Anne looked away. She wasn't afraid of him seeing her. He saw her every month.

She was terrified of seeing him.

She hadn't seen his warm brown eyes behind his tiny glasses or the harsh lighting glaring off of his bald head. She hadn't seen him smiling or looking suspicious or even worried about her.

She'd seen a death mask, the first in more than four years. The man's face was wasted, way past the skin and bone she avoided in her own mirror every morning. Skeletal, with a huge discolored mass starting on top of his head and spreading down over one side of his face. Some kind of tumor, some kind of growth.

She didn't know if it would be inside his head, in his brain, or if it would start on that smooth, hairless scalp, but whatever it was would be the end of him. She stared at her feet.

"Ms. Fincastle? May I see your ID please?"

Anne fumbled in her purse. He'd never asked for it before.

Something *was* up. That didn't matter now. She just had to get out of here.

She pulled her state ID card out of her wallet and handed it to him, looking anywhere but at the corpse in front of her.

"Okay, this is fine. It'll be a few minutes."

He handed the card back and turned away. Anne let out her breath, and she dropped the card in her purse instead of struggling with her wallet. Her hands were shaking worse than before.

No, she couldn't trust her brain, her mind, her heart, any part of her. If this was going to start again after several swallows of booze, even that tiny bit of peace was failing her.

She knew it would only get worse. It always had, for most of her life it had.

First the nightmares, then the visions, then her memories would start up again.

She'd remember the terrible thing before it happened, and just like the visions, there wouldn't be a damn thing she could do about it.

She'd see it, over and over and over again.

Then she'd have to live it.

She paced around the store, staring at greeting cards, cosmetics, random junk, trying not to look at anyone. She didn't want to know if it was happening with other people or not.

She didn't want to know.

She had to know.

She was going to go crazy in the next five minutes if she didn't.

Anne almost crashed into a little girl, squatting down in front of a bunch of toys. The girl looked up, and Anne jerked away from her.

That little girl didn't have to worry about getting old enough to need reading glasses or adult diapers. That little girl wasn't even going to make it to needing tampons.

Anne saw a mass of blood and bruises, half of the girl's brown hair torn away. The little girl was going to get killed in a car wreck before five more years went by.

Tears stood in Anne's eyes and she turned away, right into another face. This man was going to get caught in a fire, some kind of horrible fire. His whole face was red and black. She hoped he would be asleep when it happened. She covered her eyes, not wanting to see one more thing.

How much more booze could she possibly drink in one day? She was already getting terrible heartburn at night, and her face and hands were always puffy even though she was so thin. She didn't know if she could take any more.

"Ms. Fincastle?"

Anne turned and walked back to the pharmacy, looking at her feet, wiping her eyes before he could see. Maybe she should just stop the booze, not have another drop. If it wasn't going to work anymore, she could try her pills again.

The dreams had never stopped with the pills, but they hadn't been quite as bad. And sometimes she could go a little longer before she had to go to the hospital. Maybe she could do that instead.

Or maybe Joe would blow his temper so badly that Anne wouldn't care about anything anymore.

"Here you go," the pharmacist said, handing her the little white bag with blue writing on the side. "Take care now."

"Thanks." She glanced up at his tie, making sure to avoid his face.

She turned to leave, opening her purse to drop the bag in. Something slipped out of her hand, and she caught it before it could hit the floor. A folded piece of paper, something she'd never gotten with her pills before.

She stopped just inside the door. Whatever it was, she needed to look at it before she got to Joe's car. Just as surely as she knew how everyone in the store was going to die, she knew she couldn't walk out the door first.

Mostly a blank page, with her father's familiar scrawl in the middle.

Anne, please get in touch with me, sweetheart. I have to talk to you, and I'm worried about you. Please give me a call or stop by my office as soon as you get this. I love you. Dad.

This time tears streamed down her face faster than she could stop them. She hadn't spoken to her dad in months, and she couldn't remember the last time she'd seen him. He was the only one left who understood how bad it could get for her when the nightmares started.

Only her dad or Evan had ever understood. She folded the note up and put it in a tiny pocket hidden in her purse, wiped at her face, and pushed the door open.

Joe was standing, chest against his car, hands behind him. He stared into her eyes and mouthed *You fucking bitch.*

Anne drew back, but not before the police officers standing behind Joe saw her. One of them walked toward her.

Anne knew he was going to die by his own hand, by his own gun, but she pushed that to the back of her mind. She couldn't even run, not with several others standing all around him.

All she could do was stare at Joe. For the first time since she'd met him, she could see what was going to become of him.

Joe was going to prison, and Joe was going to die there. He was going to be beaten to death. Skull was caved in, eyes swollen shut, the rest of his face a mass of bruises and blood.

Anne walked out the door to meet the officer.

Whatever was going to happen, she was going to walk away from Joe, and he was never, ever going to be able to follow her again. He was never going to *see* her again.

Even if her nightmares had started again, that one long nightmare was coming to an end.

Chapter 32

The hard plastic chair hurt Anne's hips, her spine, the backs of her thighs. And the room was cold, so cold her bones were aching. The baggy cotton dress and sandals were fine out in the sun, but this place felt like a meat locker.

Anne shifted again, trying to find an unbruised place anywhere on her body. She didn't think there were any left. The officers had left the room again, but she knew someone would be watching her. There had to be cameras, and that huge mirror certainly had people on the other side.

She'd seen one of the cops glance at it way too many times when they were asking her endless questions.

The door opened slowly, and Anne cringed back against the awful chair, the bones she was sitting on crying out in protest. More questions, more accusations, more things she couldn't understand through the growing fog in her brain.

Her father walked through instead.

"Anne!"

She tried to stand to greet him, but she moved like an old, weak woman. He was around the metal table before she could get to her feet. He lifted her up, squeezing her tight. Anne was glad to see him, but she was more grateful for his warmth.

"Dad," she whispered.

"Are you okay? I've been here for over an hour, but they wouldn't let me back here to see you."

"I'm not having a great day, no." She sat as gently as she could. "I'm glad to see you."

"Listen to me, sweetheart. I can't say much, but have you told them anything? My lawyer can't handle this, but she found someone."

Anne closed her eyes, trying to remember. She walked out of the drug store, the police took Joe away forever, and then they brought her here. Her thoughts had been so hazy since then. She wasn't sure what she'd said or what she'd imagined.

All she could remember clearly was seeing how every single person in the police station was going to die. At least right now she couldn't see that with her father.

"I don't really remember, Dad. They have to know the pills were mine."

"They do. Joe sold to an undercover officer, or he was trying to. She saw the pill bottles, the empty ones he had with him. They've been after him for a while now, so that may help you."

That had to be the new score Joe was so excited about that morning, the reason he'd dragged Anne out the door so fast. She looked down at her hands on the freezing steel table. The shakes would start soon. She felt them long before she saw them.

Only one scorching cup of coffee explained her headache, and not a single bite to eat all day explained her weakness.

The biggest problem she was going to have was from only a few swallows of vodka more than three hours ago.

"What should I be saying, Dad?"

"Don't say anything else to them until the attorney gets here, okay? I talked to her just now on the phone, it shouldn't be more than half an hour. She did get them to let me see you. Do you need anything, sweetheart?"

The needs swirled through Anne's head, spinning into a mess she couldn't see the top or bottom of.

I need a soft chair. I need a warm coat. I need a gallon of coffee.

I need an entire pot of Mom's macaroni and cheese. I need a fifth of freezing cold vodka.

I need…

I need to see Evan.

The last one surprised her, but once that thought showed up it drowned out all of the others.

Years, so many years. How could she have passed so much of her life without seeing someone she'd been so close to for so long? So long without the closest friend she'd ever had?

She shook her head, trying to keep that howling empty pit where her heart should have been from taking over every other part of her.

"I could use something to eat," she finally said, looking into her father's green eyes. "And maybe a blanket?"

He leaned forward and hugged her hard again, and Anne couldn't think of how he must have been feeling. He'd always worried about her so much, always tried to do everything he could to keep her safe and warm and sane.

And now she was none of those things.

She hadn't been safe or warm or sane for so long.

"I'll see what I can do. Love you."

Anne squeezed his hand for as long as she could before he walked away.

"Love you too."

After he closed the door behind him, Anne sat forward, holding her head in her hands. Now the headache and even the cold were fading to the background.

The shaking was getting worse, so much worse, and faster than it ever had before. The trembling in her hands was spreading into her arms, her chest, every muscle and fiber in her whole body.

She hadn't gone more than three hours without a drink for… how long now? It had to be at least two years, maybe longer.

That was what usually got her out of bed in the middle of the night and again in the morning, the shivering and shaking that got so bad it woke her out of the dead sleep that had started the drinking to begin with.

After the first few times, that jittery stagger into the kitchen started to seem normal. That was the hell of it. She hadn't even thought about how fucked up that was for years now. Having to find a slug of whatever she could before she could even take a piss.

It was just how she got though the day.

The door opened again, but this time it was the police woman who'd taken Anne out of the car that morning. The full body and cavity search might have been a little bit harder if it had been a man, but she didn't think so. She didn't want to find out.

The woman put a sandwich on the table, a real sandwich from a restaurant, not one out of a vending machine. The smell of fresh bread and meat made Anne's mouth water. The officer also had a thick blanket and two pillows. Whoever this attorney was her father had found, she had some kind of pull around here.

"You getting the shakes?"

Anne looked up, trying her best to keep her eyes steady. The woman was maybe ten years older, and even in her dark, hard face, her eyes were as concerned as her voice was.

"I'm okay. The food will help, thank you."

The woman, Officer Murray according to her badge, looked Anne up and down. There was no way to hide the way her hands were trembling now.

"Want me to send someone in to help you with that?"

"No, I'll be all right."

"You realize you can't get a drink in here, don't you?" Officer Murray said, tilting her head and raising her eyebrows. "It's just going to keep getting worse. How long since you were sober, Anne?"

"I don't know," Anne whispered, staring at her jerking hands. "A long, long time."

"I'm sending someone in," the officer said, nodding once. "Just listen to her. She's not going to ask you about the pills or that guy or anything else that can get you in trouble. But she can help you with the DTs."

Anne looked back up, surprised and horrified by the word. DTs? She knew what that was, she knew what it meant. She had never thought of herself that way.

She'd been thinking a lot of bad things about herself for a while now, most of her life, but not that. That was for homeless men, bag ladies, bums she used to see hanging around digging through the dumpsters where she'd hidden the gun the day Evan's mother died.

Not her.

"Is it okay with my Dad?"

"I'll check first to make sure, I promise. I really think you need to talk to her."

"If Dad says it's okay, she can come in."

Once she got the pillows arranged on the chair and the comforter around her shoulders, Anne ate the sandwich as fast as she could. Officer Murray had left a bottle of water too, and she swallowed almost all of it in one go. That helped with her headache and with the gnawing in her belly, but if anything the shakes got worse.

The *DTs* got worse.

Anne wrapped the comforter over her head and rested her head on the table.

Was she an alcoholic? Had she crossed over that line just like she had so many others since she'd moved out of her father's house? Since she'd last seen Evan's beautiful blue eyes?

She was comfortable with lazy, worthless, whore, bitch, useless, any number of words Joe had called her over the past few months. And she'd called herself even worse words, taken those in and made them part of herself.

Crazy, loony, slut, nuts, psycho. A girl with real *issues*.

But this was a new word, and it chafed and hurt her with its sharp edges. All she'd wanted to do was make the dreams stop, give herself some kind of peace and calm for even a few hours at night. But it was those hours at night that were giving her the shakes, the fucking DTs, and Joe said the nightmares had come back already too.

If she was hooked on the booze on top of everything else, and the nightmares and visions were still coming back, what was the point of drawing another shaking, poisonous breath into her lungs?

"Ms. Fincastle?"

Anne jumped, jerking up from under the comforter. She hadn't been asleep, the shakes were way too bad for that. She hadn't heard anyone come into the room either.

"I'm Dr. Martinez."

The woman was tall, not nearly as dark as Officer Murray, and dressed in a black pantsuit instead of a blue police uniform. Even with her saying doctor, Anne thought she looked more like a lawyer than a doctor. Dr. Lewis had always worn casual clothes, slacks and a sweater, when Anne had talked to him.

But that was a long time ago.

"I'm Anne."

Anne shook her hand, embarrassed by how cold and damp her own was.

Dr. Martinez sat in the same place the police officers had when they asked her so many questions for so long.

"I just talked to your father, and I spoke to Dr. Lewis on the phone. Is it all right if I talk to you for a little while?"

Anne's eyes filled with tears. All she could do was nod.

"I can see your hands trembling, Anne. Are you coming off anything besides alcohol?"

Anne shook her head. She couldn't remember how long it had been since she'd tried anything else. Nothing Joe or anyone else had brought to her apartment had ever worked as well as the vodka had.

"Well, I hope you're telling me the truth, but it doesn't make that big of a difference today. Anything else will make you feel like shit. It's stopping the alcohol that can kill you. How long since you've had a drink?"

"Since eleven this morning."

"That's only about four hours. What about last night? Did you sleep?"

"Yeah, for a long time. But I had… I had a drink during the night."

The doctor took a deep breath, made some notes, then looked up at Anne.

"So for you to be shaking that badly you're in a pretty bad way, aren't you?"

"I'm in a bad way all around."

"I need you to listen to me, Anne. I've got some pills here that will calm the shaking down. You need to take them. If you don't, this is going to kill you."

Anne shivered again, this time from the cold settling into her stomach. The pills didn't sound like a good idea to her, not after what other pills had put her through.

She *did* want to quit the booze. She'd been wanting to quit that for a long time. Starting something else didn't seem like a good way to do that. Her very first experience with pills had put her into the hospital the first time, too.

"I just want to stop drinking. I want to stop all of this, not start something new. You said the drinking was going to kill me."

"No, not quite," the doctor said, reaching into her briefcase. "*Stopping* the alcohol could very well kill you in the shape you're in. You do need to stop drinking, but right now you've got to stop the DTs."

There was that word again. Anne hadn't heard it all that long ago, but it already fit into her inventory of herself. Dr. Martinez set a bottle of pills on the table.

"Wanting to stop drinking is great, I'm glad you said that. But letting the withdrawal take you out isn't the smartest way to do that. You have a decision to make, Anne, probably a lot of them. What you do in the next couple of hours will show me, and most of all yourself, whether you want to live or not."

Anne stared at the bottle, thinking of the day she'd gotten caught in the vision, caught up inside her own frozen body. She remembered screaming at Evan inside her head not to give up on her, but he'd walked away anyway.

Then she'd *pushed* him away, so hard her cheeks burned even now thinking about it.

For Joe. For fucking Joe.

She'd driven her best friend away for a worthless thug who only wanted her so he could sell her damn pills.

"Listen, you've got a little time yet," the doctor said. "I'm going to leave these with you. If your symptoms get much worse, it might be out of your hands before too long. You look thin and run down enough that seizures or a stroke are a real possibility. But I need you to pay attention to me now. Your best chance of turning your life around is to make the choice for yourself, Anne. Don't make us force it on you. You do it for yourself."

She put another bottle of water on the table and stood.

"If you need me, just let someone know. If I'm not here, Dr. Andrews will be. Take care."

Anne clenched her teeth, willing herself not to start humming as the doctor closed the door. That was one of the worst things that had been going on since she was eleven years old, the awful humming she had no control over.

The shakes seemed to be concentrating in her mind now, inside her fucking brain. She pushed against her eyes with the heels of her hands, bursts of purple and blue and black swirling against her eyelids.

That internal kaleidoscope faded and split into three fields, then glared into bright white. Anne kept her hands over her eyes, but she started rocking, humming and rocking even when the pillows slipped away from the terrible hard chair.

After so many years and so much drinking, she'd dared imagine this one thing would never come back, that this one bit of madness would leave her alone.

The screens exploded into life.

Anne sat on a bed on one screen, staring at the wall in front of her. Something about her eyes let her know it wasn't the same thing she'd had before, the catatonia.

Her eyes weren't frozen. They were empty.

Two nurses came in and picked Anne up, putting her in a plastic wheelchair. They moved her into a bathroom and started to undress her. They took off her diaper before they wheeled her into the shower.

At the same time, Anne walked down the stairs at her parents' house, taking each step slowly and deliberately. She listened to voices in the living room, her mother, her father, and one other, a man's voice she didn't recognize at first. Before she reached the bottom step, everyone laughed together.

Evan. Her parents were talking to Evan.

And in this memory, she was able to think and feel, and what she felt was elation. She was going to see her friend after so much time apart.

When she walked into the living room, he stood. Without a word, he had her in a huge hug, picking her up and squeezing her so tight it took her breath. In his arms, she found she could breathe again for the first time in years.

At the same time, Anne was in her stinking apartment, laying on the couch. Joe and his cigarettes were gone, but something else made her want to gag and retch. Something rotten. Something foul.

She had shit herself, but no matter how she tried she couldn't move to get away from the mess. She couldn't seem to move anything at all. Her heart pounded in her ears, making her head keep time with it.

Then her heart beat slower.

The beats were further and further apart until they gradually stopped. Anne heard her breath leave in a light gasp, almost like a sigh before falling asleep.

This was a sleep she would never wake up from.

She sat back in her police station chair and closed her eyes, her runaway muscles the least important problem she had to face. She didn't have to ask anyone what these visions meant, and she didn't need to learn a single new word.

Joe had brought a bunch of his buddies over to her apartment. From the beginning, he'd had people crashing on the couch, on the floor, anywhere they could fit.

One of the guys seemed like he was drunk every time Anne saw him, even though he never took a drink or smoked anything. He did buy her pills from Joe.

After he stopped coming around, she heard he'd poured a fifth of cheap whiskey on top of the pills. That guy would never show up anywhere on the outside of a nursing home again.

If she kept on going like this, that was how she would end up. Even if she did finally manage to stop, her mind would never recover.

Anne knew if she somehow got out of here and went back to her apartment, if that was even possible anymore, if she went back and never touched another drop, Dr. Martinez was right. Drinking was going to kill her, or at least kill her mind.

But not drinking could kill her just as dead.

She glanced down at the pills again. Her hands were probably shaking too badly to open the bottle now, but she was still afraid to touch them.

All that left was her parents' house. And Evan. Would he ever want to see her again? If she cleaned herself up and tried to make things right, would he let her?

Since that Christmas morning years ago, when she'd gotten Joe to drive her to Gwen's house to scream at him, drunk off her ass at nine in the morning, she hadn't heard a word from him.

She hadn't tried to find him either. She hadn't even really *thought* about finding him.

Up until Joe had shaken her awake that morning, she'd convinced herself Evan was nothing but a bad thing from her past, something she needed to put behind her. He'd been on her dad's side, trying to force her into rehab for a problem she didn't have in the first place.

That had been before the DTs though, before her body started trying to shake itself to pieces unless she poured more acid down her throat.

Seeing her father today, knowing he'd done everything he could to help her when it was probably already too late, had jarred her back into reality.

Of course her father didn't want to hurt her. He never had.

Had her mind gotten so twisted that she'd been thinking about Evan in the same screwed up way?

"Why would he ever want to see me?" she whispered, picking up the bottle. The pills inside rattled faintly.

Even if she did do all she could to get back to herself, to force herself back into some kind of normal life, whatever was left of it, she'd been so terrible to him. He'd turned away from her and never looked back. Why would years of no contact make him want to see her now?

The vision was so real, so deep within her. His strong arms around her, the heat of his body, the rich, safe smell of his skin, his much deeper voice whispering her name. Nothing she'd ever seen so clearly and moved toward had failed to happen.

She'd driven the visions away with the booze, but they had never been untrue.

Maybe this one was no different.

Anne had to try five times, but she finally managed to get the bottle open. The doctor said what, four of the pills?

She tried to get that many out, but a particularly vicious tremor spilled all of them onto the table.

She pushed four to the side, then went to work on the water bottle. She only spilled a little when she finally twisted the lid off.

All three of the visions were still strong inside her mind, each screen equally bright and vivid.

Anne with her brain destroyed by the vodka, people having to do every single thing for her. Anne lying dead in her own apartment, without nurses or anyone else to clean up her own shit before she died in it.

Anne walking into Evan's arms, stepping into his warm, safe embrace for the first time in so long.

She'd never known how to make one or the other of her visions come true. If she made the wrong choice now, the results could be much worse than getting picked up and going to jail.

Losing her own mind, such as it had become, would be even worse than Joe finally managing to beat her to death. But if she never made any choice at all, she wouldn't have any kind of chance.

Anne picked up four of the pills, watching them jitter in the palm of her hand. She hadn't made any kind of choice, good or bad, for longer than she could remember.

She had to make one now while she still had any mind left.

She swallowed the pills, closing her eyes as the cold water washed them down.

The only vision left found her in the arms of her friend.

PART VI

EVERYTHING TURNS

Chapter 33

ANNE FOLLOWED her mother into her childhood bedroom, caught in a waking dream that felt closer to a nightmare with every step. Back in her parents' house. Moving back home, at twenty-five years old.

Getting through the days in the hospital and weeks of rehab, gladly accepting probation instead of jail time, those certainly felt like some kind of success.

Her life was a different story, though. What kind of failure was she going to be if her life kept going like this?

"We can change anything you like, Annie. We want you to feel at home."

"I *am* at home, Mom," she said, walking over to look out the window. "Like I never even left."

She could see Evan's house from here, or at least where he used to live. His father didn't live there anymore. That was one of the things that had changed, and not in a good way. Not being able to walk into that house and even see pictures of her friend bothered her.

She wouldn't see his mother, with the same fair skin and pale blue eyes as Evan. She'd never see Evan's mom again. She wouldn't see his father, who had the same lanky body shape.

Evan's father, who'd never seemed to stop blaming Anne for the death of his wife.

Anne wasn't always sure whether knowing Mrs. Griffith was going to die had helped her, Anne, Mr. Griffith, Evan, or anyone else. The strain probably had sent Anne to the hospital just a little bit faster.

"It's going to be fine." Her mother walked in to sit on Anne's bed. "You can get your feet under you again. Take as long as you need."

"I've never had my feet under me. You know that as well as I do."

Anne regretted her words before she stopped speaking. Her mother was making an unusual effort to really talk to her, welcome her back and make her feel like she belonged here. Anne couldn't remember the last time her mother hadn't seemed afraid of her. She joined her on the bed.

"I'm sorry, Mom, thank you for coming up here. You're right. I need a safe place to stay for a while. This means a lot to me."

Her mother smiled, and Anne was surprised to see tears in her eyes. She squeezed Anne's hand.

"I mean it, Annie. Stay as long as you want. Do you need anything?"

Anne smiled herself, amazed at how her temper had adjusted in such a short time. When she'd been drinking so heavily, just a few months ago, she might have screamed that what she didn't need was her own mother not remembering how much she hated being called Annie.

Now she easily managed to keep from rolling her eyes.

"I need to get a list of local meetings together. I might need to borrow your computer."

Karen Fincastle's eyes lit up.

"You can borrow my computer anytime you want, and we can get you one soon. Let me get the list together for you, hon. I'd be happy to do that."

Anne had a nagging thought that she really needed to do that for herself, some kind of responsible step forward under her own steam. But her mother looked so happy, so excited to have a job.

It hadn't crossed her mind until just that moment how awful it must have been for her mother. When Anne's troubles started, when she was only eleven years old, her mother hadn't been able to do a thing to stop it or help. No one had, not even her father or Evan.

Her heart caught in her chest as it always did when she thought of how she'd screamed at Evan on Christmas morning years ago, how he'd walked away from her.

Anne wasn't sure anyone could help her with that or anything else now, but she did want to make her mother feel better if she could.

The clearest chance to make amends she'd had so far.

"Sure, Mom, that would be a huge help."

Her mother stood, nodding once.

"What kinds of meetings, just AA?"

"AA, NA, Al-Anon, whatever you can find close by. As many as you can find, at least for a while."

"You got it!"

Anne tried to remember when she'd last seen her mother so happy, so energized. She suspected the list would be a thing of beauty, organized by day, time, distance from the house, transit options, everything she or anyone else could ever need.

And her mother would feel better. Even if the list weren't going to be such a huge help to Anne, knowing her mother would feel better was well worth it.

She looked around her room, trying to connect herself to the things surrounding her. She hadn't been gone for decades or anything like that, but it was hard to remember being that nineteen-year-old, so full of hope and enthusiasm. Her grand experiment of living on her own hadn't been a roaring success. It had been more of a groaning failure.

"None of that, Anne F," she said under her breath.

She went to the closet, thinking the clothes might be a little big, but they should all fit eventually. She was still too thin, even after weeks of decent and regular meals in the hospital and in rehab.

Time was what she needed now. She'd heard it more than enough to finally start believing it, or at least wondering if it was true.

She hadn't gotten so low overnight. She wouldn't be fully recovered overnight either.

Nothing in the closet seemed to have been moved, but the overly fresh smell told her everything had been washed, and recently. Something else her mom had been able to do, and again, it really was a big help.

Anne hadn't kept any of her clothes from the apartment. Even if the stains or stink could be washed away, the awful memories couldn't. That was another thing her mother could do, take her shopping.

That might even be fun.

Her mother's constant patrols of her closet while Anne was growing up, digging out anything and everything that was worn or didn't fit, had gotten on her last nerve when she was a kid. For the first time, she looked forward to so much maternal attention dedicated to her appearance.

Anne sat at her desk, the same one she'd had since her very first day of school. All of her notebooks were still stacked up on the shelf, the records of her growing madness. She ran her fingertips along the metal spirals, afraid to touch them more than that.

For right now, her dreams and visions and memories were quiet and still. She wasn't sure if it was the medication, rehab, or simple exhaustion, but she was glad of the break. She worried reading the journals would bring all of them back.

Exhaustion.

That was exactly how she was feeling right now. Her mom had met her very early at the hospital, and getting everything arranged had taken longer than Anne had expected. Her dad had taken care of all of that in the past. He knew the routine of leaving a mental hospital better than any parent should have to.

Anne had been terribly nervous about him being stuck at a conference, even asking her counselor about staying an extra day so he could come get her. The woman had been right about letting her mother do this.

Anne still wished her father was home.

She sat on the bed again, then kicked her shoes off and stretched out. This wasn't the best mattress in the world, certainly not after she'd slept on it for years as a kid. But compared to the stinking pit of her apartment and the rock-like, vinyl-covered detox and rehab beds of the last six months, this felt like heaven.

Her eyes wanted to drift closed, and Anne tried to force herself to stay awake.

Keep busy, everyone had repeated that over and over again before she left.

Don't let yourself get caught up in boredom. That can lead right back into hell.

Sure, she understood that, but she remembered the other mantra that had drilled itself into her brain.

HALT. Don't get hungry, angry, lonely, or tired.

Well, right now she couldn't do a thing about being lonely, and it wasn't a good time to even think about that. But tired was starting to pull her into the void. The only thing she could do to stop being tired was to take a nap, rest for a while.

Anne didn't think she'd truly gotten any rest since she stopped sleeping in this house, this room, this bed.

She was long, long overdue.

Chapter 34

Evan jumped when his phone buzzed in his pocket, then grabbed for it before it could start ringing. He'd asked for a little time to himself so he could grade papers, and he was doing that. Anything to get some space, a break from Michelle's happy chatter about her work taking her to Seattle for a month.

The balance between how much he would miss her didn't fit well beside how much he was looking forward to having the tiny apartment to himself.

He didn't want Michelle thinking he was ready for company if he could take phone calls.

He flipped the phone open, wishing it had a caller ID box like the apartment phone did.

"Evan? Mike Fincastle here."

Before Evan's mind could quite put a person with the voice, his nerves already had. His heart pounded and a sweaty flush coved his whole body.

"Mr. Fincastle, great to hear from you," he said, walking out onto the small balcony. "How's it going?"

"Going great here. And you?"

Evan closed the sliding door behind himself. He wasn't sure why he did that, but he was sure he felt guilty about not wanting Michelle to overhear him.

"I'm good. Busy, but good."

"I don't mean to bother you, but I thought you should know Anne's coming back home. She finished up her rehab, and she's going to living with us for a while."

Evan let out his breath in a rush, closing his eyes and holding onto the railing. He shouldn't be feeling this way, not with his fiancé in the other room in a tiny apartment. His heart was ready to float the rest of him up off the balcony without asking his permission.

"I'm so glad to hear that, you have no idea. Well, you probably do. When will she get home?"

"This afternoon. I'm caught at work, Karen will pick her up."

"How is she?"

"She's good, Evan, she really is. She's been clean for six months now, and she looks so much better. Still tired and way too thin, but she's getting back to normal."

Evan closed his eyes, remembering the way Anne had looked the last time he'd seen her. Nearly skeletal but her face so awful and puffy, the furious look in her eyes and harsh sound of her voice.

He'd been so afraid that would be his last memory of her.

"Listen, are you busy tonight?" Anne's father said. "Or maybe tomorrow? I was thinking she could really use some company, a good friend she hasn't seen for a while."

"I...uh... I might be able to get away tonight. I'd love to see her."

"That's fantastic! What time should I tell her?"

Evan's mind raced, wondering what he could tell Michelle. They didn't have any particular plans for tonight, but he hadn't mentioned being out for several hours either.

He'd be going, no matter excuse he came up with. He didn't feel particularly good about that, but he knew when putting up a fight with himself would be a waste of time.

"I'll stop by around six."

"Great, I'll be home by 5:30 myself. Maybe you two can go out to dinner, somewhere where... You know..."

"I'll make sure no one's drinking, don't worry. Thank you for calling me, Mr. Fincastle."

"No problem at all, Evan. I'm glad I was able to reach you. Are you ever going to call me Mike?"

"I don't know, I'll work on it. Maybe when I turn forty."

"Okay, good enough. I'll hold you to that. See you tonight."

Evan put the phone in his pocket so he wouldn't drop it. What had he just arranged to do? Take his friend out to dinner, that's all. Nothing else.

But some deep part of him was groaning, turning over in anxiety and guilt, protesting in advance.

Anne had never seemed to return his feelings, not once since he'd fallen in love with her before he turned fourteen years old. That hadn't stopped him from feeling that way though, not even once.

He did care for Michelle, and he supposed he did love her. He surely wouldn't have asked her to marry him and been so relieved when she said yes otherwise.

He had no plans to tell her where he was going tonight, though.

He'd have to figure out what all of that meant later.

Chapter 35

Evan drove slowly through his old neighborhood, his face still burning and his heart pounding. Michelle hadn't questioned him. She was still operating under the assumption that he was trustworthy and loyal. He didn't think she suspected anything was going on but the last-minute faculty meeting Evan had plucked out of wherever lame excuses lived in his mind.

He would have felt a lot better if Michelle had grilled him under pain of deep suspicion for at least an hour before letting him go.

Whatever his own hopes or expectations might be, he wanted to get that under control before he got to Anne's house. He was too painfully aware of what happened the last time he drove through the night expecting to declare his love for her.

He kept seeing that guy's face, *Joe*, smirking at Evan with his arm around Anne. He couldn't imagine in a million years that such a weaselly asshole was still part of Anne's life. Evan snorted, glancing at his own eyes in the rear view mirror.

Who was a weasel?

He'd thought Anne was single then, unattached. Right this moment, Evan was leaving his fiancé behind to go see Anne. He knew himself well enough to know it couldn't be stopped. Not now.

He slowed as he passed the house he grew up in, the house his mother had died in. Sometimes that day didn't feel like almost fifteen years ago, not one bit. Ed had been as good as his word about selling the place. Evan had never set foot inside again after he left for college.

Seeing the house again now, he wanted to talk to his mother as badly as he ever had that awful summer when she died.

He wanted to ask Mrs. Megan Connor Griffith how she felt about that nameless guy so long ago.

He wanted to talk to her about what he was thinking and feeling about Anne, and about Michelle.

Had his Mom thought it was worth it, so many years of anger and resentment with Ed? Was Evan making the same terrible mistake right now? Was he no better than she had been, no more loyal?

Guilt warring with excitement in his belly let him know words like loyalty weren't up to this task.

All the lights were on downstairs at Anne's house, but none up where her room was. He didn't think her father would have called and then let her go out. Evan still needed to try to get a handle on his runaway hopes expectations.

Bringing Michelle's face up in his imagination helped, a little. But not enough.

"Manage your mind, Evan," he whispered as he got out of the car.

He didn't remember the walk from the sidewalk to the front door being several miles long. Evan had enough time to imagine Anne opening the door, and more than enough time to imagine Michelle opening it instead. He knocked rather than trying to aim a shaky finger at the impossibly tiny doorbell.

"Evan!"

Mike Fincastle caught him up in a huge hug, and Evan squeezed back, hoping his pounding heart didn't give him away. Anne's mother was right behind him, and even she gave him a quick hug and kiss on the cheek. Evan blinked, surprised and pleased.

~

"Anne, you have company!"

Anne opened her eyes, wondering who on earth even knew she was here. She hadn't called anybody. She didn't have any addresses or phone numbers. At least not any that weren't outdated, a bad idea, or for people who wouldn't likely want to talk to her.

"Be right there."

She had to look at the clock twice. Three hours? She felt like she'd only closed her eyes. That had been her dad's voice calling up the stairs though, so early evening did make sense.

A neat stack of paper on her desk told her just how hard she'd been sleeping. That was her list, and it was just as detailed as she'd expected. Her mother had had time to look it all up, get it all typed and printed, and bring it in without Anne noticing.

She'd needed the sleep even more than she'd thought. She hadn't even dreamed.

She took at look at herself in the mirror in the bathroom. Her hair was too long, the bangs covering half of her nose. It grew so fast, and she kept forgetting to get it cut. That was something else she could do with her mother, part of their grand shopping day.

She pushed the dark, heavy strands back, straightened out her clothes the best she could, then splashed water on her face. Even after sleeping so hard, Anne looked better than she had in a long, long time. Her face was too thin but not swollen, and her skin had a color besides death warmed over for a change.

Anne surprised herself by smiling at her reflection.

Years had passed when she couldn't stand to look at herself in the mirror at all, much less feel good about what she saw.

She took the time to rinse out her mouth to get rid of the nearly full-strength morning breath, but she didn't bother brushing her teeth. Whoever it was couldn't be expecting formal attire. Not without even a phone call.

When she was halfway down the stairs, Anne froze. She heard a man's voice, not her father, but one she knew just as well.

It wasn't the recognition that stopped her. It was the memory.

In her mind she saw Evan, sitting on the couch beside her mother. Her father had even turned off the television, a sign of how important this visit really was. She remembered going down the stairs, carefully avoiding the squeaky bottom one so no one would hear her coming.

She remembered Evan looking up, surprised to see her, his blue eyes brighter than the sun in the sky. He took three long strides to Anne and picked her up, squeezing her tight, saying her name over and over in her ear.

Anne remembered when she and Evan finally turned back to the living room, both of her parents were gone. They both laughed, and they couldn't stop looking at each other.

She knew something was going to change now, something that could never go back the way it was before. She stood still, terrified it would be another painful shift in her life that she wasn't ready for.

Was Evan married? He was twenty-seven, and unlike Anne, he was successful and out in the world. Was he moving, even further away than into Chicago or St. Louis?

She hadn't seen him for almost six years. Had he just stopped by to say goodbye?

Her heart and the memory told her it was something more joyful than that, something unexpected and true. Even the return of the memories didn't scare her the way it always had.

She couldn't recall any other strong memory that felt positive instead of terrifying.

Walking into Evan's arms, in a different way than she ever had, was going to filter out more of the noise of her in her mind than anything else ever had.

Anne knew she would find a space around herself, room to breathe and smile, room to be happy and content.

She and Evan would create that space together.

She didn't understand how yet, but she thought even her visions and nightmares were going to be calmer in that safe place with him.

Anne walked down the stairs and into her future.

～

EVAN SAT ON THE COUCH, making sure he had a clear view of the stairs. He was jittery enough. He passed what couldn't have been more than a few minutes but felt like the longest of his life, chatting with Anne's parents, trying not to watch the stairs like a stalker.

He had to accept whatever happened. He'd be overjoyed if she agreed to shake his hand after the way they'd last parted company.

Evan glanced over, not even trying to fool himself that it wasn't for at least the tenth time, and she was there. Her hair was too long, falling into her eyes. Jeans and a rumpled but clean t-shirt showed she wasn't nearly as skeletal as before.

Her cheeks were flushed, but her eyes were bright and happy.

After an endless second of being frozen into place, Evan was beside her. He never felt his feet touch the floor.

Now that it had started working again, his body wasn't consulting Evan at all. He picked Anne up and hugged her tight, all absurd ideas of a handshake long since abandoned.

How could he possibly keep himself distant when she was right here, in his arms, when he could smell her hair and her flesh again after so many years?

"Anne," he whispered, knowing he said it over and over again.

Evan finally managed to put her down and let go, and he was delighted that she held on just a second longer. He looked into her eyes, a little bloodshot with what looked like bruises under them.

She still looked a thousand times better than the last time.

"Evan. I'm so glad to see you."

They both turned to the living room, but Mike and Karen Fincastle had vanished. Their eyes met again and both were laughing, the tension of long separation dissolved in an instant.

She took his hand. "They're bored with us."

He managed not to squeeze too hard and followed her over to the couch. His arm twitched at his side, wanting so badly to be around her shoulders.

"Anne, you look great."

"Well, I look better. How did you know I was home?"

"Your Dad called me this afternoon."

She laughed again, and the sound withered a little more of the loneliness in his heart. Evan wondered, just for a second, what Michelle was doing.

"He thought you might want to go out to dinner with me."

"Of course, I'd love to," she said. "Do I need to change?"

"No, you're perfect."

Evan's face was burning, but he knew he'd told the truth. Hugging her changed the whole focus of his life. Right at that moment, he didn't give a damn what that would mean later on.

ANNE TRIED NOT to stare at Evan as he drove, forcing herself to look at her hands or out the window. He looked like a different person to her, far more than the few years could have accounted for.

He was so much more handsome than she remembered, that was part of it. All traces of his soft boyish face had faded away into high cheekbones and a strong jaw. Everything about him had gotten stronger, more solid somehow. His voice was deeper too.

Even with all of that, he felt just the same to her, just as comfortable and safe as he ever had. He kept up the conversation when she was quiet, a habit he'd picked up when she was just eleven years old.

The sound of the man's voice washed over her, reassuring as the little boy voice of her childhood friend.

"How's this look?"

She shook her head, realizing she'd been staring at his hands on the steering wheel this time. They were in front of an Italian place she'd never been with anyone but her parents before. She remembered it being nice.

"Sure, anywhere is fine."

Once they were seated across from each other, Anne no longer had to stop herself from watching him. He was so much more calm and confident than she remembered.

Her cheeks burned when she remembered why he'd looked so awful the last time she'd seen him.

"Evan, listen," she said, then she took a deep, shaky breath. "I owe you an apology."

He closed his eyes for a second.

"You don't owe me anything, but I'll listen to whatever you need to say."

She didn't want to cry in a restaurant, but she might not have any choice. No one was looking at them, no one at all. Everyone was involved in their own conversations. The room was dim enough that it didn't matter anyway.

"I'm so… I'm so sorry for the way I talked to you that day. You came over to see me and I was such a bitch. Then I was terrible to you at Gwen's house. I'm sure she hates me."

He smiled with one corner of his mouth and shook his head.

"The good thing about growing up with Gwen and my father is it takes a lot to shake me up. Upset as you were, you didn't hold a candle to her when she really gets going. She doesn't hate you at all."

Anne lowered her eyes, smiling a little herself.

"Good. I always liked her. I'm sorry I called you a son of a bitch, Evan. That was way out of line. I never should have done that."

He blinked a few times, and Anne's tears finally spilled over.

"Apology accepted. Maybe we can agree on asshole or jackass instead? Dipshit for a really bad day?"

She tried not to laugh, but that battle didn't last long. She took his hand and they giggled together, and she didn't even care when people did glance their way. They could have been in grade school again, the years between vanished in a second.

Anne could have never met Joe, gone to jail, gone to rehab. She might never have even gone to the hospital.

All she needed to do was hold Evan's hand and laugh with him.

"Listen," Evan said, wiping his eyes and squeezing her hand. "I'm not going to bug you about it, but you can tell me whatever you want to, or not a damn thing. I'm not going to judge you. I never have. If you need someone to talk to, I'm right here."

"I'll take you up on that, but you might regret it. I've gotten a lot better at talking over the past few months."

"Try me," he said, winking. "I've had a lot of practice in listening."

A strange look passed over his face, so fast she wondered if she'd imagined it. His eyebrows knotted together for the briefest second, then it was gone.

"You first. How's your job? You're teaching in the city, right?"

"Yeah, teaching history at the university, working on my doctorate. I'll probably finish up in the spring, just have to wrap up my dissertation."

"Your *doctorate*," she said, grinning. "I'm not surprised, of course it's history. What are you writing about?"

Evan rolled his eyes and shrugged.

"I'll bore you to tears if you get me started. I'm writing about the ways agriculture in the US, around the world, really, has changed with pesticides, how they've helped and hurt."

Anne stared at him again, painful chills covering her arms and legs. She couldn't even see Evan for a moment. She saw bees, piles and piles of dead bees. The images from her first nightmare flared into painful life inside of her.

Those dead bees had led to even more dead people.

Sometimes all the people.

"Bees," she whispered

"Yeah, that's a big part of it," he said, his eyebrows raised. "I'm not going to drag you through it right now, but I've been putting that data together over the past few months."

"I don't think I'd be the least bit bored if you explain all of it to me when you're finished."

Anne could remember that now, as clearly as she'd seen him picking her up in her parents' living room. Evan sitting cross-legged and barefoot on the gleaming wooden floor of his apartment, neat stacks all around him, going through every single thing with her. It made perfect, terrifying sense the way he explained it.

Despite that, knowing more about the exact problem was going to calm her fear of the future like nothing else ever had.

"Maybe I can help you practice, what is it, defending it?"

"You have no idea how much that would help," he said, running his fingers through his hair, leaving it standing on end. A flash of his younger self breaking through the confident man in front of her.

"I'm not even finished with the damn thing, and I'm already scared to death of everyone picking it apart."

"It's a deal. How are Gwen and your father? She has a kid now, doesn't she?"

"Two boys. Horrible brutes, they are," he said with a smile that made her heart melt. "They're great, so's she. Dad's the same as ever, I guess. Still a pain in the ass."

"Does he live close by you?"

"No, thank goodness. Neither one of us could stand that. We see each other at holidays, and that's plenty all around. All right, your turn. Tell me something I don't know."

Anne laughed under her breath. She wished the waiter would bring their appetizers, anything to distract him from that question. There was so much he didn't know. She was in the middle of a field of land mines.

"Anne," he said, so softly she barely heard him. "I'm not asking you to tell me gory details, though you could if you wanted. I just want to fill in some of the blanks. I've missed you."

A space inside of her opened then, like a muscle she'd forgotten clenching tight. Evan wasn't going to pressure her, and he wasn't going to leave her. He would never yell at her or hit her.

She didn't see the details of the memory, not yet. For the first time, she *felt* the memory all around her without seeing a thing.

And the memory felt like love.

Chapter 36

THE DREAMS WERE the worst of Anne's torments. Not all of her torments, to be sure, but the worst of them. The dreams told her, night after night, year after year, that life would end in disaster. Not just her own life, though that was bad enough.

Anne knew *all* life hung in that balance.

During the last few months, since she'd gotten sober, she'd learned to love the rare, precious minutes, when she hadn't quite woken up yet. Floating in warm darkness, not afraid of either a nightmare or the day to come. Drifting in the past, wandering through possible futures. Futures that weren't all scary, for the first time since she was eleven years old.

Futures full of hope. And of love.

"Time for your medication, sweetheart."

Anne did her best not to sigh or frown when she opened her eyes. Her mother had taken to her renewed role as parent like a champ. All the way to never remembering to knock on Anne's door anymore.

"Thanks, Mom."

"Any bad dreams?"

"No, none at all," Anne said, comfortable with the lie. She accepted the two orange pills. "I slept great."

"Good!" her mother said, beaming. "I'll see you downstairs."

Just as on the last many mornings, her mother was distracted enough by reports of a good night to skip watching her daughter swallow the pills.

Once the door was closed, Anne leaned over the edge of the bed. She unscrewed the lid and dumped the handful into the water jar already stained multiple colors.

Her fictional great sleep had gained her three weeks free of drugs so far. She just had to manage to keep her parents, especially her mother, from catching on.

Anne slowly got up, trying to stretch out the aches from another restless night. Every day off of the pills seemed to make her nightmares worse. What surprised her and made every terrible dream worth it was how her days were going.

For the first time in her life, Anne knew she was doing the right thing. She was doing the only thing she possibly could. For the first time in her life, her visions were calming her anxiety instead of making it worse.

She took extra care with her makeup, making sure the dark circles under her eyes were well-hidden. That would be the best way to bring this whole thing crashing down, for someone to notice how tired she looked.

Anne had studied carefully and practiced for hours before she'd ever stopped the pills. The whole thing just had to go on a little bit longer. Then she wouldn't have to worry about the medication anymore.

When her eyes looked awake and normal, Anne turned to the calendar. Wednesday, so she'd be seeing Evan today.

He was the key, she was certain of that. Everything depended on him. She'd always wondered why he'd stayed with her through so much hell, even as she was grateful for his support. The visions had given her the answer just a couple of weeks ago.

Finally satisfied with her appearance, her dark brown hair swept up into a knot that looked far more casual than it was, and her slender body as appealing as it could be with a tight skirt and fitted shirt, Anne went downstairs. She needed to have her cheerful facade firmly in place to get safely out the door.

Just a little chat with her parents, easiest thing in the world for a normal woman. Normal had always been particularly challenging for Anne, since long before she became a woman.

She managed to eat every bit of the food her mother put in front of her, and thankfully her father kept up the conversation.

Pleased with her performance, and giving her father an extra-long hug for his unwitting assistance, Anne turned to make her escape. Her mother followed her to the front door.

"What are you up to today, hon?"

"I'm working until six, then Evan's meeting me at the library. We're going to an old movie."

"That's so sweet," her mother said, handing Anne her coat. "I'm so glad you two have each other, even after… after so much time."

"I know, Mom. Me too. See you later."

Anne closed the door and leaned against it. Her mother tried, she really did. More than she ever had when Anne was younger. She'd been about to say since Anne had gone away for a while because of her problem. That's what her mother always called it, her *problem*. Like Evan's father talking about her *issues*.

That was understandable for someone who'd never had a night-mare about the end of the world, one so vivid she breathed the poisoned air and heard the dying screams all day long. All Anne's mother wanted for her was to calm down, settle down, get married, and have a family of her own, despite her *problem*. Anne had never even suspected such a thing was possible until very recently.

That was when her visions, her day visions, not her nightmares, had started to change.

Anne caught the commuter train and sat, closing her eyes. This was when she most often saw the memories now, on her hour-long ride to the university. Something about the noise and the motion lulled her and let her mind relax, even more than her stolen restful moments before she opened her eyes in the morning.

Today the vision was strong and peaceful. Anne didn't just see young boys and girls working in the fields, she was working with them. The fields were vast and well-tended, and they were full to bursting with short, leafy plants. Soybeans, that's what they were.

Anne recognized them from so many visions that she'd had to look them up to be certain. Row after row of healthy green stretched on as far as she could see in the rolling terrain. She knew it was nowhere near her home in the farmlands of Illinois. An ocean breeze was too sharp to be so far inland. That didn't matter though.

All that mattered was these people were alive, they were strong, and they were able to feed themselves.

Anne watched as the youngest children squatted beside each of the plants. Their small hands held smaller tools, and they were careful to touch each tiny purple flower. They moved from one plant to the next, making sure not to miss a single one. Anne knew the children were pollinating the beans.

Many of her nightmares gave her explanations for this, but they didn't always match up. All she knew was this work was crucial to the survival of everyone she could see. The kids were laughing and happy, seeming to enjoy such tedious and difficult work. No adults were even close enough to supervise. The children kept going of their own accord, moving in rhythm with the wind and the softly rustling leaves.

When the rumbling engine went still, Anne opened her eyes. The end of this route was her stop, a lucky coincidence she was happy to take advantage of. She followed a handful of people out.

Her job, the one Evan had helped her get, was as real as her dreamless sleep was a lie. She did work in the university library, the first job she'd ever had for longer than a couple of months.

The work was easy and repetitive, and the chance to be around so many reference books was a bonus. The Internet connection that her mother couldn't monitor was a lifesaver. She'd been free to research her medication and the risks involved in her plans over the next few days.

"I don't know how you do it, Anne."

She turned, afraid she'd been humming out loud again. Suzanne, her supervisor, smiling over what was probably her fourth cup of coffee at ten in the morning.

"What do you mean?"

"You can come in here to carts just overloaded with books, all out of order, first thing on a Monday morning, and still be happy about it."

Anne laughed, knowing she was blushing. If Suzanne or anyone else knew just how happy she was at the moment, a trip back to the psychiatric hospital might be her next step.

"I don't mind, I truly don't," she said, picking up another book. "It really does give me a chance to think."

"Well, you've taken to it like no one else I've ever seen. Keep up the great work."

Anne turned back to the shelf, effortlessly finding the spot for the book. The complicated numbering system had made sense to her from day one. Suzanne had told her that neither she nor anyone else minded the humming, but Anne was still a little embarrassed. She didn't like standing out any more than she had to, even when her days were going so well.

As clear as her visions had been lately, she wasn't sure if today or tomorrow would be her chance with Evan. She knew it was close, any time now. The increasing details in her imagination were only a part of her certainty.

She could feel the changes in her body, medication clearing out, the preparations too small for anyone else to notice. Too many negative things had come true for her to doubt something so positive. This was going to make the difficult early years of life worth living.

Anne was startled by a warm hand on her own, and she turned to look into Evan's pale blue eyes. Her whole body tingled with pleasure.

Complete surprises were rare for her, good or bad.

This one was certainly good.

"About quitting time, isn't it?"

"I hadn't even noticed," she said. "I probably would have worked all night if you hadn't shown up."

"I'll help you pack up and we'll get out of here."

Each of them grabbed an empty book cart and rolled them back toward the reference desk. Everyone else had already gone home, leaving them in warm, companionable silence.

"What did you do today, Evan?"

"Departmental meeting, I'm sorry to say, one even the lowly grad students couldn't escape. I've never understood how sitting in a room for hours on end is going to help us learn more about anything. Or teach anything."

"Was it about funding again?" Anne said, turning so he could hold her coat for her.

"Yeah, same old song. No one cares about the past when we're so busy running toward the future. The new millennium looms even over history departments, I suppose. I'm not even thirty years old, but I'm as antiquated as the books I collect."

"I wouldn't say that," Anne said. "I'm into antique books myself."

He smiled, leaning down for a quick hug. Anne felt the strange tickle of a memory about to come true, like an electric current through her nerve endings.

She kissed him on the corner of his mouth before she hugged him tight. That tickle disappeared in a blast of heat, deeper and hotter than in her most intense memories and daydreams. She felt Evan's heart pounding in that same warmth.

He drew back, looking into her eyes. Anne was pleased that her own face felt calm, especially once she saw how flushed his was. She never needed validation for something she'd seen so clearly, so many times, but she was swept up in his response all the same.

"Are you… ah, are you ready to go?" he said, taking a deep breath.

"I'm ready."

She walked beside Evan, listening to him chatter about his day. The random brush of his hand against hers didn't feel so accidental anymore. Much as she wanted to, Anne didn't grab his hand. Not yet.

She knew that time would come, maybe sooner than she thought. With so much pain and fear ahead for all of them, there was no need to rush through all of this pleasure.

They'd planned to have dinner and then see a movie, but the vision and the reality were lining up more quickly than she'd expected. A moment like this felt like a doubled photo slowly coming into focus, a lot like the truly antiquated stereo pictures he had in his apartment.

Every second brought them into alignment, an eclipse that would last for hundreds of years.

The way Evan kept looking at Anne during dinner, his eyes seeming to drink her in, left her no doubts. His knee against hers under the table intensified the heat between them.

"What time is the movie?" Anne said, knowing they were already ten minutes late.

As she'd known he would, Evan answered without looking down at his watch.

"I think we're going to miss this one."

As she knew she would, Anne laughed deep in her throat.

"Don't you have a copy of it at home? I'll bet you've seen it a dozen times."

Evan smiled and put his hand over hers.

"More than a dozen. I'd still like to watch it with you, Anne."

She looked into his eyes, the pupils wide enough to nearly obscure the lovely blue. She remembered looking into those same eyes when she told him she knew the world was going to end.

He hadn't panicked, not at first. He'd stayed with her even when he did panic later on. He'd stayed with her, remained her closest friend, through all of it, even after she did her best to push him away for years. He'd always been her way through the nightmare, even before she'd understood why.

"Let's go there now, Evan."

When they walked out of the restaurant, Evan did finally take Anne's hand. She looked up at him, trying to keep her relief and satisfaction to herself. After a lifetime of so many horrible visions, a beautiful vision was going to come true. She squeezed his hand and smiled.

His apartment was only a few blocks away, and neither of them spoke on the short walk. He didn't let go of her hand either. Anne tried to keep her memory of what was going to happen out of her mind.

She wanted to be surprised again. She wanted to have this moment for the very fist time.

Inside his apartment, Anne walked over to shelves full of books and music and movies. She knew he'd only lived here a couple of years, but so many well-loved things made it seem like he'd lived his whole life here. She ran her fingers along the row of old, leather-bound books, waiting for him.

Waiting for him to touch her.

Waiting for him to set the rest of their lives into motion. Lives filled with love from this night until the end.

She felt Evan's hands on her shoulders, and the reality obliterated all of her well-treasured and traveled memories. Her entire body was on fire, a spark lit by his flesh against her own. She turned to him.

"Anne, I've been so happy," he said, then he closed his eyes for a second. "I've been so happy to see you doing so well. I was afraid that would never happen for a long time."

Anne covered one of his hands with her own.

"So was I."

"Spending so much time with you these past two weeks has been like a dream. I keep expecting to wake up."

"This dream is real," Anne whispered, stepping into his arms. "No one knows more about dreams than I do."

She felt his heart pounding again, and this time his whole body was trembling. Anne was surprised to feel her own body doing the same, responding to Evan in a way she'd never remembered or imagined.

The joy of that, of something so simple as the natural reaction of her body to his, sent Anne's happiness spiraling around her. She was lightheaded as she turned her face up to his.

Her lips met his fully this time, and the touch turned Anne into nothing but heat. For the first time in her life, she was not terrified to be in exactly the right place at exactly the right time.

She opened her mouth and every part of her, wanting to let all of her past and her future perish in that raging heat.

Evan breathed deeply, then he pulled her against him, squeezing her body against his own. His hands were in her hair, against her back, on her face, always in motion, moving them closer together.

Anne knew this wasn't the first time for him, and she'd had plenty of her own sad attempts. Every time before, she'd been struggling, fighting against a memory she knew wasn't going to turn out well, but a memory she was unable to stop. This time she went willingly, gladly, bringing her life onto the course of her own destiny.

Evan drew back, breathing hard and holding the sides of her face. She held his hands, needing to hear what she knew he would say.

"I love you, Anne. I've never loved anyone but you."

She kissed him, trying to draw him inside of her. "I love you."

She took his hand and walked toward his bedroom, feeling and remembering the changes that would soon take place between them. Those changes would alter the courses of their own lives, and everyone around them would say it was about time.

Oh, how they'd *waited* for the two of them to get together forever, how they'd hoped. They never said once Anne got over her *problem*, and the fact that they surely thought that didn't bother her. Not anymore.

Anne knew her problem was going to be the salvation, not of all of them, but at least of enough of them.

Chapter 37

ANNE TURNED OVER, stretching and groaning. She couldn't remember the last time she'd slept so deeply and woken so easily. Nothing hurt or ached. Every single part of her felt good. She opened her eyes, and for just an instant, she wasn't sure exactly where she was.

The space was small, barely the size of her own bedroom in her parents' house. But rather than staying trapped in the painfully outdated pastels and Day-Glo of a teenaged girl in the Eighties, this was an adult's room. Deep burgundy rugs covered parts of the smooth hardwood floor, beside the queen-sized bed, in front of a plain black chest of drawers. The bed itself felt like floating in a warm cotton cloud, with the softest sheets and pillows Anne had ever slept in.

Rather than being covered with tattered posters of Duran Duran, Prince, and Pat Benatar, the rich brown walls were mostly empty. Only one picture caught Anne's eye. A woman, maybe in her thirties, and a little boy. Both of them with black hair and vivid pale blue eyes.

Anne caught her breath, remembering everything. She was in Evan's bed, and she'd spent the night with him. She'd made love with him for the first time. Her memory had been detailed and strong, but it hadn't even come close to the reality of the way their bodies moved together.

Neither Joe nor any of the other random guys had ever made her feel this way. Sex had felt good, sure, at least some of the time. It had only been sex though. Joe was always close to the line of using her, not much more than a body-sized substitute for his hand.

A couple of the other guys hadn't bothered pretending she was anything else.

She sat up against the pillowy headboard, pulling the heavy comforter up around her shoulders. She realized being with Evan was her first time actually making love. She hadn't felt like an afterthought or some kind of convenient receptacle.

She knew everything about her, every single inch of her flesh and every way she felt, was the most important and beloved thing on the face of the earth for him. Anne couldn't remember ever feeling like that before.

When she looked over at Evan's nightstand to check the time, she saw a note nearly lost in the folds of the comforter.

Went out to get breakfast, nothing here at all! Be right back. Love you, E

Anne closed her eyes, surprised to feel hot tears in her eyelashes. That was another part of her memory that had fallen short.

Words, they were just words. Her parents, her grandmother, so many people had used that word. Love. It had never affected her like this, like it altered every cell in her body.

He'd left a robe on his side of the bed too, a thick goldenrod-colored robe far too big for her, but it was warm. She looked around the neat bedroom, making a bet with herself which door would be the bathroom.

She wanted to at least be presentable when he got back, not like she'd ratted up her hair on purpose. She wanted to look as good as she felt, though that might not be possible. Her first guess was wrong, but she held the hall door open long enough to be sure the apartment was still empty. She opened the door to the tiny bathroom next. Sink crowded close against tub and toilet, but again, everything from the spotless white tiles to the recessed medicine cabinet to the matching slate gray towels and shower curtain looked so cool and stylish and grownup.

Anne wasn't sure she felt comfortable borrowing Evan's toothbrush without asking, but she at least wanted to wash her face and rinse out her mouth. She laughed at her hair in the mirror, every bit as messy and tangled as she'd imagined. She could at least clean the loose strands out of his hairbrush when she was finished.

When she touched the flat metal handle on the mirror, meaning to open the medicine cabinet and look for a brush, Anne froze.

The sense of a memory was as strong as it had ever been, the feeling of tiny bolts of lightning all over her fingers. But Anne didn't see anything. She waited for the screen to appear in her mind, three scenes, or maybe only one, but nothing happened. She blinked, then looked back at her reflection.

She'd never felt the air around her, time itself, so thick and heavy with whatever she was about to see. Not even when Evan's mother had died.

Why wasn't she seeing it? Even the most horrifying memories hadn't hesitated, keeping her waiting like this. She let go of the handle.

That didn't lessen her certainty, not one bit. If anything, dread joined anticipation to make her anxiety even worse. There was something she had to know here, something she couldn't avoid. Even if she got dressed and walked away from here forever, she wouldn't be able to leave this behind.

And she didn't think she'd be able to walk away from Evan, now or anytime in the future, no matter what she saw. Anne opened the door before she could change her mind.

Nothing seemed odd or out of place at first. She saw vitamins, aspirin, the hairbrush she'd been looking for, nail clippers, an electric razor. She picked up the brush, feeling a little guilty at looking at such an intimate space when Evan wasn't home.

This was a different intimacy than sharing his bed. This felt a lot more like snooping.

A memory did surge forward then, but it was a normal memory out of the past. Joe had found her pills in the medicine cabinet the first time he'd been in her apartment. That was the start of the long nightmare with him.

Anne started to close the door, thinking the waiting memory must be about something else. Maybe thoughts of Joe made her uneasy enough to imagine her discomfort, and it would just fade away now.

She looked back at the shelves. It was true nothing was out of place, but a lot of things seemed to be missing. More than half the cabinet was empty. That didn't make sense.

Unless…

The memory exploded around her. Anne caught herself against the sink, the brush clattering to the tiled floor.

She was back the bedroom, sitting on Evan's bed, and he was sitting beside her, both of them fully dressed. A tiny black velvet box sat between them. It looked like a jewelry box, but this wasn't a happy occasion.

The ring in that box wasn't meant for Anne. That ring had been meant, had already been given, to another. To his fiancé. The box faded away, and she knew it wasn't still here, not right now. Evan was going to get it back though, sometime in the next week or two. She groaned, sitting carefully on the edge of the bathtub.

He hadn't given this ring to some nameless girl in college, a youthful relationship long forgotten.

Evan was engaged to another woman, *right now*.

The empty space in the medicine cabinet wasn't some odd kind of OCD on his part. His fiancé's things had been there, just a few days or maybe a couple of weeks before. Gods, had he hidden them away, on the off chance Anne would be in his bathroom?

Evan was *engaged*. He'd made plans and promises to be another woman's husband. Anne held her face in her shaking hands. She hadn't had a drop to drink in over six months now, but she recognized this sensation from more hangovers than she could possibly count. She was too certain she was going to throw up to get too far away from the toilet.

"Anne?"

Too late, she remembered she hadn't closed the door behind her.

Evan stood in the doorway. His brilliant smile faded and his eyes were frightened.

She wanted to feel sad that what should have been a perfect morning was going to be such a nightmare for both of them. She wanted to mourn that loss, but she couldn't quite manage. He was in front of her now, squatting to look into her eyes.

"Anne, what's wrong? Are you sick?"

She shook her head slowly, trying to figure out what to say to him. No words seemed possible until they floated out of her mouth.

"I'm not sick."

He reached up to push her tangled hair away from her face.

"Did you have a dream?" he said, stroking her cheek now. "Did you remember something?"

"Yeah, I remembered something. It's going to happen right now. I can't stop it."

"Come in the bedroom and tell me about it. Maybe that will help."

He stood, holding out his hands to her. She couldn't think of anything else to do but let him pull her to her feet.

"I need to get dressed," she said, pulling the robe tight at her throat, trying to ignore the gut-twisting certainty that it was *her* robe. "Can you… Can you give me a minute?"

Evan looked confused, then his face went white. He closed his eyes, his eyebrows drawing down. He turned and walked through the bedroom and back out into the hall. When Anne was dressed, her hair pulled back as neatly as possible, she sat on the bed. The jewelry box wasn't there, not physically, but that didn't matter. She called him back in.

"Anne, please tell me what's going on."

"You look like you already know."

He shook his head as he sat beside her. Anne couldn't stop herself from looking at the space between them, where the ring should have been. The space felt solid, physical, like the woman was lying there instead.

"I know something's wrong, and I'm terrified of what it might be."

"You tell me then." Anne drew her knees up against her chest. "Tell me what has you so afraid."

"Did someone call?"

"No, not that I heard."

"Did you find something? See something?"

"Nothing outside my memory. Evan, just tell me the truth. Just tell me. Lying can only make it worse."

The dread in his eyes made some part of her ache. Another part of her was ready to get furious, whether he managed to tell her or not.

"There's someone else," he whispered, not dropping his gaze.

"What's her name?"

"Her name is Michelle. I… We're engaged."

This was the second time in less than twenty-four hours that the memory turned out to be a pale imitation of the reality. Anne's vision of the ring had felt like a flood of icy cold water.

Evan's words felt like a kick in the guts.

"You're *still* engaged?"

"Yes. Right now we are."

"Does she live here, Evan? Did I sleep in her bed last night after I had sex with her fiancé?"

"She's in Seattle right now."

"I didn't ask you where she is *right now*," Anne said, clenching her fists. "Does she live here or not?"

He flinched at the sound of her voice, as if she'd taken a swing at him. Anne couldn't quite manage to feel sorry for him.

"She still has her own place, but yeah, she's been staying here a lot. She's going to… She was going to move in here in a couple of weeks, when she got back."

"She doesn't know a thing about me, does she?"

Evan just shook his head, his cheeks red and his eyes lowered.

"What did you think was going to happen, Evan? When were you going to tell her? When were you going to tell me? Were you hoping we could all just get along?"

"I was going to break it off with her, I *am* going to. I should have already. I didn't want to do that over the phone. And I wanted to be with you last night. I've wanted to be with you since before I even knew what that meant."

"That doesn't mean you can treat her this way. It doesn't mean you can treat *me* this way. I didn't expect you to be a virgin any more than I am, but you're fucking engaged! You lied to me, Evan, or at least you kept a hell of a lot from me. Did you hide her things before you met me last night?"

"No, I… I mean yes. Not last night, no, but I did after I saw you again. After we went to dinner that first time." He groaned, linking his hands together around the back of his neck. "I fucked everything up."

Anne buried her face against her knees, wanting to scream. Her memories of making love to Evan hadn't been the end of what she saw, what she knew would happen.

They were going to have more than one night together. The two of them were going to spend their lives together for as long as they lived. Unless some fundamental part of her was failing, a part that had never been wrong about a memory like this before, her future was going to be with this man.

That meant she would eventually recover from the spinning pit in her middle where her stomach and her heart used to be. And he would eventually manage to stop looking and sounding so terrified.

"I don't know what you've done," she said. "I know what I have to do though."

"I have to tell her."

"That's up to you. You have to tell her if you ever want to see or talk to me again."

Evan didn't move. He just watched her gathering her things from the nightstand and dropping it all into her purse.

"Please don't go," he finally whispered.

"I don't want to go, but you didn't give me much of a choice. I never would have chosen to sleep in her bed, Evan. I never, ever would have made love to you if you'd told me the truth. Joe cheated on me all the time, did you know that? I promised myself I'd never do that to another woman. And here I am."

"I'll listen to whatever you want to say. Please don't go."

"If I don't get the hell out of here right now my next stop is going to be the liquor store. I thought I'd gotten away from guys who drove me to fucking drink!" Tears spilling from his blue eyes only twisted the fury in Anne's guts higher. "The truth god damn well hurts, doesn't it? You keep on telling yourself you're better than that, that it's justified, that you're noble, whatever it takes. I've spent almost every day of my life staring the truth dead in the face!"

"Will you at least let me drive you home?"

"I'm a big girl. I know the train schedule. And you know where to reach me, but not one single word from you until this is finished. Not one word."

Anne wished she could see what she was walking into, or out of. She had no idea if she wanted him to try to stop her, to try to hold her and kiss her and make her stay.

She didn't know if that would be worse than him sitting on that bed, *Michelle's* bed, and not saying anything.

He didn't do either. He did something far worse than what she'd been trying to prepare herself for.

"I love you, Anne. No one but you."

She walked out of his apartment without saying another word. She managed to get out the door and down to the street before sobs kept her from walking or even breathing for a long while.

Chapter 38

Evan looked at the blocky white caller ID box beside his phone, dreading at least two of the numbers it could be. He was a little relieved to see it was neither, but he wasn't sure if this was going to be a reprieve or not.

"Hi Gwen."

"What the hell have you been getting into, little brother?"

Evan laughed, knowing it wouldn't fool his sister for one second.

"Not a thing. I've been bored to death up here, nothing but work. How's your life?"

"Not nearly as dramatic as yours. I had a long talk with Michelle a couple of days ago."

He rolled his eyes, glad no one could see him.

"I'm sure she was singing my praises."

"Not exactly. Listen, I'm on the way home from Milwaukee. I can be there in about half an hour."

"I don't want to bother you with all of this."

"You're not the one who bothered me. I just want to hear your side of it."

Evan looked around the empty apartment. Still too many books, too much antique stuff on not enough shelves. Still the same angular, overly masculine furniture, now without most of the fussy pillows and hand-knit blankets that kept the place from looking like a showroom at Guys-R-Us. A whole lot more than a few things in the medicine cabinet were gone now, back to Michelle's place.

Anne still refused to talk to him, only telling him it wasn't over, whatever that meant. He doubted he'd ever hear from Michelle again after telling her the engagement was off.

He did need to talk to someone.

"In a hurry to get back home, Gwen? You can stay here tonight if you really want to know what's going on."

"Are you kidding? This week was the first break I've had in ages. Mark will be fine with the boys. At least they'll all survive without too many bruises. Need me to bring the gin?"

"Yep. I'm fresh out."

By the time Gwen walked in with two small black bottles, Evan was fairly sure he was ready to talk. Trying to figure this all out for himself was not working. Within a few minutes, they were settled on the couch, upgraded gin and tonics in hand.

"I understand you're single again."

"Subtle as usual, Gwen. I don't know. Maybe. I hope not."

"That's not how your ex-fiancé sees it."

"I'm not with her anymore, no. I may not be with anyone."

"Has she talked to you?"

Evan took a long drink to avoid answering. Michelle was one of the calls he'd been dreading, even though whatever Anne was waiting for hadn't happened yet.

"No, not for a couple of days. I doubt she will."

Gwen raised her eyebrows, shaking her head a little.

"I'd be surprised if you didn't get another call, Ev. She has a lot of questions."

"I know. What I don't know is what to tell her."

"You better figure it out. I told her to make you tell her."

"You did what?"

"Don't glare at me like that, jerk. I'm not the one who dumped my fiancé out of the blue right before she was going to move in."

Evan was quite sure he'd misheard her, or at least misunderstood her. Her words weren't making any sense.

"You told her to do what?"

"I told her I didn't know what had gotten into you, that she needed to ask you. Well, to be honest, I told her she needed to drag it out of you if she had to."

"Way to have my back, sis. Whose side are you on?"

"I'm on your side, and I do have your back. But you pushed Michelle into my life, remember? And she pushed me into this. I don't know what to tell her even if I wanted to. What the hell happened?"

"It's just not working out," he said, knowing he was wasting his time trying to get her off track. "Nothing in particular."

"Horse shit. Your relationships are your business, unless your girlfriends force me into the middle. But don't you dare lie to me."

He looked into her eyes, wondering how much he could tolerate telling her or anyone else. He wasn't thrilled with Gwen for telling Michelle to drag the truth out of him, but he knew that was the right thing to do. He needed to try to do the right thing here too.

"It's Anne. I've been seeing Anne."

Gwen hummed under her breath, then took her own long drink.

"Why am I not surprised? When did this happen?"

"She got back about a month ago. Her Dad called me."

"I'm guessing he didn't know about Michelle."

Evan shook his head, sighing.

"Neither did Anne. I didn't handle any of this right."

"I don't know if there is a right way, but you definitely got your timing wrong. Where's Anne?"

"Once she realized… Once she knew about Michelle, she left. She keeps telling me there's something I haven't done, but she won't say what."

"Well, that might be the same thing I told Michelle. I'm guessing, since I haven't seen Anne in a long time, but they both need the truth, Ev. Michelle is going to drive herself crazy trying to figure out what she did wrong. You *know* that's not fair."

"No, it's not fair. She didn't do anything wrong except be the wrong person."

"So why does she think this is because of something she did or didn't do? She has the very strong idea it was her fault."

Evan swirled the ice around in his glass, knowing stalling was useless. This was the thing he felt worst about, even more than the lying.

"I'm sure she does believe it was her fault. I didn't exactly stop her from thinking that."

Gwen snorted, shaking her head.

"You mean you told her that, or you let her decide that for herself? Answer carefully. I know where you live."

"She got there on her own, but I let her do it. And I didn't tell her otherwise."

"Why the hell did you do that? How can you be such a fucking *guy*?"

"I don't know. Maybe because I am nothing more than a standard issue fucking guy after all. I just wanted her to go. I wanted it to be over. It all made sense at the time."

"Wrong answer on that one, brother. You're *not* just a guy, and you never have been. You'd have to do quite a bit more downgrading to get there, but this is a great start."

"I hate shit like that, Gwen. I always have."

"Yeah, so? Most people hate shit like that. But we do it anyway. You turn away from things you don't like too easily, Ev. You did with Michelle, you do with Ed, and you did with Anne here too. You might have turned away with Anne a long time ago. You have to start facing things like this, going through them instead of walking away."

"Easy enough for you to say. You've always been more of a bitch than I am."

"I had to learn it. Being an only child with our parents for six years wasn't easy. I do know what I'm talking about here. Stand up for what you want. Maybe that's what Anne's waiting for, you know? She needs to know you'll stand up for her, too."

"Maybe. I'll think about it."

"Listen, how is Anne? What's been going on with her?"

Evan finished his drink and ran his fingers through his hair. This wasn't his business to tell, but he knew Gwen wasn't interested in gossip. She was worried about him. That was one of her most annoying, and endearing, traits.

"She had a tough time for a while, then she was in rehab and a hospital for six months. This is the most calm I've seen her since we were kids. Before Mom died."

"Even after she knew about Michelle?"

"Yeah, especially then. She was furious. But she hasn't started drinking, despite my best efforts to drive her to it. And she's not backing down on whatever she does want."

Gwen smiled and nodded.

"If she's been in rehab and really made some changes, I was right. She does need the truth. I've dodged that addiction bullet myself somehow, despite inheriting a love for Mom's g and ts, but I know a few people who haven't. A big part of it seems to be just telling the damn truth, to themselves and everyone else. Why should she expect any less from you?"

"I don't think I told myself the truth for a long time, Gwen. It feels crazy now, but I thought everything I was doing was all okay. I had reasons for everything. I hope I haven't fucked it up for good between us."

"Well, I'll tell you the truth. I'm not happy about the way you treated Michelle. That was an asshole move, and I think you know that. You've been in love with Anne pretty much since birth. So if you can both be happy, I hope it does work out."

She got up, reaching for Evan's empty glass. He followed her into the kitchen and got the gin and ice out of the freezer. This wasn't a night for moderation.

"I do remember the way Anne screamed at you in front of my house," she said, measuring out the gin. "I saw the way you looked when you came back in. Are you sure you know what you're getting into here, Evan?"

He'd never known for certain if Gwen knew what happened that day or not. She'd never said a word about it until this moment. Evan was so grateful he didn't mind the question now.

"Of course I'm not sure. It took me years to get over that day. I don't think I really got over it until I saw her again. Were you sure with Mark?"

She laughed, nearly spilling the bubbling tonic she was pouring into Evan's glass.

"I'm still not sure about Mark! I love him, and he drives me crazy, and I don't think anyone else would put up with either one of us. I know neither of us could raise these hellion children alone. So I guess we're stuck with each other. That might be how it happens. Inertia."

"Inertia sounds like paradise to me. I can't even imagine what that would be like."

"I can't blame you for wondering." Gwen settled herself on the couch again. "We didn't exactly grow up with anything as calm as that, did we? Speaking of chaos, have you told Hurricane Ed yet?"

"Not a word. We don't generally speak unless we're forced to. I don't have to guess how he'll feel about all of this. He really likes Michelle."

"And he really doesn't like Anne."

"Nope, never has. I'm going to have to go tell him. Much as he gets on my damn nerves, I don't want to cut off all contact with him. At least I hope I don't have to."

"I'll go with you for that. Reinforcements are always better."

"No, I need to do this myself. It's past time I stood up to him, don't you think? You were just saying I walk away from him too easily. I'm not a kid anymore, Gwen."

"You're not. You've certainly fucked up this situation like a man. You don't want to be alone for this one, though. Trust me. Ed has more of a temper than you know. And he'll be edgy about this whole thing already."

Evan nodded, moving his hips lower on the chair so he could stretch out his legs.

"He already thinks I'm too much like Mom. This will prove it."

"Neither one of them handled that in a good way, far as I can tell. I don't think Ed ever got over it. Seriously, I don't want you going over there alone. I'll stay out of the way. I have no interest in spilling these particular beans. But he can be a bastard when he gets angry enough. He won't do that if I'm there."

"I'm not going to talk to him for a while anyway. Right now I wouldn't know what to tell him."

"Just promise me you'll let me know when you are ready. Okay?"

He looked into her brown eyes, Ed's eyes, and those eyes came with Ed's temper sometimes. Gwen wouldn't joke around with something like this. She avoided their father almost as much as Evan did. If she was volunteering, even insisting, on going with him, he did need to take that seriously.

"Did he… How bad did it get, Gwen?"

She examined her nearly empty glass for a long time before answering.

"If he ever did hit Mom, I never heard or saw that. But there were times he scared the shit out of me, Ev. Then and later on, after I left home. Something in him seems like it could break loose, you know? There were reasons I hardly ever came to visit. I worried about you, but you were better at staying under his radar than I was. I hate to admit this, and I'll kill you if you repeat it, but I think we were too much alike."

"Hurricane Gwen," Evan said, grinning. "How do you think I got so good at staying out of the way? I watched you two and took notes."

"Smart kid," she said, smiling back. "You still haven't promised me."

"Okay, okay, I'll let you know," he said, getting to his feet and taking her empty glass. "I promise. I don't know about you, but these aren't quite what I'm in the mood for tonight. Make you the best dirty martini you ever tasted?"

"You're on, brother. We'll toast the disaster of your love life, then I'll tell you how to make it as good as mine."

"Good thing you brought more than one bottle."

Chapter 39

Evan had always thought his apartment was two small for more than one person. Living room with barely enough space for a sofa and two chairs. Kitchen straining to hold the basics for feeding himself and a glorified TV tray that passed as a table. Bedroom that held his bed and stereotypically dull bachelor clothing storage, and the sad attempt at a second bedroom that had forced him to buy a new desk that could be assembled inside.

Michelle had made the place more homey and welcoming some-how, but only increased his sense of not having enough room to breathe. Anne was the only person who'd ever walked in and made Evan feel like his lungs, his heart, his mind, every part of him fit better because she was there.

He was terrified Anne would never set foot inside any room with him again.

And now some little boy part of him – the fevered part who believed the sore throat was going to last the rest of his life – was afraid Michelle would sit on the sofa she'd condemned as drab and boring until they both died of shouting or cold silence.

Gwen had told him he needed to talk to Michelle, but she'd told him over and over for years that he was too damn nice. Evan thought his sister had never been more right about that second part than this moment.

Michelle wasn't crying yet, but she was getting closer. She repeated the same question, the same sharp and jagged three letters, no matter what Evan said or did in response.

"Why?"

"I'm sorry, Michelle. I don't know how else to say it. I just couldn't."

"Then why the hell did you propose to me, Evan? What were you trying to accomplish? Did you just want to see how much you could get away with?"

Evan closed his eyes, trying to think of some other words, some other thing he could do to make her understand. After nearly an hour of this, he was starting to care a lot less about understanding or about telling the truth, even after he'd promised Gwen. He just wanted her to go.

"I knew it wasn't going to work, and I couldn't keep pretending. I thought it would be worse for all of us if we got married. Do you really think that would have been better?"

"It would have been better if you'd been man enough to tell me the truth a long time ago!" she shouted, the tears starting up at last. "I wouldn't have wasted so much time with you!"

Evan could only think of one way to get this to stop. He never wanted to hurt Michelle, not in a million years. He'd loved her as much as he could.

Letting this go on was cruel to everyone. He had to let her get it out, let her be right. Let her tear him to pieces if she needed to.

He deserved it.

"You're right. I should have been more of a man. I thought I could make it work, and I was wrong. Everything I did was wrong."

She stared at him so long he was fighting the need to fidget, to look away, to do anything. Finally her eyes narrowed, and Evan tried to brace himself. He remembered all the years of fighting between his parents, partly because of his mother's affair.

Evan had grown up in the middle of those consequences. He couldn't pretend it hadn't been a disaster.

"Is it because of her?"

A wave of heat flooded through him, then he was freezing cold. He might deserve whatever Michelle said, but he'd wanted to protect her from this. He wanted to protect himself, too. And most of all, he wanted to protect Anne.

"What do you mean?"

"I mean Anne, your insane bitch of a girlfriend. Your father told me all I needed to know about her. Is she out of the loony bin again?"

Evan held his breath, trying to get his pounding heart to slow down.

His father. His fucking father. Hurricane Ed had never even pretended to like Anne from the day Evan's mother had died, and the past few years he hadn't even tolerated hearing about her.

Dealing with Michelle, breaking off their engagement after two years, that was child's play compared to standing up to his father. Even after his sister's warning about Ed's temper, Evan knew more than ever that he had to face him.

"He never should have talked to you about that. It wasn't his place or any of his concern."

"He showed a hell of a lot more concern for me than you have. Your only concern is getting me out of the way fast enough!"

"He should have let me handle this my own way. I know I've been an asshole. All I've done is make all of this worse, but that's up to me to make a mess of."

"Is it her?" she whispered, and he wished she would start shouting again.

"It's not going to change anything."

"I don't care, Evan. I know it's over. I just want to know why. I need you to tell me why. You owe me that much."

"If you knew before you came over here, why didn't you just tell me? Why did you question me for an hour first? Did you just want to torture me?"

Evan knew he wasn't being fair. Even if Michelle did just want to torture him, who would have blamed her, or stopped her? Not even Anne would have.

"I wanted you to tell me the truth. That's all. I wanted to give you a chance to tell me the truth. I wasted my time and yours waiting for that."

"You're right," he said, shrugging. "I should have told you. I doubt it'll make anything better. I'm sure it won't, but I do owe you that much. It is Anne."

Michelle closed her eyes for a long time, and Evan was afraid she was going to start crying or shouting at him again. He was afraid they were going to be here all night. When she looked at him again, she was still calm.

"When?"

"A month ago. I first saw her a month ago." He forced himself not to look away.

"And you're only telling me now. Why, Evan? What changed? Has she been here? Was she here before you broke it off with me?"

He wished he had never even picked up the phone when she'd called, and he damned himself all over again for opening the door. He couldn't marry Michelle, but he never wanted to be awful to her.

At least he never wanted to have to tell her just how awful he'd already been.

"Yes. She was here. While you were in Seattle. She was here."

"God *damn* it. God damn *you*. You're the one who talked me into going, staying the whole time, you son of a bitch! Did you do all of that just to get me out of the way so you could fuck her?"

For the first time since his Mom died, Evan didn't lose all control of his temper at those words.

Son of a bitch.

He supposed in this case he was absolutely his mother's son. And this time, if no other, the words fit them both.

"I don't... I don't know how to answer you, Michelle. What I did was wrong. I handled everything the worst way I possibly could have. I never planned for any of this to happen."

"I don't give a damn about plans, though you were happy to sit by and let me plan a wedding you had no intention of attending. You had a choice to make, a hell of a lot of choices. Every time, every single time, you chose her instead of me."

He wanted to shake his head, to argue, to create some way to make this less his fault. He couldn't. He opened his mouth, but he couldn't find a single word. Michelle seemed to be having no problems finding her own words.

"When did this start? It wasn't just a few weeks ago, was it?" Evan shook his head, looking at the floor. "That wasn't a yes or no question!"

He didn't dare point out that the last one had been. Even he wouldn't be that big of a jackass.

"It started when we were in middle school. A long time ago."

"Jesus," Michelle said, her face going white. "Did you ever care about me at all?"

For the first time since she'd walked in the door, really the first time since he'd picked Anne up and held her in his arms, Evan wanted to hug Michelle. He wanted to take away all the pain he'd caused.

"Of course I did, Michelle. That's what's so hard about this. I do care about you. I'm not devoid of feelings here, I know this is awful for you. I didn't know it would be so awful for me."

Michelle's jaw dropped.

"Oh, *poor* Evan. Having a hard time with stabbing me in the fucking back? That must be just terrible. If you're suffering so deeply, why did you do it, why?"

Evan covered his face with his hands, wishing this would all go away. He'd created it, but he wasn't sure if he could live with the fallout. Even after Michelle left and went on with her life, and he knew she would, he would still have to live with what he'd put her through. He was afraid the damage to himself, and to his life with Anne, would be too big.

"I don't want to make it worse," he said, speaking from behind his hands. "Can't we just stop this now?"

"No, Evan, we can't stop this now. You got what you wanted. You got her, and you got me for a while too. You got to convince me you were worthy of being my husband for a long time. We're not going to stop until I say we stop. You tell me why."

He lowered his hands and took a deep breath, then looked into her eyes. She did need to tear him to pieces. He was sure he'd done the same to her, just like his mother had done to his father.

An ache twisted through his guts and his heart, the strongest need to talk to his mother he'd felt since he was thirteen. If she could answer that question, tell him *why*, maybe he could manage to tell Michelle now.

"Because… Because I fell in love with her when I was thirteen years old. I didn't think there was a chance, and I fell in love with you, too, Michelle, I did. I wasn't lying or trying to hurt you or trick you. I did want to marry you."

"You *did* want to. At least you're honest enough to use past tense." She wiped her eyes. "If you wanted to be with me, why did you go see her at all?"

"Her father called to let me know she was home. He thought she'd like to see an old friend. That's all. That's how it started, anyway."

"Before I went to Seattle," she said, her brow furrowing. "The day I was here with you, and out of the blue you told me you had a faculty meeting. A faculty meeting at night. That was it. That was when you went to see her."

Evan nodded, wishing he could send this whole day away.

"And none of them cared that you were engaged?"

"They didn't know. I wasn't trying to hide it. I just hadn't talked to any of them in years."

"Did you tell her when you saw her, Evan? Does she know I exist?"

"I don't want to do this, please."

"I don't care what you want anymore! I want you to tell me the truth. I want to know all of it, so I'll remember just what a nasty piece of work you turned out to be."

Evan took a deep breath, holding it until his head pounded. Maybe if he got it out, he'd be able to remember it too, and never, ever do something like this again. Not to Anne, not to anyone.

Most of all, not to himself.

"All right. You asked. I didn't tell her, no. Once I saw her, I decided not to tell her or her family. I was wrong from the second I picked up the phone and talked to her Dad, and that only got worse. She didn't figure it out until after, 'til we were together the first time."

"How? Did you tell her? Did she find something of mine?"

Evan shook his head, not wanting to say one more word. Everything got worse from here. He wasn't about to tell Michelle or anyone else how exactly Anne figured things out.

He was going to have to take the hit himself. Fair enough.

"She didn't find anything. I… I hid it all. I guess it was the way I acted the next morning."

"You hid my things," she whispered. "You got your inconvenient fiancé out of here then you hid the evidence. Were you protecting her or yourself? You sure as hell weren't protecting me."

"Myself. I didn't want… I didn't want what's going on right now, and what went on with her."

"What did she say, Evan? What did she say when she found out about me? That you'd lied to her too?"

"She wasn't happy with me. She was furious. She's not going to see me again until…unless I tell you everything."

"She was a lot more honorable than you are. That's why you agreed to talk to me, isn't it? For her."

Evan hadn't thought he could feel worse until that second, those words. Until he saw the heartbroken look in Michelle's eyes, all of it his doing. Even if what she said was the truth, he had to try to make this better.

"No, not just for her. It was making me sick to hide so many things from you. I knew it wasn't right. When you called, I wanted to make it a little easier if I could. I don't think I have, but I had to try."

"Does she know we were engaged now?"

All he could do was nod.

"Were you at least careful, Evan? Your father told me where she's been, what kind of life she's led. Do I need to go get tested?"

None of that had crossed his mind, not for one second, that first night with Anne. If he thought about it rationally at any point, he would have assumed she'd been treated for anything she had in the hospital. Once again, the truth was harder than he'd imagined.

"You can if you want, if it makes you feel better. You and I were never together after I was with Anne. You're safe."

Michelle smiled, and Evan thought it was the saddest smile he'd ever seen.

"I'm safe now, as long as I stay away from you. As long as I stay away from you as long as I live." She stood, picking up her coat and her purse. Evan stood but he didn't move toward her. "I hope she's worth it, I really do. Sounds to me like you're going to have your hands full with this one."

"Michelle, do you want…" He reached into his pocket and pulled out the ring box. "This is yours. I want you to keep it."

"Why the hell would I want that, Evan? You think I want to remember you or anything to do with you?"

"I'm sure you don't. Sell it, give it away, whatever you want to do. It's yours."

"Fuck you," she said, shaking her head. "Flush it down the toilet, shove it up your ass, give it to *her*. You did this. You decide what to do with the mess you left behind." She turned and walked toward the door. "I have to thank you for getting this over with before we did get married, I guess. The same thing would have happened if you'd seen her in ten years, wouldn't it?"

She looked back at him, her eyes overly bright. One more slice of her, one more shred of him.

"It probably would have. I'm sorry, Michelle. I truly am."

She laughed, a harsh grunt that broke Evan's heart at last.

"Yeah, so am I. Good luck to both of you. You're going to need it."

She closed the door quietly, and she was gone. Evan was tempted to slam it himself, to slam it over and over again until his ears were numb, or maybe to slam it on his own fingers.

Fair wasn't making him feel better, not anymore. All he had left was the guilt and shame he was nearly choking on.

He opened the box, turning it so the ring caught the light. He knew he'd never give this to Anne or anyone else. It didn't matter how much it had cost or if he did decide to flush it. The ring was pretty enough, but he'd never buy something so typical, so common, for Anne.

Just a big white diamond with smaller ones all around, nothing special at all. Michelle had loved everything about it, crying when he'd slipped it onto her finger.

She'd cried even harder when she threw it at him two weeks ago.

Evan put the box back in his pocket. He did the only thing he could think of, even if he didn't deserve comfort or support. He needed it too badly not to.

She picked up on the first ring.

"Evan."

"Anne. She just left. She knows everything."

"Are you okay?"

"No, not really."

"Come get me."

"I'll be right there."

Chapter 40

Evan sat in the passenger seat of Gwen's minivan, the smell of stale fries and little boy sweat rising all around him, staring up at an ivy-covered brick apartment building. Hurricane Ed's second floor windows stood open to catch the warm May breeze. Sensible tan curtains stirred in most, but three rippled with bright cartoon characters.

The small, tree-lined park across the street echoed with little kid yells and laughter, perfect for Ed's frequent weekends with his grandsons. Evan sometimes wondered if his father had more adult company, but he'd never felt brave enough to find out. Gwen probably knew, with her willingness to ask questions no one else would even consider.

Right now she only sat quietly beside him.

They'd been parked for several minutes without saying a word.

"I don't know if I'm ready for this," he said, looking at his sister.

"I'm never ready to see him, not even when I have the boys with me. We can get out of there at any time, Ev. You don't live with him, and you don't have to. This isn't even the house you grew up in. You never lived here. He isn't in charge of your life anymore."

"He is until I stand up to him. Even if he never speaks to me again, I have to stand up to him now."

"Okay. Let's go."

They walked up the perfectly maintained wood and marble stair-case together, and Gwen squeezed his hand for just a second when they got to 2C. Evan smiled at her, glad she was with him after all. He couldn't remember ever being so nervous or afraid as he was at that moment. Anger at his father for talking to Michelle was the only thing that kept him moving forward.

He pressed the old-fashioned engraved brass doorbell, listening for the charming three-note tone. Neither Evan nor Gwen had ever listened when their father told them they could just walk in. Evan knew neither of them ever would.

After just a few seconds, Ed Griffith opened the door.

"Hey, two for the price of one!" he said, smiling and stepping back. "Come on in."

Evan and Gwen followed their father through a living room that seemed bigger than Evan's whole apartment, past a mix of heavy wood furniture from their childhood home and grandson-friendly beanbags and chairs. Shelves jammed full of games, toys, and video-cassettes, most of the kid variety, took up one brick wall.

The kitchen was just as spacious and comfortable, with room for the big oak dining room table from the house and a sleek granite island. Ed opened a glass-fronted cabinet and brought out a huge St. Louis souvenir coffee mug for Gwen. Ed's hair was still thick, but it was almost completely gray now. His shoulders were a bit rounded, his back not as strong. He looked so much smaller to Evan, so much less intimidating.

But some part of him was still scared to death of his father.

A steel carafe of strong coffee waited on the table. Gwen winked at Evan and reached into the fridge to get something for it. Evan was the only one who could tolerate Ed's coffee black.

"Well, this is a treat," their father said, sitting down across from his children. "What brings you both out here?"

"Evan's so damned cheap he conned me into driving," Gwen said, pouring milk into her mug. "No, I was hoping to borrow a few more books for the boys. They both read like fiends, thank goodness. You still have a few here, don't you?"

"Yeah, piles of them. You're not borrowing, hon, they belong to the boys here or at your house. The two of you will just have to work it out if your brother… Take as many as you want."

Evan didn't miss that hesitation, and neither did Gwen. She smiled at him before turning to Ed.

"They'll bring some back when they're here for Memorial Day weekend, if that's still on?"

"Absolutely it's still on. They're welcome here any time."

Evan watched the two of them, trying to hide his smile, and his confusion. He'd never imagined his father turning into such a stereotypical grandpa, unrecognizable from the father he'd once been. Even with Gwen's uneasiness about talking to Ed herself, she was perfectly comfortable with their father keeping her sons. Evan had seen Ed with his grandsons more than enough to know she was right about that.

"I'll just finish my coffee and go take a look," Gwen said.

"Is there any coffee in there?" their father said with a half smile. "Looks like mostly milk to me."

"A few drops of your coffee keeps me awake for days."

Gwen glanced at Evan then, her eyebrows raised just a little. He closed his eyes and nodded. He wasn't ready to face talking to his father, but sitting here drinking purified caffeine wasn't going to help.

"I'll be back," she said, walking toward the boys' bedrooms.

Evan turned back to his father, trying to gather all of his wits and his calm about him. He wouldn't be able to keep Anne and Ed from crossing paths forever, much as he might want to. He couldn't stay so angry about his father talking to Michelle, or angry at her either.

He owed it to her, to Anne, and to himself, to at least try to get through this. Before he was ready, his time ran out.

"What's been going on with you, son?"

"It's been an interesting few weeks."

"That's what I hear. Michelle called me a little while back."

"Yeah, she told me about that. You two had quite a talk."

Ed shook his head, then refilled both their cups.

"You don't have to tell me a thing, you know that. But she was pretty upset."

"I know. I didn't handle things very well. But I did what I had to."

"Want to tell me why?"

Evan stared at his hands for a few seconds, then closed his eyes.

No, he didn't want to. Not at all. But that was the whole point of coming over here in the first place.

"It was never going to work out between us, Dad. That's all."

"Did she know that?"

"No, she didn't know. Not before it was over."

Ed rubbed his face, a habit Evan hadn't noticed they shared until just then.

"You seemed happy with her, Evan. I know she was happy with you. What happened?"

"Michelle just wasn't the one for me. No matter how hard I tried, she never would have been. Going on that way didn't seem fair to anyone."

His father crossed his arms and sighed. Evan tried to brace himself. Too many conversations with Ed went downhill after that aggressive gesture.

"What made you suddenly realize she wasn't the one? Is there someone else?"

Evan forced himself not to sigh in return. His anger was trying to jump in and take over the whole conversation.

"You *know* this, Dad. You know this. You knew it well enough to tell Michelle what was going on."

"She called me, son, crying so hard I could barely understand a word she said. She'd just left your place, which she thought was her place until she got back from Seattle. What was I supposed to tell her? 'Easy come, easy go?'"

"You could have told her to talk to me about it. You could have said you were sorry, or tried to make her feel better. Anything else was up to me to tell her."

Ed narrowed his eyes and turned his head a little to the side.

"Is there someone else, Evan?"

The sharp tone in his father's voice tensed up all the muscles in Evan's neck and shoulders. That tone had almost always been the end of conversations that had already gone downhill. Either he got up and walked away, or the shouting started. He wasn't sure Gwen being in the next room was going to make any difference.

"It's Anne. It's always been Anne. No one else has ever come close. We're really happy, Dad."

For the first time, he honestly wished he had visions, like Anne did. Even if they weren't true, and Evan was starting to suspect they actually were, he might have some idea what to expect here. His father stared at him, and Evan could see him trying to keep his face neutral.

"That's nonsense. You were engaged for over two years, up until a few weeks ago. I know she wasn't pregnant, and you've never done much of anything on a whim, much less getting engaged or getting unengaged. You had to care about Michelle at some point."

"I did care about her, yes. Of course I do. But I didn't love her. No matter how hard I tried, I never could. That wasn't fair to her, or to me."

"I didn't even know Anne was back from the hospital. Again."

"She's been back for a few months now," Evan said, stretching the truth enough to be uncomfortable. Not quite eight weeks had passed. "She's doing really well."

"She always seems to, in the beginning." Ed at least had the grace to drop his gaze, and a few seconds later Evan understood why. "When did this happen, Evan? Exactly when did you realize you'd been waiting for Anne all these years?"

Evan chewed the insides of his cheeks, wanting desperately to avoid the question. Even such relative civility wouldn't last once they got into this.

"I've known that since I was thirteen years old. Time hasn't changed it at all."

"That's not what I asked you, and I know you heard me. When...did this...happen?"

Gwen somehow managed to use her anger and not let it get away from her, not let it take over. She'd used that anger to keep this man from controlling her the way he'd always managed to control Evan. Maybe that was the part he was missing now. His own anger.

"Two months ago. I first saw her two months ago."

"That was while you were still engaged, wasn't it?" Ed said, one of his eyebrows raised.

"Yeah, Dad, I was still engaged."

"So on top of everything else, Anne didn't give a shit that you already had a fiancé."

"She didn't know, not for a while."

"Hid that from her, did you?" Ed tapped his fingers against his biceps. "So you're starting this disaster on a good path already. Did she even care when she finally did find out?"

"She wasn't happy with me at all. She was furious. She refused to see me again until I ended things and told Michelle the truth."

"Well, good for Anne for having at least that much integrity. She wasn't unhappy enough to let you be though, to let you go back to your fiancé."

"I told you it's going really well, Dad, more than it ever could have with Michelle. Didn't you hear me?"

"You have to work at it, Evan, that's the whole point. It feels oh so exciting right now, sure. But time passes. The newness wears off."

Evan felt the mistake, the bad judgment, somewhere at the bottom of his brain. Somewhere in the old part. He knew how bad it was going to be, and it didn't matter. He couldn't stop the words once they started. They just kept moving, from his throat to his mouth out into the corrosive, dangerous air between himself and his father.

"The way you worked at it with Mom? Is that what you mean? The way you never, ever let her forget her mistakes until the day she died?"

Ed folded his hands on the table, and he kept his eyes focused on them.

"Son, be careful where you're going here. You don't have any idea what you're getting into with me."

"Maybe not, but I do know what you're getting into with me."

"Is that right?" his father said, glancing up.

"Yeah, that's right. I did everything wrong, and I'm not trying to deny that. But I'm not going to let you make this Anne's fault like you've done so many other things. I made the bad choices, not her."

"She didn't just have some kind of mental breakdown this time, Evan. She had to go to rehab to clean up before she could even go to the hospital. I'd say that counts as some pretty god damn bad choices. What makes you think she's going to stay clean now?"

Evan breathed deeply, trying to slow the pulse he could feel in his ears.

"That's not what I'm talking about, Dad, listen to me. Whatever she did in the past is her business. What I'm telling you is she wouldn't let me keep being such a jackass, not if I wanted to be with her. Doing the right things so I could be with her is the first good decision I've made for a long time."

"You broke a good woman's heart for a girl who'll probably end up back in the hospital before the end of the year. For a grade school crush."

Evan stood and shoved his chair forward. Everything on the heavy oak table rattled.

"That's enough, Dad, enough! This is not some kind of crush, no matter how much you want it to be. It's not a crush any more than Gwen and Mark are, or you and Mom were. I love her. I always have. If you can't deal with that, I won't bother you anymore."

"So you think if Gwen left Mark for some guy she knew twenty years ago, I'd be happy about that?"

Ed's voice had risen to full volume, his hands clenched into fists on the table. That voice had Evan wanting to shrink away and cover his ears forever. He managed to stop himself after only a few steps toward the door.

"I never loved Michelle or anyone else. Not like this. I never *want* to. This is the my life and my decision. If you're going to keep this up, I can't be around you anymore."

The two men stared at each other long enough for Evan to lose count of his own breaths. Ed finally leaned over and pulled the chair back out.

"Sit down, son. I might not like this, but I'm not going to turn my back on you. Sit."

Evan opened his mouth and breathed in until he couldn't anymore, then let it out in a sigh as he sat.

"I know Mom broke your heart, Dad. I understand now that it wasn't because she didn't love us or you. It was because she was human. She made mistakes just like all of us do. I know I have."

Evan wasn't sure if he should be heartbroken or frightened at fierce agitation he saw in his father's eyes. Ed had hardly spoken about his wife since the day she died. When he did, it was always "your mother," never my wife or even Megan.

Evan was afraid everything hidden away or forced inside his father would burst out in just a few seconds.

"Your mother's choices, and mine, were between us. That's just where they're going to stay. That was part of *our* life, not yours. It's not your or your sister's business."

"But it all affected us, Dad, you have to understand that. Knowing what she did, seeing how it changed both of you, I grew up with that. I can't pretend it wasn't part of my life too."

"Then why the hell did you treat Michelle that way?" Ed shouted, pounding his fists on the table, loud enough that Evan shrank back in his chair. "If you had even the slightest idea what that would do to her, how the hell *could* you?"

Evan felt the hand on his shoulder before he realized Gwen had walked into the room. His ears were still ringing, of course she would have heard it too. He was thankful she was there, and even more thankful that she didn't say anything.

"Because I made a terrible mistake, that's why. I got carried away with seeing Anne, with being so happy she was okay. Then when I realized she wanted me after so many years, I think I just lost my head. I didn't mean to be such an ass, but I know I was."

"If you know it was a mistake," his father said, "why did you keep making it? Why are you still making it?"

Evan winced at the entirely different sound of his father's voice. He was no longer threatening. He was heartbroken. Evan wasn't ready to feel sympathy, not after that shout and the awful things Ed had said about Anne. He wasn't ready, but he was feeling it deep in his guts.

"Because I didn't love Michelle, not the same way I love Anne. I was making the mistake by…by thinking…"

He watched his sister walk around to sit at the table. He wanted her to speak now as badly as he hadn't wanted her to just a few seconds before.

"It wasn't the same thing, Dad," she said. "I remember more about that time than you think I do. Evan was wrong, but he wasn't doing the same thing Mom did, not at all. For a while, Mom forgot the one she really loved was you. She stayed with you, didn't she?"

Their father blew out his breath, shaking his head.

"I think she regretted that more often than not."

"It doesn't matter though, she stayed," Gwen said. "Pain in the ass that you are, she stayed."

"Right back at you, kid." Ed turned back to Evan. "Are you just dating her, or what?"

Evan tried to keep his smile to himself. Of course there wouldn't be any happily ever after in this conversation, not with Hurricane Ed. Gwen winked at him again, flashing a crooked smile of her own too fast for their father to notice.

"We've been dating since right after she got back."

"Where's she living now, with her parents?"

"For now."

Ed scowled. "You want her to move in with you already?"

"Yeah, Dad, I really do. I hope she does soon. It's going beautifully, since you didn't ask."

"Does she even have a job, son? Or are you just supporting her?"

"Of course she has a job, but if I wanted to support her instead I would do just that. I just told you we're really happy, more than once. Why can't you hear me?"

Ed took a deep breath, looking at Gwen, then back at Evan.

"I heard you say you want to move in with a girl who's had issues since she was eleven years old, and I don't mean just bad moods sometimes. She's been in and out of hospitals her whole life, Evan. What makes you think she's going to get better? What can possibly have changed after all this time?"

"Maybe the change is she has someone who loves her. Maybe not having someone say she's crazy all the time is making a difference."

"I never said she was crazy," his dad said, his cheeks turning red. "I just think this is a lot for you to take on, son. Have you thought this through?"

Evan looked at the floor, gritting his teeth. He'd heard those words, have you thought it through, his whole life. Thinking it through had been related to jobs, school, renting an apartment, buying a car. Big decisions that made sense to take his time with.

What bugged the crap out of him was hearing it about going on vacation, going to a movie, ordering dinner, even buying a book. Evan couldn't remember if his father been like that before his mother died, or at least he hadn't noticed. Now everything in Ed's life seemed to be about thinking it through, whatever *it* happened to be.

And never, ever doing a damn thing about it.

"You know what, Dad? I didn't need to think it through. I've loved Anne since I was thirteen years old. Probably before that. That's never changed, not even for a minute. I've already thought through how much I missed her and how much every other woman I've ever dated isn't her. That wasn't Michelle's or anyone one else's fault. That's just the way it is. I've thought through how empty my life feels when Anne's not in it. No amount of thinking is ever going to change the way I feel about her."

His father shook her head, sighing again.

"What do you think about this, Gwen?" Ed said, turning to her. She shook her head, smiling a little.

"No way, I'm not getting in the middle of you two. You're both grownups. As long as you don't start throwing punches, you just have to work it out."

Ed narrowed his eyes, then turned back to Evan.

"What if she leaves you? What if she does have to go back to the hospital and leaves you alone?"

"I'll do my best to keep that from happening, but I know it could. That's the way life works, isn't it? None of us knows anything for sure. You didn't know when you met Mom, or when Gwen and I were born."

"Don't tell me you want to have kids with her." Ed scrubbed at his chin. "You never know with things like this."

"You're right," Evan said. "You never know with *anything*, Dad. That's just how it is. You had no way to know what would happen with Mom."

"Son, your mother had an aneurism. She never had to stay in a hospital because she was imagining things or because she tried to drink herself to death. You can't be telling me you want the mother of your children to be suicidal. And all the medication Anne must be on can't be good."

Evan hated feeling like this, his guts churning and cold sweat working down his back. Despite Gwen calming everything down, he was starting to hate this conversation even more.

If there was one thing his father did know, it was how hard raising two kids alone had been.

"We haven't really talked about kids, Dad. I don't know how she feels about it. I'm not the only one who'll make that decision."

"But how do *you* feel about it, Evan?"

He stared at his hands before looking into his father's eyes. That gentle tone was something he did remember from his childhood, from before his mother died. His father had hardly ever talked that way since.

"I honestly haven't thought about it," Evan said. "All I know is I want to be with Anne. The rest will work itself out. If she doesn't want kids, I don't want them. That's all."

Ed held Evan's gaze for a long time, longer than he had since Evan was a little boy. He was painfully aware his father probably didn't do that very often because Evan's eyes were exactly like his his mother's.

"Just tell me you're happy," Ed finally said. "I'm going to worry about you no matter what. Both of you. But I want you to be happy."

Evan smiled, surprised it was so natural and easy.

"I am, Dad. It has been a rough few weeks, but I don't think I've ever been this happy before."

PART VII

MENDING THE FUTURE

Chapter 41

Anne sat in the chilly white waiting room, staring at the ring finger on her left hand. Nothing was there, not yet. Even with a marriage so well-known and remembered to her, six months wasn't quite enough time for that. She knew exactly how her hand was going to look, though.

Evan was going to search his beloved antique shops for weeks, all the way into Chicago, until he found a ring with four matching stones the exact color of Anne's eyes. She didn't have to say a word to him about not wanting a diamond like he'd given Michelle, and she loved him all the more for that.

He would be trembling and nervous, and he would admit later that he'd been scared she wouldn't want a ring from him at all after what had happened. Anne would tell him the truth: that she'd been dreaming of a ring exactly like this.

The nurse sat behind her bullet-proof glass, calmly calling one name after another. Some women were here for an abortion, to end the life growing inside of them.

Anne wondered if any of them were like her. Did they know the dreadful fate awaiting the children they were never going to have? Years ago she'd wished she'd meet another person like her, just once. Now she didn't want to, not ever if she could help it.

If one other woman knew what was coming and decided to terminate her pregnancy, Anne was afraid she would lose her resolve. Her dreams and memories told her everything and everyone depended on what she was going to do tonight, but she still mourned the fate of their child. A child she would never know.

She looked at her hand again. Before another year passed, a thin white gold wedding ring would join the beautiful green stones. Evan would wear a thicker one to match, they would both wear them for the rest of their lives. Her engagement ring had already been worn and loved for well over one hundred years. Anne hoped to love it herself as long as she could, then send it further on into the future.

Her phone buzzed in her pocket, pulling her out of visions of her wedding day.

Her mother had managed to stop herself from calling Anne every day only this week. She might not ever be able to stop sending text messages. Anne didn't mind. After only a few months of living with her parents, such a short time of calm after so many years of screaming nightmares, Anne had abruptly moved into Evan's apartment three months ago.

She'd never been able to see such a joyful and incredible turn of events when she'd returned to her parents' house. Even remembering and reliving the visions after she started spending so many nights with Evan hadn't prepared Anne for the overwhelming reality of waking up beside him every morning.

Anne replied to her mother that she was doing fine, no nightmares, and she and Evan would be there for Sunday dinner. She'd lied about the nightmares, of course. She'd been lying to her mother about that for a long while now. Only Evan, the one who slept beside her, knew how often and how badly Anne had the dreams.

He was the one woken as often as she was, holding her close in the middle of the night as she trembled and cried. Anne tried not to let visions of Evan's death bring her to tears right now.

She felt terrible about interrupting his sleep in such an awful way. She dutifully took her medication out of the bottles, making sure he saw her do that much. She dissolved all of them in hot water and poured them into the toilet when he couldn't see her. Anne didn't like putting such strong medicine into the water supply, but that wouldn't matter for much longer.

The poison in the air was going to kill far more people than the poison in the water.

She'd be able to solve the problem of Evan's sleep and of the dissolved pills in just a few short hours. Once she was finished here, Anne would be taking her medication, at least some of it, once again.

"Anne F?"

Anne stood, nodding at the nurse. A sign beside the nurse's window announced the new experimental harvest procedure, the chance to share life with a couple who wanted to share love. Anne had dreamt about this for weeks now, but the sign announced the start date of only a couple of days ago.

The idea of even more people being born on a doomed planet nearly made Anne cry again. No matter how many desperate hours she'd spent thinking about that, hours that added up to years of her own life, she couldn't do a thing to stop it. She hoped her choices somehow made it better.

The only thing she could do was walk through the door and into her future.

The young woman was very kind and efficient as she took Anne's vital signs.

"Have you used a pregnancy test?"

"Yes," Anne lied. "I did last week."

"How far along do you think you are?"

Anne pretended to think back, to count the days since her last period. She knew the day and the hour she had conceived this baby, but she couldn't let this no-nonsense woman know that.

"About five weeks, I think."

"And you want the experimental harvest procedure?"

"Yes. That's exactly what I want."

The nurse made notes for a few seconds, then she looked up into Anne's eyes. Her brown eyes were warm and concerned.

"Have you talked to your partner about this?"

An unexpected tear rolled down Anne's cheek, and she knew the woman saw before she could hide it. Talking to Evan about this was one thing she had only imagined, never remembered. Her imagination had been painful enough, more than painful enough.

Anne had to tell a lie that hurt even worse.

"I don't have a partner. This was all a mistake. I don't want to carry a mistake inside my body anymore."

The nurse nodded, then she touched Anne's shoulder. Anne smiled, and she didn't try to fight her tears any longer.

She wanted to cry out that she wanted this baby, she wanted this baby more than she wanted to draw her next breath. She wanted to see what she and Evan had made together, what the most perfect joining of them would look like, smell like, sound like.

She wanted to see this baby, this new person inside of her, grow up and learn and explore and find out about the world.

Anne knew she couldn't do any of those things, no matter how badly she wanted to. The agony of this moment had come out of nowhere, stronger than the faint regret she remembered about this night. The memory was what she had to do though, even if she left her own heart in this lonely room along with Evan's baby.

The procedure was much easier than Anne expected. Less uncomfortable than the routine examinations she'd always hated. She wasn't sure if it was because she knew this one had a purpose, and she didn't care.

She was going to take the birth control the doctor offered. Evan would be sad about her not wanting to have children with him, but he would understand. Anne's parents would understand too. Of course she didn't want to pass her problem along to a child. Of course.

The secret that Anne would never tell anyone, not for the rest of her life, was that she was not going to pass her problem along.

Just as he had been in every other way, Evan was the key.

Something about him, maybe his own firm sanity, maybe his genes, maybe just the love between the two of them, was going to let their baby be almost normal. This child would have part of Anne's problem, the part that would somehow let life on Earth continue after so much disaster. But this child would not be driven crazy by her own mind.

Anne's breath caught at her first glimpse of the baby's gender, the first hint that she and Evan had made a little girl together.

"It's all right, we're all finished here," the doctor said, misunderstanding. "You can sit up and get comfortable."

Anne got dressed and watched the doctor working. She looked into a microscope, making notes with her left hand. She couldn't have been any older than Anne herself, maybe even younger.

"Do you have any requests for the donation?"

"I want the donation held for at least twenty years. Can you do that?"

The doctor looked at her, eyes wide, but Anne knew her request would be honored. She stood, ready to walk out of this room and away from this sad reality.

"That's an unusual request, but I will make a note of that," the doctor said, turning back to the microscope. "You were carrying twins."

Anne's jaw dropped and she sat down again, hard.

Twins? She'd never remembered that, not one time, not ever. Leaving them behind was more than twice as hard.

"Are you... Are you sure?"

"I'm certain. I see two perfectly healthy embryos here. You're giving an amazing gift, Anne."

Anne stood, this time on shaking legs. For the first time, she had no idea what was about to happen. She'd known she would be donating the child she carried, but finding out they were twins plunged her deep into the unknown. She'd longed for that ignorance, the ability to wonder what the future had in store, for most of her life. Now she wanted only to know what lay ahead for all of them.

"Thank you," she managed to whisper.

Anne turned and walked out of the room and into her unknown future.

Chapter 42

Evan lay still in the cozy darkness of his bedroom, his hand on Anne's waist. She was sleeping quietly, but he knew that wouldn't last much longer. He didn't need to look at the clock to be sure. His own body's clock woke him most nights just before she did.

The first couple of months had been rough, and Evan could admit that to himself now. He'd been red-eyed and bleary enough that people at work had asked him if he was sick. He'd just said he had a new girlfriend. Thankfully they'd just laughed and patted him on the back instead of asking any more questions.

He knew they assumed he was losing sleep because of all the sex, and that part had definitely been nice. Better than he'd imagined, actually, and he'd been imagining making love to Anne since he'd learned what that meant. What made him lose sleep was her nightmares.

She'd tried to warn him about that the first time she'd spent the night on purpose, that she might wake him. He'd been too dazed and happy that she'd come back to pay attention to what she was saying, but she'd been telling the truth. Just a few hours after they'd fallen asleep, Anne had started moaning, the most awful sound Evan had ever heard.

Her face, barely visible in the faint light from his clock that night and so many nights since, was what brought him to full awareness. Even with her eyes closed, she clearly saw the most dreadful thing anyone could imagine. Her face would look like she was crying, brow drawn down, eyes squeezed tight, sweet mouth pushed out and trembling.

Evan knew she saw visions about the end of the world, she had for years now. So maybe it *was* the very worst thing.

When she finally woke from her dreams, gasping and jerking, Evan was afraid to move at first. With her eyes open, the horrified look was a thousand times worse. She stared for a few seconds, then drew in a shuddering breath. Then she always moved against him, holding on tighter than he would have thought she could.

All he could do for a long time was stroke her hair and whisper that it was all going to be okay. Evan hadn't noticed the time that first night, but he knew now that she took almost ten minutes to calm down and get back to sleep. That first night, he'd fallen back asleep with her.

It wasn't until the third night that Evan really understood the worst part of Anne's nightmares. He hadn't asked her, but he had a pretty strong idea she'd slept alone almost all of her life. The hospitals she'd been in and out of certainly had single beds. She'd told him more about her time with Joe that he'd wanted to hear, and part of that had been drinking enough to stop the dreams. At least for a while.

So for most of her life, the woman he loved so dearly had woken up from those horrible nightmares all by herself. She hadn't had anyone to comfort her once she outgrew going into her parents' room. Joe certainly wouldn't have bothered, and he didn't have to ask about the others.

From that night on, Evan knew he would do whatever he had to to keep her from being so alone and afraid in the middle of the night.

He got into the habit of taking an hour long nap during the day to make up for the lost sleep, locking his office door and stretching out on the couch. That had turned into an unexpected pleasure he wasn't sure he'd give up if he had the chance to.

The two of them had started going to bed a little earlier to make up for the interruption. He'd tried to talk to her about the dreams, but she hadn't wanted to tell him. She told him her medicine helped sometimes, but she got into phases when it didn't. She thought this would pass before long.

The last two nights had been the worst he'd ever seen in her or anyone else. The first night she'd started thrashing around before she woke up, and she fought him when he tried to hold her.

Then last night, she'd woken screaming.

Evan decided then and there to find out what was making the dreams worse. He'd be heartbroken to have to stop sharing her bed, but if having him there was making it worse, that's what he would do. He was afraid he was disturbing her somehow, intruding on her space too much.

If she needed different medication, he would help with that. A noise machine, a different pillow, even a different apartment, anything at all within his power to make this better for her. Whatever it took would be worth it.

Evan focused on Anne again when she shifted, turning onto her back and moving closer to him. She wasn't dreaming, not yet.

Something about her, something he couldn't put words to even now, drew Evan to Anne like a moth to a flame. Even if he did burn up in that flame, like his father feared, Evan simply didn't care. Being in that fire with her, even for the briefest instant, would be worth everything.

Anne twitched against Evan's side, pulling him out of his thoughts and into his much more complicated reality. He watched her, determined to catch her before she started screaming this time.

Her memories sometimes were too accurate for him to doubt, but he'd never figured out where to put that inside of himself. He just knew to trust what she saw. He had to at least try to help her.

Her face crumpled up again, and she seemed to be shaking her head. She drew a sharp breath. Evan pulled her close.

"Anne, sweetie, you're dreaming," he whispered, bracing himself for whatever happened. "Wake up, you're dreaming. Everything is okay."

She pushed against him for a second, then all the tension drained away with her breath. When she breathed in, she squeezed him back.

"I'm sorry, Evan," she said against his chest. "I didn't meant to wake you."

He moved back enough to see her eyes. She still looked upset, but the horror had left her, at least for the moment. He wished she could be free of it forever.

"I want you to tell me about it," he said, brushing her hair back. "Tell me about the dream. You've never done that before. Maybe it'll help."

Anne looked at him without saying anything. He wondered if she was remembering that same day, that long ago day on the playground when she had first trusted him with her terrible secret.

He could only hope she knew he was as unable to turn away from her now as he'd been that incredible, awful day.

"The dreams change. I don't always have the same one."

"What about just now? Was that a new one?"

She nodded, rolling her eyes closed again.

"A new one. A bad one."

"Tell me about it. I'm not going anywhere."

She smiled at him, and Evan's heart knew that leaving him to stay with Anne all those years ago had been the right choice. The best choice. The only choice he ever could have made.

"You're not, are you?" she said, then she took a deep breath. "I got my medication adjusted a couple of days ago. That always makes them stop in a couple of weeks."

"But they start up again eventually, right? Maybe if you tell me, they won't come back."

"I'll try. I was dreaming about a volcano just now. A really big one. The sky turned black for a long, long time."

"What happened?"

"A whole lot of people starve to death. Most of the people do."

"Most of the people this time though, not all of them?"

She shrugged, then put her arm around his waist.

"That part changes too, it always has. It's been most of the people for a long while now."

"What do you think the difference is?" he said. "Is it random, or can you tell?"

She smiled a tiny bit, one he could barely see in the dim light. He was sure he saw her cheeks turning red.

"It's too sappy."

"Oh come on, you don't know anyone more sappy than I am. I do that part so you don't have to, remember? I'll tell you whether it's sappy or not, dear."

Anne smiled, then tried to hide a huge yawn.

"Okay, you asked for it. I've spent a lot of time thinking about this one, might be kinda nice to tell someone else. The dreams seem to shift depending on whether I'm with you or not."

"With me?" Evan was too pleased to be embarrassed. "Did that always happen?"

"Yeah, I think it always has. When we were apart for whatever reason, or when I was about to go into the hospital, dreams, visions, memories, everything I saw was *everybody* dying. When we were together, even as friends, at least a few people seem to make it."

"Do you know why?"

Evan had a wild theory about what the two of them could do together, a deeply held secret dream, but he wasn't about to tell her or anyone else that just yet.

"Who knows? I don't even know why I see these crazy things to begin with, much less what makes them change. Sometimes I see three things all at once, but I have no idea what to do about it. I do know they've always been easier to tolerate when I'm with you."

Evan spoke before his sleepy mind could stop him.

"Well, we'll have to make sure that never changes."

Anne laughed low in her throat, the same way she did when they were making love, and Evan felt his own face burning. He was hardly playing it cool about wanting to marry her, but he was nowhere near ready to ask her yet. He hadn't even found the ring despite searching high and low everywhere short of Chicago.

"I... I mean..."

"It's okay, Evan. It's all going to work out just fine."

"Have you seen something? Something about us?"

That was the second of the internal think-before-you-speak rules so carefully instilled by his father to fail Evan in just a few seconds. He wasn't sure he truly wanted to know about his own future, and he hated to bug her about something that tormented her so horribly. She raised up on one elbow and kissed him.

"Do you really want to know?"

"I do, I think. You said you love to be surprised, though, I remember that. Does it help to know what's coming?"

"Most of the time it's been awful." She held her cheek against his. "Most of the time what's coming has been something I would have stopped if I could have. Sometimes it's good to look forward to things. But I do love to be surprised."

"Then don't tell me," Evan said, relieved. "I'll be surprised enough for both of us. I'll just change the subject now so I don't keep putting my foot in my mouth if you don't mind. You said you have choices sometimes. Did you dream about choices just now?"

Anne lay with her head on his chest, her fingers playing with his curling hair.

"No, not this one. It went straight through. Not a thing I can do about this one. It might not happen, though. It didn't feel quite the same as the rest. It's hard to explain."

"Try me. I'm a good listener. At least you've told me that before. Maybe if you tell me, you'll be able to get back to sleep."

She shook her head against him. "I'm afraid you won't be able to, though."

"That's my problem, not yours. I'm tougher than I look. Tell me about your dream, sweetie. What makes it feel like it won't happen?"

"The other dreams feel heavier, more substantial, like something I could almost touch. They stay with me, some of them for years now. Decades. But this one feels like it'll be gone before morning."

"Tell me anyway. I want to know what you dream about, Anne."

By the time she finished talking, Evan understood why she'd woken up looking so upset and afraid. So many people suffering, fighting, dying, and all she could do was watch and wonder if only a few would live or none at all.

He could almost see the unsettling scenes playing out like a movie in his mind's eye. He was afraid he wouldn't be able to go to sleep after all, but he didn't dare tell her that. As long as she was calm enough to sleep, he was more than glad to let her. He only hoped he didn't wake her with a nightmare of his own.

"Are you okay, Evan? Tell me the truth."

"I will be. Do you feel any better at all for talking about it?"

"I do, actually. It's all faded. I don't know if I could remember well enough to tell you again."

"It's all worth it then," he said, "if telling me takes it away. I want you to tell me the others too, the ones that feel real." His heart ached almost as much as his stomach twisted at the thought of her having dreams worse than this one, but he'd just have to deal with that when the time came. "Will you do that?"

"Promise to tell me if you start getting too upset, or if you start having bad dreams too?"

"I promise. Think you can sleep now?"

This time her laugh, her deep sexy laugh, started heat in his belly that he couldn't ignore. That was the best way he could imagine to clear the terrible images out of his mind. Hopefully out of hers, too.

Her hand drifting lower, across his belly and into the thicker hair below, told him Anne was thinking the same thing.

"Maybe in a little while."

Chapter 43

Anne drew in a deep breath, closing her eyes so she could focus on the scent of Lake Michigan on the morning breeze. She caught a sharp, clean trace of last night's fog cutting through the sweet spring lilacs down in the courtyard .

All the windows in the apartment she'd shared with Evan for the last two years stayed open as soon as the two of them could stand the cold in spring until they couldn't stand the cold in autumn. Anne loved the faint rattle of the old-fashioned counterweights when she lifted the bottom panes or lowered the top ones. One of the many advantages of a building built before the Second World War.

Thick walls that shut out almost all the noise of neighbors and city alike were another. She'd been afraid of the sounds of so many people, that their presence jammed in around her would make the nightmares worse for her and for Evan. But the solidity of the stones around them, the broad hardwood beams under their feet, even the comfort of Evan loving his teaching position at the university so much, gave Anne the best sleep of her life.

Sleeping beside Evan, the man she'd happily vowed to sleep beside for the rest of her life, did more than a quiet bedroom ever could.

Evan shifted on the long couch beside her, tucking his bare, chilly feet under her leg. Anne opened one eye and caught his grin before he could hide it behind a book. He sometimes joked she was trying to freeze him to death with the open windows, but he never closed them when she wasn't home.

He wore a midnight blue terrycloth robe just like her own, the set an unusually thoughtful anniversary gift from Evan's father the year before. Hurricane Ed had surprised them both with the way he'd welcomed Anne into the family on their wedding day. Maybe he'd had a few dreams or memories of his own.

Anne's dreams over the past few weeks had turned as sweet as the lilac downstairs, as fresh and clean as the breeze off the lake.

"What's on your mind?" Evan said. "Did you have a bad dream last night?"

Anne shook her head. "I haven't had a bad dream without you waking up for a long time now. I hate to interrupt your sleep like that, but it's helped more than you know."

Evan got up and poured more coffee for both of them, but he kept staring at her, a strange, crooked smile on his face. She wondered if he knew he looked like his father in that moment if at no other time.

"You look like you want to say something," he said. "I'd swear I'm seeing the future for you right now. Want to just tell me?"

"I don't feel quite like I can do that, but maybe you can help. You told me once you didn't want to know what was coming. This time I think… I want to be sure about this one."

He shook his head, still smiling. "That's not quite what I said. I *do* want to know, sometimes I'm jealous of you for that. But I still want the surprises. Way too much to ask, isn't it?"

"Maybe not in this case. Tell me something, sweetie. Tell me how you feel about children."

Evan blinked and sat back, his pale blue eyes wide. Anne was afraid she'd misread him. That hadn't really happened in all the years she'd known him, all her life, but everything could always change.

"How I feel… You mean in general?"

Anne laughed, harder than she meant to, and she was relieved when Evan laughed with her. The memories of their baby, of their child they would raise together, grew ever stronger and more clear. But she'd never seen the slightest hint of this conversation.

"Well, yeah," she said. "In general, sure. If you hate all children on sight, this will go pretty quickly."

"No, I don't hate them on sight, not usually. You know as well as I do that our nephews are turning into surly beasts from the foul land of the teenager, but I still like them. I pretty much like most kids once I get to know them, if that makes any sense at all."

"That makes perfect sense. I feel the same way most of the time."

"Now that we've got that out of the way, I still don't know what you're asking me about."

Anne moved his feet into her lap, rubbing his cool skin between her hands.

"How do you feel about having children, Evan?"

"Is there something I need to know right now?"

"No, nothing like that. I know you like surprises, but that would be a big one."

He still looked confused, but he didn't seem upset at all.

"I haven't really thought about it much, not seriously. No more than daydreams. You told me a long time ago you never wanted any kids. You didn't want to…"

"It's okay, I remember what I said. I'm still worried about what would happen to them, what *will* happen to them, when everything falls apart. That's still true."

"Has something else changed, Anne? Do you feel differently now?"

Anne closed her eyes. Gathering her thoughts about all the things that had changed felt impossible, much less trying to find the words for any of it. That fear was still there, her dread about so many people dying. But somehow she felt stronger anyway.

The future felt less heavy inside of her, like Evan was carrying part of the burden.

And his strength was deeper and more steady than she'd ever imagined.

"I'm afraid," she said. "But I don't know if that's any different than anyone feels talking about this. If it's something you want, I don't want my fear to keep us from it. Just feeling so much better about it might mean things have shifted. You know?"

Evan moved until he was close beside her, arm around her shoulders. The solid comfort of his body reached every part of her.

"I do know," he said, kissing her cheek. "Have you seen something you need to tell me about?"

"Only that it's all going to work out just fine. Do you want to know more than that?"

Evan kissed her mouth hard then, hard and long enough that she forgot all about the dreams and visions and memories. All Anne could hold onto was how much she loved him, how much she wanted him. A lazy Sunday morning on this sofa in the sunny living room of their apartment felt like the perfect time and place to start bringing her memories into reality. He drew back, breathing as hard as she was.

"All I want to know is if we're going to be happy if we do this. That's all. If *you're* going to be happy. I know I am as long as I'm with you. I don't even have to ask about that."

"I won't tell you it's all going to be easy. I have a pretty good feeling a lot of it won't be. But I know this is the right thing, Evan. I don't have to see the future to know that."

"That's more than enough for me. Yes, Anne, I want to have children with you. I have for a long, long time. I'll tell you something else I've thought about for a while now, but I didn't think the time would ever be right to tell you. Maybe you feel better because this is what we're *supposed* to do. Maybe that's why you don't see everyone dying anymore."

"Maybe that's true," she said. "Maybe you make all the difference."

Anne was startled, amazed that he was saying what she'd so clearly seen. This was a gift she'd never expected to have when she donated her embryos, the first children they'd made together. Those babies, removed from her and from Evan forever, were going to be part of that chance of survival, but now she knew they could do the same thing right here.

She'd have the joy of seeing how Evan was with this child, how he took all the pain and struggle between himself and his father and turned it into love. And she knew if this baby, this sweet little boy, did turn out to have her issues, her gift, she'd make sure he understood what it was and how to deal with it.

What Anne didn't tell him, what she never planned to tell her husband or anyone else, was that she *did* know.

Parts of it were going to be hard, terribly hard. But most of their lives together, and the life of their son, were going to be good. Even after they were gone, and that felt further away than it ever had for her, their son would live on just like her grandmother had told her.

Back when Anne couldn't believe anything would ever be good again, her Gemaw had known. She'd seen this happening.

Her Gemaw had seen those beautiful blue eyes she was staring into, Evan's eyes, in her own baby's face. But what Anne saw now was a healthy boy, a strong and dependable man, with her own green eyes. The same as her father's and her grandmother's.

And even further away, so distant in time that she could only catch glimpses, a grandson who would help bring Anne's rare, sweet dreams of humanity surviving into reality. A grandson who would somehow have need of the four flashing hunter green stones of the engagement ring she wore alongside her wedding band.

Need, and necessity she couldn't quite understand.

And all of it out of love.

Chapter 44

THE RECOVERY ROOM at the university hospital felt more like a modern apartment. Maybe one of the new lake view buildings, the location for so many expensive faculty parties and endless fundraisers. Warm beige and gold walls, thick rugs on the tile floor, soft lighting. A sitting area by wide floor to ceiling windows crowded with comfortable chairs.

The bed beside Evan's plush recliner had a discreet monitoring panel tucked into a gleaming wooden enclosure, but the sheets and comforters were rich shades of green and blue instead of blinding sick room white. And the much smaller bed in the sitting area looked more like a high-end bassinet than a standard infant hospital bed.

Neither he nor Anne had imagined being friends with faculty and staff because of all those parties would make such a difference on the day their lives changed forever.

Evan watched Anne sleeping in that comfortable bed, the pleasant buzz of low voices only adding to the awe-struck, dazed state of his mind.

Nothing he'd ever read or heard had prepared him for this day. Nothing ever could have.

"Come on over here, Dad."

He blinked and turned toward the other side of the room, where Gwen sat with Mark, Ed, Mike, and Karen. The most important people in his life had all been there to meet the newest member of their family. His father spoke again.

"Evan, you asleep with your eyes open?"

"I'm sorry, what did you say? Did you mean me?"

Everyone laughed, and Evan smiled, not quite sure what the joke was yet. His father shook his head, but he was smiling too.

"I mean you, Dad, come on over. I think you're about to be on duty."

All the air in Evan's lungs escaped, and he felt a little light-headed. Even though Ed had been speaking to him, Evan had just assumed that word, *Dad*, was meant for that corner of the room. After all, the three fathers he knew best were all right there.

Until that moment, Evan hadn't quite grasped that he was one of them now.

He glanced at Anne again, still sound asleep, her hands together under her face like the little girl he still remembered so well. The only thing as beautiful in the entire world was in that tiny bed. Evan walked over and stood beside his father.

"He's about to wake up," Ed said, his hand on Evan's shoulder. "He has the same look on his face you always did. I'd bet if you pick him up, he won't cry and wake Mom over there."

Evan looked up, right at his sister. She had a crooked, smartass grin on her face, but her eyes, so much like Ed's, were overly bright. Ed showed no signs of the weepiness both his children were caught up in, but Evan couldn't remember the last time he'd seen his father so calm. So happy.

Content, that was the word he was looking for. Ed might not be on the verge of sobbing, or even dignified blotting at the corners of his eyes, but he was content.

"Go on, he's about to let loose full blast," Ed whispered. "You'll get to be an expert at knowing every little thing that sound means eventually, so you might as well get to know the warning signs."

"I'm not sure…"

"Just pick him up, Ev," Gwen said, Mark nodding beside her.

"Mark was impossible the first few times too, but we didn't have any real disasters. You can handle it, little brother."

Evan leaned down, watching for those signs his father was talking about, wondering if their son would rise up out of sleep the same way Anne did when she had a nightmare. His head was full of all the advice and warnings about picking up a newborn. Support his neck, hand under his puffy diapered backside, hold him close to your body.

Evan doubted he'd ever be natural and easy picking his own son up, able to move without the litany of advice running through his head.

Connor's rosy little brow wrinkled, then smoothed, and he seemed to be pursing his mouth, like he disapproved of the situation all around him. Just as his eyes fluttered open, Evan snuggled Connor close against his chest.

So warm. So *small.*

"See, you're a natural," Mike Fincastle said, standing on Evan's other side. "He's already settling down."

"I'm here, Connor. Daddy's here."

At his whisper, Connor's dark blue eyes seemed to focus on Evan's. He was sure he'd read somewhere that a newborn wouldn't be able to do that for a long time yet, but Evan felt the contact, the connection.

No one else existed in the room, in the entire world, but the two of them in that moment.

Whatever beat out time in his chest after his heart had gone to Anne's so many years ago left him to join their son, but Evan had never felt more whole and full. Connor blinked a few times, pursed his lips again, then drifted back into sleep.

"What's he saying, Evan?" Anne's mother said. He smiled at his mother-in-law, at Connor's grandmother, trying not to laugh and wake his son.

"I'm in over my head with this guy. He has no idea what the hell he's doing."

Everyone laughed softly, and Gwen put her arm around Evan.

"Go sit down, relax. You look about as sleepy as my nephew there."

Evan started to hand Connor to Gwen, much as he didn't want to, but she shook her head.

"He's fine right where he is."

Evan walked with exaggerated care, wondering again if he'd ever be brave enough to just pick up the baby and go like he'd seen Gwen and Mark and so many other people do.

Gwen followed him, waiting until he sat in the recliner beside Anne's bed as carefully as he could. His sister grabbed an impossibly soft blanket from a chest of drawers and covered him with it.

"Here, let me put these pillows around you. I'm going to lean the chair back. No, you're fine. You're not going to drop him, Ev."

By the time she finished adjusting him and the chair, Evan felt like he was in his own warm cradle, Connor secure in his arms, tiny head on his shoulder.

Gwen kissed her nephew's forehead, then Evan's. He thought she'd last done that when he was thirteen, on one of those long, awful nights after their mother died.

"Mama Gwen."

"Well, you're Daddy Evan now, so we're even. Get some rest. You're going to need it."

"I wish…"

"I know, me too. Mrs. Megan Connor Griffith would have been over the moon right about now. We'll just have to make up the difference." She glanced at the rest of them, then spoke barely above a whisper. "We'll all be here for anything you need, okay? But you're going to do just fine."

She gave the blanket one final tuck under his shoulder, then rejoined the others. Evan watched them, trying to fight the sleepiness that seemed to flow from his wife and their son into his own mind and body.

All of them sitting together like that, like family.

Like *their* family, the strange and jumbled and fractured and pulled together bunch he and Anne had drawn around themselves. He didn't think any of them could have possibly imagined this quiet room, this completely unexpected turn in his life, even a few short years ago.

He couldn't wait until Anne woke up so he could tell her about it. He couldn't wait until the three of them were at home, really starting out on their new adventure.

"I'm here, sweetheart," he whispered, no longer sure if he was talking to Anne or to their little boy. Probably both. "I'm not going anywhere. You're safe. We're all safe."

Evan turned toward Connor, shifting until the baby was breathing into his face. That incredible sweet smell pushed away the tiny bit of consciousness Evan had left.

He hoped Anne's dreams were as sweet as their baby's breath against his cheek, as sweet as flowers after the rain.

Evan had a feeling his own dreams would be, too.

ABOUT KARI

Kari Kilgore's wanderlust and imagination lead her all over the world on grand adventures. Her heart and family bring her home to her native Appalachian Mountains of Virginia. From that solid base, she and her husband Jason A. Adams bring those adventures to life in fiction.

Kari writes science fiction, fantasy, horror, and contemporary fiction, and she's happiest when she surprises herself. She lives at the end of a long dirt road in the middle of the woods with Jason, various house critters, and wildlife they're better off not knowing more about.

The Confidential Adventure Club

For Kari's exclusive free After The End stories and deleted scenes (including from the Storms of Future Past Series), discounts, early pre-sale releases, adorable pet photos, and a whole lot more not available anywhere else, visit The Confidential Adventure Club at www.smarturl.it/sofp-welcome.

Hope to see you there!

www.karikilgore.com
www.spiralpublishing.net

ALSO BY KARI KILGORE

I hope you enjoyed reading *Dreaming the Storm* as much as I enjoyed writing it. For more of the Storms of Future Past series, including Book Two, *Joining the Storm*, swing by www.smarturl.it/storms-series. Check out more of my fiction at www.karikilgore.com.

The Confidential Adventure Club

Curious what happened to Connor, the baby born at the end of *Dreaming the Storm*, and before the beginning of *Joining the Storm*?

Want more fiction from Kari, including stories, discounts, and box sets not available anywhere else? Want to hear about locations, research, and other cool things that inspired this story and beyond? All that and adorable pet photos, too?

Join The Confidential Adventure Club and get a thank you gift of *In the Eye of the Storm*, an exclusive short story from after The End of *Dreaming the Storm*, and a whole lot more at www.smarturl.it/sofp-welcome.

Hope to see you there!

Novels:

Until Death

The Dream Thief

Joining the Storm: Book Two of the Storms of Future Past Series

Fighting the Storm: Book Four of the Storms of Future Past Series

Novellas:

Songs in the Mountain

Legacy of the Land

Restricted Species

The Becalmed

In the Pines

Into the Storm: Book Three of the Storms of Future Past Series

Short Stories:

Renovations

Intentions

The Garbage Belt

The Seeds of Love

Wicked Bone

The Sound of Murder

Terminalia

Little Five: A Terminalia Story

Reflections

Collections:

Fantastic Women: A Dark Fantasy Novella Trio

Fantastic Shorts: Volume 1 - A Fantasy Short Story Collection

"Kari Kilgore is an author to watch—her lyrical voice a siren song; her insight, conjured voodoo."

—Richard Thomas, author of *Breaker* and *Tribulations*